the
brethren

John Grisham is the author of twenty-two novels,
one work of non-fiction, a collection of stories,
and a novel for young readers. He is on the Board
of Directors of the Innocence Project in New
York and is the Chairman of the Board of Directors
of the Mississippi Innocence Project at the
University of Mississippi School of Law. He lives
in Virginia and Mississippi.

john grisham
the brethren

arrow books

Reissued in the United Kingdom by Arrow Books in 2011

27 29 30 28 26

Copyright © Belfry Holdings, Inc. 2000

John Grisham has asserted his right under the Copyright, Designs
and Patents Act, 1988, to be identified as the author of this work

First published in the United Kingdom in 2000 by Century
First published in paperback in 2000 by Arrow books

Arrow Books
The Random House Group Limited
20 Vauxhall Bridge Road, London, SW1V 2SA

www.randomhouse.co.uk

Addresses for companies within The Random House Group Limited can
be found at: www.randomhouse.co.uk/offices.htm

The Random House Group Limited Reg. No. 954009

A CIP catalogue record for this book
is available from the British Library

Penguin Random House is committed to a sustainable future for
our business, our readers and our planet. This book is made from
Forest Stewardship Council® certified paper.

Printed and bound in Great Britain by Clays Ltd, Elcograf S.p.A.

THE BRETHREN

ONE

For the weekly docket the court jester wore his standard garb of well-used and deeply faded maroon pajamas and lavender terry-cloth shower shoes with no socks. He wasn't the only inmate who went about his daily business in his pajamas, but no one else dared wear lavender shoes. His name was T. Karl, and he'd once owned banks in Boston.

The pajamas and shoes weren't nearly as troubling as the wig. It parted at the middle and rolled in layers downward, over his ears, with tight curls coiling off into three directions, and fell heavily onto his shoulders. It was a bright gray, almost white, and fashioned after the Old English magistrate's wigs from centuries earlier. A friend on the outside had found it at a secondhand costume store in Manhattan, in the Village.

T. Karl wore it to court with great pride, and, odd as it was, it had, with time, become part of the show. The other inmates kept their distance from T. Karl anyway, wig or not.

He stood behind his flimsy folding table in the prison cafeteria, tapped a plastic mallet that served

1

as a gavel, cleared his squeaky throat, and announced with great dignity: 'Hear ye, hear ye, hear ye. The Inferior Federal Court of North Florida is now in session. Please rise.'

No one moved, or at least no one made an effort to stand. Thirty inmates lounged in various stages of repose in plastic cafeteria chairs, some looking at the court jester, some chatting away as if he didn't exist.

T. Karl continued: 'Let all ye who search for justice draw nigh and get screwed.'

No laughs. It had been funny months earlier when T. Karl first tried it. Now it was just another part of the show. He sat down carefully, making sure the rows of curls bouncing upon his shoulders were given ample chance to be seen, then he opened a thick red leather book which served as the official record for the court. He took his work very seriously.

Three men entered the room from the kitchen. Two of them wore shoes. One was eating a saltine. The one with no shoes was also bare-legged up to his knees, so that below his robe his spindly legs could be seen. They were smooth and hairless and very brown from the sun. A large tattoo had been applied to his left calf. He was from California.

All three wore old church robes from the same choir, pale green with gold trim. They came from the same store as T. Karl's wig, and had been presented by him as gifts at Christmas. That was how he kept his job as the court's official clerk.

There were a few hisses and jeers from the spectators as the judges ambled across the tile floor, in full regalia, their robes flowing. They took their places behind a long folding table, near T. Karl but not too near, and faced the weekly gathering. The short round one sat in the middle. Joe Roy Spicer was his name, and by default he acted as the Chief Justice of the tribunal. In his previous life, Judge Spicer had been a Justice of the Peace in Mississippi, duly elected by the people of his little county, and sent away when the feds caught him skimming bingo profits from a Shriners club.

'Please be seated,' he said. Not a soul was standing.

The judges adjusted their folding chairs and shook their robes until they fell properly around them. The assistant warden stood to the side, ignored by the inmates. A guard in uniform was with him. The Brethren met once a week with the prison's approval. They heard cases, mediated disputes, settled little fights among the boys, and had generally proved to be a stabilizing factor amid the population.

Spicer looked at the docket, a neat hand-printed sheet of paper prepared by T. Karl, and said, 'Court shall come to order.'

To his right was the Californian, the Honorable Finn Yarber, age sixty, in for two years now with five to go for income tax evasion. A vendetta, he still maintained to anyone who would listen. A crusade by a Republican governor who'd managed to rally the voters in a recall drive to remove Chief Justice Yarber from the California Supreme Court. The rallying point had been Yarber's opposition to the death penalty, and his high-handedness in delaying every execution. Folks wanted blood,

3

Yarber prevented it, the Republicans whipped up a frenzy, and the recall was a smashing success. They pitched him onto the street, where he floundered for a while until the IRS began asking questions. Educated at Stanford, indicted in Sacramento, sentenced in San Francisco, and now serving his time at a federal prison in Florida.

In for two years and Finn was still struggling with the bitterness. He still believed in his own innocence, still dreamed of conquering his enemies. But the dreams were fading. He spent a lot of time on the jogging track, alone, baking in the sun and dreaming of another life.

'First case is Schneiter versus Magruder,' Spicer announced as if a major antitrust trial was about to start.

'Schneiter's not here,' Beech said.

'Where is he?'

'Infirmary. Gallstones again. I just left there.'

Hatlee Beech was the third member of the tribunal. He spent most of his time in the infirmary because of hemorrhoids, or headaches, or swollen glands. Beech was fifty-six, the youngest of the three, and with nine years to go he was convinced he would die in prison. He'd been a federal judge in East Texas, a hardfisted conservative who knew lots of Scripture and liked to quote it during trials. He'd had political ambitions, a nice family, money from his wife's family's oil trust. He also had a drinking problem which no one knew about until he ran over two hikers in Yellowstone. Both died. The car Beech had been driving was owned by a young lady he was not married to. She was found naked in the front seat, too drunk to walk.

4

They sent him away for twelve years.

Joe Roy Spicer, Finn Yarber, Hatlee Beech. The Inferior Court of North Florida, better known as the Brethren around Trumble, a minimum security federal prison with no fences, no guard towers, no razor wire. If you had to do time, do it the federal way, and do it in a place like Trumble.

'Should we default him?' Spicer asked Beech.

'No, just continue it until next week.'

'Okay. I don't suppose he's going anywhere.'

'I object to a continuance,' Magruder said from the crowd.

'Too bad,' said Spicer. 'It's continued until next week.'

Magruder was on his feet. 'That's the third time it's been continued. I'm the plaintiff. I sued him. He runs to the infirmary every time we have a docket.'

'What're ya'll fightin over?' Spicer asked.

'Seventeen dollars and two magazines,' T. Karl said helpfully.

'That much, huh?' Spicer said. Seventeen dollars would get you sued every time at Trumble.

Finn Yarber was already bored. With one hand he stroked his shaggy gray beard, and with the other he raked his long fingernails across the table. Then he popped his toes, loudly, crunching them into the floor in an efficient little workout that grated on the nerves. In his other life, when he had titles – Mr. Chief Justice of the California Supreme Court – he often presided while wearing leather clogs, no socks, so that he could exercise his toes during the dull oral arguments. 'Continue it,' he said.

5

'Justice delayed is justice denied,' Magruder said solemnly.

'Now that's original,' said Beech. 'One more week, then we'll default Schneiter.'

'So ordered,' Spicer said, with great finality. T. Karl made a note in the docket book. Magruder sat down in a huff. He'd filed his complaint in the Inferior Court by handing to T. Karl a one-page summary of his allegations against Schneiter. Only one page. The Brethren didn't tolerate paperwork. One page and you got your day in court. Schneiter had replied with six pages of invective, all of which had been summarily stricken by T. Karl.

The rules were kept simple. Short pleadings. No discovery. Quick justice. Decisions on the spot, and all decisions were binding if both parties submitted to the jurisdiction of the court. No appeals; there was nowhere to take one. Witnesses were not given an oath to tell the truth. Lying was completely expected. It was, after all, a prison.

'What's next?' Spicer asked.

T. Karl hesitated for a second, then said, 'It's the Whiz case.'

Things were suddenly still for a moment, then the plastic cafeteria chairs rattled forward in one noisy offensive. The inmates scooted and shuffled until T. Karl announced, 'That's close enough!' They were less than twenty feet away from the bench.

'We shall maintain decorum!' he proclaimed.

The Whiz matter had been festering for months at Trumble. Whiz was a young Wall Street crook who'd bilked some rich clients. Four million dollars had never been accounted for, and legend held that Whiz had stashed it offshore and managed it from inside Trumble. He had six years left, and would be almost forty when paroled. It was widely assumed that he was quietly serving his time until one glorious day when he would walk free, still a young man, and fly off in a private jet to a beach where the money was waiting.

Inside, the legend only grew, partly because Whiz kept to himself and spent long hours every day studying financials and technical charts and reading impenetrable economic publications. Even the warden had tried to cajole him into sharing market tips.

An ex-lawyer known as Rook had somehow got next to Whiz, and had somehow convinced him to share a small morsel of advice with an investment club that met once a week in the prison chapel. On behalf of the club, Rook was now suing the Whiz for fraud.

Rook took the witness chair, and began his narrative. The usual rules of procedure and evidence were dispensed with so that the truth could be arrived at quickly, whatever form it might take.

'So I go to the Whiz and I ask him what he thinks about ValueNow, a new online company I read about in *Forbes*,' Rook explained. 'It was about to go public, and I liked the idea behind the company. Whiz said he'd check it out for me. I heard nothing. So I went back to him and said, "Hey, Whiz, what about ValueNow?" And he said he thought it was a solid company and the stock would go through the roof.'

'I did not say that,' the Whiz inserted quickly.

He was seated across the room, by himself, his arms folded over the chair in front.

'Yes you did.'

'I did not.'

'Anyway, I go back to the club and tell them that Whiz is high on the deal, so we decide we want to buy some stock in ValueNow. But little guys can't buy because the offering is closed. I go back to Whiz over there and I say, "Look, Whiz, you think you could pull some strings with your buddies on Wall Street and get us a few shares of ValueNow?" And Whiz said he thought he could do that.'

'That's a lie,' said Whiz.

'Quiet,' said Justice Spicer. 'You'll get your chance.'

'He's lying,' Whiz said, as if there was a rule against it.

If Whiz had money, you'd never know it, at least not on the inside. His eight-by-twelve cell was bare except for stacks of financial publications. No stereo, fan, books, cigarettes, none of the usual assets acquired by almost everyone else. This only added to the legend. He was considered a miser, a weird little man who saved every penny and was no doubt stashing everything offshore.

'Anyway,' Rook continued, 'we decided to gamble by taking a big position in ValueNow. Our strategy was to liquidate our holdings and consolidate.'

'Consolidate?' asked Justice Beech. Rook sounded like a portfolio manager who handled billions.

'Right, consolidate. We borrowed all we could

from friends and family, and had close to a thousand bucks.'

'A thousand bucks,' repeated Justice Spicer. Not bad for an inside job. 'Then what happened?'

'I told Whiz over there that we were ready to move. Could he get us the stock? This was on a Tuesday. The offering was on a Friday. Whiz said no problem. Said he had a buddy at Goldman Sux or some such place that could take care of us.'

'That's a lie,' Whiz shot from across the room.

'Anyway, on Wednesday I saw Whiz in the east yard, and I asked him about the stock. He said no problem.'

'That's a lie.'

'I got a witness.'

'Who?' asked Justice Spicer.

'Picasso.'

Picasso was sitting behind Rook, as were the other six members of the investment club. Picasso reluctantly waved his hand.

'Is that true?' Spicer asked.

'Yep,' Picasso answered. 'Rook asked about the stock. Whiz said he would get it. No problem.'

Picasso testified in a lot of cases, and had been caught lying more than most inmates.

'Continue,' Spicer said.

'Anyway, Thursday I couldn't find Whiz anywhere. He was hiding from me.'

'I was not.'

'Friday, the stock goes public. It was offered at twenty a share, the price we could've bought it for if Mr. Wall Street over there had done what he promised. It opened at sixty, spent most of the day at eighty, then closed at seventy. Our plans were to sell it as soon as possible. We could've bought fifty shares at twenty, sold them at eighty, and walked away from the deal with three thousand dollars in profits.'

Violence was very rare at Trumble. Three thousand dollars would not get you killed, but some bones might be broken. Whiz had been lucky so far. There'd been no ambush.

'And you think the Whiz owes you these lost profits?' asked ex-Chief Justice Finn Yarber, now plucking his eyebrows.

'Damned right we do. Look, what makes the deal stink even worse is that Whiz bought Value-Now for himself.'

'That's a damned lie,' Whiz said.

'Language, please,' Justice Beech said. If you wanted to lose a case before the Brethren, just offend Beech with your language.

The rumors that Whiz had bought the stock for himself had been started by Rook and his gang. There was no proof of it, but the story had proved irresistible and had been repeated by most inmates so often that it was now established as fact. It fit so nicely.

'Is that all?' Spicer asked Rook.

Rook had other points he wanted to elaborate on, but the Brethren had no patience with windy litigants. Especially ex-lawyers still reliving their glory days. There were at least five of them at Trumble, and they seemed to be on the docket all the time.

'I guess so,' Rook said.

'What do you have to say?' Spicer asked the Whiz.

10

Whiz stood and took a few steps toward their table. He glared at his accusers, Rook and his gang of losers. Then he addressed the court. 'What's the burden of proof here?'

Justice Spicer immediately lowered his eyes and waited for help. As a Justice of the Peace, he'd had no legal training. He'd never finished high school, then worked for twenty years in his father's country store. That's where the votes came from. Spicer relied on common sense, which was often at odds with the law. Any questions dealing with legal theory would be handled by his two colleagues.

'It's whatever we say it is,' Justice Beech said, relishing a debate with a stockbroker on the court's rules of procedure.

'Clear and convincing proof?' asked the Whiz.

'Could be, but not in this case.'

'Beyond a reasonable doubt?'

'Probably not.'

'Preponderance of the evidence?'

'Now you're getting close.'

'Then, they have no proof,' the Whiz said, waving his hands like a bad actor in a bad TV drama.

'Why don't you just tell us your side of the story?' said Beech.

'I'd love to. ValueNow was a typical online offering, lots of hype, lots of red ink on the books. Sure Rook came to me, but by the time I could make my calls, the offering was closed. I called a friend who told me you couldn't get near the stock. Even the big boys were shut out.'

'Now, how does that happen?' asked Justice Yarber.

The room was quiet. The Whiz was talking money, and everyone was listening.

'Happens all the time in IPOs. That's initial public offerings.'

'We know what an IPO is,' Beech said.

Spicer certainly did not. Didn't have many of those back in rural Mississippi.

The Whiz relaxed, just a little. He could dazzle them for a moment, win this nuisance of a case, then go back to his cave and ignore them.

'The ValueNow IPO was handled by the investment banking firm of Bakin-Kline, a small outfit in San Francisco. Five million shares were offered. Bakin-Kline basically presold the stock to its preferred customers and friends, so that most big investment firms never had a shot at the stock. Happens all the time.'

The judges and the inmates, even the court jester, hung on every word.

He continued. 'It's silly to think that some disbarred yahoo sitting in prison, reading an old copy of *Forbes*, can somehow buy a thousand dollars' worth of ValueNow.'

And at that very moment it did indeed seem very silly. Rook fumed while his club members began quietly blaming him.

'Did you buy any of it?' asked Beech.

'Of course not. I couldn't get near it. And besides, most of the high-tech and online companies are built with funny money. I stay away from them.'

'What do you prefer?' Beech asked quickly, his curiosity getting the better of him.

'Value. The long haul. I'm in no hurry. Look,

this is a bogus case brought by some boys looking for an easy buck.' He waved toward Rook, who was sinking in his chair. The Whiz sounded perfectly believable and legitimate.

Rook's case was built on hearsay, speculation, and the corroboration of Picasso, a notorious liar.

'You got any witnesses?' Spicer asked.

'I don't need any,' the Whiz said and took his seat.

Each of the three justices scribbled something on a slip of paper. Deliberations were quick, verdicts instantaneous. Yarber and Beech slid theirs to Spicer, who announced, 'By a vote of two to one, we find for the defendant. Case dismissed. Who's next?'

The vote was actually unanimous, but every verdict was officially two to one. That allowed each of the three a little wiggle room if later confronted.

But the Brethren were well regarded around Trumble. Their decisions were quick and as fair as they could make them. In fact, they were remarkably accurate in light of the shaky testimony they often heard. Spicer had presided over small cases for years, in the back of his family's country store. He could spot a liar at fifty feet. Beech and Yarber had spent their careers in courtrooms, and had no tolerance for lengthy arguments and delays, the usual tactics.

'That's all today,' T. Karl reported. 'End of docket.'

'Very well. Court is adjourned until next week.'

T. Karl jumped to his feet, his curls again vibrating across his shoulders, and declared, 'Court's adjourned. All rise.'

13

No one stood, no one moved as the Brethren left the room. Rook and his gang were huddled, no doubt planning their next lawsuit. The Whiz left quickly.

The assistant warden and the guard eased away without being seen. The weekly docket was one of the better shows at Trumble.

TWO

Though he'd served in Congress for fourteen years, Aaron Lake still drove his own car around Washington. He didn't need or want a chauffeur, or an aide, or a bodyguard. Sometimes an intern would ride with him and take notes, but for the most part Lake enjoyed the tranquillity of sitting in D.C. traffic while listening to classical guitar on the stereo. Many of his friends, especially those who'd achieved the status of a Mr. Chairman or a Mr. Vice Chairman, had larger cars with drivers. Some even had limos.

Not Lake. It was a waste of time and money and privacy. If he ever sought higher office, he certainly didn't want the baggage of a chauffeur wrapped around his neck. Besides, he enjoyed being alone. His office was a madhouse. He had fifteen people bouncing off the walls, answering phones, opening files, serving the folks back in Arizona who'd sent him to Washington. Two more did nothing but raise money. Three interns managed to further clog his narrow corridors and take up more time than they deserved.

He was single, a widower, with a quaint little

15

townhouse in Georgetown that he was very fond of. He lived quietly, occasionally stepping into the social scene that had attracted him and his late wife in the early years.

He followed the Beltway, the traffic slow and cautious because of a light snow. He was quickly cleared through CIA security at Langley, and was very pleased to see a preferred parking space waiting for him, along with two plainclothes security personnel.

'Mr. Maynard is waiting,' one of them said gravely, opening his car door while the other took his briefcase. Power did have its perks.

Lake had never met with the CIA director at Langley. They'd conferred twice on the Hill, years earlier, back when the poor guy could get around. Teddy Maynard was in a wheelchair and in constant pain, and even senators got themselves driven out to Langley anytime he needed them. He'd called Lake a half-dozen times in fourteen years, but Maynard was a busy man. His light-lifting was usually handled by associates.

Security barriers collapsed all around the congressman as he and his escorts worked their way into the depths of the CIA headquarters. By the time Lake arrived at Mr. Maynard's suite, he was walking a bit taller, with just a trace of a swagger. He couldn't help it. Power was intoxicating.

Teddy Maynard had sent for him.

Inside the room, a large, square, windowless place known unofficially as the bunker, the Director was sitting alone, looking blankly at a large screen upon which the face of Congressman Aaron Lake was frozen. It was a recent photo, one taken at a black-tie fund-raiser three months earlier where Lake had half a glass of wine, ate baked chicken, no dessert, drove himself home, alone, and went to bed before eleven. The photo was appealing because Lake was so attractive – light red hair with almost no gray, hair that was not colored or tinted, a full hairline, dark blue eyes, square chin, really nice teeth. He was fifty-three years old and aging superbly. He did thirty minutes a day on a rowing machine and his cholesterol was 160. They hadn't found a single bad habit. He enjoyed the company of women, especially when it was important to be seen with one. His steady squeeze was a sixty-year-old widow in Bethesda whose late husband had made a fortune as a lobbyist.

Both his parents were dead. His only child was a schoolteacher in Santa Fe. His wife of twenty-nine years had died in 1996 of ovarian cancer. A year later, his thirteen-year-old spaniel died too, and Congressman Aaron Lake of Arizona truly lived alone. He was Catholic, not that that mattered anymore, and he attended Mass at least once a week. Teddy pushed the button and the face disappeared.

Lake was unknown outside the Beltway, primarily because he'd kept his ego in check. If he had aspirations to higher office, they were closely guarded. His name had been mentioned once as a potential candidate for governor of Arizona, but he enjoyed Washington too much. He loved Georgetown – the crowds, the anonymity, the city life – good restaurants and cramped bookstores and espresso bars. He liked theater and music, and he and his late wife had never missed an event at the Kennedy Center.

On the Hill, Lake was known as a bright and hardworking congressman who was articulate, fiercely honest, and loyal, conscientious to a fault. Because his district was the home of four large defense contractors, he had become an expert on military hard-ware and readiness. He was Chairman of the House Committee on Armed Services, and it was in that capacity that he had come to know Teddy Maynard.

Teddy pushed the button again, and there was Lake's face. For a fifty-year veteran of intelligence wars, Teddy seldom had a knot in his stomach. He'd dodged bullets, hidden under bridges, frozen in mountains, poisoned two Czech spies, shot a traitor in Bonn, learned seven languages, fought the cold war, tried to prevent the next one, had more adventures than any ten agents combined, yet looking at the innocent face of Congressman Aaron Lake he felt a knot.

He – the CIA – was about to do something the agency had never done before.

They'd started with a hundred senators, fifty governors, four hundred and thirty-five congressmen, all the likely suspects, and now there was only one. Representative Aaron Lake of Arizona.

Teddy flicked a button and the wall went blank. His legs were covered with a quilt. He wore the same thing every day – a V-necked navy sweater, white shirt, subdued bow tie. He rolled his wheelchair to a spot near the door, and prepared to meet his candidate.

*

During the eight minutes Lake was kept waiting, he was served coffee and offered a pastry, which he declined. He was six feet tall, weighed one-seventy, was fastidious about his appearance, and had he taken the pastry Teddy would've been surprised. As far as they could tell, Lake never ate sugar. Never.

His coffee was strong, though, and as he sipped it he reviewed a little research of his own. The purpose of the meeting was to discuss the alarming flow of black market artillery into the Balkans. Lake had two memos, eighty pages of double-spaced data he'd crunched until two in the morning. He wasn't sure why Mr. Maynard wanted him to appear at Langley to discuss such a matter, but he was determined to be prepared.

A soft buzzer sounded, the door opened, and the Director of the CIA rolled out, wrapped in a quilt and looking every day of his seventy-four years. His handshake was firm, though, probably because of the strain of pushing himself around. Lake followed him back into the room, leaving the two college-educated pit bulls to guard the door.

They sat opposite each other, across a very long table that ran to the end of the room where a large white wall served as a screen. After brief preliminaries, Teddy pushed a button and another face appeared. Another button, and the lights grew dim. Lake loved it – push little buttons, high-tech images flash instantly. No doubt the room was wired with enough electronic junk to monitor his pulse from thirty feet.

'Recognize him?' Teddy asked.

'Maybe. I think I've seen the face before.'

'He's Natli Chenkov. A former general. Now a member of what's left of the Russian parliament.'

'Also known as Natty,' Lake said proudly.

'That's him. Hard-line Communist, close ties to the military, brilliant mind, huge ego, very ambitious, ruthless, and right now the most dangerous man in the world.'

'Didn't know that.'

A flick, another face, this one of stone under a gaudy military parade hat. 'This is Yuri Goltsin, second in command of what's left of the Russian army. Chenkov and Goltsin have big plans.' Another flick, a map of a section of Russia north of Moscow. 'They're stockpiling arms in this region,' Teddy said. 'They're actually stealing them from themselves, looting the Russian army, but, and more important, they're buying them on the black market.'

'Where's their money coming from?'

'Everywhere. They're swapping oil for Israeli radar. They're trafficking in drugs and buying Chinese tanks through Pakistan. Chenkov has close ties with some mobsters, one of whom recently bought a factory in Malaysia where they make nothing but assault rifles. It's very elaborate. Chenkov has a brain, a very high IQ. He's probably a genius.'

Teddy Maynard was a genius, and if he bestowed that title on another, then Congressman Lake certainly believed it. 'So who gets attacked?'

Teddy dismissed the question because he wasn't ready to answer it. 'See the town of Vologda. It's about five hundred miles east of Moscow. Last week we tracked sixty Vetrov to a warehouse there. As you know, the Vetrov –'

'Is equivalent to our Tomahawk Cruise, but two feet longer.'

'Exactly. That makes three hundred they've moved in during the last ninety days. See the town of Rybinsk, just southwest of Vologda?'

'Known for its plutonium.'

'Yes, tons of it. Enough to make ten thousand nuclear warheads. Chenkov and Goltsin and their people control the entire area.'

'Control?'

'Yes, through a web of regional mobsters and local army units. Chenkov has his people in place.'

'In place for what?'

Teddy squeezed a button and the wall was blank. But the lights stayed dim, so that when he spoke across the table he did so almost from the shadows. 'The coup is right around the corner, Mr. Lake. Our worst fears are coming true. Every aspect of Russian society and culture is cracking and crumbling. Democracy is a joke. Capitalism is a nightmare. We thought we could McDonaldize the damned place, and it's been a disaster. Workers are not getting paid, and they're the lucky ones because they have jobs. Twenty percent do not. Children are dying because there are no medicines. So are many adults. Ten percent of the population are homeless. Twenty percent are hungry. Each day things get worse. The country has been looted by the mobsters. We think at least five hundred billion dollars has been stolen and taken out of the country. There's no relief in sight. The time is perfect for a new strongman, a new

21

dictator who'll promise to lead the people back to stability. The country is crying for leadership, and Mr. Chenkov has decided it's up to him.'

'And he has the army.'

'He has the army, and that's all it takes. The coup will be bloodless because the people are ready for it. They'll embrace Chenkov. He'll lead the parade into Red Square and dare us, the United States, to stand in his way. We'll be the bad guys again.'

'So the cold war is back,' Lake said, his words fading at the end.

'There'll be nothing cold about it. Chenkov wants to expand, to recapture the old Soviet Union. He desperately needs cash, so he'll simply take it in the form of land, factories, oil, crops. He'll start little regional wars, which he'll easily win.' Another map appeared. Phase One of the new world order was presented to Lake. Teddy didn't miss a word. 'I suspect he'll roll through the Baltic States, toppling governments in Estonia, Latvia, Lithuania, etc. Then he'll go to the old Eastern bloc and strike a deal with some of the Communists there.'

The congressman was speechless as he watched Russia expand. Teddy's predictions were so certain, so precise.

'What about the Chinese?' Lake asked.

But Teddy wasn't finished with Eastern Europe. He flicked; the map changed. 'Here's where we get sucked in.'

'Poland?'

'Yep. Happens every time. Poland is now a member of NATO, for some damned reason.

22

Imagine that. Poland signing on to help protect us and Europe. Chenkov solidifies Russia's old turf, and casts a longing eye westward. Same as Hitler, except he was looking to the east.'

'Why would he want Poland?'

'Why did Hitler want Poland? It was between him and Russia. He hated the Poles, and he was ready to start a war. Chenkov doesn't give a damn about Poland, he just wants to control it. And he wants to destroy NATO.'

'He's willing to risk a third world war?'

Buttons were pushed; the screen became a wall again; lights came on. The audiovisuals were over and it was time for an even more serious conversation. Pain shot through Teddy's legs, and he couldn't keep from frowning.

'I can't answer that,' he said. 'We know a lot, but we don't know what the man's thinking. He's moving very quietly, putting people in place, setting things up. It's not completely unexpected, you know.'

'Of course not. We've had these scenarios for the last eight years, but there's always been hope that it wouldn't happen.'

'It's happening, Congressman. Chenkov and Goltsin are eliminating their opponents as we speak.'

'What's the timetable?'

Teddy shifted again under the quilt, tried another position to stop the pain. 'It's difficult to say. If he's smart, which he certainly is, he'll wait until there's rioting in the streets. I think that a year from now Natty Chenkov will be the most famous man in the world.'

'A year,' Lake said to himself, as if he'd just been given his own death sentence.

There was a long pause as he contemplated the end of the world. Teddy certainly let him. The knot in Teddy's stomach was significantly smaller now. He liked Lake a lot. He was indeed very handsome, and articulate, and smart. They'd made the right choice.

He was electable.

After a round of coffee and a phone call Teddy had to take – it was the Vice President – they reconvened their little conference and moved forward. The congressman was pleased that Teddy had so much time for him. The Russians were coming, yet Teddy seemed so calm.

'I don't have to tell you how unprepared our military is,' he said gravely.

'Unprepared for what? For war?'

'Perhaps. If we are unprepared, then we could well have a war. If we are strong, we avoid war. Right now the Pentagon could not do what it did in the Gulf War in 1991.'

'We're at seventy percent,' Lake said with authority. This was his turf.

'Seventy percent will get us a war, Mr. Lake. A war we cannot win. Chenkov is spending every dime he can steal on new hardware. We're cutting budgets and depleting our military. We want to push buttons and launch smart bombs so that no American blood is shed. Chenkov will have two million hungry soldiers, anxious to fight and die if necessary.'

For a brief moment Lake felt proud. He'd had

the guts to vote against the last budget deal because it decreased military spending. The folks back home were upset about it. 'Can't you expose Chenkov now?' he asked.

'No. Absolutely not. We have excellent intelligence. If we react to him, then he'll know that we know. It's the spy game, Mr. Lake. It's too early to make him a monster.'

'So what's your plan?' Lake asked boldly. It was quite presumptuous to ask Teddy about his plans. The meeting had accomplished its purpose. One more congressman had been sufficiently briefed. At any moment Lake could be asked to leave so that another committee chairman of some variety could be shown in.

But Teddy had big plans, and he was anxious to share them. 'The New Hampshire primary is two weeks away. We have four Republicans and three Democrats all saying the same thing. Not a single candidate wants to increase defense spending. We have a budget surplus, miracle of all miracles, and everyone has a hundred ideas about how to spend it. A bunch of imbeciles. Just a few years ago we had huge budget deficits, and Congress spent money faster than it could be printed. Now there's a surplus. They're gorging themselves on the pork.'

Congressman Lake looked away for a second, then decided to let it pass.

'Sorry about that,' Teddy said, catching himself. 'Congress as a whole is irresponsible, but we have many fine congressmen.'

'You don't have to tell me.'

'Anyway, the field is crowded with a bunch of

clones. Two weeks ago we had different front-runners. They're slinging mud and knifing each other, all for the benefit of the country's forty-fourth largest state. It's silly.' Teddy paused and grimaced and tried to reshift his useless legs. 'We need someone new, Mr. Lake, and we think that someone is you.'

Lake's first reaction was to suppress a laugh, which he did by smiling, then coughing. He tried to compose himself, and said, 'You must be kidding.'

'You know I'm not kidding, Mr. Lake,' Teddy said sternly, and there was no doubt that Aaron Lake had walked into a well-laid trap.

Lake cleared his throat and completed the job of composing himself. 'All right, I'm listening.'

'It's very simple. In fact, its simplicity makes it beautiful. You're too late to file for New Hampshire, and it doesn't matter anyway. Let the rest of the pack slug it out there. Wait until it's over, then startle everyone by announcing your candidacy for President. Many will ask, "Who the hell is Aaron Lake?" And that's fine. That's what we want. They'll find out soon enough.

'Initially, your platform will have only one plank. It's all about military spending. You're a doom-sayer, with all sorts of dire predictions about how weak our military is becoming. You'll get everybody's attention when you call for doubling our military spending.'

'Doubling?'

'It works, doesn't it? It got your attention. Double it during your four-year term.'

'But why? We need more military spending, but a twofold increase would be excessive.'

'Not if we're facing another war, Mr. Lake. A war in which we push buttons and launch Tomahawk missiles by the thousands, at a million bucks a pop. Hell, we almost ran out of them last year in that Balkan mess. We can't find enough soldiers and sailors and pilots, Mr. Lake. You know this. The military needs tons of cash to recruit young men. We're low on everything – soldiers, missiles, tanks, planes, carriers. Chenkov is building now. We're not. We're still downsizing, and if we keep it up through another Administration, then we're dead.'

Teddy's voice rose, almost in anger, and when he stopped with 'we're dead,' Aaron Lake could almost feel the earth shake from the bombing.

'Where does the money come from?' he asked.

'Money for what?'

'The military.'

Teddy snorted in disgust, then said, 'Same place it always comes from. Need I remind you, sir, that we have a surplus?'

'We're busy spending the surplus.'

'Of course you are. Listen, Mr. Lake, don't worry about the money. Shortly after you announce, we'll scare the hell out of the American people. They'll think you're half-crazy at first, some kind of wacko from Arizona who wants to build even more bombs. But we'll jolt them. We'll create a crisis on the other side of the world, and suddenly Aaron Lake will be called a visionary. Timing is everything. You make a speech about how weak we are in Asia, few people listen. Then

27

we'll create a situation over there that stops the world, and suddenly everyone wants to talk to you. It will go on like that, throughout the campaign. We'll build the tension on this end. We'll release reports, create situations, manipulate the media, embarrass your opponents. Frankly, Mr. Lake, I don't expect it to be that difficult.'

'You sound like you've been here before.'

'No. We've done some unusual things, all in an effort to protect this country. But we've never tried to swing a presidential election.' Teddy said this with an air of regret.

Lake slowly pushed his chair back, stood, stretched his arms and legs, and walked along the table to the end of the room. His feet were heavier. His pulse was racing. The trap had been sprung; he'd been caught.

He returned to his seat. 'I don't have enough money,' he offered across the table. He knew it was received by someone who'd already thought about it.

Teddy smiled and nodded and pretended to give this some thought. Lake's Georgetown home was worth $400,000. He kept about half that much in mutual funds and another $100,000 in municipal bonds. There were no significant debts. He had $40,000 in his reelection account.

'A rich candidate would not be attractive,' Teddy said, then reached for yet another button. Images returned to the wall, sharp and in color. 'Money will not be a problem, Mr. Lake,' he said, his voice much lighter. 'We'll get the defense contractors to pay for it. Look at that,' he said, waving with his right hand as if Lake wasn't sure what to look at. 'Last year the aerospace and defense industry did almost two hundred billion in business. We'll take just a fraction of that.'

'How much of a fraction?'

'As much as you need. We can realistically collect a hundred million dollars from them.'

'You also can't hide a hundred million dollars.'

'Don't bet on it, Mr. Lake. And don't worry about it. We'll take care of the money. You make the speeches, do the ads, run the campaign. The money will pour in. By the time November gets here, the American voters will be so terrified of Armageddon they won't care how much you've spent. It'll be a landslide.'

So Teddy Maynard was offering a landslide. Lake sat in a stunned but giddy silence and gawked at all that money up there on the wall – $194 billion, defense and aerospace. Last year's military budget was $270 billion. Double that to $540 billion in four years, and the contractors would get fat again. And the workers! Wages soaring through the roof! Jobs for everyone!

Candidate Lake would be embraced by executives with the cash and unions with the votes. The initial shock began to fade, and the simplicity of Teddy's plan became clear. Collect the cash from those who will profit. Scare the voters into racing to the polls. Win in a landslide. And in doing so save the world.

Teddy let him think for a moment, then said, 'We'll do most of it through PACs. The unions, engineers, executives, business coalitions – there's no shortage of political groups already on the books. And we'll form some others.'

Lake was already forming them. Hundreds of PACs, all flush with more cash than any election had ever seen. The shock was now completely gone, replaced by the sheer excitement of the idea. A thousand questions raced through his mind: Who'll be my Vice President? Who'll run the campaign? Chief of staff? Where to announce? 'It might work,' he said, under control.

'Oh yes. It'll work, Mr. Lake. Trust me. We've been planning this for some time.'

'How many people know about it?'

'Just a few. You've been carefully chosen, Mr. Lake. We examined many potential candidates, and your name kept rising to the top. We've checked your background.'

'Pretty dull, huh?'

'I suppose. Although your relationship with Ms. Valotti concerns me. She's been divorced twice and likes painkillers.'

'Didn't know I had a relationship with Ms. Valotti.'

'You've been seen with her recently.'

'You guys are watching, aren't you?'

'You expect something less?'

'I guess not.'

'You took her to a black-tie cry-a-thon for oppressed women in Afghanistan. Gimme a break.' Teddy's words were suddenly short and dripping with sarcasm.

'I didn't want to go.'

'Then don't. Stay away from that crap. Leave it for Hollywood. Valotti's nothing but trouble.'

'Anybody else?' Lake asked, more than a little defensive. His private life had been pretty dull since he'd become a widower. He was suddenly proud of it.

'Not really,' Teddy said. 'Ms. Benchly seems to be quite stable and makes a lovely escort.'

'Oh, thank you very much.'

'You'll get hammered on abortion, but you won't be the first.'

'It's a tired issue,' Lake said. And he was tired of grappling with it. He'd been for abortions, against abortions, soft on reproductive rights, tough on reproductive rights, pro-choice, pro-child, anti-women, embraced by the feminists. In his fourteen years on Capitol Hill he'd been chased all over the abortion minefield, getting bloodied with each new strategic move.

Abortion didn't scare him anymore, at least not at the moment. He was much more concerned with the CIA sniffing through his background.

'What about GreenTree?' he asked.

Teddy waved his right hand as if it was nothing. 'Twenty-two years ago. Nobody got convicted. Your partner went bankrupt and got himself indicted, but the jury let him walk. It'll come up; everything will come up. But frankly, Mr. Lake, we'll keep the attention diverted elsewhere. There's an advantage in jumping in at the last minute. The press won't have too much time to dig up dirt.'

'I'm single. We've elected an unmarried president only once.'

'You're a widower, the husband of a very lovely lady who was well respected both here and back home. It won't be an issue. Trust me.'

'So what worries you?'

'Nothing, Mr. Lake. Not a thing. You're a solid candidate, very electable. We'll create the issues and the fear, and we'll raise the money.'

Lake stood again, walked around the room rubbing his hair, scratching his chin, trying to clear his head. 'I have a lot of questions,' he said.

'Maybe I can answer some of them. Let's talk again tomorrow, right here, same time. Sleep on it, Mr. Lake. Time is crucial, but I suppose a man should have twenty-four hours before making such a decision.' Teddy actually smiled when he said this.

'That's a wonderful idea. Let me think about it. I'll have an answer tomorrow.'

'No one knows we've had this little chat.'

'Of course not.'

THREE

In terms of space, the law library occupied exactly one fourth of the square footage of the entire Trumble library. It was in a corner, partitioned off by a wall of red brick and glass, tastefully done at taxpayer expense. Inside the law library, shelves of well-used books stood packed together with barely enough room for an inmate to squeeze between them. Around the walls were desks covered with typewriters and computers and sufficient research clutter to resemble any big-firm library.

The Brethren ruled the law library. All inmates were allowed to use it, of course, but there was an unwritten policy that one needed permission to stay there for any length of time. Maybe not permission, but at least notice.

Justice Joe Roy Spicer of Mississippi earned forty cents an hour sweeping the floors and straightening the desks and shelves. He also emptied the trash, and was generally considered to be a pig when it came to his menial tasks. Justice Hatlee Beech of Texas was the official law librarian, and at fifty cents an hour was the highest paid. He was fastidious about 'his volumes,' and often bickered

33

with Spicer about their care. Justice Finn Yarber, once of the California Supreme Court, was paid twenty cents an hour as a computer technician. His pay was at the bottom of the scale because he knew so little about computers.

On a typical day, the three spent between six and eight hours in the law library. If a Trumble inmate had a legal problem, he simply made an appointment with one of the Brethren and visited their little suite. Hatlee Beech was an expert on sentencing and appeals. Finn Yarber did bankruptcies, divorces, and child support cases. Joe Roy Spicer, with no formal legal training, had no real specialty. Nor did he want one. He ran the scams.

Strict rules prohibited the Brethren from charging fees for their legal work, but the strict rules meant little. They were, after all, convicted felons, and if they could quietly pick up some cash on the outside then everyone would be happy. Sentencing was a moneymaker. About a fourth of the inmates who arrived at Trumble had been improperly sentenced. Beech could review the records overnight and find the loopholes. A month earlier, he had knocked four years off the sentence of a young man who'd been given fifteen. The family had agreed to pay, and the Brethren earned $5,000, their biggest fee to date. Spicer arranged the secret deposit through their lawyer in Neptune Beach.

There was a cramped conference room in the back of the law library, behind the shelves and barely visible from the main room. The door to it had a large glass window, but no one bothered to look in. The Brethren retired there for quiet business. They called it their chamber.

Spicer had just met with their lawyer and he had mail, some really good letters. He closed the door and removed an envelope from a file. He waved it for Beech and Yarber to see. 'It's yellow,' he said. 'Ain't that sweet? It's for Ricky.'

'Who's it from?' Yarber asked.

'Curtis from Dallas.'

'The banker?' Beech asked excitedly.

'No, Curtis owns the jewelry stores. Listen.' Spicer unfolded the letter, also on soft yellow stationery. He smiled and cleared his throat and began to read: ' "Dear Ricky: Your letter of January eighth made me cry. I read it three times before I put it down. You poor boy. Why are they keeping you there?" '

'Where is he?' asked Yarber.

'Ricky's locked down in a fancy drug rehab unit his rich uncle is paying for. He's been in for a year, is clean and fully rehabbed, but the terrible people who run the place won't release him until April because they've been collecting twenty thousand dollars a month from his rich uncle, who just wants him locked away and won't send any spending money. Do you remember any of this?'

'Now I do.'

'You helped with the fiction. May I proceed?'

'Please do.'

Spicer continued reading: ' "I'm tempted to fly down there and confront those evil people myself. And your uncle, what a loser! Rich people like him think they can just send money and not get involved. As I told you, my father was quite wealthy, and he was the most miserable person I've ever known. Sure he bought me things – objects that were temporary and meant nothing when they were gone. But he never had time for me. He was a sick man, just like your uncle. I've enclosed a check for a thousand dollars if you need anything from the commissary.

' "Ricky, I can't wait to see you in April. I've already told my wife that there is an international diamond show in Orlando that month, and she has no interest in going with me." '

'April?' asked Beech.

'Yep. Ricky is certain he will be released in April.'

'Ain't that sweet,' Yarber said with a smile. 'And Curtis has a wife and kids?'

'Curtis is fifty-eight, three adult children, two grandchildren.'

'Where's the check?' asked Beech.

Spicer flipped the sheets of stationery and went to page two. ' "We have to make certain you can meet me in Orlando," ' he read. ' "Are you sure you'll finally be released in April? Please tell me you will. I think about you every hour. I keep your photo hidden in my desk drawer, and when I look into your eyes I know that we should be together." '

'Sick, sick, sick,' Beech said, still smiling. 'And he's from Texas.'

'I'm sure there are a lot of sweet boys in Texas,' Yarber said.

'And none in California?'

'The rest of it is just mush,' Spicer said, scanning quickly. There would be plenty of time to read it later. He held up the $1,000 check for his colleagues to see. In due course, it would be

36

smuggled out to their attorney and he would deposit it in their hidden account.

'When are we gonna bust him?' Yarber asked.

'Let's swap a few more letters. Ricky needs to share some more misery.'

'Maybe one of the guards could beat him up, or something like that,' Beech said.

'They don't have guards,' replied Spicer. 'It's a designer rehab clinic, remember? They have counselors.'

'But it's a lockdown facility, right? That means gates and fences, so surely there's a guard or two around. What if Ricky got attacked in the shower or the locker room by some goon who wanted his body?'

'It can't be a sexual attack,' Yarber said. 'That might scare Curtis. He might think Ricky caught a disease or something.'

And so the fiction went for a few minutes as they created more misery for poor Ricky. His picture had been lifted from the bulletin board of a fellow inmate, copied at a quick print by their lawyer, and had now been sent to more than a dozen pen pals across North America. The photo was of a smiling college grad, in a navy robe with a cap and gown, holding a diploma, a very handsome young man.

It was decided that Beech would work on the new story for a few days, then write a rough draft of the next letter to Curtis. Beech was Ricky, and at that moment their little tormented fictional boy was writing his tales of misery to eight different caring souls. Justice Yarber was Percy, also a young man locked away for drugs but now clean and nearing release and looking for an older sugar daddy with whom to spend meaningful time. Percy had five hooks in the water, and was slowly reeling them in.

Joe Roy Spicer didn't write very well. He coordinated the scam, helped with the fiction, kept the stories straight, and met with the lawyer who brought the mail. And he handled the money.

He pulled out another letter and announced, 'This, Your Honors, is from Quince.'

Everything stopped as Beech and Yarber stared at the letter. Quince was a wealthy banker in a small town in Iowa, according to the six letters he and Ricky had swapped. Like the rest, they'd found him through the personals of a gay magazine now hidden in the law library. He'd been their second catch, the first having become suspicious and disappearing. Quince's photo of himself was a snapshot taken at a lake, with the shirt off, the potbelly, the skinny arms, the receding hairline of a fifty-one-year-old – his family all around him. It was a bad photo, no doubt selected by Quince because it might be difficult to identify him, if anyone ever tried.

'Would you like to read it, Ricky boy?' Spicer asked, handing the letter to Beech, who took it and looked at the envelope. Plain white, no return address, typed lettering.

'Have you read it?' Beech asked.

'No. Go ahead.'

Beech slowly removed the letter, a plain sheet of white paper with tight single-spaced paragraphs produced by an old typewriter. He cleared his voice, and read: ' "Dear Ricky: It's done. I can't believe I did it, but I pulled it off. I used a pay phone and a money order so nothing could be traced – I think my trail is clean. The company you suggested in New York was superb, very discreet and helpful. I have to be honest, Ricky, it scared the hell out of me. Booking a gay cruise is something I never dreamed of doing. And you know what? It was exhilarating. I am so proud of myself. We have a cabin suite, a thousand bucks a night, and I can't wait." '

Beech stopped and glanced above his reading glasses halfway down his nose. Both of his colleagues were smiling, savoring the words.

He continued: ' "We set sail on March tenth, and I have a wonderful idea. I will arrive in Miami on the ninth, so we won't have much time to get together and introduce ourselves. Let's meet on the boat, in our suite. I'll get there first, check in, get the champagne on ice, then wait for you. Won't that be fun, Ricky? We'll have three days to ourselves. I say we don't leave the room." '

Beech couldn't help but smile, and he somehow managed to do so while shaking his head in disgust.

He continued: ' "I am so excited about our little trip. I have finally decided to discover who I really am, and you've given me the courage to take the first step. Though we haven't met, Ricky, I can never thank you enough.

' "Please write me back immediately and confirm. Take care, my Ricky. Love, Quince." '

'I think I'm gonna vomit,' Spicer said, but he wasn't convincing. There was too much to do.

'Let's bust him,' Beech said. The others quickly agreed.

'How much?' asked Yarber.

'At least a hundred thousand,' said Spicer. 'His family has owned banks for two generations. We know his father is still active in the business, so you have to figure the old man might go nuts if his boy gets outed. Quince can't afford to get booted from the family gravy train, so he'll pay whatever we demand. It's a perfect situation.'

Beech was already taking notes. So was Yarber. Spicer began pacing around the small room like a bear stalking prey. The ideas came slowly, the language, the opinions, the strategy, but before long the letter took shape.

In rough draft, Beech read it: '"Dear Quince: So nice to get your letter of January fourteenth. I'm so happy you got the gay cruise booked. It sounds delightful. One problem, though. I won't be able to make it, and there are a couple of reasons for this. One is that I won't be released for a few more years. I'm in a prison, not a drug treatment clinic. And I'm not gay, far from it. I have a wife and two kids, and right now they're having a difficult time financially because I'm sitting here in prison, unable to support them. That's where you come in, Quince. I need some of your money. I want a hundred thousand dollars. We can call it hush money. You send it, and I'll forget the Ricky business and the gay cruise and no one in Bakers, Iowa, will ever know anything about it. Your wife and your children and your father and the rest of your rich family will never know about Ricky. If you don't send the money, then I'll flood your little town with copies of our letters.

' "It's called extortion, Quince, and you're

caught. It's cruel and mean and criminal, and I don't care. I need money, and you have it." '

Beech stopped and looked around the room for approval.

'It's beautiful,' said Spicer, already spending the loot.

'It's nasty,' said Yarber. 'But what if he kills himself?'

'That's a long shot,' said Beech.

They read the letter again, then debated whether the timing was right. They did not mention the illegality of their scam, or the punishment if they got caught. Those discussions had been laid to rest months earlier when Joe Roy Spicer had convinced the other two to join him. The risks were insignificant when weighed against the potential returns. The Quinces who got themselves snared were not likely to run to the police and complain of extortion.

But they hadn't busted anyone yet. They were corresponding with a dozen or so potential victims, all middle-aged men who'd made the mistake of answering this simple ad:

> SWM in 20s looking for kind and
> discreet gentleman in 40s or 50s
> to pen pal with.

One little personal in small print in the back of a gay magazine had yielded sixty responses, and Spicer had the chore of sifting through the rubbish and identifying rich targets. At first he'd found the work disgusting, then he became amused by it. Now it was a business because they were about to extort a hundred thousand bucks from a perfectly innocent man.

Their lawyer would take a third, the usual cut but a frustrating percentage nonetheless. They had no choice. He was a critical player in their crimes.

They worked on the letter to Quince for an hour, then agreed to sleep on it and do a final draft the next day. There was another letter from a man using the pseudonym of Hoover. It was his second, written to Percy, and rambled on for four paragraphs about bird-watching. Yarber would be forced to study birds before writing back as Percy and professing a great interest in the subject. Evidently, Hoover was afraid of his shadow. He revealed nothing personal, and there was no indication of money.

Give him some more rope, the Brethren decided. Talk about birds, then try to nudge him to the subject of physical companionship. If Hoover didn't take the hint, and if he didn't reveal something about his financial situation, then they'd drop him.

Within the Bureau of Prisons, Trumble was officially referred to as a camp. Such a designation meant there were no fences around the grounds, no razor wire, no watchtowers, no guards with rifles waiting to nail escapees. A camp meant minimum security, so that any inmate could simply walk away if he chose. There were a thousand at Trumble, but few walked away.

It was nicer than most public schools. Air-conditioned dorms, clean cafeteria serving three squares a day, a weight room, billiards, cards, racquetball, basketball, volleyball, jogging track, library, chapel, ministers on duty, counselors, caseworkers, unlimited visiting hours.

Trumble was as good as it could get for prisoners, all of whom were classified as low risk. Eighty percent were there for drug crimes. About forty had robbed banks without hurting or really scaring anyone. The rest were white-collar types whose crimes ranged from small-time scams to Dr. Floyd, a surgeon whose office had bilked Medicare out of $6 million over two decades.

Violence was not tolerated at Trumble. Threats were rare. There were plenty of rules and the administration had little trouble enforcing them. If you screwed up, they sent you away, to a medium-security prison, one with razor wire and rough guards.

Trumble's prisoners were content to behave themselves and count their days, the federal way.

Pursuing serious criminal activity on the inside was unheard of, until the arrival of Joe Roy Spicer. Before his fall, Spicer had heard stories about the Angola scam, named for the infamous Louisiana state penitentiary. Some inmates there had perfected the gay-extortion scheme, and before they were caught they had fleeced their victims of $700,000.

Spicer was from a rural county near the Louisiana line, and the Angola scam was a notorious affair in his part of the state. He never dreamed he'd copy it. But he woke up one morning in a federal pen, and decided to shaft every living soul he could get close enough to.

He walked the track every day at 1 P.M., usually

43

alone, always with a pack of Marlboros. He hadn't smoked for ten years before his incarceration; now he was up to two packs a day. So he walked to negate the damage to his lungs. In thirty-four months he'd walked 1,242 miles. And he'd lost twenty pounds, though probably not from exercise, as he liked to claim. The prohibition against beer was more responsible for the weight loss.

Thirty-four months of walking and smoking, twenty-one months to go.

Ninety thousand dollars of the stolen bingo money was literally buried in his backyard, a half a mile behind his house next to a toolshed – entombed in a homemade concrete vault his wife knew nothing about. She'd helped him spend the rest of the loot, $180,000 altogether, though the feds had traced only half of it. They'd bought Cadillacs and flown to Las Vegas, first class out of New Orleans, and they'd been driven around by casino limos and put up in suites.

If he had any dreams left, one was to be a professional gambler, headquartered out of Vegas but known and feared by casinos everywhere. Blackjack was his game, and though he'd lost a ton, he was still convinced he could beat any house. There were casinos in the Caribbean he'd never seen. Asia was heating up. He'd travel the world, first class, with or without his wife, stay in fancy suites, order room service, and terrorize any blackjack dealer dumb enough to deal him cards.

He'd take the $90,000 from his backyard, add it to his share of the Angola scam, and move to Vegas. With or without her. She hadn't been to Trumble in four months, although she used to come every three weeks. He had nightmares of her plowing up the backyard looking for his buried treasure. He was almost convinced she didn't know about the money, but there was room for doubt. He'd been drinking two nights before being shipped off to prison, and had said something about the $90,000. He couldn't remember his exact words. Try as he might, he simply could not recall what he'd told her.

He lit another Marlboro at mile one. Maybe she had a boyfriend now. Rita Spicer was an attractive woman, a little chunky in places but nothing $90,000 couldn't hide. What if she and a new squeeze had found the money and were already spending it? One of Joe Roy's worst recurring nightmares was a scene from a bad movie – Rita and some unknown male with shovels digging like idiots in the rain. Why the rain, he didn't know. But it was always at night, in the middle of a thunderstorm, and the lightning would flash and he would see them slogging their way through the backyard, each time getting nearer and nearer to the toolshed.

In one dream the new mystery boyfriend was on a bulldozer, pushing piles of dirt all over the Spicer farm while Rita stood nearby, pointing here and there with her shovel.

Joe Roy craved the money. He could feel the cash in his hands. He would steal and extort all he could while he counted his days at Trumble, then he would rescue his buried loot and head for Vegas. No one in his hometown would have the pleasure of pointing and whispering and saying,

'There's old Joe Roy. Guess he's out of the pen now.' No sir.

He'd be living the high life. With or without her.

FOUR

Teddy looked at his pill bottles lined along the edge of his table, like little executioners ready to take away his misery. York was seated across from him, reading from his notes.

York said, 'He was on the phone until three this morning, talking to friends in Arizona.'

'Who?'

'Bobby Lander, Jim Gallison, Richard Hassel, the usual gang. His money people.'

'Dale Winer?'

'Yes, him too,' York said, amazed at Teddy's recall. Teddy had his eyes closed now, and was rubbing his temples. Somewhere between them, somewhere deep in his brain, he knew the names of Lake's friends, his contributors, his confidants, his poll workers, and his old high school teachers. All of it neatly tucked away, ready to be used if necessary.

'Anything unusual?'

'No, not really. Just the typical questions you'd expect from a man contemplating such an unexpected move. His friends were surprised, even

47

shocked, and somewhat reluctant, but they'll come around.'

'Did they ask about money?'

'Of course. He was vague, said it would not be a problem, though. They are skeptical.'

'Did he keep our secrets?'

'He certainly did.'

'Was he worried about us listening?'

'I don't think so. He made eleven calls from his office and eight from his home. None from his cell phones.'

'Faxes? E-mail?'

'None. He spent two hours with Schiara, his –'

'Chief of staff.'

'Right. They basically planned the campaign. Schiara wants to run it. They like Nance of Michigan as VP.'

'Not a bad choice.'

'He looks fine. We're already checking him. Had a divorce when he was twenty-three, but that was thirty years ago.'

'Not a problem. Is Lake ready to commit?'

'Oh yes. He's a politician, isn't he? He's been promised the keys to the kingdom. He's already writing speeches.'

Teddy removed a pill from a bottle and swallowed it without the aid of anything liquid. He frowned as if it was bitter. He squeezed the wrinkles in his forehead and said, 'York, tell me we're not missing anything on this guy. No skeletons.'

'No skeletons, Chief. We've examined his dirty underwear for six months. There's nothing that can hurt us.'

'He's not going to marry some fool, is he?'

'No. He dates several women, but nothing serious.'

'No sex with his interns?'

'None. He's clean.'

They were repeating a dialogue they'd had many times. Once more wouldn't hurt.

'No shady financial deals from another lifetime?'

'This is his life, Chief. There's nothing back there.'

'Booze, drugs, prescription pills, gambling on the Internet?'

'No sir. He's very clean, sober, straight, bright, pretty remarkable.'

'Let's talk to him.'

Aaron Lake was once again escorted to the same room deep inside Langley, this time with three handsome young men guarding him as if danger lurked at every corner. He walked even quicker than the day before, his head even taller, his back without the slightest curve. His stature was rising by the hour.

Once again he said hello to Teddy and shook his calloused hand, then followed the quilt-laden wheelchair into the bunker and sat across the table. Pleasantries were exchanged. York watched from a room down the hall where three monitors hooked to hidden cameras relayed every word, every movement. Next to York were two men who spent their time studying tapes of people as they talked and breathed and moved their hands and eyes and heads and feet, in an effort to determine what the speakers really meant.

'Did you sleep much last night?' Teddy asked, managing a smile.

'Yes, actually,' Lake lied.

'Good. I take it you're willing to accept our deal.'

'Deal? I didn't know it was exactly a deal.'

'Oh yes, Mr. Lake, it's exactly a deal. We promise to get you elected, and you promise to double defense spending and get ready for the Russians.'

'Then you have a deal.'

'That's good, Mr. Lake. I'm very pleased. You'll make an excellent candidate and a fine President.'

The words rang through Lake's ears, and he couldn't believe them. President Lake. President Aaron Lake. He'd paced the floor until five that morning trying to convince himself that the White House was being offered to him. It seemed too easy.

And as hard as he tried, he couldn't ignore the trappings. The Oval Office. All those jets and helicopters. The world to be traveled. A hundred aides at his beck and call. State dinners with the most powerful people in the world.

And, above all, a place in history.

Oh yes, Teddy had himself a deal.

'Let's talk about the campaign itself,' Teddy said. 'I think you should announce two days after New Hampshire. Let the dust settle. Let the winners get their fifteen minutes and let the losers sling more mud, then announce.'

'That's pretty fast,' Lake said.

'We don't have a lot of time. We ignore New

Hampshire and get ready for Arizona and Michigan on February twenty-second. It's imperative that you win those two states. When you do, you establish yourself as a serious candidate, and you're set for the month of March.'

'I was thinking of announcing back home, somewhere in Phoenix.'

'Michigan's better. It's a bigger state, fifty-eight delegates, compared to twenty-four for Arizona. You'll be expected to win at home. If you win in Michigan on the same day, then you're a candidate to be reckoned with. Announce in Michigan first, then do it again hours later in your home district.'

'An excellent idea.'

'There's a helicopter plant in Flint, D-L Trilling. They have a large hangar, four thousand workers. The CEO is a man I can talk to.'

'Book it,' Lake said, certain that Teddy had already chatted with the CEO.

'Can you start filming ads day after tomorrow?'

'I can do anything,' Lake said, settling into the passenger's seat. It was becoming obvious who was driving the bus.

'With your approval, we'll hire an outside consulting group to front the ads and publicity. But we have better people here, and they won't cost you anything. Not that money will be a problem, you understand.'

'I think a hundred million should cover things.'

'It should. Anyway, we'll start working on the TV ads today. I think you'll like them. They're total gloom and doom – the miserable shape of our military, all sorts of threats from abroad. Armageddon, that sort of stuff. They'll scare the hell out of people. We'll plug in your name and face and a few brief words, and in no time you'll be the most famous politician in the country.'

'Fame won't win the election.'

'No, it won't. But money will. Money buys television and polls, and that's all it takes.'

'I'd like to think the message is important.'

'Oh, it is, Mr. Lake, and our message is far more important than tax cuts and affirmative action and abortion and trust and family values and all the other silliness we're hearing. Our message is life and death. Our message will change the world and protect our affluence. That's all we really care about.'

Lake was nodding his agreement. Protect the economy, keep the peace, and American voters would elect anyone. 'I have a good man to run the campaign,' Lake said, anxious to offer something.

'Who?'

'Mike Schiara, my chief of staff. He's my closest adviser, a man I trust implicitly.'

'Any experience on the national level?' Teddy asked, knowing full well there was none.

'No, but he's quite capable.'

'That's fine. It's your campaign.'

Lake smiled and nodded at the same time. That was good to hear. He was beginning to wonder.

'What about Vice President?' Teddy asked.

'I have a couple of names. Senator Nance of Michigan is an old friend. There's also Governor Guyce from Texas.'

Teddy received the names with careful deliberation. Not bad selections, really, though Guyce would never work. He was a rich boy who'd skated through college and golfed through his thirties, then spent a fortune of his father's money to purchase the governor's mansion for four years. Besides, they wouldn't have to worry about Texas.

'I like Nance,' Teddy said.

Then Nance it would be, Lake almost said.

They talked about money for an hour, the first wave from the PACs and how to accept instant millions without creating too much suspicion. Then the second wave from the defense contractors. Then the third wave of cash and other untraceables.

There'd be a fourth wave Lake would never know about. Depending on the polls, Teddy Maynard and his organization would be prepared to literally haul boxes filled with cash into union halls and black churches and white VFWs in places like Chicago and Detroit and Memphis and throughout the Deep South. Working with locals they were already identifying, they would be prepared to buy every vote they could find.

The more Teddy pondered his plan, the more convinced he became that the election would be won by Mr. Aaron Lake.

Trevor's little law office was in Neptune Beach, several blocks from Atlantic Beach, though no one could tell where one beach stopped and the other started. Jacksonville was several miles to the west and creeping toward the sea every minute. The office was a converted summer rental, and from his sagging back porch Trevor could see the beach and the ocean and hear the seagulls. Hard to believe he'd been renting the place for twelve years now.

Early in the lease he'd enjoyed hiding on the porch, away from the phone and the clients, staring endlessly at the gentle waters of the Atlantic two blocks away.

He was from Scranton, and like all snowbirds, he'd finally grown weary of gazing at the sea, roaming the beaches barefoot, and throwing bread crumbs to the birds. Now he preferred to waste time locked in his office.

Trevor was terrified of courtrooms and judges. While this was unusual and even somewhat honorable, it made for a different style of lawyering. It relegated Trevor to paperwork – real estate closings, wills, leases, zoning – all the mundane, nondazzling, smalltime areas of the profession no one told him about in law school. Occasionally he handled a drug case, never one involving a trial, and it was one of his unfortunate clients at Trumble who'd connected him with the Honorable Joe Roy Spicer. In short order he'd become the official attorney for all three – Spicer, Beech, and Yarber. The Brethren, as even Trevor referred to them.

He was a courier, nothing more or less. He smuggled them letters disguised as official legal documents and thus protected by the lawyer-client privilege. And he sneaked their letters out. He gave them no advice, and they sought none. He ran their bank account offshore and handled phone calls from the families of their clients inside Trumble. He fronted their dirty little deals, and in doing so avoided courtrooms and judges and other lawyers, and this suited Trevor just fine.

He was also a member of their conspiracy, easily

indictable should they ever be exposed, but he wasn't worried. The Angola scam was absolutely brilliant because its victims couldn't complain. For an easy fee with potential rewards, he'd gamble with the Brethren.

He eased from his office without seeing his secretary, then sneaked away in his restored 1970 VW Beetle, no air-conditioning. He drove down First Street toward Atlantic Boulevard, the ocean visible through homes and cottages and rentals. He wore old khakis, a white cotton shirt, a yellow bow tie, a blue seersucker jacket, all of it heavily wrinkled. He passed Pete's Bar and Grill, the oldest watering hole along the beaches and his personal favorite even though the college kids had discovered the place. He had an outstanding and very past-due bar tab there of $361, almost all for Coors longnecks and lemon daiquiris, and he really wanted to clear the debt.

He turned west on Atlantic Boulevard, and began fighting the traffic into Jacksonville. He cursed the sprawl and the congestion and the cars with Canadian plates. Then he was on the bypass, north past the airport and soon deep into the flat Florida countryside.

Fifty minutes later he parked at Trumble. You gotta love the federal system, he told himself again. Lots of parking close to the front entrance, nicely landscaped grounds tended daily by the inmates, and modern, well-kept buildings.

He said, 'Hello, Mackey,' to the white guard at the door, and 'Hello, Vince,' to the black one. Rufus at the front desk X-rayed the briefcase while

Nadine did the paperwork for his visit. 'How're the bass?' he asked Rufus.

'Ain't biting,' Rufus said.

No lawyer in the brief history of Trumble had visited as much as Trevor. They took his picture again, stamped the back of his hand with invisible ink, and led him through two doors and a short hallway. 'Hello, Link,' he said to the next guard.

'Mornin, Trevor,' Link said. Link ran the visitors' area, a large open space with lots of padded chairs and vending machines against one wall, a playground for youngsters, and a small outdoor patio where two people could sit at a picnic table and share a moment. It was cleaned and shined and completely empty. It was a weekday. Traffic picked up on Saturdays and Sundays, but for the rest of the time Link observed an empty area.

They went to the lawyers' room, one of several private cubbyholes with doors that shut and windows through which Link could do his observing, if he were so inclined. Joe Roy Spicer was waiting and reading the daily sports section where he played the odds on college basketball. Trevor and Link stepped into the room together, and very quickly Trevor removed two twenty-dollar bills and handed them to Link. The closed-circuit cameras couldn't see them if they did this just inside the door. As part of the routine, Spicer pretended not to see the transaction.

Then the briefcase was opened and Link made a pretense of looking through it. He did this without touching a thing. Trevor removed a large manila envelope which was sealed and marked in bold

'Legal Papers.' Link took it and squeezed it to make sure it held only papers and not a gun or a bottle of pills, then he gave it back. They'd done this dozens of times.

Trumble regulations required a guard to be present in the room when all papers were removed and all envelopes were opened. But the two twenties got Link outside where he posted himself at the door because there was simply nothing else to guard at the moment. He knew letters were being passed back and forth, and he didn't care. As long as Trevor didn't traffic in weapons or drugs, Link wouldn't get involved. The place had so many silly regulations anyway. He leaned on the door, with his back to it, and before long was drifting into one of his many horse naps, one leg stiff, the other bent at the knee.

In the lawyers' room, little legal work was being done. Spicer was still absorbed in point spreads. Most inmates welcomed their guests. Spicer only tolerated his.

'Got a call last night from the brother of Jeff Daggett,' Trevor said. 'The kid from Coral Gables.'

'I know him,' Spicer said, finally lowering his newspaper because money was on the horizon. 'He got twelve years in a drug conspiracy.'

'Yep. His brother says that there's this ex-federal judge inside Trumble who's looked over his papers and thinks he might be able to knock off a few years. This judge wants a fee, so Daggett calls his brother, who calls me.' Trevor removed his rumpled blue seersucker jacket and flung it on a chair. Spicer hated his bow tie.

'How much can they pay?'

'Have you guys quoted a fee?' Trevor asked.

'Beech may have, I don't know. We try to get five thousand for a two-two-five-five reduction.' Spicer said this as if he had practiced criminal law in the federal courts for years. Truth was, the only time he'd actually seen a federal courtroom was the day he was sentenced.

'I know,' Trevor said. 'I'm not sure they can pay five thousand. The kid had a public defender for a lawyer.'

'Then squeeze whatever you can, but get at least a thousand up front. He's not a bad kid.'

'You're getting soft, Joe Roy.'

'No. I'm getting meaner.'

And in fact he was. Joe Roy was the managing partner of the Brethren. Yarber and Beech had the talent and the training, but they'd been too humiliated by their fall to have any ambition. Spicer, with no training and little talent, possessed enough manipulative skills to keep his colleagues on track. While they brooded, he dreamed of his comeback.

Joe Roy opened a file and withdrew a check. 'Here's a thousand bucks to deposit. Came from a pen pal in Texas named Curtis.'

'What's his potential?'

'Very good, I think. We're ready to bust Quince in Iowa.' Joe Roy withdrew a pretty lavender envelope, tightly sealed and addressed to Quince Garbe in Bakers, Iowa.

'How much?' Trevor asked, taking the envelope.

'A hundred thousand.'

'Wow.'

'He's got it, and he'll pay it. I've given him the wiring instructions. Alert the bank.'

In twenty-three years of practicing law, Trevor had never earned a fee anywhere close to $33,000. Suddenly, he could see it, touch it, and, though he tried not to, he began spending it – $33,000 for doing nothing but shuttling mail.

'You really think this will work?' he asked, mentally paying off the tab at Pete's Bar and telling MasterCard to take this check and shove it. He'd keep the same car, his beloved Beetle, but he might spring for an air conditioner.

'Of course it will,' Spicer said, without a trace of doubt.

He had two more letters, both written by Justice Yarber posing as young Percy in rehab. Trevor took them with anticipation.

'Arkansas is at Kentucky tonight,' Spicer said, returning to his newspaper. 'The line is fourteen. Whatta you think?'

'Much closer than that. Kentucky is very tough at home.'

'Are you in?'

'Are you?'

Trevor had a bookie at Pete's Bar, and though he gambled little he had learned to follow the lead of Justice Spicer.

'I'll put a hundred on Arkansas,' Spicer said.

'I think I will too.'

They played blackjack for half an hour, with Link occasionally glancing in and frowning his disapproval. Cards were prohibited during visitation, but who cared? Joe Roy played the game hard because he was training for his next career. Poker and gin rummy were the favorites in the rec room, and Spicer often had trouble finding a blackjack opponent.

Trevor wasn't particularly good, but he was always willing to play. It was, in Spicer's opinion, his only redeeming quality.

FIVE

The announcement had the festive air of a victory party, with red, white, and blue banners and bunting draped from the ceiling and parade music blasting through the hangar. Every D-L Trilling employee was required to be present, all four thousand of them, and to heighten their spirits they had been promised a full day of extra vacation. Eight hours paid, at an average wage of $22.40, but management didn't care because they had found their man. The hastily built stage was also covered in banners and packed with every suit in the company, all smiling broadly and clapping wildly as the music whipped the crowd into a frenzy. Three days earlier no one had heard of Aaron Lake. Now he was their savior.

He certainly looked like a candidate, with a new slightly trimmer haircut suggested by one consultant and a dark brown suit suggested by another. Only Reagan had been able to wear brown suits, and he'd won two landslides.

When Lake finally appeared, and strode purposefully across the stage, shaking vigorously the hands of corporate honchos he'd never see again, the laborers went wild. The music was carefully ratcheted up a couple of notches by a sound consultant who was a member of a sound team Lake's people had hired for $24,000 for the event. Money was of little concern.

Balloons fell like manna. Some were popped by workers who'd been asked to pop them, so for a few seconds the hangar sounded like the first wave of a ground attack. Get ready for it. Get ready for war. Lake Before It's Too Late.

The Trilling CEO clutched him as if they were fraternity brothers, when in fact they'd met two hours earlier. The CEO then took the podium and waited for the noise to subside. Working with notes he'd been faxed the day before, he began a long-winded and quite generous introduction of Aaron Lake, future President. On cue, the applause interrupted him five times before he finished.

Lake waved like a conquering hero and waited behind the microphone, then with perfect timing stepped forward and said, 'My name is Aaron Lake, and I am now running for President.' More roaring applause. More piped-in parade music. More balloons drifting downward.

When he'd had enough, he launched into his speech. The theme, the platform, the only reason for running was national security, and Lake hammered out the appalling statistics proving just how thoroughly the current Administration had depleted our military. No other issues were really that important, he said bluntly. Lure us into a war we can't win, and we'll forget about the tired old quarrels over abortion, race, guns, affirmative action, taxes. Concerned about family values? Start losing our sons and daughters in combat and you'd see some families with real problems.

Lake was very good. The speech had been written by him, edited by consultants, polished by other professionals, and the night before he'd delivered it to Teddy Maynard, alone, deep inside Langley. Teddy had approved, with minor changes.

Teddy was tucked under his quilts and watching the show with great pride. York was with him, silent as usual. The two often sat alone, staring at screens, watching the world grow more dangerous.

'He's good,' York said quietly at one point.

Teddy nodded, even managing a slight smile.

Halfway through his speech, Lake became wonderfully angry at the Chinese. 'Over a twenty-year period, we allowed them to steal forty percent of our nuclear secrets!' he said, and the laborers hissed.

'Forty percent!' he shouted.

It was closer to fifty, but Teddy chose to downplay it just a little. The CIA had received its share of blame for the Chinese thievery.

For five minutes Aaron Lake blistered the Chinese, and their looting and their unprecedented military buildup. The strategy was Teddy's. Use the Chinese to scare the American voters, not the Russians. Don't tip them. Protect the real threat until later in the campaign.

Lake's timing was near-perfect. His punch line brought down the house. When he promised to double the defense budget in the first four years of his Administration, the four thousand D-L Trilling employees who built military helicopters exploded in a frenzy.

Teddy watched it quietly, very proud of his creation. They had managed to upstage the spectacle in New Hampshire by simply snubbing it. Lake's name had not been on the ballot, and he was the first candidate in decades to be proud of that fact. 'Who needs New Hampshire?' he'd been quoted as saying. 'I'll take the rest of the country.'

Lake signed off amid thunderous applause, and reshook all the hands on the stage. CNN returned to its studio where the talking heads would spend fifteen minutes telling the viewers what they had just witnessed.

On his table, Teddy pushed buttons and the screen changed. 'Here's the finished product,' he said. 'The first installment.'

It was a television ad for candidate Lake, and it began with a brief glimpse of a row of grim Chinese generals standing rigidly at a military parade, watching massive hardware roll by. 'You think the world's a safer place?' a deep, rich ominous voice asked off-camera. Then, glimpses of the world's current madmen, all watching their armies parade by – Hussein, Qaddafi, Milosevic, Kim in North Korea. Even poor Castro, with the last of his ragtag army lumbering through Havana, got a split second of airtime. 'Our military could not now do what it did in 1991 during the Gulf War,' the voice said as gravely as if another war had already been declared. Then a blast, an atomic mushroom, followed by thousands of Indians dancing in the streets. Another blast, and the Pakistanis were dancing next door.

'China wants to invade Taiwan,' the voice continued as a million Chinese soldiers marched in perfect step.'North Korea wants South Korea,' the voice said, as tanks rolled through the DMZ. 'And the United States is always an easy target.'

The voice changed quickly into one with a high pitch, and the ad shifted to a congressional hearing of some sort, with a heavily bemedaled general lecturing some subcommittee. 'You, the Congress,' he was saying, 'spend less on the military each year. This defense budget is smaller than it was fifteen years ago. You expect us to be ready for war in Korea, the Middle East, and now Eastern Europe, yet our budget keeps shrinking. The situation is critical.' The ad went blank, nothing but a dark screen, then the first voice said, 'Twelve years ago there were two superpowers. Now there are none.' The handsome face of Aaron Lake appeared, and the ad finished with the voice saying, 'Lake, Before It's Too Late.'

'I'm not sure I like it,' York said after a pause.

'Why not?'

'It's so negative.'

'Good. Makes you feel uncomfortable, doesn't it?'

'Very much so.'

'Good. We're going to flood television for a week, and I suspect Lake's soft numbers will get even softer. The ads will make people squirm, and they won't like them.'

York knew what was coming. The people would indeed squirm and dislike the ads, then get the hell scared out of them, and Lake would suddenly become a visionary. Teddy was working on the terror.

There were two TV rooms on each wing at Trumble; two small bare rooms where you could smoke and watch whatever the guards wanted you to watch. No remote – they'd tried that at first but it had caused too much trouble. By far the nastiest disagreements occurred when the boys couldn't agree on what to watch. So the guards made the selections.

Rules prohibited inmates from having their own TVs.

The guard on duty happened to like basketball. There was a college game on ESPN, and the room was packed with inmates. Hatlee Beech hated sports, and he sat alone in the other TV room and watched one banal sitcom after another. When he was on the bench and working twelve hours a day, he had never watched television. Who had the time? He'd had an office in his home where he dictated opinions until late while everyone else was glued to prime time. Now, watching the mindless crap, he realized how lucky he'd been. In so many ways.

He lit a cigarette. He hadn't smoked since college, and for the first two months at Trumble he'd resisted the temptation. Now it helped with the boredom, but only a pack a day. His blood pressure was up and down. Heart disease ran in the family. At fifty-six with nine years to go, he would leave in a box, he was certain.

Three years, one month, one week, and Beech

was still counting the days in as opposed to the days to go. Just four years ago he'd been building his reputation as a tough young federal judge who was going places. Four rotten years. When he traveled from one courthouse to the next in East Texas, he did so with a driver, a secretary, a clerk, and a U.S. Marshal. When he walked into a courtroom people stood out of respect. Lawyers gave him high marks for his fairness and hard work. His wife had been an unpleasant woman, but with her family's oil trust he'd managed to live peacefully with her. The marriage was stable, not exactly warm, but with three fine kids in college they had reason to be proud. They had weathered some rough times and were determined to grow old together. She had the money. He had the status. Together they'd raised a family. Where was there to go?

Certainly not to prison.

Four miserable years.

The drinking came from nowhere. Maybe it was pressure from work, maybe it was to escape his wife's bickering. For years, after law school, he'd been a light social drinker, nothing serious. Certainly not a habit. Once when the kids were small, his wife took them to Italy for two weeks. Beech was left alone, which suited him fine. For some reason he could never determine, or remember, he turned to bourbon. Lots of it, and he never stopped. The bourbon became important. He kept it in his study and sneaked it late at night. They had separate beds so he seldom got caught.

The trip to Yellowstone had been a three-day judicial conference. He'd met the young lady in a bar in Jackson Hole. After hours of drinking they made the sad decision to take a ride. While Hatlee drove she took off her clothes, but for no other reason than to just do it. Sex had not been discussed, and at that point he was completely harmless.

The two hikers were from D.C., just college kids returning from the trails. Both died at the scene, slaughtered on the shoulder of a narrow road by a drunken driver who never saw them. The young lady's car was found in a ditch with Beech hugging the steering wheel, unable to remove himself. She was naked and knocked out.

He remembered nothing. When he awoke hours later he saw for the first time the inside of a cell. 'Better get used to it,' the sheriff had said with a sneer.

Beech called in every favor and pulled every string imaginable, all to no avail. Two young people were dead. He'd been caught with a naked woman. His wife had the oil money so his friends ran like scared dogs. In the end, no one stood up for the Honorable Hatlee Beech.

He was lucky to get twelve years. MADD mothers and SADD students protested outside the courthouse when he made his first official appearance. They wanted a life sentence. Life!

He himself, the Honorable Hatlee Beech, was charged with two counts of manslaughter, and there was no defense. There was enough alcohol in his blood to kill the next guy. A witness said he'd been speeding on the wrong side of the road.

Looking back, he'd been lucky his crime was on federal lands. Otherwise he would have been shipped away to some state pen where things were much tougher. Say what you want, but the feds knew how to run a prison.

He smoked alone in the semidarkness, watching prime-time comedy written by twelve-year-olds, and there was a political ad, one of many those days. It was one Beech had never seen, a menacing little segment with a somber voice predicting doom if we didn't hurry and build more bombs. It was very well done, ran for a minute and a half, cost a bundle, and delivered a message no one wanted to hear. Lake Before It's Too Late.

Who the hell's Aaron Lake?

Beech knew his politics. It had been his passion in another life, and at Trumble he was known as a fellow who watched Washington. He was one of the few who cared what happened there.

Aaron Lake? Beech had missed the guy. What an odd strategy, to enter the race as an unknown after New Hampshire. Never a shortage of clowns who want to be President.

Beech's wife kicked him out before he pled guilty to two counts of manslaughter. Quite naturally, she was angrier over the naked woman than the dead hikers. The kids sided with her because she had the money and because he'd screwed up so badly. It was an easy decision on their part. The divorce was final a week after he arrived at Trumble.

His youngest had been to see him twice in three years, one month, and one week. Both visits were on the sly, lest the mother find out about them. She had prohibited the kids from going to Trumble.

Then he got sued, two wrongful death cases brought by the families. With no friends willing to step forward, he'd tried to defend himself from prison. But there wasn't much to defend. A judgment of $5 million had been entered against him by the trial court. He appealed from Trumble, lost from Trumble, and appealed again.

In the chair beside him, next to his cigarettes, was an envelope brought earlier by Trevor, the lawyer. The court had rejected his final appeal. The judgment was now written in stone.

Didn't really matter, because he'd also filed for bankruptcy. He'd typed the papers himself in the law library and filed them with a pauper's oath, sent them to the same courthouse in Texas where he was once a god.

Convicted, divorced, disbarred, imprisoned, sued, bankrupt.

Most of the losers at Trumble handled their time because their falls had been so short. Most were repeat offenders who'd blown third and fourth chances. Most liked the damned place because it was better than any other prison they'd visited.

But Beech had lost so much, had fallen so far. Just four years ago he'd had a wife with millions and three kids who loved him and a big home in a small town. He was a federal judge, appointed by the President for life, making $140,000 a year, which was a lot less than her oil royalties but still not a bad salary. He got himself called to Washington twice a year for meetings at Justice. Beech had been important.

An old lawyer friend had been to see him twice,

on his way to Miami where he had kids, and he stayed long enough to deliver the gossip. Most of it was worthless, but there was a strong rumor that the ex-Mrs. Beech was now seeing someone else. With a few million bucks and slender hips it was only a matter of time.

Another ad. Lake Before It's Too Late again. This one began with a grainy video of men with guns slithering through the desert, dodging and shooting and undergoing some type of training. Then the sinister face of a terrorist – dark eyes and hair and features, obviously some manner of Islamic radical – and he said in Arabic with English subtitles, 'We will kill Americans wherever we find them. We will die in our holy war against the great Satan.' After that, quick videos of burning buildings. Embassy bombings. A busload of tourists. The remains of a jetliner scattered through a pasture.

A handsome face appeared, Mr. Aaron Lake himself. He looked directly at Hatlee Beech and said, 'I'm Aaron Lake, and you probably don't know me. I'm running for President because I'm scared. Scared of China and Eastern Europe and the Middle East. Scared of a dangerous world. Scared of what's happened to our military. Last year the federal government had a huge surplus, yet spent less on defense than we did fifteen years ago. We're complacent because our economy is strong, but the world today is far more dangerous than we realize. Our enemies are legion, and we cannot protect ourselves. If elected, I will double defense spending during my term of office.'

No smiles, no warmth. Just plain talk from a

71

man who meant what he said. A voice over said, 'Lake, Before It's Too Late.'

Not bad, thought Beech.

He lit another cigarette, his last of the night, and stared at the envelope on the empty chair – $5 million lodged against him by the two families. He'd pay the money if he could. Never saw the kids, not before he killed them. The paper the next day had their happy photos, a boy and a girl. Just college kids, enjoying the summer.

He missed the bourbon.

He could bankrupt half the judgment. The other half was for punitive damages, nonbankruptable. So it would follow wherever he went, which he assumed was nowhere. He'd be sixty-five when his sentence was over, but he'd be dead before then. They'd carry him out of Trumble in a box, send him home to Texas, where they'd bury him behind the little country church where he'd been baptized. Maybe one of the kids would spring for a headstone.

Beech left the room without turning off the TV. It was almost ten, time for lights-out. He bunked with Robbie, a kid from Kentucky who'd broken into 240 houses before they caught him. He sold the guns and microwaves and stereos for cocaine. Robbie was a four-year veteran of Trumble, and because of his seniority he had chosen the bottom bunk. Beech crawled into the top one, said, 'Good night, Robbie,' and turned off the light.

'Night, Hatlee,' came the soft response.

Sometimes they chatted in the dark. The walls were cinderblock, the door was metal, their words were confined to their little room. Robbie was twenty-five and would be forty-five before he left Trumble. Twenty-four years – one for every ten houses.

The time between bed and sleep was the worst of the day. The past came back with a vengeance – the mistakes, the misery, the could-haves and should-haves. Try as he might, Hatlee could not simply close his eyes and go to sleep. He had to punish himself first. There was a grandchild he'd never seen, and he always started with her. Then his three kids. Forget the wife. But he always thought about her money. And the friends. Ah, the friends. Where were they now?

Three years in, and with no future there was only the past. Even poor Robbie below dreamed of a new beginning at the age of forty-five. Not Beech. At times he almost longed for the warm Texas soil, layered upon his body, behind the little church.

Surely someone would buy him a headstone.

SIX

For Quince Garbe, February 3 would be the worst day of his life. It was almost the last, and it would've been had his doctor been in town. He couldn't get a prescription for sleeping pills, and he didn't have the courage to use a gun on himself.

It began pleasantly enough with a late breakfast, a bowl of oatmeal by the fire in the den, alone. His wife of twenty-six years had already left for town, for another day of charity teas and fund-raising and frantic small-town volunteerism that kept her busy and away from him.

It was snowing when he left their large and pretentious banker's home on the edge of Bakers, Iowa, and drove ten minutes to work in his long black Mercedes, eleven years old. He was an important man about town, a Garbe, a member of a family that had owned the bank for generations. He parked in his reserved spot behind the bank, which faced Main Street, and made a quick detour to the post office, something he did twice a week. For years he'd had a private box there, away from his wife and especially away from his secretary.

Because he was rich and few others were in

Bakers, Iowa, he seldom spoke to people on the street. He didn't care what they thought. They worshiped his father and that was enough to keep their business.

But when the old man died, would he have to change his personality? Would he be forced to smile on the sidewalks of Bakers and join the Rotary Club, the one founded by his grandfather?

Quince was tired of being dependent on the whims of the public for his security. He was tired of relying on his father to keep their customers happy. He was tired of banking and tired of Iowa and tired of snow and tired of his wife, and what Quince wanted more than anything that morning in February was a letter from his beloved Ricky. A nice, brief little note confirming their rendezvous.

What Quince really wanted was three warm days on a love boat with Ricky. He might never come back.

Bakers had eighteen thousand people, so the central post office on Main was usually busy. And there was always a different clerk behind the counter. That's how he'd rented the box – he'd waited until a new postal worker was on duty. CMT Investments was the official lessee. He went straight to the box, around a corner to a wall with a hundred others.

There were three letters, and as he snatched them and stuffed them in his coat pocket his heart froze as he saw that one was from Ricky. He hurried onto Main, and minutes later entered his bank, at exactly 10 A.M. His father had been there for four hours, but they had long since stopped bickering over Quince's work schedule. As always, he stopped at his secretary's desk to hurriedly remove his gloves as if important matters were waiting. She handed him his mail, his two phone messages, and reminded him that he had lunch in two hours with a local real estate agent.

He locked his door behind him, flung his gloves one way and his coat the other, and ripped open the letter from Ricky. He sat on his sofa and put on his reading glasses, breathing heavily not from the walk but from anticipation. He was on the verge of arousal when he started reading.

The words hit like bullets. After the second paragraph, he emitted a strange, painful 'Awwww.' Then a couple of 'Oh my gods.' Then a low, hissing 'Sonofabitch.'

Quiet, he told himself, the secretary is always listening. The first reading brought shock, the second disbelief. Reality began settling in with the third reading, and Quince's lip started to quiver. Don't cry, dammit, he told himself.

He threw the letter on the floor and paced around his desk, ignoring as best he could the cheerful faces of his wife and children. Twenty years' worth of class photos and family portraits were lined along his credenza, just under the window. He looked out and watched the snow, now heavier and accumulating on the sidewalks. God how he hated Bakers, Iowa. He'd thought he might leave and escape to the beach, where he could frolic with a handsome young pal and maybe never come home.

Now he would leave under different circumstances.

It was a joke, a hoax, he told himself, but he

instantly knew better. The scam was too tight. The punch line was too perfect. He'd been set up by a professional.

All his life he'd fought his desires. Somehow he'd finally found the nerve to crack the closet door, and now he got shot between the eyes by a con man. Stupid, stupid, stupid. How could this be so difficult?

Random thoughts hit from every direction as he watched the snow. Suicide was the easy answer, but his doctor was gone and he really didn't want to die. At least not at the moment. He wasn't sure where he'd find a hundred thousand bucks he could send off without raising suspicions. The old bastard next door paid him a pittance and kept his thumb on every dime. His wife insisted on balancing their checkbook. There was some money in mutuals, but he couldn't move it without her knowing. The life of a rich banker in Bakers, Iowa, meant a title and a Mercedes and a large mortgaged house and a wife with social activities. Oh how he wanted to escape!

He'd go to Florida anyway, and track the letter somehow, and confront this con man, expose his extortion attempt, find some justice. He, Quince Garbe, had done nothing wrong. Surely a crime was being perpetrated here. Perhaps he could hire an investigator, and maybe a lawyer, and they'd protect him. They'd get to the bottom of this scam.

Even if he found the money, and wired it as instructed, the gate would be opened and Ricky, whoever in hell Ricky was, might want more. What would stop Ricky from extorting again, and again?

If he had guts he'd run off anyway, run to Key

West or some hot spot where it never snowed and live any damn way he wanted to live, and let the pitiful little people of Bakers, Iowa, gossip about him for the next half-century. But he didn't have the guts, and that's what made Quince so sad.

His children were staring at him, freckled smiles with teeth wrapped in silver braces. His heart sank, and he knew he'd find the money and wire it precisely as directed. He had to protect them. They had done nothing wrong.

The bank's stock was worth about $10 million, all of it still tightly controlled by the old man, who at the moment was barking in the hallway. The old man was eighty-one, very much alive but still eighty-one. When he was gone, Quince would have to contend with a sister in Chicago, but the bank would be his. He'd sell the damned thing as fast as he could and leave Bakers with a few million in his pocket. Until then, though, he'd be forced to do what he'd always done, keep the old man content.

Quince's getting yanked out of the closet by some con man would devastate his father, and pretty much take care of the stock. Sister in Chicago would get all of it.

When the barking stopped outside, he eased through the door and passed his secretary for a cup of coffee. He ignored her as he returned to his room, locked his door, read the letter for the fourth time, and collected his thoughts. He'd find the money, and he'd wire it just as instructed, and he'd hope and pray with a fury that Ricky would go away. If not, if he came back for more, Quince would call his doctor and get some pills.

The real estate agent he was meeting for lunch was a high-roller who took chances and cut corners, probably a crook. Quince began to make plans. The two of them would arrange a few shady loans; overappraise some land, lend the money, sell to a strawman, etc. He would know how to do it.

Quince would find the money.

The Lake campaign's doomsday ads landed with a thud, at least in public opinion. Massive polling through the first week showed a dramatic increase in name recognition, from 2 to 20 percent, but the ads were universally disliked. They were frightening and people just didn't want to think about wars and terrorism and old nukes getting hauled across mountains in the dark. People saw the ads (they were impossible to miss), and they heard the message, but most voters simply didn't want to be bothered. They were too busy making money and spending it. When issues were confronted in the midst of a roaring economy, they were limited to the old standbys of family values and tax cuts.

Candidate Lake's early interviewers treated him as just another flake until he announced, live on the air, that his campaign had received in excess of $11 million in less than a week.

'We expect to have twenty million in two weeks,' he said without boasting, and real news started to happen. Teddy Maynard had assured him the money would be there.

Twenty million in two weeks had never been done before, and by the end of that day Washington was consumed with the story. The frenzy reached its peak when Lake was interviewed, live yet again, by two of the three networks on the evening news. He looked great; big smile, smooth words, nice suit and hair. The man was electable.

Final confirmation that Aaron Lake was a serious candidate came late in the day, when one of his opponents took a shot at him. Senator Britt of Maryland had been running for a year and had finished a strong second in New Hampshire. He'd raised $9 million, spent a lot more than that, and was forced to waste half of his time soliciting money rather than campaigning. He was tired of begging, tired of cutting staff, tired of worrying about TV ads, and when a reporter asked him about Lake and his $20 million Britt shot back, 'It's dirty money. No honest candidate can raise that much that fast.' Britt was shaking hands in the rain at the entrance to a chemical plant in Michigan.

The dirty money comment was seized with great gusto by the press and soon splattered all over the place.

Aaron Lake had arrived.

Senator Britt of Maryland had other problems, though he'd tried to forget them.

Nine years earlier he'd toured Southeast Asia to find some facts. As always, he and his colleagues from the Congress flew first class, stayed in nice hotels, and ate lobster, all in an effort to study poverty in the region and to get to the bottom of the raging controversy brought about by Nike and its use of cheap foreign labor. Early in the journey, Britt met a girl in Bangkok, and, feigning illness, decided to stay behind while his buddies continued their fact-finding into Laos and Vietnam.

Her name was Payka, and she was not a prostitute. She was a twenty-year-old secretary in the U.S. embassy in Bangkok, and because she was on his country's payroll Britt felt a slight proprietary interest. He was far away from Maryland, from his wife and five kids and his constituents. Payka was stunning and shapely, and anxious to study in the United States.

What began as a fling quickly turned into a romance, and Senator Britt had to force himself to return to Washington. Two months later he was back in Bangkok on, as he told his wife, pressing but secret business.

In nine months he made four trips to Thailand, all first class, all at taxpayer expense, and even the globe-trotters in the Senate were beginning to whisper. Britt pulled strings with the State Department and Payka appeared to be headed for the United States.

She never made it. During the fourth and final rendezvous, Payka confessed that she was pregnant. She was Catholic and abortion was not an option. Britt stiff-armed her, said he needed time to think, then fled Bangkok in the middle of the night. The fact-finding was over.

Early in his Senate career, Britt, a fiscal hardliner, had grabbed a headline or two by criticizing CIA wastefulness. Teddy Maynard said not a word, but certainly didn't appreciate the grandstanding. The rather thin file on Senator Britt was dusted off and given priority, and when he went to Bangkok for the second time the CIA went with him. Of course he didn't know it, but they sat near him on the flight, first class also, and they had people on the ground in Bangkok. They watched the hotel where the two lovebirds spent three days. They took pictures of them eating in fine restaurants. They saw everything. Britt was oblivious and stupid.

Later, when the child was born, the CIA obtained the hospital records, then the medical records to link the blood and DNA. Payka kept her job at the embassy, so she was easy to find.

When the child was a year old, he was photographed sitting on Payka's knee in a downtown park. More photos followed, and by the time he was four he was beginning to remotely favor Senator Dan Britt of Maryland.

His daddy was long gone. Britt's zeal for finding facts in Southeast Asia had faded dramatically, and he'd turned his attention to other critical areas of the world. In due course he was seized with presidential ambitions, the old senatorial affliction that sooner or later gets them all. He'd never heard from Payka, and that nightmare had been easy to forget.

Britt had five legitimate children, and a wife with a big mouth. They were a team, Senator and Mrs. Britt, both leading the juggernaut of family values and 'We've Got to Save Our Kids!' Together they wrote a book on how to raise children in a sick American culture, though their oldest was only thirteen. When the President was embarrassed by sexual misadventures, Senator Britt became the biggest virgin in Washington.

He and his wife struck a nerve, and the money

rolled in from conservatives. He did well in the
Iowa caucuses, ran a close second in New Hampshire, but was running out of money and sinking in
the polls.

He would sink even more. After a brutal day of
campaigning, his entourage settled into a motel in
Dearborn, Michigan, for a short night. It was there
that the senator finally came face to face with child
number six, though not in person.

The agent's name was McCord, and he'd been
following Britt with phony press credentials for a
week. He said he worked for a newspaper in
Tallahassee, but in fact he'd been a CIA agent for
eleven years. There were so many reporters
swarming around Britt that no one thought to
check.

McCord befriended a senior aide, and over a
late drink in the Holiday Inn bar he confessed that
he had something in his possession that would
destroy candidate Britt. He said it was given to him
by a rival camp, Governor Tarry's. It was a
notebook, with a bomb on every page: an affidavit
from Payka setting forth the broad details of their
affair; two photos of the child, the last of which
had been taken a month earlier and the child, now
seven, looking more and more like his dad; blood
and DNA summaries indelibly linking father and
son; and travel records which showed in black and
white that Senator Britt had burned $38,600 in
taxpayers' money to carry on his affair on the other
side of the world.

The deal was simple and straightforward: With-
draw from the race immediately, and the story
would never be told. McCord, the journalist, was

83

ethical and didn't have the stomach for such trash. Governor Tarry would keep it quiet if Britt disappeared. Quit, and not even Mrs. Britt would know.

Shortly after 1 A.M., in Washington, Teddy Maynard took the call from McCord. The package had been delivered. Britt was planning a press conference for noon the next day.

Teddy had dirt files on hundreds of politicians, past and present. As a group they were an easy bunch to trap. Place a beautiful young woman in their path, and you generally gathered something for the file. If women didn't work, money always did. Watch them travel, watch them crawl in bed with the lobbyists, watch them pander to any foreign government smart enough to send lots of cash to Washington, watch them set up their campaigns and committees to raise funds. Just watch them, and the files always grew thicker. He wished the Russians were so easy.

Though he despised politicians as a group, he did respect a handful of them. Aaron Lake was one. He'd never chased women, never drank much or picked up habits, never seemed preoccupied with cash, never had been inclined to grandstand. The more he watched Lake, the more he liked him.

He took his last pill of the night and rolled himself to bed. So Britt was gone. Good riddance. Too bad he couldn't leak the story anyway. The pious hypocrite deserved a good thrashing. Save it, he told himself. And use it again. President Lake might need Britt one day, and that little boy over in Thailand might come in handy.

SEVEN

Picasso was suing Sherlock and other unnamed defendants for injunctive relief in an effort to stop them from urinating on his roses. A little misdirected urine was not going to upset the balance of life at Trumble, but Picasso also wanted damages in the amount of five hundred dollars. Five hundred dollars was a serious matter.

The dispute had been festering since the past summer, when Picasso caught Sherlock in the act, and the assistant warden had finally intervened. He asked the Brethren to settle the matter. Suit was filed, then Sherlock hired an ex-lawyer named Ratliff, yet another tax evader, to stall, delay, postpone, and file frivolous pleadings, the usual routine for those practicing the art of law on the outside. But Ratliff's tactics didn't sit well with the Brethren, and neither Sherlock nor his lawyer was held in high esteem by the panel.

Picasso's rose garden was a carefully tended patch of dirt next to the gym. It had taken him three years of bureaucratic wars to convince some mid-level paper-pusher in Washington that such a hobby was and always had been therapeutic, since

Picasso suffered from several disorders. Once the garden was approved, the warden quickly signed off, and Picasso dug in with both hands. He got his roses from a supplier in Jacksonville, which in itself took another box of paperwork.

His real job was that of a dishwasher in the cafeteria, for which he earned thirty cents an hour. The warden refused his request to be classified as a gardener, so the roses were deemed a hobby. During the season, Picasso could be seen early and late in his little patch, on all fours, tilling and digging and watering. He even talked to his flowers.

The roses in question were Belinda's Dream, a pale pink rose, not particularly beautiful, but loved by Picasso nonetheless. When they arrived from the supplier everybody at Trumble knew that the Belindas were there. He lovingly planted them in the front and center of his garden.

Sherlock began urinating on them just for the sheer hell of it. He wasn't fond of Picasso anyway because he was a notorious liar, and peeing on the man's roses just seemed appropriate for some reason. Others caught on. Sherlock encouraged them by assuring that they were in fact helping the roses by adding fertilizer.

The Belindas lost their pinkness and began to fade, and Picasso was horrified. An informant left a note under his door, and the secret was out. His beloved garden had become a favorite watering hole. Two days later, he ambushed Sherlock, caught him in the act, and the two chubby middle-aged white men had an ugly wrestling match on the sidewalk.

The plants turned a dull yellow, and Picasso filed suit.

When it finally reached trial, after months of delays by Ratliff, the Brethren were already tired of it. They had quietly preassigned the case to Justice Finn Yarber, whose mother had once raised roses, and after a few hours of research he had informed the other two that urine would, in fact, not change the color of the plants. So two days before the hearing they reached their decision: They would grant the injunction to keep Sherlock and the other pigs from spraying Picasso's roses, but they would not award damages.

For three hours they listened to grown men bicker about who peed where and when, and how often. At times, Picasso, acting as his own attorney, was near tears as he begged his witnesses to squeal on their friends. Ratliff, counsel for the defense, was cruel and abrasive and redundant, and after an hour it was obvious he deserved his disbarment, whatever his crimes may have been.

Justice Spicer passed the time by studying the point spreads on college basketball games. When he couldn't contact Trevor he placed make-believe bets, every game. He was up $3,600 in two months, on paper. He was on a roll, winning at cards, winning at sports, and he had trouble sleeping at night dreaming about his next life, in Vegas or in the Bahamas, doing it as a pro. With or without his wife.

Justice Beech frowned with deep judicial deliberation and appeared to be taking exhaustive notes, when in fact he was drafting another letter to Curtis in Dallas. The Brethren had decided to bait him again. Writing as Ricky, Beech explained that a cruel guard at the rehab unit was threatening all sorts of vile physical attacks unless Ricky could produce some 'protection money.' Ricky needed $5,000 to secure his safety from the beast, and could Curtis lend it to him?

'Could we move this along?' Beech said loudly, interrupting ex-lawyer Ratliff once again. When he was a real judge, Beech had mastered the practice of reading magazines while half-listening to lawyers drone on before juries. A blaring and well-timed admonition from the bench kept everyone sharp.

He wrote: 'It is such a vicious game they play here. We arrive broken into tiny pieces. Slowly, they clean us up, dry us out, put us back together, piece by piece. They clear our heads, teach us discipline and confidence, and prepare us for our return to society. They do a good job of this, yet they allow these ignorant thugs who guard the grounds to threaten us, fragile as we still are, and in doing so break down what we've worked so hard to produce. I am so scared of this man. I hide in my room when I'm supposed to be tanning and lifting weights. I cannot sleep. I long for booze and drugs as a means of escape. Please, Curtis, loan me the $5,000 so I can buy this guy off, so I can complete my rehab and leave here in one piece. When we meet, I want to be healthy and in great shape.'

What would his friends think? The Honorable Hatlee Beech, federal judge, writing prose like a faggot, extorting money out of innocent people.

He had no friends. He had no rules. The law he

once worshiped had placed him where he was, which, at the moment, was in a prison cafeteria wearing a faded green choir robe from a black church, listening to a bunch of angry convicts argue over urine.

'You've already asked that question eight times,' he barked at Ratliff, who'd obviously been watching too many bad lawyer shows on television.

Since the case was Justice Yarber's, he was expected to at least appear as if he were paying attention. He was not, nor was he concerned about appearances. As usual, he was naked under his robe, and he sat with his legs crossed wide, cleaning his long toenails with a plastic fork.

'You think they'd turn brown if I crapped on them?' Sherlock yelled at Picasso, and the cafeteria erupted with laughter.

'Language, please,' Justice Beech admonished.

'Order in the court,' said T. Karl, the court jester, under his bright gray wig. It was not his role in the courtroom to demand order, but it was something he did well and the Brethren let it slide. He rapped his gavel, said, 'Order, gentlemen.'

Beech wrote: 'Please help me, Curtis. I have no one else to turn to. I'm breaking again. I fear another collapse. I fear I will never leave this place. Hurry.'

Spicer put a hundred dollars on Indiana over Purdue, Duke over Clemson, Alabama over Vandy, Wisconsin over Illinois. What did he know about Wisconsin basketball? he asked himself. Didn't matter. He was a professional gambler, and a damned good one. If the $90,000 was still buried behind the toolshed he'd parlay it into a million within a year.

'That's enough,' Beech said, holding up his hands.

'I've heard enough too,' Yarber said, forgetting his toenails and leaning on the table.

The Brethren huddled and deliberated as if the outcome might set a serious precedent, or at least have some profound impact on the future of American jurisprudence. They frowned and scratched their heads and appeared to even argue over the merits of the case. Meanwhile, poor Picasso sat by himself, ready to cry, thoroughly exhausted by Ratliff's tactics.

Justice Yarber cleared his throat and said, 'By a vote of two to one, we have reached a decision. We are issuing an injunction against all inmates urinating on the damned roses. Anyone caught doing so will be fined fifty dollars. No damages will be assessed at this time.'

With perfect timing T. Karl slammed his gavel and yelled, 'Court's adjourned until further notice. All rise.'

Of course, no one moved.

'I want to appeal,' Picasso yelled.

'So do I,' said Sherlock.

'Must be a good decision,' Yarber said, collecting his robe and standing. 'Both sides are unhappy.'

Beech and Spicer stood too, and the Brethren paraded out of the cafeteria. A guard walked into the middle of the litigants and witnesses and said, 'Court's over, boys. Get back to work.'

★

The CEO of Hummand, a company in Seattle which made missiles and radar-jamming machinery, had once been a congressman who'd been quite close to the CIA. Teddy Maynard knew him well. When the CEO announced at a press conference that his company had raised $5 million for the Lake campaign, CNN interrupted a liposuction segment to carry the story Live! Five thousand Hummand workers had written checks for $1,000 each, the maximum allowed under federal law. The CEO had the checks in a box that he showed to the cameras, then he flew with them on a Hummand jet to Washington, where he took them to the Lake headquarters.

Follow the money, and you'll find your winner. Since Lake's announcement, over eleven thousand defense and aerospace workers from thirty states had contributed just over $8 million. The Postal Service was delivering their checks in boxes. Their unions had sent almost that much, with another $2 million promised. Lake's people hired a D.C. accounting firm just to process and count the money.

The Hummand CEO arrived in Washington amid as much fanfare as could be generated. Candidate Lake was on another private jet, a Challenger freshly leased at $400,000 a month. When he landed in Detroit he was met by two black Suburbans, both brand new, both just leased at $1,000 a month each. Lake now had an escort, a group of people moving in sync with him wherever he went, and though he was certain he'd soon get used to it, it was unnerving at first. Strangers around him all the time. Grave young men in dark

91

suits with little microphones in their ears, guns strapped to their bodies. Two Secret Service agents were on the flight with him, and three more waited with the Suburbans.

And he had Floyd from his congressional office. Floyd was a dull-witted young man from a prominent family back in Arizona who was good for nothing but running errands. Now Floyd was a driver. Floyd took the wheel of one Suburban, Lake in the front seat, two agents and a secretary sitting behind. Two aides and three agents piled into the other, and away they went, headed for downtown Detroit where serious local TV journalists were waiting.

Lake had no time for stumping or walking neighborhoods or eating catfish or standing in the rain outside busy factories. He couldn't hike for the cameras or stage town meetings or stand amid rubble in ghettos and decry failed policies. There wasn't enough time to do all the things candidates were expected to do. He was entering late, with no groundwork in place, no grass roots, no local support of any kind. Lake had a handsome face, a pleasant voice, nice suits, an urgent message, and lots of cash.

If buying TV could buy an election, Aaron Lake was about to get himself a new job.

He called Washington, talked to his moneyman, and was given the news about the $5 million announcement. He'd never heard of Hummand. 'Is it a public company?' he asked. No, came the answer. Very private. Just under a billion in annual sales. An innovator in radar jamming. Could make billions if the right man took charge of the military and started spending again.

Nineteen million dollars was now in hand, a record, of course. And they were revising their projections. The Lake campaign would collect thirty million in its first two weeks.

There was no way to spend money that fast.

He folded the cell phone, handed it back to Floyd, who appeared to be lost in traffic. 'From now on we use helicopters,' Lake announced over his shoulder to the secretary, who actually wrote down the directive: Find helicopters.

Lake hid behind his sunglasses and tried to analyze thirty million bucks. The transition from a fiscal conservative to a freewheeling candidate was awkward, but the money had to be spent. It wasn't squeezed from the taxpayers; rather, it was freely given. He could rationalize. Once elected, he'd continue his fight for the workingman.

He thought again about Teddy Maynard, sitting in some dark room deep inside Langley, legs wrapped in a quilt, face squinting from pain, pulling strings only he could pull, making money fall from trees. Lake would never know the things Teddy was doing on his behalf, nor did he want to.

The Director of Middle East Operations was named Lufkin, a twenty-year man Teddy trusted implicitly. Fourteen hours earlier he'd been in Tel Aviv. Now he was in Teddy's war room, somehow looking fresh and alert. His message had to be delivered in person, mouth to mouth, no wires or signals or satellites. And what was said between them would never be repeated. It had been that way for many years.

'An attack on our embassy in Cairo is now imminent,' Lufkin said. No reaction from Teddy; no frown, no surprise, no cutting of the eyes, nothing. He'd gotten such news many times before.

'Yidal?'

'Yes. His top lieutenant was seen in Cairo last week.'

'Seen by whom?'

'The Israelis. They've also followed two truck-loads of explosives from Tripoli. Everything seems to be in place.'

'When?'

'Imminent.'

'How imminent?'

'Within a week, I'd guess.'

Teddy pulled an earlobe and closed his eyes. Lufkin tried not to stare, and he knew better than to ask questions. He would leave soon, and return to the Middle East. And he would wait. The attack on the embassy might proceed with no warning. Dozens would be killed and maimed. A crater in the city would smolder for days, and in Washington fingers would point and accusations would fly. The CIA would be blamed again.

None of it would faze Teddy Maynard. As Lufkin had learned, sometimes Teddy needed the terror to accomplish what he wanted.

Or maybe the embassy would be spared, the attack thwarted by Egyptian commandos working with the United States. The CIA would be praised for its excellent intelligence. That wouldn't faze Teddy either.

'And you're certain?' he asked.

'Yes, as certain as one can be in these situations.'

Lufkin, of course, had no clue that the Director was now plotting to elect a President. Lufkin had barely heard of Aaron Lake. Frankly, he didn't care who won the election. He'd been in the Middle East long enough to know it didn't really matter who set American policy there.

He'd leave in three hours, on the Concorde to Paris, where he'd spend a day before going to Jerusalem.

'Go to Cairo,' Teddy said without opening his eyes.

'Sure. And do what?'

'Wait.'

'Wait for what?'

'Wait for the ground to shake. Stay away from the embassy.'

York's initial reaction was one of horror. 'You can't run this damned ad, Teddy,' he said. 'It's R-rated. I've never seen so much blood.'

'I like that,' Teddy said, pushing a button on the remote. 'An R-rated campaign ad. It's never been done before.'

They watched it again. It began with the sound of a bomb, then footage of the Marine barracks in Beirut; smoke, rubble, chaos, Marines being pulled from debris, mangled bodies, Marines lying dead in a neat row. President Reagan addressing the press and vowing revenge. But the threat

95

sounded hollow. Then the photo of an American soldier standing between two masked gunmen. A heavy, ominous voiceover said, 'Since 1980, hundreds of Americans have been murdered by terrorists around the world.' Another bomb scene, more bloody and dazed survivors, more smoke and chaos. 'We always vow revenge. We always threaten to find and punish those responsible.' Quick clips of President Bush on two separate occasions angrily promising retaliation – another attack, more bodies. Then footage of a terrorist standing in the door of a jetliner, dragging off the body of an American soldier. President Clinton, near tears, his voice ready to crack, saying, 'We will not rest until we find those responsible.' Next the handsome but serious face of Aaron Lake, looking sincerely at the camera, coming into our homes, saying, 'The fact is, we don't retaliate. We react with words, we swagger and threaten, but in reality we bury our dead, then forget about them. The terrorists are winning the war because we have lacked the guts to fight back. When I'm your President, we will use our new military to fight terrorism wherever we find it. No American death will go unanswered. I promise. We will not be humiliated by ragtag little armies hiding in mountains. We will destroy them.'

The ad ran for exactly sixty seconds, cost very little to make because Teddy already had the footage, and would start running during prime time in forty-eight hours.

'I don't know, Teddy,' York said. 'It's gruesome.'

'It's a gruesome world.'

Teddy liked the ad and that's all that mattered. Lake had objected to the blood, but came around quickly. His name recognition was up to 30 percent, but his ads were still disliked.

Just wait, Teddy kept telling himself. Wait until there are more bodies.

EIGHT

Trevor was sipping a carry-out double latte from Beach Java and debating whether to add a generous shot or two of Amaretto to help soothe away the morning's cobwebs when the call came. His cramped suite had no intercom system; one was not needed. Jan could simply yell any message down the hall, and he could yell back if he wanted. For eight years he and this particular secretary had been barking at each other.

'It's some bank in the Bahamas!' she announced. He almost spilled the coffee as he lunged for the phone.

It was a Brit whose accent had been softened by the islands. A substantial wire had been received, from a bank in Iowa.

How substantial, he wanted to know, covering his mouth so Jan couldn't hear.

A hundred thousand dollars.

Trevor hung up and added the Amaretto, three shots of it, and sipped the delightful brew while smiling goofily at the wall. In his career he'd never come close to a fee of $33,000. He'd settled a car wreck once for $25,000, taken a fee of $7,500, and within two months had spent all of it.

Jan knew nothing about the offshore account and the scam that diverted money to it, so he was forced to wait an hour, make a bunch of useless phone calls, and try to look busy before announcing he had to take care of some crucial business in downtown Jacksonville, then he was needed at Trumble. She didn't care. He disappeared all the time and she had some reading to keep her occupied.

He raced to the airport, almost missed his shuttle, and drank two beers during the thirty-minute flight to Fort Lauderdale, then two more on the way to Nassau. On the ground, he fell into the back of a cab, a 1974 Cadillac painted gold, without air-conditioning and with a driver who'd also been drinking. The air was hot and wet, the traffic slow, and Trevor's shirt was sticking to his back by the time they stopped downtown near the Geneva Trust Bank Building.

Inside, Mr. Brayshears came forward eventually and led Trevor to his small office. He presented a sheet of paper which gave the bare details: a $100,000 wire originating from the First Iowa Bank in Des Moines, remitter being a faceless entity named CMT Investments. The payee was another generic entity named Boomer Realty, Ltd. Boomer was the name of Joe Roy Spicer's favorite bird dog.

Trevor signed the forms to transfer $25,000 to his own, separate account with Geneva Trust, money he kept hidden from his secretary and from the IRS. The remaining $8,000 was handed to him in a thick envelope, cash. He stuffed it deep into his khaki pants pocket, shook Brayshears' soft little hand, and raced out of the building. He was tempted to stay a couple of days, find a room on the beach, get a chair by the pool, and drink rum until they stopped bringing it to him. The temptation grew to the point that he almost bolted from the gate at the airport and raced to get another cab. But he reached deep, determined not to squander his money this time.

Two hours later he was in the Jacksonville airport, drinking strong coffee, without liquor, and making his plans. He drove to Trumble, arriving at four-thirty, and he waited for Spicer for almost half an hour.

'A pleasant surprise,' Spicer said dryly as he stepped into the attorney-conference room. Trevor had no briefcase to inspect, so the guard patted his pockets and stepped outside. His cash was hidden under the floor mat of his Beetle.

'We received a hundred thousand dollars from Iowa,' Trevor said, glancing at the door.

Spicer was suddenly happy to see his lawyer. He resented the 'we' in Trevor's announcement, and he resented the healthy cut he raked off the top. But the scam wouldn't work without help from the outside, and, as usual, the lawyer was a necessary evil. So far, Trevor could be trusted.

'It's in the Bahamas?'

'Yes. I just left there. The money's tucked away, all sixty-seven thousand of it.'

Spicer breathed deeply and savored the victory. A third of the loot gave him $22,000 and change. It was time to write some more letters!

100

He reached into the pocket of his olive prison shirt and removed a folded newspaper clipping. He stretched his arms, studied it for a second, then said, 'Duke's at Tech tonight. The line is eleven. Put five thousand bucks on Tech.'

'Five thousand?'

'Yep.'

'I've never put five thousand on a game before.'

'What kinda bookie you got?'

'Small time.'

'Look, if he's a bookie, he can handle the numbers. Call him as soon as you can. He may have to make a few calls, but he can do it.'

'All right, all right.'

'Can you come back tomorrow?'

'Probably.'

'How many other clients have ever paid you thirty-three thousand bucks?'

'None.'

'Right, so be here at four tomorrow. I'll have some mail for you.'

Spicer left him and walked quickly from the administration building with only a nod at a guard in a window. He walked with a purpose across the finely manicured lawn, the Florida sun heating the sidewalk even in February. His colleagues were deep in their unhurried labors in their little library, alone as always, so Spicer did not hesitate to announce: 'We got the hundred thousand from ole Quince in Iowa!'

Beech's hands froze on his keyboard. He peered over his reading glasses, his jaw dropping, and managed to say, 'You're kidding.'

'Nope. Just talked to Trevor. The money was

wired in exactly as instructed, arrived in the Bahamas this morning. Quincy baby came through.'

'Let's hit him again,' Yarber said, before the others could think of it.

'Quince?'

'Sure. The first hundred was easy, let's squeeze him one more time. What could we lose?'

'Not a damned thing,' Spicer said with a smile. He wished he'd said it first.

'How much?' asked Beech.

'Let's try fifty,' Yarber said, pulling numbers from the air as if anything was possible.

The other two nodded and pondered the next fifty thousand, then Spicer took charge and said, 'Look, let's evaluate where we are now. I think Curtis in Dallas is ripe. We'll hit Quince again. This thing is working, and I think we should shift gears, get more aggressive, know what I mean? Let's take each pen pal, analyze them one by one, and step up the pressure.'

Beech turned off his computer and reached for a file. Yarber cleared his small desk. Their little Angola scam had just received a fresh infusion of capital, and the smell of ill-gotten cash was intoxicating.

They began reading all the old letters, and drafting new ones. More victims were needed, they quickly decided. More ads would be placed in the back pages of those magazines.

Trevor made it as far as Pete's Bar and Grill, arriving there just in time for happy hour, which at Pete's began at 5 P.M. and ran until the first fistfight. He found Prep, a thirty-two-year-old sophomore at North Florida, shooting nine-ball for twenty bucks a game. Prep's dwindling trust fund required the family lawyer to pay him $2,000 a month as long as he was enrolled as a full-time student. He'd been a sophomore for eleven years.

Prep was also the busiest bookie at Pete's, and when Trevor whispered that he had serious money to place on the Duke-Tech game, Prep asked, 'How much?'

'Fifteen thousand,' Trevor said, then gulped his longneck beer.

'You serious?' Prep asked, chalking his cue stick and glancing around the smoky table. Trevor had never bet more than a hundred bucks on any game.

'Yep.' Another long pull on the bottle. He was feeling lucky. If Spicer had the guts to lay $5,000 on the game, Trevor would double it. He'd just earned 33,000 tax-free dollars. So what if he lost ten? That much belonged to the IRS anyway.

'I'll have to make a call,' Prep said, pulling out a cell phone.

'Hurry. The game starts in thirty minutes.'

The bartender was a local who'd never left the state of Florida but had somehow developed an intense passion for Australian Rules Football. A game was on from Down Under, and it took a $20 bribe from Trevor to get the channel changed to ACC basketball.

With $15,000 riding on Georgia Tech, there was no way Duke could miss a shot, at least not in the first half. Trevor ate french fries, drank one bottle after another, and tried to ignore Prep, who was

103

standing near a pool table in a dark corner, watching.

In the second half, Trevor almost bribed the bartender to switch back to the Aussie game. He was getting drunker, and with ten minutes to go was openly cursing Joe Roy Spicer to anyone who would listen. What did that redneck know about ACC basketball? Duke led by twenty with nine minutes to go, when Tech's point guard got hot and nailed four straight threes. Trevor had Tech and eleven.

The game was tied with a minute to go. Trevor didn't care who won. He'd beat the spread. He paid his tab, tipped the bartender another $100, then flashed a smart-ass salute to Prep as he walked out the door. Prep flipped him the bird.

In the cool darkness, Trevor skipped along Atlantic Boulevard, away from the lights, past the cheap summer rentals packed tightly together, past the neat little retirement homes with their fresh paint and perfect lawns, down the old wooden steps to the sand, where he took off his shoes and strolled along the edge of the water. The temperature was in the forties, not unusual for Jacksonville in February, and before long his feet were cold and wet.

Not that he felt much – $43,000 in one day, tax-free, all hidden from the government. Last year after expenses he'd cleared $28,000, and that was working practically full time – haggling with clients too poor or too cheap to pay, avoiding courtrooms, dealing with penny-ante real estate agents and bankers, bickering with his secretary, cutting corners on taxes.

Ah, the joy of quick cash. He'd been suspicious of the Brethren's little scam, but now it seemed so brilliant. Extort from those who can't complain. How thoroughly clever.

And since it was working so well, he knew Spicer would turn up the heat. The mail would get heavier, the visits to Trumble more frequent. Hell, he'd be there every day if necessary, hauling letters in and out, bribing guards.

He splashed his feet in the water as the wind picked up and the waves roared in.

Even more clever would be to steal from the extortionists, court-certified crooks who certainly couldn't complain. It was a nasty thought, one he was almost ashamed of, but a valid one nonetheless. All options would be kept open. Since when were thieves known for their loyalty?

He needed a million dollars, nothing more or less. He'd done the math many times, driving to Trumble, drinking at Pete's, sitting at his desk with the door locked. A lousy million bucks, and he could close his sad little office, surrender his law license, buy a sailboat, and spend eternity drifting with the winds around the Caribbean.

He was closer than he would ever be.

Justice Spicer rolled over again on the bottom bunk. Sleep was a rare gift in his tiny room, on his tiny bed with a small, smelly roommate named Alvin snoring above him. Alvin had roamed North America as a hobo for decades, but late in life had grown weary and hungry. His crime had been the robbery of a rural mail carrier in Oklahoma. His apprehension had been aided mightily when Alvin walked into the FBI office in Tulsa and declared, 'I did it.' The FBI scrambled for six hours to find the crime. Even the judge knew Alvin planned it all. He wanted a federal bed, certainly not one provided by the state.

Sleep was even more difficult than usual because Spicer was worried about the lawyer. Now that the scam had hit its stride, there was serious cash lying around. And more on the way. The more Boomer Realty collected in the Bahamas, the more tempting it would become for Trevor. He and he alone could steal their ill-gotten loot and get away with it.

But the scam worked only with an outside conspirator. Someone had to sneak the mail back and forth. Someone had to collect the money.

There had to be a way to bypass the lawyer, and Joe Roy was determined to find it. If he didn't sleep for a month, he didn't care. No slimy lawyer would take a third of his money, then steal the rest.

NINE

Defensepac, or D-PAC as it would quickly and widely become known, made a roaring entry onto the loose and murky field of political finance. No political-action committee in recent history had appeared with as much muscle behind it.

Its seed money came from a Chicago financier named Mitzger, an American with dual Israeli citizenship. He put up the first $1 million, which lasted about a week. Other Jewish high-rollers were quickly brought into the fold, though their identities were shielded by corporations and offshore accounts. Teddy Maynard knew the dangers of having a bunch of rich Jews contribute openly and in an organized fashion to Lake's campaign. He relied on old friends in Tel Aviv to organize the money in New York.

Mitzger was a liberal when it came to politics, but no issue was as dear as the security of Israel. Aaron Lake was much too moderate on social matters, but he was also dead serious about a new military. Middle East stability depended on a strong America, at least in Mitzger's opinion.

He rented a suite at the Willard in D.C. one day,

and by noon the next he had leased an entire floor
of an office building near Dulles. His staff from
Chicago worked around the clock plowing through
the myriad details required to instantly outfit forty
thousand square feet with the latest technology.
He had a 6 A.M. breakfast with Elaine Tyner, a
lawyer/lobbyist from a gigantic Washington firm,
one she'd built with her own iron will and lots of
oil clients. Tyner was sixty years old and currently
regarded as the most powerful lobbyist in town.
Over bagels and juice she agreed to represent D-
PAC for an initial retainer of $500,000. Her firm
would immediately dispatch twenty associates and
that many clerks to the new D-PAC offices where
one of her partners would take charge. One section
would do nothing but raise money. One would
analyze congressional support for Lake and begin,
gently at first, the delicate process of lining up
endorsements from senators and representatives
and even governors. It would not be easy; most
were already committed to other candidates. Yet
another section would do nothing but research –
military hardware, its costs, new gadgets, futuristic
weapons, Russian and Chinese innovations –
anything that candidate Lake might need to know.

Tyner herself would work on raising money
from foreign governments, one of her specialties.
She was very close to the South Koreans, having
been their presence in Washington for the past
decade. She knew the diplomats, the businessmen,
the big shots. Few countries would sleep easier
with a beefed-up United States military than South
Korea.

'I feel sure they'll be good for at least five million,' she said confidently. 'Initially, anyway.'

From memory, she made a list of twenty French and British companies that derived at least a fourth of their annual sales from the Pentagon. She'd start working on them immediately.

Tyner was very much the Washington lawyer these days. She hadn't seen a courtroom in fifteen years, and every meaningful world event originated within the Beltway and somehow affected her.

The challenge at hand was unprecedented – electing an unknown, last-minute candidate who, at the moment, enjoyed 30 percent name recognition and 12 percent positives. What their candidate had, though, unlike the other flakes who dropped in and out of the presidential derby, was seemingly unlimited cash. Tyner had been well paid to elect and defeat scores of politicians, and she held the unwavering belief that money would always win. Give her the money, and she could elect or beat anybody.

During the first week of its existence, D-PAC buzzed with unbridled energy. The offices were open twenty-four hours a day as Tyner's people set up shop and charged forward. Those raising money produced an exhaustive computerized list of 310,000 hourly workers in defense and related industries, then hit them hard with a slick mail-out pleading for money. Another list had the names of twenty-eight thousand white-collar defense workers who earned in excess of $50,000 a year. They were mailed a different type of solicitation.

The D-PAC consultants looking for endorsements found the fifty members of Congress with the most defense jobs in their districts. Thirty-seven were up for reelection, which would make the arm-twisting that much easier. D-PAC would go to the grassroots, to the defense workers and their bosses, and orchestrate a massive phone campaign in support of Aaron Lake and more military spending. Six senators from defense-heavy states had tough opponents in November, and Elaine Tyner planned a lunch with each of them.

Unlimited cash cannot go unnoticed for long in Washington. A rookie congressman from Kentucky, one of the lowest of the 435, desperately needed money to fight what appeared to be a losing campaign back home. No one had heard of the poor boy. He hadn't said a word during his first two years, and now his rivals back home had found an attractive opponent. No one would give him money. He heard rumors, tracked down Elaine Tyner, and their conversation went something like this:

'How much money do you need?' she asked.

'A hundred thousand dollars.' He flinched, she did not.

'Can you endorse Aaron Lake for President?'

'I'll endorse anybody if the price is right.'

'Good. We'll give you two hundred thousand and run your campaign.'

'It's all yours.'

Most were not that easy, but D-PAC managed to buy eight endorsements in the first ten days of its existence. All were insignificant congressmen who'd served with Lake and liked him well enough. The strategy was to line them up before the cameras a week or two before big Super Tuesday, March 7. The more the merrier.

Most, however, had already committed to other candidates.

Tyner hurriedly made the rounds, sometimes eating three power meals a day, all happily covered by D-PAC. Her goal was to let the town know that her brand-new client had arrived, had plenty of money, and was backing a dark horse soon to break from the pack. In a city where talk was an industry in itself, she had no trouble spreading her message.

Finn Yarber's wife arrived unannounced at Trumble, her first visit in ten months. She wore fraying leather sandals, a soiled denim skirt, a baggy blouse adorned with beads and feathers, and all sorts of old hippie crap around her neck and wrists and head. She had a gray butch cut and hair under her arms, and looked very much like the tired, worn-out refugee from the sixties that she really was. Finn was less than thrilled when word got to him that his wife was waiting up front.

Her name was Carmen Topolski-Yocoby, a mouthful that she had used as a weapon all of her adult life. She was a radical feminist lawyer in Oakland whose speciality was representing lesbians suing for sexual harassment at work. So every single client was an angry woman battling an angry employer. Work was a bitch.

She had been married to Finn for thirty years – married, but not always living together. He'd lived with other women; she'd lived with other men.

111

Once when they were newlyweds, they lived with an entire houseful of others, different combinations each week. Both came and went. For one six-year stretch they lived together in chaotic monogamy, and produced two children, neither of whom had amounted to much.

They'd met on the battlefields of Berkeley in 1965, both protesting the war and all other evils, both law students, both committed to the high moral ground of social change. They worked diligently to register voters. They fought for the dignity of migrant workers. They got arrested during the Tet Offensive. They chained themselves to redwoods. They fought the Christians in the schools. They sued on behalf of the whales. They marched the streets of San Francisco in every parade, for any and every cause.

And they drank heavily, partied with great enthusiasm, and relished the drug culture; they moved in and out and slept around, and this was okay because they defined their own morality. They were fighting for the Mexicans and the redwoods, dammit! They had to be good people!

Now they were just tired.

She was embarrassed that her husband, a brilliant man who'd somehow stumbled his way onto the California Supreme Court, was now locked away in a federal prison. He was quite relieved that the prison was in Florida and not California; otherwise she might visit more often. His first digs had been near Bakersfield, but he managed to get himself transferred away.

They never wrote each other, never called. She

was passing through because she had a sister in Miami.

'Nice tan,' she said. 'You're looking good.'

And you're shriveling like an old prune, he thought. Damn, she looked ancient and tired.

'How's life?' he asked, not really caring.

'Busy. I'm working too hard.'

'That's good.' Good that she was working and making a living, something she'd done off and on for many years. Finn had five years to go before he could shake Trumble's dust from his gnarled and bare feet. He had no intention of returning to her, or to California. If he survived, something he doubted every day, he'd leave at the age of sixty-five, and his dream was to find a land where the IRS and the FBI and all the rest of those alphabetized government thugs had no jurisdiction. Finn hated his own government so much he planned to renounce his citizenship and find another nationality.

'Are you still drinking?' he asked. He, of course, was not, though he did manage a little pot occasionally from one of the guards.

'I'm still sober, thanks for asking.'

Every question was a barb, every reply a retort. He honestly wondered why she had stopped by. Then he found out.

'I've decided to get a divorce,' she said.

He shrugged as if to say, 'Why bother?' Instead he said, 'Probably not a bad idea.'

'I've found someone else,' she said.

'Male or female?' he asked, more curious than anything else. Nothing would surprise him.

'A younger man.'

He shrugged again and almost said, 'Go for it, old girl.'

'He's not the first,' Finn said.

'Let's not go there,' she said.

Fine with Finn. He had always admired her exuberant sexuality, her stamina, but it was difficult to imagine this old woman doing it with any regularity. 'Show me the papers,' he said. 'I'll sign them.'

'They'll be here in a week. It's a clean break, since we own so little these days.'

At the height of his rise to power, Justice Yarber and Ms. Topolski-Yocoby had jointly applied for a mortgage on a home in the marina district of San Francisco. The application, properly sanitized to remove any hint of chauvinism or sexism or racism or ageism, blandly worded by spooked California lawyers terrified of being sued by some offended soul, showed a gap between assets and liabilities of almost a million dollars.

Not that a million dollars had mattered to either one of them. They were too busy fighting timber interests and ruthless farmers, etc. In fact, they'd taken pride in the scantness of their assets.

California was a community property state, which roughly meant an equal split. The divorce papers would be easy to sign, for many reasons.

And there was one reason Finn would never mention. The Angola scam was producing money, hidden and dirty, and off-limits to any and every greedy agency. Ms. Carmen would damned sure never know about it.

Finn wasn't certain how the tentacles of community property might reach a secret bank account in the Bahamas, but he had no plans to find out. Show him the papers, he'd be happy to sign.

They managed to chat a few minutes about old friends, a brief conversation indeed because most friends were gone. When they said good-bye, there was no sadness, no remorse. The marriage had been dead for a long time. They were relieved at its passing.

He wished her well, without so much as a hug, then went to the track, where he stripped to his boxers and walked an hour in the sun.

TEN

Lufkin was finishing his second day in Cairo with dinner at a sidewalk café on Shari' el-Corniche, in the Garden City section of the city. He sipped strong black coffee and watched the merchants close their shops – sellers of rugs and brass pots and leather bags and linens from Pakistan, all for the tourists. Less than twenty feet away, an ancient vendor meticulously folded his tent, then left his spot without a trace.

Lufkin looked very much the part of a modern Arab – white slacks, light khaki jacket, a white vented fedora with the bill down close to his eyes. He watched the world from behind a hat and a pair of sunshades. He kept his face and arms tanned and his dark hair cut very short. He spoke perfect Arabic and moved with ease from Beirut to Damascus to Cairo.

His room was at the Hotel El-Nil on the edge of the Nile River, six crowded blocks away, and as he drifted through the city he was suddenly joined by a tall thin foreigner of some breed with only passable English. They knew each other well enough to trust each other, and continued their walk.

'We think tonight is the night,' the contact said, his eyes also hidden.

'Go on.'

'There's a party at the embassy.'

'I know.'

'Yes, a nice setting. Lots of traffic. The bomb will be in a van.'

'What kind of van?'

'We don't know.'

'Anything else?'

'No,' he said, then vanished in a swarming crowd.

Lufkin drank a Pepsi in a hotel bar, alone, and thought about calling Teddy. But it had been four days since he'd seen him at Langley, and Teddy had made no contact. They'd been through this before. Teddy was not going to intervene. Cairo was a dangerous place for Westerners these days, and no one could effectively blame the CIA for not stopping an attack. There would be the usual grandstanding and finger pointing, but the terror would quickly be shoved into the recesses of the national memory, then forgotten. There was a campaign at hand, and the world moved fast anyway. With so many attacks, and assaults, and mindless violence both at home and abroad, the American people had become hardened. Twenty-four-hour news, nonstop flash points, the world always with a crisis somewhere. Late-breaking stories, a shock here and a shock there, and before long you couldn't keep up with events.

Lufkin left the bar and went to his room. From

his window on the fourth floor the city rambled forever, built helter-skelter over the centuries. The roof of the American embassy was directly in front of him, a mile away.

He opened a paperback Louis L'Amour, and waited for the fireworks.

The truck was a two-ton Volvo panel van, loaded from floor to ceiling with three thousand pounds of plastic explosives made in Romania. Its door happily advertised the services of a well-known caterer in the city, a company which made frequent visits to most of the Western embassies. It was parked near the service entrance, in the basement.

The driver of the truck had been a large, friendly Egyptian called Shake by the Marines who guarded the embassy. Shake passed through often, hauling food and supplies to and from social events. Shake was now dead on the floor of his truck, a bullet in his brain.

At twenty minutes after ten, the bomb was detonated by a remote device, operated by a terrorist hiding across the street. As soon as he pushed the right buttons, he ducked behind a car, afraid to look.

The explosion ripped out supporting columns deep in the basement, so the embassy fell to one side. Debris rained for blocks. Most of the nearby buildings suffered structural damage. Windows within a quarter of a mile were cracked.

Lufkin was napping in his chair when the quake came. He jumped to his feet, walked onto his narrow balcony, and watched the cloud of dust.

The roof of the embassy was no longer visible. Within minutes flames were seen and the interminable sirens began. He propped his chair against the railing of the balcony, and settled in for the duration. There would be no sleep. Six minutes after the explosion, the electricity in Garden City went out, and Cairo was dark except for the orange glow of the American embassy.

He called Teddy.

When the technician, Teddy's sanitizer, assured Lufkin the line was secure, the old man's voice came through as clearly as if they were chatting from New York to Boston. 'Yes, Maynard here.'

'I'm in Cairo, Teddy. Watching our embassy go up in smoke.'

'When did it happen?'

'Less than ten minutes ago.'

'How big –'

'Hard to tell. I'm in a hotel a mile away. Massive, I'd say.'

'Call me in an hour. I'll stay here at the office tonight.'

'Done.'

Teddy rolled himself to a computer, punched a few buttons, and within seconds found Aaron Lake. The candidate was en route from Philadelphia to Atlanta, aboard his shiny new airplane. There was a phone in Lake's pocket, a secure digital unit as slim as a cigarette lighter.

Teddy punched more numbers, the phone was summoned, and Teddy spoke to his monitor. 'Mr. Lake, it's Teddy Maynard.'

Who else could it be? Lake thought. No one else could use the phone.

'Are you alone?' Teddy asked.

'Just a minute.'

Teddy waited, then the voice returned. 'I'm in the kitchen now,' Lake said.

'Your plane has a kitchen?'

'A small one, yes. It's a very nice plane, Mr. Maynard.'

'Good. Listen, sorry to bother you, but I have some news. They bombed the American embassy in Cairo fifteen minutes ago.'

'Who?'

'Don't ask that.'

'Sorry.'

'The press will be all over you. Take a moment, prepare some remarks. It will be a good time to express concern for the victims and their families. Keep the politics to a minimum, but also keep the hard line. Your ads are prophetic now, so your words will be repeated many times.'

'I'll do it right now.'

'Call me when you get to Atlanta.'

'Yes, I will.'

Forty minutes later, Lake and his group landed in Atlanta. The press had been duly notified of his arrival, and with the dust just settling in Cairo, there was a crowd waiting. No live pictures had yet emerged of the embassy, yet several agencies were already reporting that 'hundreds' had been killed.

In the small terminal for private aircraft, Lake stood before an eager group of reporters, some with cameras and mikes, others with slim recorders, others still with just plain old notepads. He spoke solemnly, without notes: 'At this moment, we should be in prayer for those who've been injured and killed by this act of war. Our thoughts and prayers are with them and their families, and also with the rescue people. I am not going to politicize this event, but I will say that it is absurd for this country to once again suffer at the hands of terrorists. When I am President, no American life will go unaccounted for. I will use our new military to track down and annihilate any terrorist group that preys upon innocent Americans. That's all I have to say.'

He walked off, ignoring the shouts and questions from the pack of shaggy dogs.

Brilliant, thought Teddy, watching live from his bunker. Quick, compassionate, yet tough as hell. Superb! He once again patted himself on the back for choosing such a wonderful candidate.

When Lufkin called again it was past midnight in Cairo. The fires had been extinguished and they were hauling out bodies as fast as they could. Many were buried in the rubble. He was a block away, behind an army barricade, watching with thousands of others. The scene was chaos, smoke and dust thick in the air. Lufkin had been to several bomb sites in his career, and this was a bad one, he reported.

Teddy rolled around his room and poured another decaf coffee. The Lake terror ads would begin at prime time. On this very night the campaign would spend $3 million in a coast-to-coast deluge of fear and doom. They'd pull the ads tomorrow, and announce it beforehand. Out of respect for the dead and their families, the Lake campaign would temporarily suspend its little prophecies. And they'd start polling at noon tomorrow, massive polling.

High time candidate Lake's positives shot upward. The Arizona and Michigan primaries were less than a week away.

The first pictures from Cairo were of a harried reporter with his back to an army barricade, soldiers watching him fiercely, as he might get shot if he tried once more to charge forward. Sirens wailed all around; lights flashed. But the reporter knew little. A massive bomb had exploded deep in the embassy at ten-twenty when a party was breaking up; no idea of the casualties, but there'd be plenty, he promised. The area was cordoned off by the army, and for good measure they'd sealed the airspace so, dammit, there'd be no helicopter shots. As of yet, no one had claimed responsibility, but for good measure he gave the names of three radical groups as the usual suspects.

'Could be one of these, could be someone else,' he said helpfully. With no carnage to film, the camera was forced to stay with the reporter, and since he had nothing to say he prattled on about how dangerous the Middle East had become, as if this were breaking news and he was there to report it!

Lufkin called around 8 P.M. D.C. time to tell Teddy that the American ambassador to Egypt could not be located, and they were beginning to fear he might be in the rubble. At least that was the word on the street. While talking to Lufkin on the phone, Teddy watched the muted reporter; a Lake terror ad appeared on another screen. It showed the rubble, the carnage, the bodies, the radicals from some other attack, then the smooth but earnest voice of Aaron Lake promising revenge.

How perfect the timing, Teddy thought.

An aide woke Teddy at midnight with lemon tea and a vegetable sandwich. As he so often did, he'd napped in his wheelchair, the wall of TV screens alive with images but no sound. When the aide left, he pushed a button and listened.

The sun was well up in Cairo. The ambassador had not been found, and it was now being assumed he was somewhere in the rubble.

Teddy had never met the ambassador to Egypt, an absolute unknown anyway, who was now being idolized by the chattering reporters as a great American. His death didn't particularly bother Teddy, though it would increase the criticism of the CIA. It would also add gravity to the attack, which, in the scheme of things, would benefit Aaron Lake.

Sixty-one bodies had been recovered so far. The Egyptian authorities were blaming Yidal, the likeliest of suspects because his little army had bombed three Western embassies in the past sixteen months, and because he was openly calling for war against the United States. The current CIA dossier on Yidal gave him thirty soldiers and an annual budget of around $5 million, almost all originating from Libya and Saudi Arabia. But to the press, the leaks suggested an army of a thousand with unlimited funds with which to terrorize innocent Americans.

The Israelis knew what Yidal had for breakfast and where he ate it. They could've taken him out a dozen times, but so far he'd kept his little war away from them. As long as he killed Americans and Westerners, the Israelis really didn't care. It was to their benefit for the West to loathe the Islamic radicals.

Teddy ate slowly, then napped some more. Lufkin called before noon Cairo time with the news that the bodies of the ambassador and his wife had been found. The count was now at eighty-four; all but eleven were Americans.

The cameras caught up with Aaron Lake outside a plant in Marietta, Georgia, shaking hands in the dark as the shift changed, and when asked about events in Cairo, he said: 'Sixteen months ago these same criminals bombed two of our embassies, killing thirty Americans, and we've done nothing to stop them. They're operating with impunity because we lack the commitment to fight. When I'm President, we'll declare war on these terrorists and stop the killing.'

The tough talk was contagious, and as America woke up to the terrible news in Cairo, the country was also treated to a brash chorus of threats and ultimatums from the other seven candidates. Even the more passive among them now sounded like gunslingers.

ELEVEN

It was snowing again in Iowa, a steady swirl of snow and wind that turned to slush on the streets and sidewalks and made Quince Garbe once again long for a beach. He covered his face on Main Street as if to protect himself, but the truth was he didn't want to speak to anyone. Didn't want anyone to see him darting yet again into the post office.

There was a letter in the box. One of those letters. His jaw fell and his hands froze when he saw it, just lying there with some junk mail, innocent, like a note from an old friend. He glanced over both shoulders – a thief racked with guilt – then yanked it out and thrust it into his coat.

His wife was at the hospital planning a ball for crippled children, so the house was empty except for a maid who spent her day napping down in the laundry room. He hadn't given her a raise in eight years. He took his time driving there, fighting the snow and the drifts, cursing the con man who'd entered his life under the ruse of love, anticipating

125

the letter, which grew heavier near his heart with each passing minute.

No sign of the maid as he entered the front door, making as much noise as possible. He went upstairs to his bedroom, where he locked the door. There was a pistol under the mattress. He flung his overcoat and his gloves onto an armchair, then his jacket, and he sat on the edge of his bed and examined the envelope. Same lavender paper, same handwriting, same everything with a Jacksonville postmark, two days old. He ripped it open and removed a single page.

Dear Quince:
Thanks so much for the money. So that you won't think I'm a total thug, I think you should know the money went to my wife and children. They are suffering so. My incarceration has left them destitute. My wife is clinically depressed and cannot work. My four children are fed by welfare and food stamps.
(A hundred thousand bucks should certainly fatten them up, Quince thought.)
They live in government housing and have no dependable transportation. So, thanks again for your help. Another $50,000 should get them out of debt and start a nice college fund.
Same rules as before; same wiring instructions; same promises to expose your secret life if the money is not received quickly. Do it now, Quince, and I swear this is my last letter.

Thanks again, Quince.

Love, Ricky

He went to the bathroom, to the medicine cabinet, where he found his wife's Valium. He took two, but thought about eating all of them. He needed to lie down but he couldn't use the bed because it would be wrinkled and someone would ask questions. So he stretched himself out on the floor, on the worn but clean carpet, and waited for the pills to work.

He'd begged and scraped and even lied a little to borrow the first installment for Ricky. There was no way he could squeeze another $50,000 from a personal balance sheet already heavily padded and still teetering on the edge of insolvency. His nice large house was choked with a fat mortgage held by his father. His father signed his paychecks. His cars were large and imported, but they had a million miles on them and little value. Who in Bakers, Iowa, would want to buy an eleven-year-old Mercedes?

And what if he managed to somehow steal the money? The criminal otherwise known as Ricky would simply thank him again, then demand more.

It was over.

Time for the pills. Time for the gun.

The phone startled him. Without thinking, he scrambled to his feet and grabbed the receiver. 'Hello,' he grunted.

'Where the hell are you?' It was his father, with a tone he knew so well.

'I'm, uh, not feeling well,' he managed to say,

staring at his watch and now remembering the ten-thirty meeting with a very important inspector from the FDIC.

'I don't give a damn how you feel. Mr. Colthurst from the FDIC has been waiting in my office for fifteen minutes.'

'I'm vomiting, Dad,' he said, and cringed again with the word Dad. Fifty-one years old, still using the word Dad.

'You're lying. Why didn't you call if you're sick? Gladys told me she saw you just before ten walking toward the post office. What the hell's going on here?'

'Excuse me. I gotta go to the toilet. I'll call you later.' He hung up.

The Valium rolled in like a pleasant fog, and he sat on the edge of his bed staring at the lavender squares scattered on the floor. Ideas were slow in coming, hampered by the pills.

He could hide the letters, then kill himself. His suicide note would place the bulk of the blame on his father. Death was not an altogether unpleasant prospect; no more marriage, no more bank, no more Dad, no more Bakers, Iowa, no more hiding in the closet.

But he would miss his children and grandchildren.

And what if this Ricky monster didn't learn of the suicide, and sent another letter, and they found it, and somehow Quince got himself outed anyway, long after his funeral?

The next lousy idea involved a conspiracy with his secretary, a woman he trusted marginally to begin with. He would tell her the truth, then ask her to write a letter to Ricky and break the news of Quince Garbe's suicide. Together, Quince and his secretary could scheme and fake their way through a suicide, and in the process take some measure of revenge against Ricky.

But he'd rather be dead than tell his secretary.

The third idea occurred after the Valium had settled in at full throttle, and it made him smile. Why not try a little honesty? Write a letter to Ricky and plead poverty. Offer another $10,000 and tell him that's all. If Ricky was determined to destroy him, then he, Quince, would have no choice but to come after Ricky. He'd inform the FBI, let them track the letters and the wire transfers, and both men would go down in flames.

He slept on the floor for thirty minutes, then gathered his jacket, gloves, and overcoat. He left the house without seeing the maid. As he drove to town, flush with the desire to confront the truth, he admitted aloud that only the money mattered. His father was eighty-one. The bank's stock was worth about $10 million. Someday it would be his. Stay in the closet until the cash was in hand, then live any way he damned well pleased.

Don't screw up the money.

Coleman Lee owned a taco hut in a strip mall on the outskirts of Gary, Indiana, in a section of town now ruled by the Mexicans. Coleman was forty-eight, with two bad divorces decades earlier, no children, thank God. Because of all the tacos, he was thick and slow, with a drooping stomach and large fleshy cheeks. Coleman was not pretty, but he was certainly lonely.

His employees were mainly young Mexican boys, illegal immigrants, all of whom he, sooner or later, tried to molest, or seduce, or whatever you'd call his clumsy efforts. Rarely was he successful, and his turnover was high. Business was slow too because people talked and Coleman was not well regarded. Who wanted to buy tacos from a pervert?

He rented two small boxes at the post office at the other end of the strip mall – one for his business, the other for his pleasure. He collected porno and gathered it almost daily from the post office. The mail carrier at his apartment was a curious type, and it was best to keep some things as quiet as possible.

He strolled along the dirty sidewalk at the edge of the parking lot, past the discount stores for shoes and cosmetics, past a XXX video dive he'd been banned from, past a welfare office, one brought to the suburbs by a desperate politician looking for votes. The post office was crowded with Mexicans taking their time because it was cold out.

His daily haul was two hard-core magazines sent to him in plain brown wrappers, and a letter which looked vaguely familiar. It was a square yellow envelope, no return address, postmarked in Atlantic Beach, Florida. Ah, yes, he remembered as he held it. Young Percy in rehab.

Back in his cramped little office between the kitchen and the utility room, he quickly flipped through the magazines, saw nothing new, then stacked them in a pile with a hundred others. He opened the letter from Percy. Like the two before,

it was handprinted, and addressed to Walt, a name
he used to collect all his porn. Walt Lee.

Dear Walt:

I really enjoyed your last letter. I've read it
many times. You have a nice way with words.
As I told you, I've been here for almost
eighteen months, and it gets very lonely. I
keep your letters under my mattress, and
when I feel really isolated I read them over
and over. Where did you learn to write like
that? Please send another one as soon as
possible.

With a little luck, I'll be released in April.
I'm not sure where I'll go or what I'll do. It's
frightening, really, to think that I'll just walk
out of here after almost two years, and have
no one to be with. I hope we're still pen pals
by then.

I was wondering, and I really hate to ask
this, but since I have no one else I'll do it
anyway, and please feel free to say no, it
won't hurt our friendship, but could you loan
me a thousand bucks? They have this little
book and music shop here at the clinic, and
they let us buy paperbacks and CDs on
credit, and, well, I've been here so long that
I've run up quite a tab.

If you can make the loan, I'd really
appreciate it. If not, I completely understand.

Thanks for being there, Walt. Please write
me soon. I treasure your letters.

Love, Percy

A thousand bucks? What kinda little creep was this? Coleman smelled a con. He ripped the letter into pieces and threw them in the trash.

'A thousand bucks,' he mumbled to himself, reaching for the magazines again.

Curtis was not the real name of the jeweler in Dallas. Curtis worked fine when corresponding with Ricky in rehab, but the real name was Vann Gates.

Mr. Gates was fifty-eight years old, on the surface happily married, the father of three and the grandfather of two, and he and his wife owned six jewelry stores in the Dallas area, all located in malls. On paper they had $2 million, and they'd made it themselves. They had a very nice new home in Highland Park, with separate bedrooms at opposite ends. They met in the kitchen for coffee and in the den for TV and grandkids.

Mr. Gates ventured from the closet now and then, always with excruciating caution. No one had a clue. His correspondence with Ricky was his first attempt at finding love through the want ads, and so far he'd been thrilled with the results. He rented a small box in a post office near one of the malls, and used the name Curtis V. Cates.

The lavender envelope was addressed to Curtis Cates, and as he sat in his car and carefully opened it, he at first had no clue anything was wrong. Just another sweet letter from his beloved Ricky. Lightning hit, though, with the first words:

Dear Vann Gates:
    The party's over, pal. My name ain't Ricky,

and you're not Curtis. I'm not a gay boy
looking for love. You, however, have an awful
secret, which I'm sure you want to keep. I
want to help.

Here's the deal: Wire $100,000 to Geneva
Trust Bank, Nassau, Bahamas, account
number 144-DXN-9593, for Boomer Realty,
Ltd., routing number 392844-22.

Do so immediately! This is not a joke. It's
a scam, and you've been hooked. If the
money is not received within ten days, I will
send to your wife, Ms. Glenda Gates, a little
packet filled with copies of all letters, photos,
etc.

Wire the money, and I'll simply go away.

Love, Ricky

With time, Vann found the Dallas I-635 loop,
and before long he was on the I-820 loop around
Fort Worth, then back to Dallas, driving at exactly
fifty-five, in the right-hand lane, oblivious to the
traffic stacked up behind him. If crying would
help, then he would've certainly had a good one.
He had no qualms about weeping, especially in the
privacy of his Jaguar.

But he was too angry to cry, too bitter to be
wounded. And he was too frightened to waste time
yearning for someone who did not exist. Action
was needed – quick, decisive, secretive.

Heartache, though, overcame him, and he
finally pulled onto the shoulder and parked with
the engine running. All those wonderful dreams of
Ricky, those countless hours staring at his handsome face with his crooked little smile, and reading

his letters – sad, funny, desperate, hopeful – how could so many emotions be conveyed with the written word? He'd practically memorized the letters.

And he was just a boy, so young and virile, yet lonely and in need of mature companionship. The Ricky he'd come to love needed the loving embrace of an older man, and Curtis/Vann had been making plans for months. The ploy of a diamond show in Orlando while his wife was in El Paso at her sister's. He'd sweated the details and left no tracks.

He did, finally, cry. Poor Vann shed tears without shame or embarrassment. No one could see him; the other cars were flying past at eighty miles per hour.

He vowed revenge, like any jilted lover. He'd track down this beast, this monster who'd posed as Ricky and broken his heart.

When the sobbing began to subside, he thought of his wife and family and that helped greatly in drying up the tears. She'd get all six stores and the $2 million and the new house with separate bedrooms, and he would get nothing but ridicule and scorn and gossip in a town that loved it so. His children would follow the money, and for the rest of their lives his grandchildren would hear the whispers about their grandfather.

Back in the right lane at fifty-five, back through Mesquite for the second time, reading the letter again as eighteen-wheelers roared past.

There was no one to call, no banker he could trust to check out the account in the Bahamas, no lawyer to run to for advice, no friend to hear his sorry tale.

For a man who'd carefully lived a double life, the money would not be insurmountable. His wife watched every dime, both at home and at the stores, and for that reason Vann had long since mastered the scheme of hiding money. He did it with gems, rubies and pearls and sometimes small diamonds he placed aside and later sold to other dealers for cash. It was common in the business. He had boxes of cash – shoe boxes neatly stacked in a fireproof safe in a mini-storage out in Plano. Post-divorce cash. Cash for the afterlife when he and Ricky would sail the world and spend it all in one endless voyage.

'Sonofabitch!' he said through gritted teeth. And again and again.

Why not write this con man and plead poverty? Or threaten to expose his little extortion scheme? Why not fight back?

Because the sonofabitch knew exactly what he was doing. He'd tracked Vann well enough to learn his real name, and the name of his wife. He knew Vann had the money.

He pulled into his driveway and there was Glenda sweeping the sidewalk. 'Where have you been, honey?' she asked pleasantly.

'Running errands,' he said with a smile.

'Took a long time,' she said, still sweeping.

He was so sick of it. She timed his movements! For thirty years he'd been under her thumb, with a stopwatch clicking in the palm of her hand.

He pecked her on the cheek out of habit, then went to the basement where he locked a door and

135

began to cry again. The house was his prison (with a mortgage of $7,800 a month, it certainly felt like it). She was the guard, the keeper of the keys. His sole means of escape had just collapsed, replaced by a cold-blooded extortionist.

TWELVE

Eighty coffins required a lot of space. They were laid in perfect rows, all neatly wrapped in red, white, and blue, all the same length and width. They'd arrived thirty minutes earlier aboard an Air Force cargo plane, and were removed with great pomp and ceremony. Almost a thousand friends and relatives sat on folding chairs, on the concrete floor of the hangar, and stared in shock at the sea of flags arranged before them. They were outnumbered only by the shaggy dogs, all quarantined behind barricades and military police.

Even for a country well accustomed to foreign policy boondoggles, it was an impressive body count. Eighty Americans, eight Brits, eight Germans – no French because they'd been boycotting Western diplomatic functions in Cairo. Why were eighty Americans still in the embassy after 10 P.M.? That was the question of the hour, and so far no good answer had surfaced. So many of those who made such decisions were now lying in their coffins. The best theory buzzing around D.C. was that the caterer had been late, and the band even later.

But the terrorists had proved all too well that they would strike at any hour, so what difference did it make how late the ambassador and his wife and their staff and colleagues and guests wanted to party?

The second great question of the hour was just exactly why did we have eighty people in our embassy in Cairo to begin with? The State Department had yet to acknowledge the question.

After some mournful music from an Air Force band, the President spoke. His voice broke and he managed to summon a tear or two, but after eight years of such theatrics the act had worn thin. He'd already promised revenge many times, so he dwelt on comfort and sacrifice and the promise of a better life in the hereafter.

The Secretary of State called the names of the dead, a morbid recitation designed to capture the gravity of the moment. The sobbing increased. Then some more music. The longest speech was delivered by the Vice President, fresh from the campaign trail and filled with a newly discovered commitment to eradicate terrorism from the face of the earth. Though he'd never worn a military uniform, he seemed eager to start tossing grenades.

Lake had them all on the run.

Lake watched the grim ceremony while flying from Tucson to Detroit, late for another round of interviews. On board was his pollster, a newly acquired magician who now traveled with him. While Lake and his staff watched the news, the pollster worked feverishly at the small conference

138

table upon which he had two laptops, three phones, and more printouts than any ten people could digest.

The Arizona and Michigan primaries were three days away, and Lake's numbers were climbing, especially in his home state, where he was in a dead heat with the long-established front-runner, Governor Tarry of Indiana. In Michigan, Lake was ten points down, but people were listening. The fiasco in Cairo was working beautifully in his favor.

Governor Tarry was suddenly scrambling for money. Aaron Lake was not. It was coming in faster than he could spend it.

When the Vice President finally finished, Lake left the screen and returned to his leather swivel recliner and picked up a newspaper. A staff member brought him coffee, which he sipped while watching the flatlands of Kansas eight miles below him. Another staff member handed him a message – one that was supposed to require an urgent call from the candidate. Lake glanced around the plane, and counted thirteen people, pilots not included.

For a private man who still missed his wife, Lake was not adjusting well to the complete lack of privacy. He moved with a group, every half hour slotted by someone, every action coordinated by a committee, every interview preceded by written guesses about the questions and suggested responses. He got six hours each night alone, in his hotel room, and damned if the Secret Service wouldn't sleep on the floor if he'd allow it. Because of the fatigue, he slept like an infant. His only true moments of quiet reflection occurred in the bath-room, either in the shower or on the toilet.

But he wasn't kidding himself. He, Aaron Lake, quiet congressman from Arizona, had become an overnight sensation. He was charging while the rest were faltering. Big money was aimed at him. The press followed like bloodhounds. His words got repeated. He had very powerful friends, and as the pieces were falling in place the nomination looked realistic. He hadn't dreamed of such things a month earlier.

Lake was savoring the moment. The campaign was madness, but he could control the tempo of the job itself. Reagan was a nine-to-five President, and he'd been far more effective than Carter, an avid workaholic. Just get to the White House, he told himself over and over, suffer these fools, gut it through the primaries, endure with a smile and a quick wit, and one day very soon he'd sit in the Oval Office, alone, with the world at his feet.

And he would have his privacy.

Teddy sat with York in his bunker, watching the live scene from Andrews Air Force Base. He preferred York's company when things were rough. The accusations had been brutal. Scape-goats were in demand, and many of the idiots chasing the cameras blamed the CIA because that's who they always blamed.

If they only knew.

He'd finally told York of Lufkin's warnings, and York understood completely. Unfortunately, they'd been through this before. When you police the world you lose a lot of cops, and Teddy and

140

York had shared many sad moments watching the flag-covered coffins roll off the C-130s, evidence of another debacle abroad. The Lake campaign would be Teddy's final effort at saving American lives.

Failure seemed unlikely. D-PAC had collected more than $20 million in two weeks, and was in the process of hauling the money around Washington. Twenty-one congressmen had been recruited for Lake endorsements, at a total cost of $6 million. But the biggest prize so far was Senator Britt, the ex-candidate, the father of a little Thai boy. When he abandoned his quest for the White House he owed close to $4 million, with no viable plan to cover his deficit. Money tends not to follow those who pack up and go home. Elaine Tyner, the lawyer running D-PAC, met with Senator Britt. It took her less than an hour to cut the deal. D-PAC would pay off all his campaign debts, over a three-year period, and he would make a noisy endorsement of Aaron Lake.

'Did we have a projection of casualties?' York asked.

After a while Teddy said, 'No.'

Their conversations were never hurried.

'Why so many?'

'Lots of booze. Happens all the time in the Arab countries. Different culture, life is dull, so when our diplomats throw a party, they throw a good one. Many of the dead were quite drunk.'

Minutes passed. 'Where's Yidal?' asked York.

'Right now he's in Iraq. Yesterday, Tunisia.'

'We really should stop him.'

'We will, next year. It'll be a great moment for President Lake.'

Twelve of the sixteen congressmen endorsing Lake wore blue shirts, a fact that was not lost on Elaine Tyner. She counted such things. When a D.C. politician got near a camera, odds were he'd put on his best blue cotton shirt. The other four wore white.

She arranged them before the reporters in a ballroom of the Willard Hotel. The senior member, Representative Thurman of Florida, opened things up by welcoming the press to this very important occasion. Working from prepared notes, he offered his opinions on the current state of world events, commented on things in Cairo and China and Russia, and said that the world was a lot more dangerous than it looked. He rattled off the usual statistics about our reduced military. Then he launched into a long soliloquy about his close friend Aaron Lake, a man he'd served with for ten years and whom he knew better than most. Lake was a man with a message, one we didn't particularly want to hear, but a very important one nonetheless.

Thurman was breaking ranks with Governor Tarry, and though he did so with great reluctance and no small feeling of betrayal, he had become convinced through painful soul-searching that Aaron Lake was needed for the safety of our nation. What Thurman didn't say was that a recent poll showed Lake becoming very popular back in Tampa-St. Pete.

The mike was then passed to a congressman

from California. He covered no new territory, but rambled for ten minutes anyway. In his district north of San Diego were forty-five thousand defense and aerospace workers, and all of them, it seemed, had written or called. He'd been an easy convert; the pressure from home plus $250,000 from Ms. Tyner and D-PAC, and he had his marching orders.

When the questions started, the sixteen bunched together in a tight little pack, all anxious to answer and say something, all afraid their faces might not get wedged into the picture.

Though there were no committee chairmen, the group was not unimpressive. They managed to convey the image that Aaron Lake was a legitimate candidate, a man they knew and trusted. A man the nation needed. A man who could be elected.

The event was well staged and well covered, and instantly made news. Elaine Tyner would trot out five more the following day, then save Senator Britt for the day before big Super Tuesday.

The letter in Ned's glove box was from Percy, young Percy in rehab who got his mail through Laurel Ridge, Post Office Box 4585, Atlantic Beach, FL 32233.

Ned was in Atlantic Beach, had been for two days, with the letter and with the determination to track down young Percy because he smelled a hoax. He had nothing better to do. He was retired with plenty of money, no family to speak of, and besides, it was snowing in Cincinnati. He had a room at the Sea Turtle Inn, on the beach, and at night he hit the bars along Atlantic Boulevard.

He'd found two excellent restaurants, crowded little places with lots of young pretty girls and boys. He'd discovered Pete's Bar and Grill a block away, and for the last two nights he'd staggered from the place, drunk on cold drafts. The Sea Turtle was just around the corner.

During the day Ned watched the post office, a modern brick and glass government job on First Street, parallel to the beach. A small, windowless box midway from the floor, 4585 was on a wall with eighty others, in an area of medium traffic. Ned had inspected the box, tried to open it with keys and wire, and had even asked questions at the front desk. The postal workers had been most unhelpful. Before leaving the first day, he had stuck a two-inch strand of thin black thread to the bottom of the box's door. It was imperceptible to anyone else, but Ned would know if the mail was checked.

He had a letter in there, in a bright red envelope, one he'd mailed three days earlier from Cincinnati, then raced south. In it he'd sent Percy a check for $1,000, money the boy needed for a set of artist's supplies. In an earlier letter, Ned had revealed that he had once owned a modern art gallery in Greenwich Village. It was a lie, he had not, but he doubted everything Percy said too.

Ned had been suspicious from the beginning. Before he answered the solicitation, he had tried to verify Laurel Ridge, the fancy detox unit supposedly holding Percy. There was a telephone, a private number he'd been unable to pry out of directory assistance. There was no street address. Percy had explained in his first letter that the place was top-secret because many of its patients were high-powered corporate executives and top-level government officials, all of whom had, in one way or another, succumbed to chemicals. It sounded good. The boy had a way with words.

And a very pretty face. That's why Ned kept writing. The photo was something he admired every day.

The request for money had caught him by surprise, and since he was bored he decided to make the drive to Jacksonville.

From his spot in the parking lot, low behind the steering wheel of his car, with his back to First Street, he could watch the wall of boxes and the postal customers as they came and went. It was a long shot, but what the hell. He used a small pair of foldable binoculars, and on occasion caught a stare from someone walking by. The task grew monotonous after two days, but as the time passed he became more and more convinced that his letter would be retrieved. Surely someone checked the box at least once every three days. A rehab clinic with patients would get plenty of mail, wouldn't it? Or was it simply a front for a con man who dropped by once a week to check his traps?

The con man showed up late in the afternoon of the third day. He parked a Beetle next to Ned, then ambled into the post office. He wore wrinkled khakis, white shirt, straw hat, bow tie, and had the disheveled air of a would-be beach Bohemian.

Trevor had enjoyed a long midday break at Pete's, then slept off his liquid lunch with an hour nap at his desk, and was just stirring about, making his rounds. He put the key in Box 4585 and removed a handful of correspondence, most of it junk mail, which he threw away as he flipped through the letters on his way out of the building.

Ned watched every move. After three days of tedium, he was thrilled that his surveillance had paid off. He followed the Beetle, and when it parked and the driver walked into a small, run-down law office, Ned drove away, scratching his temple, repeating out loud, 'A lawyer?'

He kept driving, down Highway A1A, along the shore, away from the sprawl of Jacksonville, south through Vilano Beach and Crescent Beach and Beverly Beach and Flagler Beach and finally to a Holiday Inn outside Port Orange. He went to the bar before he went to his room.

It wasn't the first scam he'd flirted with. In fact, it was the second. He'd sniffed the other one out too before any damage was done. Over his third martini he swore it would be his last.

THIRTEEN

The day before the Arizona and Michigan primaries, the Lake campaign unleashed a media blitz, the likes of which had never been seen before in presidential politics. For eighteen hours, the two states were bombarded with one ad after another. Some were fifteen seconds, little softies with not much more than his handsome face and the promises of decisive leadership and a safer world. Others were one-minute documentaries on the dangers of the post-cold war. Still others were macho, in-your-face promises to the terrorists of the world – kill people simply because they are Americans, and you will pay a very dear price. Cairo was still very fresh, and the assurances hit their mark.

The ads were bold, put together by high-powered consultants, and the only downside was oversaturation. But Lake was too new to the scene to bore anyone, not now anyway. His campaign spent $10 million on television in the two states, a staggering amount.

They ran at a slower clip during voting hours on Tuesday, February 22, and when the polls closed the exit analysts predicted Lake would win his home state and run a close second in Michigan. Governor Tarry, after all, was from Indiana, another midwestern state, and he'd spent weeks in Michigan during the previous three months.

Evidently, he hadn't spent enough time there. The voters in Arizona opted for their native son, and those in Michigan liked the new fellow too. Lake got 60 percent at home, and 55 percent in Michigan where Governor Tarry got a paltry 31 percent. The balance was divided among the noncontenders.

It was a devastating loss for Governor Tarry, just two weeks before big Super Tuesday and three weeks before the little one.

Lake watched the vote counting from on board his airplane, en route from Phoenix, where'd he'd voted for himself. An hour from Washington, CNN declared him the surprise winner in Michigan, and his staff opened the champagne. He savored the moment, even allowed himself two glasses.

History was not lost on Lake. No one had ever started so late, and come so far so fast. In the darkened cabin, they watched the analysts on four screens, the experts all marveling at this man Lake and what he'd done. Governor Tarry was gracious, but also worried about the enormous sums of money being spent by his heretofore unknown opponent.

Lake chatted politely with the small group of reporters waiting for him at Reagan National Airport, then rode in yet another black Suburban to his national campaign headquarters where he thanked his highly paid staff and told them to go home and get some sleep.

It was almost midnight when he got to Georgetown, to his quaint little rowhouse on Thirty-fourth, near Wisconsin. Two Secret Service agents got out of the car behind Lake, and two more were waiting on the front steps. He had adamantly refused an official request to put guards inside his home.

'I do not want to see you people lurking around here,' he said harshly at his front door. He resented their presence, didn't know their names, and didn't care if they disliked him. They had no names, as far as he was concerned. They were simply 'You people,' said with as much contempt as possible.

Once he was locked inside, he went upstairs to his bedroom and changed clothes. He turned out the lights as if he were asleep, waited fifteen minutes, then eased downstairs to the den to see if anyone was looking in, then down another flight to the small basement. He climbed through a window, and stepped into the cold night near his tiny patio. He paused, listened, heard nothing, then quietly opened a wooden gate and darted between the two buildings behind his. He surfaced on Thirty-fifth Street, alone, in the dark, dressed like a jogger with a running cap pulled low to his brow. Three minutes later he was on M Street, in the crowds. He found a taxi and disappeared into the night.

Teddy Maynard had gone to sleep reasonably

content with his candidate's first two victories, but he was awakened by the news that something had gone wrong. When he rolled himself into the bunker at ten minutes after 6 A.M., he was more frightened than angry, though his emotions had run the gamut in the past hour. York was waiting, along with a supervisor named Deville, a tiny nervous man who'd obviously been wired for many hours.

'Let's hear it,' Teddy growled, still rolling and looking for coffee.

Deville did the talking. 'At twelve-o-two this morning he said good-bye to the Secret Service and entered his house. At twelve-seventeen he exited through a small window in the basement. We, of course, have wires and timers on every door and window. We've leased a rowhouse across the street, and we were on alert anyway. He hasn't been home in six days.' Deville waved a small pill, the size of an aspirin. 'This is a little device known as a T-Dec. They're in the soles of all of his shoes, including his jogging shoes. So if he's not barefoot we know where he is. Once pressure is applied from the foot, the bug emits a signal that is broadcast for two hundred yards without a transmitter. When pressure is relaxed, it will continue to provide a signal for fifteen minutes. We scrambled and picked him up on M Street. He was dressed in sweats with a cap over his eyes. We had two cars in place when he jumped in a cab. We followed him to Chevy Chase, to a suburban shopping center. While the cab waited, he darted into a place called Mailbox America, one of these new places where you can send and receive mail outside the Postal Service. Some, including this one, are open twenty-four hours for mail pickup. He was inside for less than a minute, just long enough to open his box with a key, remove several pieces of mail, throw it all away, then return to the cab. One of our cars followed him back to M Street, where he got out and sneaked back home. The other car stayed at the mailbox place. We went through the waste can just inside the door, and found six pieces of junk mail, evidently his. The address is A1 Konyers, Box 455, Mailbox America, 39380 Western Avenue, Chevy Chase.'

'So he didn't find what he was looking for?' Teddy asked.

'It looks as though he tossed everything he took from his box. Here's the video.'

A screen dropped from the ceiling as the lights faded. Footage from a video camera zoomed across a parking lot, past the cab, and onto the figure of Aaron Lake in his baggy sweats as he disappeared around a corner inside Mailbox America. Seconds later he reappeared, flipping through letters and papers in his right hand. He stopped briefly at the door and then dumped everything in a tall wastebasket.

'What the hell's he looking for?' Teddy mumbled to himself.

Lake left the building and quickly ducked inside the cab. The video stopped; the lights became brighter.

Deville resumed his narrative. 'We're confident we found the right papers in the trash can. We were there within seconds, and no one else entered the premises while we waited. The time was twelve fifty-eight. An hour later, we entered again and keyed the lock to Box 455, so we'll have access anytime we need it.'

'Check it every day,' Teddy said. 'Inventory every piece of mail. Leave the junk, but when something arrives I want to know it.'

'You got it. Mr. Lake reentered the basement window at one twenty-two and stayed at home for the rest of the night. He's there now.'

'That's all,' Teddy said, and Deville left the room.

A minute passed as Teddy stirred his coffee. 'How many addresses does he have?'

York knew the question was coming. He glanced at some notes. 'He gets most of his personal mail at his home in Georgetown. He has at least two addresses on Capitol Hill, one at his office, the other at the Armed Services Committee. He has three offices back home in Arizona. That's six that we know about.'

'Why would he need a seventh?'

'I don't know the reason, but it can't be good. A man who has nothing to hide does not use an alias or a secret address.'

'When did he rent the box?'

'We're still working on that.'

'Maybe he rented the box after he decided to enter the race. He's got the CIA doing his thinking for him, so maybe he figures we're watching everything too. And he figures he might need a little privacy, thus the box. Maybe it's a girlfriend we missed somehow. Maybe he likes dirty magazines or videos, something that is shipped through the mail.'

After a long pause, York said, 'Could be. What

if the box was rented months ago, long before he entered the race?'

'Then he's not hiding from us. He's hiding from the world, and his secret is truly dreadful.'

They silently contemplated the dreadfulness of Lake's secret, neither wanting to venture a guess. They decided to step up surveillance even more, and to check the mailbox twice a day. Lake would be leaving town in a matter of hours, off to do battle in other primaries, and they would have the box to themselves.

Unless someone else was also checking it for him.

Aaron Lake was the man of the hour in Washington. From his office on Capitol Hill he graciously granted live interviews to the early morning news programs. He received senators and other members of Congress, friends and former enemies alike, all bearing tidings of great joy and congratulations. He had lunch with his campaign staff, and followed it with long meetings on strategy. After a quick dinner with Elaine Tyner, who brought wonderful news of tons of new cash over at D-PAC, he left the city and flew to Syracuse to make plans for the New York primary.

A large crowd welcomed him. He was, after all, now the front-runner.

FOURTEEN

The hangovers were becoming more frequent, and as Trevor opened his eyes for another day he told himself that he simply had to get a grip. You can't lay out at Pete's every night, drinking cheap longnecks with coeds, watching meaningless basketball games just because you've got a thousand bucks on them. Last night it had been Logan State and somebody, some team with green uniforms. Who the hell cared about Logan State?

Joe Roy Spicer, that's who. Spicer put $500 on them, Trevor backed it up with a thousand of his own, and Logan won it for them. In the past week, Spicer had picked ten out of twelve winners. He was up $3,000 in real cash, and Trevor, happily following along, was up $5,500 for himself. His gambling was proving to be much more profitable than his lawyering. And someone else was picking the winners!

He went to the bathroom and splashed water on his face without looking at the mirror. The toilet was still clogged from the day before, and as he stomped around his dirty little house looking for a plunger the phone rang. It was a wife from a previous life, a woman he loathed and one who loathed him, and when he heard her voice he knew she needed money. He said no angrily and got in the shower.

Things were worse at the office. A divorcing couple had arrived in separate cars to finish the negotiations for their property settlement. The assets they were fighting over were of no consequence to anyone else – pots, pans, a toaster – but since they had nothing, they had to fight over something. The fights are nastiest when the stakes are smallest.

Their lawyer was an hour late, and they had used the time to simmer and boil until finally Jan had separated them. The wife was parked in Trevor's office when he stumbled in from the back door.

'Where the hell you been?' she demanded loud enough for husband to hear up front. Husband charged down the hall, past Jan, who did not give chase, and burst into Trevor's small office.

'We've been waiting for an hour!' he announced.

'Shut up, both of you!' Trevor screamed, and Jan left the building. His clients were stunned at the volume.

'Sit down!' he screamed again, and they fell into the only empty chairs. 'You people pay five hundred bucks for a lousy divorce and you think you own the place!'

They looked at his red eyes and red face and decided this was not a man to mess with. The phone started ringing and no one answered it. Nausea hit again, and Trevor bolted out of his office and across the hall to the bathroom, where he puked, as quietly as possible. The toilet failed to flush, the little metal chain clinking harmlessly inside the tank.

The phone was still ringing. He staggered down the hall to fire Jan, and when he couldn't find her he left the building too. He walked to the beach, took off his shoes and socks, and splashed his feet in the cool salt water.

Two hours later, Trevor sat motionless at his desk, door locked to keep out clients, bare feet on the desk, with sand still wedged between the toes. He needed a nap and he needed a drink, and he stared at the ceiling trying to organize his priorities. The phone rang, this time duly answered by Jan, who was still employed but secretly checking want ads.

It was Brayshears, in the Bahamas. 'We have a wire, sir,' he said.

Trevor was instantly on his feet. 'How much?'

'A hundred thousand, sir.'

Trevor glanced at his watch. He had about an hour to catch a flight. 'Can you see me at three-thirty?' he asked.

'Certainly, sir.'

He hung up and yelled toward the front, 'Cancel my appointments for today and tomorrow. I'm leaving.'

'You don't have any appointments,' Jan yelled back. 'You're losing money faster than ever.'

He wouldn't bicker. He slammed the back door and drove away.

The flight to Nassau stopped first in Fort Lauderdale, though Trevor hardly knew it. After two quick beers he was sound asleep. Two more over the Atlantic, and a flight attendant had to wake him when the plane was empty.

The wire was from Curtis in Dallas, as expected. It was remitted by a Texas bank, payable to Boomer Realty, care of Geneva Trust Bank, Nassau. Trevor raked his one third off the top, again hiding $25,000 in his own secret account, and taking $8,000 in cash. He thanked Mr. Brayshears, said he hoped to see him soon, and staggered out of the building.

The thought of going home had not crossed his mind. He headed for the shopping district, where packs of heavy American tourists choked the sidewalks. He needed shorts and a straw hat and a bottle of sunscreen.

Trevor eventually made it to the beach, where he found a room in a nice hotel, $200 a night but what did he care? He lathered himself in oil and stretched out by the pool, close enough to the bar. A waitress in a thong fetched him drinks.

He woke up after dark, sufficiently cooked but not burned. A security guard escorted him to his room, where he fell on the bed and returned to his coma. The sun was up again before he moved.

After such a long period of rest, he awoke surprisingly clear-headed, and very hungry. He ate some fruit and went looking for sailboats, not exactly shopping for one, but paying close attention to the details. A thirty-footer would be sufficient, just large enough to live on yet manageable by a crew of one. There would be no passengers; just the lonely skipper hopping from

157

island to island. The cheapest one he found was $90,000 and it needed some work.

Noon found him back at the pool with a cell phone trying to placate a client or two, but his heart wasn't in it. The same waitress brought another drink. Off the phone, he hid behind dark sunshades and tried to crunch the numbers. But things were wonderfully dull between his ears.

In the past month he'd earned about $80,000 in tax-free graft. Could the pace continue? If so, he'd have his million bucks in a year, and he could abandon his office and what was left of his career, and he could buy his little boat and hit the sea.

For the first time ever, the dream almost seemed real. He could see himself at the wheel, shirtless, shoeless, cold beer at the ready, gliding across the water from St. Barts to St. Kitts, from Nevis to St. Lucia, from one island to a thousand others, wind popping his mainsail, not a damned thing in the world to worry about. He closed his eyes and longed even harder for an escape.

His snoring woke him. The thong was nearby. He ordered some rum and checked his watch.

Two days later Trevor finally made it back to Trumble. He arrived with mixed feelings. First, he was quite anxious to pick up the mail and facilitate the scam, anxious to keep the extortion going and the money rolling in. On the other hand, he was tardy and Judge Spicer would not be happy.

'Where the hell you been?' Spicer growled at him as soon as the guard left the attorney-conference room. It seemed to be the standard question these days. 'I've missed three games because of you, and I picked nothing but winners.'

'The Bahamas. We got a hundred thousand from Curtis in Dallas.'

Spicer's mood changed dramatically. 'It took three days to check on a wire in the Bahamas?' he asked.

'I needed a little rest. Didn't know I was supposed to visit this place every day.'

Spicer was mellowing by the second. He'd just picked up another $22,000. It was safely tucked away with his other loot, in a place no one could find, and as he handed the lawyer yet another stack of pretty envelopes he was thinking of ways to spend the money.

'Aren't we busy,' Trevor said, taking the letters.

'Any complaints? You're making more than we are.'

'I have more to lose than you do.'

Spicer handed over a sheet of paper. 'I've picked ten games here. Five hundred bucks on each.'

Great, thought Trevor. Another long weekend at Pete's, watching one game after another. Oh well, there could be worse things. They played blackjack at a dollar a hand until the guard broke up the meeting.

Trevor's increased visits had been discussed by the warden and the higher-ups at the Bureau of Prisons in Washington. Paperwork had been created on the subject. Restrictions had been contemplated, but then abandoned. The visits were useless, and besides, the warden didn't want to alienate the Brethren. Why pick a fight?

The lawyer was harmless. After a few phone

calls around Jacksonville they decided that Trevor was basically unknown and probably had nothing better to do than hang out in the attorney-conference room of a prison.

The money gave new life to Beech and Yarber. Spending it would necessarily entail getting to it, and that would require they one day walk away as free men, free to do whatever they wanted with their growing fortunes.

With $50,000 or so now in the bank, Yarber was busy plotting an investment portfolio. No sense letting it sit there at 5 percent per annum, even if it was tax-free. One day very soon he'd roll it over into aggressive growth funds, with emphasis on the Far East. Asia would boom again, and his little pile of dirty money would be there to share in the wealth. He had five years to go, and if he earned between 12 and 15 percent on his money until then the $50,000 would grow to roughly $100,000 by the time he left Trumble. Not a bad start for a man who would be sixty-five, and hopefully still in good health.

But if he (and Percy and Ricky) could keep adding to the principal, he might indeed be rich when they turned him loose. Five lousy years – months and weeks he'd been dreading. Now he was suddenly wondering if he had enough time to extort all he needed. As Percy, he was writing letters to over twenty pen pals across North America. No two were in the same town. It was Spicer's job to keep the victims separated. Maps were being used in the law library to make certain neither Percy nor Ricky was corresponding with men who appeared to live near one another.

When he wasn't writing letters, Yarber caught himself thinking about the money. Thankfully, the divorce papers from his wife had come and gone. He'd be officially single in a few months, and by the time he was paroled she'd have long since forgotten about him. Nothing would be shared. He'd be free to walk away without a single string attached.

Five years, and he had so much work to do. He'd cut out the sugar and walk an extra mile each day.

In the darkness of his top bunk, during sleepless nights, Hatlee Beech had done the same math as his colleagues. Fifty thousand dollars in hand, a healthy rate of return somewhere, add to the principal by squeezing from as many victims as they could catch, and one day there'd be a fortune. Beech had nine years, a marathon that once seemed endless. Now there was a flicker of hope. The death sentence they'd handed him was slowly becoming a time of harvest. Conservatively, if the scam netted him only $100,000 a year for the next nine years, plus a healthy rate of return, then he'd be a multimillionaire when he danced through the gates, also at the age of sixty-five.

Two, three, four million was not out of the question.

He knew exactly what he'd do. Since he loved Texas, he'd go to Galveston and buy one of those ancient Victorians near the sea, and he'd invite old friends to stop by and see how rich he was. Forget the law, he'd put in twelve-hour days working the

161

money, nothing but work, nothing but money, so that by the time he was seventy he'd have more than his ex-wife.

For the first time in years, Hatlee Beech thought he might live to see sixty-five, maybe seventy.

He, too, gave up sugar, and butter, and he cut his cigarettes in half with the goal of going cold turkey real soon. He vowed to stay away from the infirmary and stop taking pills. He began walking a mile every day, in the sun, like his colleague from California. And he wrote his letters, he and Ricky.

And Justice Spicer, already equipped with sufficient motivation, was finding it difficult to sleep. He wasn't plagued by guilt or loneliness or humiliation, nor was he depressed by the indignity of prison. He was simply counting money, and juggling rates of return, and analyzing point spreads. With twenty-one months to go, he could see the end.

His lovely wife Rita had passed through the week before, and they'd spent four hours together over two days. She'd cut her hair, stopped drinking, and lost eighteen pounds, and she promised to be even skinnier when she picked him up at the front gate in less than two years. After four hours with her, Joe Roy was convinced the $90,000 was still buried behind the toolshed.

They'd move to Vegas, buy a new condo, and say to hell with the rest of the world.

With the Percy-and-Ricky scam working so well, Spicer had found a new worry. He'd leave Trumble first, happily, gladly, without looking back. But what about the money to be made after he was gone? If the scam was still printing money, what would happen to his share of the future earnings, money he was clearly entitled to? It had been, after all, his idea, one he'd borrowed from the prison in Louisiana. Beech and Yarber had been reluctant conspirators at first.

He had time to devise an exit strategy, just as he had time to contrive a way to get rid of the lawyer. But it would cost him some sleep.

The letter from Quince Garbe in Iowa was read by Beech: "'Dear Ricky (or whoever the hell you are): I don't have any more money. The first $100,000 was borrowed from a bank using a bogus financial statement. I'm not sure how I'll pay it back. My father owns our bank and all its money. Why don't you write him some letters, you thug! I can possibly scrape together $10,000 if we can agree that the extortion will stop there. I'm on the verge of suicide, so don't push. You're scum, you know that. I hope you get caught. Sincerely, Quince Garbe.'"

'Sounds pretty desperate,' Yarber said, looking up from his own pile of mail.

Spicer said, toothpick hanging from his bottom lip, 'Tell him we'll take twenty-five thousand.'

'I'll write him and tell him to wire it,' Beech said, opening another envelope addressed to Ricky.

FIFTEEN

During lunch, when experience had shown that traffic picked up somewhat at Mailbox America, an agent nonchalantly entered the place behind two other customers, and for the second time that day placed a key in Box 455. Lying on top of three pieces of junk mail – one from a pizza carryout, one from a car wash, one from the U.S. Postal Service – he noticed something new. It was an envelope, light orange in color, five by eight. With a pair of tweezers he kept on his key ring, he clamped the end of the envelope, slid it quickly from the box, and dropped it in a small leather briefcase. The junk mail was left undisturbed.

At Langley, it was carefully opened by experts. Two handwritten pages were removed, and copied.

An hour later, Deville entered Teddy's bunker, holding a file. Deville was in charge of what was commonly referred to, deep inside Langley, as the 'Lake mess.' He gave copies of the letter to Teddy and York, then scanned it to a large screen, where Teddy and York at first just stared at it. The printing was bold, in block form, easily readable, as if the author had labored over each word. It read:

Dear Al:

Where you been? Did you get my last letter? I wrote three weeks ago and I haven't heard a word. I guess you're busy, but please don't forget about me. I get very lonely here, and your letters have always inspired me to keep going. They give me strength and hope because I know somebody out there cares. Please don't give up on me, Al.

My counselor says that I might be released in two months. There's a halfway house in Baltimore, actually a few miles from where I grew up, and the people here are trying to get me a spot there. It would be for ninety days, enough time for me to find a job, some friends, etc., you know, get used to society again. It's a lockdown place at night, but I'd be free during the day.

There aren't many good memories, Al. Every person who ever loved me is now dead, and my uncle, the guy who's paying for this rehab, is very rich but very cruel.

I need friends so desperately, Al.

By the way, I've lost another five pounds, and my waist is now a thirty-two. The photo I sent you is getting outdated. I've never liked the way my face looks in it – too much flesh on the cheeks.

I'm much leaner now, and tanned. They let us tan for up to two hours a day here, weather permitting. It's Florida, but some days are too cool. I'll send you another photo, maybe one from the chest up. I'm lifting weights like crazy. I think you'll like the next photo.

You said you would send me one of you. I'm still waiting. Please don't forget me, Al. I need one of your letters.

Love, Ricky

Since York had had the responsibility of investigating every aspect of Lake's life, he felt compelled to try and speak first. But he could think of nothing to say. They read the letter in silence again, and again.

Finally, Deville broke the ice by saying, 'Here's the envelope.' He flashed it on the wall. It was addressed to Mr. Al Konyers, at Mailbox America. The return address was: Ricky, Aladdin North, P.O. Box 44683, Neptune Beach, FL 32233.

'It's a front,' Deville said. 'There's no such place as Aladdin North. There's a telephone number, and you get an answering service. We've called ten times with questions, but the operators know nothing. We've called every rehab and treatment clinic in North Florida, and no one's heard of this place.'

Teddy was silent, still staring at the wall.

'Where's Neptune Beach?' York grunted.

'Jacksonville.'

Deville was excused, but told to stand by. Teddy began making notes on a green legal pad. 'There are other letters, and at least one photo,' he said, as if the problem were just part of the routine. Panic was a state unknown to Teddy Maynard.

'We have to find them,' he said.

'We've done two thorough searches of his home,' York said.

'Then do a third. I doubt if he would keep such stuff at his office.'

'How soon – '

'Do it now. Lake is in California looking for votes. We have no time on this, York. There may be other secret boxes, other men writing letters and bragging about their tans and waistlines.'

'Do you confront him?'

'Not yet.'

Since they had no sample of Mr. Konyers' handwriting, Deville made a suggestion that Teddy eventually liked. They would use the ruse of a new laptop, one with a built-in printer. The first draft was composed by Deville and York, and after an hour or so the fourth draft read as follows:

Dear Ricky:

I got your letter of the twenty-second; forgive me for not writing sooner. I've been on the road a lot lately, and I'm behind on everything. In fact, I'm writing this letter at thirty-five thousand feet, somewhere over the Gulf, en route to Tampa. And I'm using a new laptop, one so small it almost fits in my pocket. Amazing technology. The printer leaves something to be desired. I hope you can read it okay.

Wonderful news about your release, and the halfway house in Baltimore. I have some business interests there, and I'm sure I can help you find a job.

Keep your head up, only two months to go. You're a much stronger person now, and you're ready to live life to its fullest. Don't be discouraged.

I'll help in any way possible. When you get to Baltimore, I'll be happy to spend some time with you, show you around, you know.

I promise I'll write sooner. I can't wait to hear from you.

Love, Al

They decided Al was in a hurry and forgot to sign his name. The letter was marked up, revised, redrafted, pored over with more care than a treaty. The final version was printed on a piece of stationery from the Royal Sonesta Hotel in New Orleans, and placed in a thick, plain brown envelope with optic wiring hidden along the bottom edge. In the lower right-hand corner, in a spot that looked as if it had been slightly damaged and knotted in transit, a tiny transmitter the size of a pinhead was installed. When activated, it would send a signal a hundred yards for up to three days.

Since Al was traveling to Tampa, the envelope was stamped with a Tampa postmark, dated that day. This was done in less than half an hour by a team of very strange people down in Documents on the second floor.

At 4 P.M., a green van with many miles on it stopped at the curb in front of Aaron Lake's townhouse, near one of the many shade trees on Thirty-fourth, in a lovely section of Georgetown.

Its door advertised a plumbing company in the District. Four plumbers got out and began removing tools and equipment.

After a few minutes, the only neighbor who'd noticed grew bored and returned to her television. With Lake in California, the Secret Service was with him, and his home had yet to qualify for round-the-clock surveillance, at least by the Secret Service. That scrutiny would come quickly, though.

The ploy was a clogged sewer line in the small front lawn, something that could be done without entering the home. An outside job, one that would pacify the Secret Service in case they happened to drop by.

But two of the plumbers did indeed enter the home, with their own keys. Another van stopped by to check on progress, and to drop off a tool. Two plumbers from the second van mixed with those already there, and a regular unit began to form.

Inside the house, four of the agents began their tedious search for hidden files. They moved from room to room, inspecting the obvious, prying for the secrets.

The second van left, and a third one came from the other direction and parked with its tires on the sidewalk, as service vans often do. Four more plumbers joined the sewer cleaning, and two eventually drifted inside. After dark, a spotlight was rigged in the front yard, over the sewer cover, and directed into the home so the lights inside would not be noticed. The four men left outside sipped coffee and told jokes and tried to stay warm. Neighbors hurried by on foot.

After six hours the sewer was clean, as was the home. Nothing unusual was found, certainly no hidden file with correspondence from one Ricky in rehab. No sign of a photo. The plumbers turned off their lights, packed their tools, and disappeared without a trace.

At eight-thirty the next morning, when the doors opened at the Neptune Beach post office, an agent named Barr walked hurriedly in as if he were late for something. Barr was an expert on locks and keys, and he'd spent five hours the previous afternoon at Langley studying various boxes used by the Postal Service. He had four master keys, one of which he was certain would open number 44683. If not, he'd be forced to key it, which might take sixty seconds or so and could possibly draw attention. The third key worked, and Barr placed the brown envelope, postmarked the day before from Tampa, addressed to Ricky with no last name, care of Aladdin North, inside the box. There were two other letters already there. For good measure, he removed a piece of junk mail, then closed the door to the box, wadded up the mail, and threw it in the wastebasket.

Barr and two others waited patiently in a van in the parking lot, sipping coffee and videoing every postal customer. They were seventy yards away from the box. Their handheld receiver beeped with the faint signal from the envelope. A diverse group came and went with the flow – a black female in a short brown dress, a white male with a beard and leather jacket, a white female in a jogging suit, a black male in jeans – all agents of the CIA, all watching the box without a clue about who wrote the letter or where it was going. Their job was simply to find the person who'd rented the box.

They found him after lunch.

Trevor drank his lunch at Pete's, but only two beers. Cold drafts with salty peanuts from the community bowl, consumed while losing fifty bucks on a dogsled race in Calgary. Back at the office, he napped for an hour, snoring so loudly his long-suffering secretary finally had to close his door. She slammed it actually, but not loud enough to wake him.

Dreaming of sailboats, he made his trek to the post office, this time choosing to walk because the day was beautiful, he had nothing better to do, and his head needed clearing. He was delighted to find four of the little treasures angled neatly in Aladdin North's box. He placed them carefully in the pocket of his well-worn seersucker jacket, straightened his bow tie, and ambled forth, certain that another payday was fast approaching.

He'd never been tempted to read the letters. Let the Brethren do the dirty work. He could keep his hands clean, shuttle the mail, rake his third off the top. And besides, Spicer would kill him if he delivered mail that had been tampered with.

Seven agents watched him stroll back to his office.

Teddy was napping in his wheelchair when Deville

entered. York had gone home; it was after 10 P.M. York had a wife, Teddy did not.

Deville delivered his narrative while referring to pages of scribbled notes: 'The letter was removed from the box at one-fifty P.M. by a local lawyer named Trevor Carson. We followed him to his office in Neptune Beach, where he stayed for eighty minutes. It's a small one-man office, one secretary, not a lot of clients. Carson is a small-timer along the beaches, does divorces, real estate, two-bit stuff. He's forty-eight, divorced at least twice, native of Pennsylvania, college at Furman, law school at Florida State, got his license suspended eleven years ago for commingling client funds, then got it back.'

'All right, all right,' Teddy said.

'At three-thirty, he left his office, drove an hour to the federal prison at Trumble, Florida. Took the letters with him. We followed but lost the signal when he entered the prison. Since then, we've gathered some information about Trumble. It's a minimum-security prison, commonly referred to as a camp. No walls or fences, very low risk inmates. A thousand of them at Trumble. According-ing to a source within the Bureau of Prisons here in Washington, Carson visits all the time. No other lawyer, no other person visits as much as Carson. Up until a month ago he went once a week, now it's at least three times a week. Sometimes four. All visits are official attorney-client conferences.'

'Who is his client?'

'It's not Ricky. He is the attorney of record for three judges.'

'Three judges?'

'Yes.'

'Three judges in prison?'

'That's right. They call themselves the Brethren.'

Teddy closed his eyes and rubbed his temples. Deville let things sink in for a moment, then continued: 'Carson was in the prison for fifty-four minutes, and when he exited we could not pick up the signal from the envelope. By this time, we were parked next to his car. He walked within five feet of our receiver, and we're certain he did not have the letter. We followed him back to Jacksonville, back to the beaches. He parked near a place called Pete's Bar and Grill, where he stayed for three hours. We searched his car, found his briefcase, and inside there were eight letters addressed to various men all over the country. All letters were outbound from the prison, none were inbound. Evidently, Carson shuttles mail back and forth to his clients. As of thirty minutes ago, he was still in the bar, quite drunk, betting on college basketball games.'

'A loser.'

'Very much so.'

The loser staggered out of Pete's after the second overtime of a game on the West Coast. Spicer had picked three out of four winners. Trevor had dutifully followed suit, and was up a thousand bucks for the night.

Drunk as he was, he was smart enough not to drive. His DUI three years earlier was still a painful memory, and besides the damned cops were all over the place. The restaurants and bars around the Sea Turtle Inn attracted the young and restless, thus the cops.

Walking was a challenge, though. He made it well enough to his office, a straight shot south, past the quiet little summer rentals and retirement cottages, all dark and tucked in for the night. He carried his briefcase with the letters from Trumble.

He pressed onward, searching for his house. He crossed the street for no reason, and half a block later recrossed it. There was no traffic. When he began to circle back, he came within twenty yards of an agent who'd ducked behind a parked car. The silent army watched him, suddenly fearful that the drunken fool might stumble into one of them.

At some point he gave up, and managed to find his office again. He rattled keys on the front steps, dropped his briefcase and forgot about it, and less than a minute after opening the door he was at his desk, sprawled in his swivel rocker, fast asleep, the front door half open.

The back door had been unlocked throughout the night. Following orders from Langley, Barr and company had entered the office and wired everything. There was no alarm system, no locks on the windows, nothing of value to attract thievery in the first place. Tapping the phones and bugging the walls had been an easy task, made so by the obvious fact that no one on the outside observed anything inside the offices of L. Trevor Carson, Attorney and Counselor-at-Law.

The briefcase was emptied, its contents cataloged at Langley's instructions. Langley wanted a precise record of the letters the lawyer had taken from Trumble. When everything had been inspected and photographed, the briefcase was placed in the hallway near his office. The snoring was impressive, and uninterrupted.

Shortly before 2, Barr managed to start the Beetle parked near Pete's. He drove it down the empty street and left it innocently on the curb in front of the law office, so that the drunk would rub his eyes in a few hours and pat himself on the back for such a nice job of driving. Or maybe he would shrink in horror at the thought of having driven while intoxicated once again. Either way, they'd be listening.

SIXTEEN

Thirty-seven hours before the polls opened in Virginia and Washington, the President appeared live on national television to announce that he had ordered an air attack in and around the Tunisian city of Talah. The Yidal terrorist unit was believed to train there, in a well-stocked compound on the edge of town.

And so the country became glued to yet another mini-war, one of pushbuttons and smart bombs and retired generals on CNN prattling on about this strategy or that. It was dark in Tunisia, thus no footage. The retired generals and their clueless interviewers did a lot of guessing. And waiting. Waiting for sunlight so the smoke and rubble could be broadcast to a jaded nation.

But Yidal had its sources, most likely the Israelis. The compound was empty when the smart bombs dropped in from nowhere. They hit their targets, shook the desert, destroyed the compound, but killed not a single terrorist. A couple strayed, however, one venturing into the center of Talah, where it hit a hospital. Another hit a small house where a family of seven was fast asleep. Fortunately, they never knew what happened.

Tunisian television was quick to cover the burning hospital, and at daybreak on the East Coast the country learned that the smart bombs weren't so smart after all. At least fifty bodies had been recovered, all very innocent civilians.

At some point during the early morning, the President developed a sudden uncharacteristic aversion to reporters, and could not be reached for comment. The Vice President, a man who'd said plenty when the attack started, was in seclusion with his staff somewhere in Washington.

The bodies piled up, the cameras kept rolling, and by midmorning world reaction was swift, brutal, and unanimous. The Chinese were threatening war. The French seemed inclined to join them. Even the Brits said the United States was trigger-happy.

Since the dead were nothing more than Tunisian peasants, certainly not Americans, the politicians were quick to politicize the debacle. The usual finger-pointing and grandstanding and calls for investigations happened before noon in Washington. And on the campaign circuit, those still in the race took a few moments to reflect on just how ill-fated the mission had been. None of them would have engaged in such desperate retaliation without better intelligence. None but the Vice President, who was still in seclusion. As the bodies were being counted, not a single candidate thought the raid was worthy of the risks. All condemned the President.

But it was Aaron Lake who attracted the most

attention. He found it difficult to move without tripping over cameramen. In a carefully worded statement, he said, without notes, 'We are inept. We are helpless. We are feeble. We should be ashamed of our inability to wipe out a ragtag little army of less than fifty cowards. You cannot simply push buttons and run for cover. It takes guts to fight wars on the ground. I have the guts. When I am President, no terrorist with American blood on his hands will be safe. That is my solemn promise.'

In the fury and chaos of the morning, Lake's words found their mark. Here was a man who meant what he said, who knew precisely what he would do. We wouldn't slaughter innocent peasants if a man with guts were making the decisions. Lake was the man.

In the bunker, Teddy weathered another storm. Bad intelligence was blamed for every disaster. When the raids were successful, the pilots and the brave boys on the ground and their commanders and the politicians who sent them into battle got the credit. But when the raids went wrong, as they usually did, the CIA got the blame.

He had advised against the attack. The Israelis had a tenuous and very secret agreement with Yidal – don't kill us, and we won't kill you. As long as the targets were Americans and an occasional European, then the Israelis would not get involved. Teddy knew this, but it was information he had not shared. Twenty-four hours before the attack, he had advised the President, in writing, that he doubted the terrorists would be in the compound when the bombs arrived. And, because of the

178

target's proximity to Talah, there was an excellent chance of collateral damage.

Hatlee Beech opened the brown envelope without noticing that the right lower corner was somewhat wadded and slightly damaged. He was opening so many personal envelopes these days, he looked only at the return address to see who and where they came from. Nor did he notice the Tampa postmark.

He hadn't heard from Al Konyers in several weeks. He read the letter through without stopping, and found little if no interest in the fact that Al was using a new laptop. It was perfectly believable that Ricky's pen pal had taken a sheet of stationery from the Royal Sonesta in New Orleans, and was pecking out the letter at thirty-five thousand feet.

Wonder if he was flying first class? he asked himself. Probably so. They wouldn't have computer hookups back in coach, would they? Al had been in New Orleans on business, stayed at a very nice hotel, then flew first class to his next destination. The Brethren were interested in the financial conditions of all their pen pals. Nothing else mattered.

After he read the letter, he handed it to Finn Yarber, who was in the process of writing another one as poor Percy. They were working in the small conference room in the corner of the law library, their table littered with files and mail and a pretty assortment of soft pastel correspondence cards. Spicer was outside, at his table, guarding the door and studying point spreads.

'Who's Konyers?' Finn asked.

Beech was flipping through some files. They kept a neat folder on every pen pal, complete with the letters they received and copies of all letters they'd sent.

'Don't know much,' Beech said. 'Lives in the D.C. area, fake name, I'm sure. Uses one of those mailbox services. That's his third letter, I think.'

From the Konyers file Beech pulled out the first two letters. The one from December 11 read:

Dear Ricky:

Hello. My name is Al Konyers. I'm in my fifties. I like jazz, old movies, Humphrey Bogart, and I like to read biographies. I don't smoke and don't like people who do. Fun is Chinese take-out, a little wine, a black-and-white western with a good friend. Drop me a line.

Al Konyers

It was typewritten on plain white paper, the way most of them were at first. Fear was stamped between every line – fear of getting caught, fear of starting a long-distance relationship with a complete stranger. Every letter of every word was typewritten. He didn't even sign his name.

Ricky's first response was the standard letter Beech had written a hundred times now: Ricky's twenty-eight, in rehab, bad family, rich uncle, etc. And dozens of the same enthusiastic questions: What kind of work do you do? How about your family? Do you like to travel? If Ricky could bare his soul, then he needed something in return. Two pages of the same crap Beech had been writing for five months. He wanted so desperately to simply Xerox the damned thing. But he couldn't. He was forced to personalize each one, on nice pretty paper. And he sent Al the same handsome photo he'd sent to the others. The picture was the bait that hooked almost all of them.

Three weeks passed. On January 9, Trevor had delivered a second letter from Al Konyers. It was as clean and sterile as the first, probably typed with rubber gloves.

Dear Ricky:

I enjoyed your letter. I have to admit I felt sorry for you at first, but you seem to have adjusted well to rehab and know where you're going. I've never had problems with drugs and alcohol, so it's difficult for me to understand. It sounds as though you're getting the best treatment money can buy. You shouldn't be so harsh on your uncle. Think of where you might be if not for him.

You ask many questions about me. I'm not ready to discuss a lot of personal matters, but I understand your curiosity. I was married for thirty years, but not anymore. I live in D.C., and work for the government. My job is challenging and fulfilling.

I live alone. I have few close friends and prefer it that way. When I travel, it's usually to Asia. I adore Tokyo.

I'll keep you in my thoughts in the days to come.

Al Konyers

Just above the typewritten name, he'd scribbled the name 'Al,' with a black-felt pen, fine point.

The letter was most unimpressive for three reasons. First, Konyers did not have a wife, or at least he said he didn't. A wife was crucial for extortion. Threaten to tell the wife, to send her copies of all the letters from the gay pen pal, and the money rolled in.

Second, Al worked for the government, so he probably didn't have a lot of money.

Third, Al was much too scared to waste time with. Getting information was like pulling teeth. The Quince Garbes and Curtis Cateses were much more fun because they'd spent their lives in the closet and were now anxious to escape. Their letters were long and windy and filled with all the damning little facts an extortionist might need. Not Al. Al was boring. Al wasn't sure what he wanted.

So Ricky raised the stakes with his second letter, another piece of boilerplate Beech had perfected with practice. Ricky had just learned that he would be released in a few months! And he was from Baltimore. What a coincidence! And he might need some help getting a job. His rich uncle was refusing to help anymore, he was afraid of life on the outside without the help of friends, and he really couldn't trust his old friends because they were still on drugs, etc., etc.

The letter went unanswered, and Beech assumed that Al Konyers was frightened by it. Ricky was on his way to Baltimore, just an hour from Washington, and that was too close for Al.

While waiting for an answer from Al, the Quince

Garbe money landed, followed by the wire from Curtis in Dallas, and the Brethren found renewed energy in their scam. Ricky wrote Al the letter that was intercepted and analyzed at Langley.

Now, suddenly, Al's third letter had a very different tone. Finn Yarber read it twice, then reread the second letter from Al. 'Sounds like a different person, doesn't it?' he said.

'Yes, it does,' Beech said, looking at both letters. 'I think the old boy is finally excited about meeting Ricky.'

'I thought he worked for the government.'

'Says he does.'

'Then what's this about having business interests in Baltimore?'

'We worked for the government, didn't we?'

'Sure.'

'What was your highest salary on the bench?'

'When I was chief justice I made a hundred and fifty thousand.'

'I made a hundred and forty. Some of those professional bureaucrats make more than that. Plus, he's not married.'

'That's a problem.'

'Yeah, but let's keep pushing. He's got a big job, which means he's got a big boss, lots of colleagues, typical Washington hotshot. We'll find a pressure point somewhere.'

'What the hell,' Finn said.

What the hell, indeed. What was there to lose? So what if they pushed a little too hard, and Mr. Al got scared or got mad and decided to throw the letters away? You can't lose what you don't have.

Serious money was being made here. It was not

a time to be timid. Their aggressive tactics were producing spectacular results. The mail was growing each week, as was their offshore account. Their scam was foolproof because their pen pals lived double lives. Their victims had no one to complain to.

Negotiations were quick because the market was ripe. It was still winter in Jacksonville, and because the nights were chilly and the ocean was too cool to swim in, the busy season was a month away. There were hundreds of small rentals available along Neptune Beach and Atlantic Beach, including one almost directly across the street from Trevor. A man from Boston offered $600 cash for two months, and the real estate agent snatched it. The place was furnished with odds and ends no flea market would handle. The old shag carpet was well worn and emitted a permanent musty smell. It was perfect.

The renter's first chore was to cover the windows. Three of them faced the street and looked across to Trevor's, and during the first few hours of surveillance it became obvious how few clients came and went. There was so little business over there! When work surfaced it was usually done by the secretary, Jan, who also read a lot of magazines.

Others quietly moved into the rental, men and women with old suitcases and large duffel bags filled with electronic wizardry. The fragile furnishings were shoved to the rear of the cottage, and the front rooms were quickly filled with screens and monitors and listening devices of a dozen varieties.

Trevor himself would make an interesting case study for third-year law students. He arrived around 9 A.M., and spent the first hour reading newspapers. His morning client seemed to always arrive at ten-thirty, and after an exhaustive half-hour conference he was ready for lunch, always at Pete's Bar and Grill. He carried a phone with him, to prove his importance to the bartenders there, and he usually made two or three unnecessary calls to other lawyers. He called his bookie a lot.

Then he walked back to his office, past the rental where the CIA monitored every step, back to his desk where it was time for a nap. He came to life around three, and hit it hard for two hours. By then he needed another longneck from Pete's.

The second time they followed him to Trumble, he left the prison after an hour and returned to his office about 6 P.M. While he was having dinner in an oyster bar on Atlantic Boulevard, alone, an agent entered his office and found his old brief-case. In it were five letters from Percy and Ricky.

The commander of the silent army in and around Neptune Beach was a man named Klockner, the best Teddy had in the field of domestic street spying. Klockner had been instructed to intercept all mail flowing through the law office.

When Trevor went straight home after leaving the oyster bar, the five letters were taken across the street to the rental, where they were opened, copied, then resealed and replaced in Trevor's briefcase. None of the five was for Al Konyers.

At Langley, Deville read the five letters as they came off the fax. They were examined by two handwriting experts who agreed that Percy and

185

Ricky were not the same people. Using samples taken from their court files, it was determined, without much effort, that Percy was really former Justice Finn Yarber, and that Ricky was former U.S. District Judge Hatlee Beech.

Ricky's address was the Aladdin North box at the Neptune Beach post office. Percy, to their surprise, used a postal box in Atlantic Beach, one rented to an outfit called Laurel Ridge.

SEVENTEEN

For his next visit to Langley, the first in three weeks, the candidate arrived in a caravan of shiny black vans, all going too fast but who would complain. They were cleared and waved onward, deeper into the complex, until they roared to a collective stop near a very convenient door where all sorts of grim-faced, thick-necked young men were waiting. Lake rode the wave into the building, losing escorts as he went until finally he arrived not at the usual bunker but in Mr. Maynard's formal office, with a view of a small forest. Everyone else was left at the door. Alone, the two great men shook hands warmly and actually appeared happy to see one another.

Important things first. 'Congratulations on Virginia,' Teddy said.

Lake shrugged as if he wasn't sure. 'Thank you, in more ways than one.'

'It's a very impressive win, Mr. Lake,' Teddy said. 'Governor Tarry worked hard there for a year. Two months ago he had commitments from every precinct captain in the state. He looked unbeatable. Now, I think he's fading fast. It's often a disadvantage to be the front-runner early in the race.'

'Momentum is a strange animal in politics,' Lake observed wisely.

'Cash is even stranger. Right now, Governor Tarry can't find a dime because you've got it all. Money follows momentum.'

'I'm sure I'll say this many times, Mr. Maynard, but, well, thanks. You've given me an opportunity I'd hardly dreamed of.'

'Are you having any fun?'

'Not yet. If we win, the fun will come later.'

'The fun starts next Tuesday, Mr. Lake, with big Super Tuesday. New York, California, Massachusetts, Ohio, Georgia, Missouri, Maryland, Maine, Connecticut, all in one day. Almost six hundred delegates!' Teddy's eyes were dancing as if he could almost count the votes. 'And you're ahead in every state, Mr. Lake. Can you believe it?'

'No, I cannot.'

'It's true. You're neck and neck in Maine, for some damned reason, and it's close in California, but you're going to win big next Tuesday.'

'If you believe the polls,' Lake said, as if he didn't trust them himself. Fact was, like every candidate, Lake was addicted to the polls. He was actually gaining in California, a state with 140,000 defense workers.

'Oh, I believe them. And I believe that a landslide is coming on little Super Tuesday. They love you down South, Mr. Lake. They love guns and tough talk and such, and right now they're falling in love with Aaron Lake. Next Tuesday will be fun, but the following Tuesday will be a romp.'

Teddy Maynard was predicting a romp, and Lake couldn't help but smile. His polls showed the same trends, but it just sounded better coming from Teddy. He lifted a sheet of paper and read the latest polling data from around the country. Lake was ahead by at least five points in every state.

They reveled in their momentum for a few minutes, then Teddy turned serious. 'There's something you should know,' he said, and the smile was gone. He flipped a page and glanced at some notes. 'Two nights ago, in the Khyber Pass in the mountains of Afghanistan, a Russian long-range missile with nuclear warheads was moved by truck into Pakistan. It is now en route to Iran, where it will be used for God knows what. The missile has a range of three thousand miles, and the capability of delivering four nuclear bombs. The price was about thirty million dollars U.S., cash up front paid by the Iranians through a bank in Luxembourg. It's still there, in an account believed to be controlled by Natty Chenkov's people.'

'I thought he was stockpiling, not selling.'

'He needs cash, and he's getting it. In fact, he's probably the only man we know who's collecting it faster than you.'

Teddy didn't do humor well, but Lake laughed out of politeness anyway.

'Is the missile operational?' Lake asked.

'We think so. It originated from a collection of silos near Kiev, and we believe it's of a recent make and model. With so many lying around, why would the Iranians buy an old one? Yes, it's safe to assume it's fully operational.'

'Is it the first?'

'There've been some spare parts and plutonium, to Iran and Iraq and India and others, but I think this is the first fully assembled, ready-to-shoot missile.'

'Are they anxious to use it?'

'We don't think so. It appears as if the transaction was instigated by Chenkov. He needs the money to buy other kinds of weapons. He's shopping his wares, things he doesn't need.'

'Do the Israelis know it?'

'No. Not yet. You have to be careful with them. Everything is give and take. Someday, if we need something from them, then we might tell them about this transaction.'

For a moment, Lake longed to be President, and immediately. He wanted to know everything Teddy knew, then he realized he probably never would. There was, after all, a sitting President right then, at that moment, albeit a lame duck, and Teddy wasn't chatting with him about Chenkov and his missiles.

'What do the Russians think about my campaign?' he asked.

'At first, they weren't concerned. Now they're watching closely. But you have to remember, there is no such thing as a Russian voice anymore. The free marketers speak favorably of you because they fear the Communists. The hard-liners are scared of you. It's very complex.'

'And Chenkov?'

'I'm ashamed to say we're not that close to him,

yet. But we're working on it. We should have some ears in the vicinity soon.'

Teddy tossed his papers onto his desk, and rolled himself closer to Lake. The many wrinkles in his forehead pinched closer together, downward. His bushy eyebrows fell hard on his sad eyes. 'Listen to me, Mr. Lake,' he said, his voice much more somber. 'You have this thing won. There will be a bump or two in the road, things we cannot foresee, and even if we could we'd be powerless to prevent them. We'll ride them out together. The damage will be slight. You're something brand new and the people like you. You're doing a marvelous job and communicating. Keep the message simple – our security is at risk, the world is not as safe as it looks. I'll take care of the money, and I'll certainly keep the country frightened. That missile in the Khyber Pass, we could've detonated it. Five thousand people would've been killed, five thousand Pakistanis. Nuclear bombs exploding in the mountains. You think we'd wake up and worry about the stock market? Not a chance. I'll take care of the fear, Mr. Lake. You keep your nose clean and run hard.'

'I'm running as hard as I can.'

'Run harder, and no surprises, okay?'

'Certainly not.'

Lake wasn't sure what he meant by surprises, but he let it pass. Just a bit of grandfatherly wisdom, perhaps.

Teddy rolled away again. He found his buttons and a screen dropped from the ceiling. They spent twenty minutes viewing rough cuts of the next series of Lake ads, then said their goodbyes.

191

Lake sped away from Langley, two vans in front and one behind, all racing to Reagan National Airport, where the jet was waiting. He wanted a quiet night in Georgetown, at home where the world was held at bay, where he could read a book in solitude, with no one watching or listening. He longed for the anonymity of the streets, the nameless faces, the Arab baker on M Street who made a perfect bagel, the used-book dealer on Wisconsin, the coffeehouse where they roasted beans from Africa. Would he ever be able to walk the streets again, like a normal person, doing whatever he pleased? Something told him no, that those days were gone, probably forever.

When Lake was airborne, Deville entered the bunker and announced to Teddy that Lake had come and gone without trying to check the mailbox. It was time for the daily briefing on the Lake mess. Teddy was spending more time than he'd planned worrying about what his candidate might do next.

The five letters Klockner and his group intercepted from Trevor had been thoroughly researched. Two had been written by Yarber as Percy; the other three by Beech as Ricky. The five pen pals were in different states. Four were using fictitious names; one was bold enough not to hide behind an alias. The letters were basically the same: Percy and Ricky were troubled young men in rehab, trying desperately to pull their lives together, both talented and still able to dream big dreams, but in need of moral and physical support from new friends because the old ones were dangerous. They freely divulged their sins and foibles, their weaknesses and heartaches. They rambled about their lives after rehab, their hopes and dreams of all the things they wanted to do. They were proud of their tans and their muscles, and seemed anxious to show their new hardened bodies to their pen pals.

Only one letter asked for money. Ricky wanted a loan of $1,000 from a correspondent named Peter in Spokane, Washington. He said the money was needed to cover some expenses his uncle was refusing to pay.

Teddy had read the letters more than once. The request for money was important because it began to shed light on the Brethren's little game. Perhaps it was just a two-bit enterprise someone taught them, some other con who'd finished his time at Trumble and was now roaming at large stealing anew.

But the size of the stakes was not the issue. It was a flesh game – thinner waists and bronze skin and firm biceps – and their candidate was in the middle of it.

There were still questions, but Teddy was patient. They would watch the mail. The pieces would fall into place.

With Spicer guarding the door to the conference room, and daring anyone to use the law library, Beech and Yarber labored away with their mail. To Al Konyers, Beech wrote:

Dear Al:
Thanks for your last letter. It means so much to me to hear from you. I feel like I've

been living in a cage for months, and I'm slowly seeing daylight. Your letters help to open the door. Please don't stop writing.

I'm sorry if I've bored you with too much personal stuff. I respect your privacy and hope I haven't asked too many questions. You seem like a very sensitive man who enjoys solitude and the finer things of life. I thought about you last night when I watched *Key Largo*, the old Bogart and Bacall film. I could almost taste the Chinese carry-out. The food here is pretty good, I guess, but they simply can't do Chinese.

I have a great idea. In two months when I get out of here, let's rent *Casablanca and African Queen*, get the carry-out, get a bottle of nonalcoholic wine, and spend a quiet evening on the sofa. God, I get excited just thinking about life on the outside and doing real things again.

Forgive me if I'm going too fast, Al. It's just that I've done without a lot of things here, and not just booze and good food. Know what I mean?

The halfway house in Baltimore is willing to take me if I can find a part-time job of some type. You said you had some interests there. I know I'm asking a lot because you don't know me, but can you arrange this? I will be forever grateful.

Please write me soon, Al. Your letters, and the hopes and dreams of leaving here in two months with a job on the outside, sustain me in my darkest hours.

Thanks, friend.

Love, Ricky

The one to Quince Garbe had a very different tone. Beech and Yarber had kicked it around for several days. The final draft read:

Dear Quince:
   Your father owns a bank, yet you say you can only raise another $10,000. I think you're lying, Quince, and it really ticks me off. I'm tempted to send the file to your father and wife anyway.
   I'll settle for $25,000, immediately, same wiring instructions.
   And don't threaten suicide. I really don't care what you do. We'll never meet, and I think you're a sicko anyway.
   Wire the damned money, Quince, and now!

Love, Ricky

Klockner worried that Trevor might visit Trumble one day before noon, then drop off the mail at some point along the way before returning to his office or his home. There was no way to intercept it while en route. It was imperative that he haul it back, and leave it overnight so they could get their hands on it.

He worried, but at the same time Trevor was proving to be a late starter. He showed few signs of life until after his two o'clock nap.

So when he informed his secretary that he was about to leave for Trumble at 11 A.M., the rental across the street sprang into action. A call was immediately placed to Trevor's office by a middle-aged woman claiming to be a Mrs. Beltrone, who explained to Jan that she and her rich husband were in dire need of a quick divorce. The secretary put her on hold, and yelled down the hallway for Trevor to wait a second. Trevor was gathering papers from his desk and placing them in his briefcase. The camera in the ceiling above him caught his look of displeasure at having been interrupted by a new client.

'She says she's rich!' Jan yelled, and Trevor's frown disappeared. He sat down and waited.

Mrs. Beltrone unloaded on the secretary. She was wife number three, the husband was much older, they had a home in Jacksonville but spent most of their time at their home in Bermuda. Also had a home in Vail. They'd been planning the divorce for some time, everything had been agreed upon, no fighting at all, very amicable, just needed a good lawyer to handle the paperwork. Mr. Carson had come highly recommended, but they had to act fast for some undisclosed reason.

Trevor took over and listened to the same story. Mrs. Beltrone was sitting across the street in the rental, working from a script the team had put together just for this occasion.

'I really need to see you,' she said after fifteen minutes of baring her soul.

'Well, I'm awfully busy,' Trevor said, as if he were flipping pages in half a dozen daily appointment books. Mrs. Beltrone was watching him on the monitor. His feet were on the desk, his eyes closed, his bow tie crooked. The life of an awfully busy lawyer.

'Please,' she begged. 'We need to get this over with. I must see you today.'

'Where's your husband?'

'He's in France, but he'll be here tomorrow.'

'Well, uh, let's see,' Trevor mumbled, playing with his bow tie.

'What's your fee?' she asked, and his eyes flew open.

'Well, this is obviously more complicated than your simple no-fault. I'd have to charge a fee of ten thousand dollars.' He grimaced when he said it, holding his breath for the response.

'I'll bring it today,' she said. 'Can I see you at one?'

He was on his feet, hovering over the phone. 'How about one-thirty?' he managed to say.

'I'll be there.'

'Do you know where my office is?'

'My driver can find it. Thanks, Mr. Carson.'

Just call me Trevor, he almost said. But she was gone.

They watched as he wrung his hands together, then pumped his fists, gritted his teeth, said, 'Yes!' He'd hooked a big one.

Jan appeared from the hall and said, 'Well?'

'She'll be here at one-thirty. Get this place cleaned up a little.'

'I'm not a maid. Can you get some money up front? I need to pay bills.'

'I'll get the damned money.'

Trevor attacked his bookshelves, straightening volumes he hadn't touched in years, dusting the planks with a paper towel, stuffing files in drawers.

197

When he charged his desk, Jan finally felt a twinge of guilt and began vacuuming the reception area.

They labored through lunch, their bitching and straining making for great amusement across the street.

No sign of Mrs. Beltrone at one-thirty.

'Where the hell is she?' Trevor barked down the hall just after two.

'Maybe she checked around, got some more references,' Jan said.

'What did you say?' he yelled.

'Nothing, boss.'

'Call her,' he demanded at two-thirty.

'She didn't leave a number.'

'You didn't get a number?'

'That's not what I said. I said she didn't leave a number.'

At three-thirty, Trevor stormed out of his office, still trying desperately to uphold his end of a raging argument with a woman he'd fired at least ten times in the past eight years.

They followed him straight to Trumble. He was in the prison for fifty-three minutes, and when he left it was after five, too late to drop off mail in either Neptune Beach or Atlantic Beach. He returned to his office and left his briefcase on his desk. Then, predictably, he went to Pete's for drinks and dinner.

EIGHTEEN

The unit from Langley flew to Des Moines, where the agents rented two cars and a van, then drove forty minutes to Bakers, Iowa. They arrived in the quiet, snowbound little town two days before the letter. By the time Quince picked it up at the post office, they knew the names of the postmaster, the mayor, the chief of police, and the short-order cook at the pancake house next to the hardware store. But no one in Bakers knew them.

They watched Quince hurry to the bank after leaving the post office. Thirty minutes later, two agents known only as Chap and Wes found the corner of the bank where Mr. Garbe, Jr., did business, and they presented themselves to his secretary as inspectors from the Federal Reserve. They certainly looked official – dark suits, black shoes, short hair, long overcoats, clipped speech, efficient manners.

Quince was locked inside, and at first seemed unwilling to come out. They impressed upon his secretary the urgency of their visit, and after almost forty minutes the door opened slightly. Mr. Garbe looked as though he'd been crying. He was pale, shaken, unhappy with the prospect of entertaining anyone. But he showed them in anyway, too unnerved to ask for identification. He didn't even catch their names.

He sat across the massive desk, and looked at the twins facing him. 'What can we do for you?' he asked, with a very faint smile.

'Is the door locked?' Chap asked.

'Why yes, it is.' The twins got the impression that most of Mr. Garbe's day was spent behind locked doors.

'Can anyone hear us?' Wes asked.

'No.' Quince was even more rattled now.

'We're not reserve officials,' Chap said. 'We lied.'

Quince wasn't sure if he should be angry or relieved or even more frightened, so he just sat there for a second, mouth open, frozen, waiting to be shot.

'It's a long story,' Wes said.

'You've got five minutes.'

'Actually, we have as long as we want.'

'This is my office. Get out.'

'Not so fast. We know some things.'

'I'll call security.'

'No you won't.'

'We've seen the letter,' Chap said. 'The one you just got from the post office.'

'I picked up several.'

'But only one from Ricky.'

Quince's shoulders sagged, his eyes closed slowly. Then they opened again and looked at the tormentors in total, absolute defeat. 'Who are you?' he mumbled.

200

'We're not enemies.'

'You're working for him, aren't you?'

'Him?'

'Ricky, or whoever the hell he is.'

'No,' Wes said. 'He's our enemy too. Let's just say that we have a client who's in the same boat you're in, more or less. We've been hired to protect him.'

Chap pulled a thick envelope from his coat pocket and tossed it on the desk. 'There's twenty-five thousand cash. Send it to Ricky.'

Quince stared at the envelope, his mouth open wide. His poor brain was choked with so many thoughts he was dizzy. So he closed his eyes again, and squinted fiercely in a vain effort to organize things. Forget the question of who they were. How did they read the letter? Why were they offering him money? How much did they know?

He sure as hell couldn't trust them.

'The money's yours,' Wes said. 'In return, we need some information.'

'Who is Ricky?' Quince asked, his eyes barely open.

'What do you know about him?' Chap asked.

'His name's not Ricky.'

'True.'

'He's in prison.'

'True,' Chap said again.

'Says he has a wife and children.'

'Partially true. The wife is now an ex-wife. The children are still his.'

'Says they're destitute, and that's why he's scamming people.'

'Not exactly. His wife is quite wealthy, and his

children have followed the money. We're not sure why he's scamming people.'

'But we'd like to stop him,' Chap added. 'We need your help.'

Quince suddenly realized that for the first time in his life, in all of his fifty-one years, he was sitting in the presence of two living, breathing people who knew he was a homosexual. The knowledge terrified him. For a second he wanted to deny it, to concoct some story of how he came to know Ricky, but invention failed him. He was too scared to be inspired.

Then he realized that these two, whoever they were, could ruin him. They knew his little secret, and they had the power to wreck his life.

And they were offering $25,000 cash?

Poor Quince covered his eyes with his knuckles and said, 'What do you want?'

Chap and Wes thought he was about to cry. They didn't particularly care, but there was no need for it. 'Here's the deal, Mr. Garbe,' said Chap. 'You take the money lying there on your desk, and you tell us everything about Ricky. Show us your letters. Show us everything. If you have a file or a box or some secret place where you've hidden everything, we'd like to see it. Once we've gathered all we need, then we'll leave. We'll disappear as quickly as we've come, and you'll never know who we are or who we're protecting.'

'And you'll keep the secrets?'

'Absolutely.'

'There's no reason for us to tell anyone about you,' Wes added.

'Can you make him stop?' Quince asked, staring at them.

Chap and Wes paused and glanced at each other. Their responses had been perfect so far, but this question had no clear answer. 'We can't promise, Mr. Garbe,' Wes said. 'But we'll try our best to put this Ricky character out of business. As we said, he's upsetting our client too.'

'You've got to protect me on this.'

'We'll do all we can.'

Suddenly Quince stood and leaned forward with his palms flat on the desk. 'Then I have no choice,' he announced. He didn't touch the money, but walked a few steps to an ancient glass bookcase filled with weathered and peeling volumes. With one key he unlocked the case, and with another he opened a small, hidden safe on the second shelf from the floor. Carefully, he withdrew a thin, letter-sized folder, which he delicately placed next to the envelope filled with cash.

Just as he opened the file, an offensive, high-pitched voice squawked through the intercom, 'Mr. Garbe, your father would like to see you immediately.'

Quince bolted upright in horror, his cheeks instantly pale, his face contorted in panic. 'Uh, tell him I'm in a meeting,' he said, trying to sound reassuring but coming off as a hopeless liar.

'You tell him,' she said, and the intercom clicked.

'Excuse me,' he said, actually trying to smile. He picked up the receiver, punched three numbers, and turned his back on Wes and Chap so that maybe they wouldn't hear.

'Dad, it's me. What's up?' he said, head low.

A long pause as the old man filled his ear.

Then, 'No, no, they're not from the Federal Reserve. They're, uh, they're lawyers from Des Moines. They represent the family of an old college buddy of mine. That's all.'

A shorter pause.

'Uh, Franklin Delaney, you wouldn't remember him. He died four months ago, without a will, a big mess. No, Dad, uh, it has nothing to do with the bank.'

He hung up. Not a bad piece of lying. The door was locked. That's all that mattered.

Wes and Chap stood and moved in tandem to the edge of the desk, where they leaned forward together as Quince opened the file. The first thing they noticed was the photo, paper-clipped to the inside flap. Wes gently removed it, and said, 'Is this supposed to be Ricky?'

'That's him,' Quince said, ashamed but determined to get through it.

'A nice-looking young man,' Chap said, as if they were staring at a *Playboy* centerfold. All three were immediately uncomfortable.

'You know who Ricky is, don't you?' Quince asked.

'Yes.'

'Then tell me.'

'No, it's not part of the deal.'

'Why can't you tell me? I'm giving you everything you want.'

'That's not what we agreed on.'

'I want to kill the bastard.'

'Relax, Mr. Garbe. We have a deal. You get the money, we get the file, nobody gets hurt.'

'Let's go back to the beginning,' Chap said, looking down at the fragile and suffering little man in the oversized chair. 'How did it all start?'

Quince moved some papers around in the file and produced a thin magazine. 'I bought this at a bookstore in Chicago,' he said, sliding it around so they could read it. The title was *Out and About*, and it described itself as a publication for mature men with alternative lifestyles. He let them take in the cover, then flipped to the back pages. Wes and Chap didn't try to touch it, but their eyes took in as much as possible. Very few pictures, lots of small print. It wasn't pornography by any means.

On page forty-six was a small section of personals. One was circled with a red pen. It read:

> SWM in 20s looking for kind and
> discreet gentleman in 40s or 50s
> to pen pal with.

Wes and Chap leaned lower to read it, then came back up together. 'So you answered this ad?' Chap said.

'I did. I sent a little note, and about two weeks later I heard from Ricky.'

'Do you have a copy of your note?'

'No. I didn't copy my letters. Nothing left this office. I was afraid to make copies around here.'

Wes and Chap frowned in disbelief, then great disappointment. What kind of dumb ass were they dealing with here?

'Sorry,' Quince said, tempted to grab the cash before they changed their minds.

Moving things along, he removed the first letter from Ricky and thrust it at them. 'Just lay it down,' Wes said, and they leaned in again, inspecting without touching. They were very slow readers, Quince noticed, and they read with incredible concentration. His mind was beginning to clear, and a glimmer of hope emerged. How sweet it was to have the money and not have to worry about another crooked loan, another pack of lies to cover his trail. And now he had allies, Wes and Chap here, and God knows who else working against Ricky. His heart slowed a little and his breathing was not as labored.

'The next letter please,' Chap said.

Quince laid them out in sequence, one beside the other, three lavender in color, one a soft blue, one yellow, all written in the tedious block handwriting of a person with plenty of time. When they finished one page, Chap would carefully arrange the next one with a pair of tweezers. Their fingers touched nothing.

The odd thing about the letters, as Chap and Wes would whisper to each other much later, was that they were so thoroughly believable. Ricky was wounded and tortured and in dire need of someone to talk to. He was pitiful and sympathetic. And there was hope because the worst was over for him and he would soon be free to pursue new friendships. The writing was superb!

After a deafening silence, Quince said, 'I need to make a phone call.'

'To whom?'

'It's business.'

Wes and Chap looked at each other with uncertainty, then nodded. Quince walked with the phone to his credenza and watched Main Street below while talking to another banker.

At some point, Wes began making notes, no doubt in preparation for the cross-examination to come. Quince loitered by the bookcase, trying to read a newspaper, trying to ignore the note-taking. He was calm now, thinking as clearly as possible, plotting his next move, the one after these goons left him.

'Did you send a check for a hundred thousand dollars?' Chap asked.

'I did.'

Wes, the grimmer-faced of the two, glared at him with contempt, as if to say, 'What a fool.'

They read some more, took a few notes, whispered and mumbled between themselves.

'How much money has your client sent?' Quince asked, just for the hell of it.

Wes got even grimmer and said, 'We can't say.'

No surprise to Quince. The boys had no sense of humor.

They sat down after an hour, and Quince took his seat in his banker's chair.

'Just a couple of questions,' Chap said, and Quince knew they'd be talking for another hour.

'How'd you book the gay cruise?'

'It's in the letter there. This thug gave me the name and number of a travel agency in New York. I called, then sent a money order. It was easy.'

'Easy? Have you done it before?'

'Are we here to talk about my sex life?'

'No.'

'So let's stick to the issues,' Quince said like a real ass, and he felt good again. The banker in him boiled for a moment. Then he thought of something he simply couldn't resist. With a straight face, he said, 'The cruise is still paid for. You guys wanna go?'

Fortunately, they laughed. It was a quick flash of humor, then back to business. Chap said, 'Did you consider using a pseudonym?'

'Yes, of course. It was stupid not to. But I'd never done this before. I thought the guy was legitimate. He's in Florida, I'm in Podunk, Iowa. It never crossed my mind the guy was a fraud.'

'We'll need copies of all this,' Wes said.

'That could be a problem.'

'Why?'

'Where would you copy it?'

'The bank doesn't have a copier?'

'It does, but you're not copying that file in this bank.'

'Then we'll take it to a quick print somewhere.'

'This is Bakers. We don't have a quick print.'

'Do you have an office supply store?'

'Yes, and the owner owes my bank eighty thousand dollars. He sits next to me at the Rotary Club. You're not copying it there. I'm not going to be seen with that file.'

Chap and Wes looked at each other, then at Quince. Wes said, 'Okay, look. I'll stay here with you. Chap will take the file and find a copier.'

'Where?'

'The drugstore,' Wes said.

'You've found the drugstore?'

'Sure, we needed some tweezers.'

'That copier's twenty years old.'

'No, they have a new one.'

'You must be careful, okay? The pharmacist is my secretary's second cousin. This is a very small town.'

Chap took the file and walked to the door. It clicked loudly when he unlocked it, and when he stepped through he was immediately under scrutiny. The secretary's desk was crowded with older women, all busy doing nothing until Chap emerged and they froze and gawked. Old Mr. Garbe was not far away, holding a ledger, pretending to be busy but himself consumed with curiosity. Chap nodded to them all and eased away, passing as he went virtually every employee of the bank.

The door clicked loudly again as Quince locked the damned thing before anyone could barge in. He and Wes chatted awkwardly about this and that for a few minutes, the conversation almost dying at times for lack of common ground. Forbidden sex had brought them together, and they certainly had to avoid that subject. Life in Bakers was of little interest. Quince could ask nothing about Wes' background.

Finally, he said, 'What should I say in my letter to Ricky?'

Wes warmed to the idea immediately. 'Well, I would wait, first of all. Wait a month. Let him sweat. If you hurry back with a response, and with the money, he might think it's too easy.'

'What if he gets mad?'

'He won't. He has plenty of time, and he wants the money.'

'Do you see all his mail?'

'We think we have access to most of it.'

Quince was overcome with curiosity. Sitting with a man who now knew his deepest secret, he felt as though he could prod. 'How will you stop him?'

And Wes, for no reason he would ever understand, said simply, 'We'll probably just kill him.'

A radiant peace broke out around the eyes of Quince Garbe, a warm calming glow that spread through his tortured countenance. His wrinkles softened. His lips spread into a tiny smile. His inheritance would be safe after all, and when the old man was gone and the money was his he'd flee this life and live as he pleased.

'How nice,' he said softly. 'How very nice.'

Chap took the file to a motel room where a leased color copier was waiting with other members of the unit. Three sets were made, and thirty minutes later he was back at the bank. Quince inspected his originals; everything was in order. He carefully relocked the file, then said to his guests, 'I think it's time for you to go.'

They left without shaking hands or the usual good-byes. What was there to say?

A private jet was waiting at the local airport, whose runway was barely long enough. Three hours after leaving Quince, Chap and Wes reported to Langley. Their mission was a resounding success.

*

210

A summary of the account in the Geneva Trust Bank was procured with a bribe of $40,000 to a Bahamian banking official, a man they'd used before. Boomer Realty had a balance of $189,000. Its lawyer had about $68,000 in his account. The summary listed all the transactions – money wired in, money taken out. Deville's people were trying desperately to track down the originators of the wires. They knew about Mr. Garbe's remitting bank in Des Moines, and they knew that another wire of $100,000 had been sent from a bank in Dallas. They could not, however, find out who'd originated that wire.

They were scrambling on many fronts when Teddy summoned Deville to the bunker. York was with him. The table was covered with copies of Garbe's file and copies of the bank summaries.

Deville had never seen his boss so dejected. York too had little to say. York was bearing the brunt of the Lake screwup, though Teddy was blaming himself.

'The latest,' Teddy said softly.

Deville never sat while in the bunker. 'We're still tracking the money. We've made contact with the magazine *Out and About*. It's published in New Haven, a very small outfit, and I'm not sure if we'll be able to penetrate. Our contact in the Bahamas is on retainer and we'll know if and when any wires are received. We have a unit ready to search Lake's offices on Capitol Hill, but that's a long shot. I'm not optimistic. We have twenty people on the ground in Jacksonville.'

'How many of our people are shadowing Lake?'

'We've just gone from thirty to fifty.'

'He must be watched. We cannot turn our backs. He is not the person we thought he was, and if we lose sight of him for one hour he might mail a letter, or buy another magazine.'

'We know. We're doing the best we can.'

'This is our highest domestic priority.'

'I know.'

'What about planting someone inside the prison?' Teddy asked. It was a new idea, one hatched by York within the past hour.

Deville rubbed his eyes and chewed his nails for a moment, then said, 'I'll go to work on it. We'll have to pull strings we've never pulled before.'

'How many prisoners are in the federal system?' York asked.

'One hundred thirty-five thousand, give or take,' Deville said.

'Surely we could slip in another, couldn't we?'

'I'll give it a look.'

'Do we have contacts at the Bureau of Prisons?'

'It's new territory, but we're working on it. We're using an old friend at Justice. I'm optimistic.'

Deville left them for a while. He'd get called back in an hour or so. York and Teddy would have another checklist of questions and thoughts and errands for him to tend to.

'I don't like the idea of searching his office on Capitol Hill,' York said. 'It's too risky. And besides, it would take a week. Those guys have a million files.'

'I don't like it either,' Teddy said softly.

'Let's get our guys in Documents to write a

letter from Ricky to Lake. We'll wire the envelope, track it, maybe it will lead us to his file.'

'That's an excellent idea. Tell Deville.'

York made a note on a pad filled with many other notes, most of which had been scratched through. He scribbled to pass the time, then asked the question he'd been saving. 'Will you confront him?'

'Not yet.'

'When?'

'Maybe never. Let's gather the intelligence, learn all we can. He seems to be very quiet about his other life, perhaps it came about after his wife died. Who knows? Maybe he can keep it quiet.'

'But he has to know that you know. Otherwise, he might take another chance. If he knows we're always watching, he'll behave himself. Maybe.'

'Meanwhile the world's going to hell. Nuclear arms are bought and sold and sneaked across borders. We're tracking seven small wars with three more on the brink. A dozen new terrorist groups last month alone. Maniacs in the Middle East building armies and hoarding oil. And we sit here hour after hour plotting against three felonious judges who are at this very moment probably playing gin rummy.'

'They're not stupid,' York said.

'No, but they're clumsy. Their nets have snared the wrong person.'

'I guess we picked the wrong person.'

'No, they did.'

NINETEEN

The memo arrived by fax from the Regional Supervisor, Bureau of Prisons, Washington. It was directed to M. Emmitt Broon, the warden of Trumble. In terse but standard language the supervisor said he'd reviewed the logs from Trumble and was bothered by the number of visits by one Trevor Carson, attorney for three of the inmates. Lawyer Carson had reached the point of logging in almost every day.

While every inmate certainly had a constitutional right to meet with his attorney, the prison likewise had the power to regulate the traffic. Beginning immediately, attorney-client visits would be restricted to Tuesdays, Thursdays, and Saturdays, between the hours of 3 and 6 P.M. Exceptions would be granted liberally for good cause shown.

The new policy would be utilized for a period of ninety days, after which time it would be reviewed.

Fine with the warden. He too had grown suspicious of Trevor's almost daily appearances. He'd questioned the front desk and the guards in a vain effort to determine what, exactly, was the nature of all this legal work. Link, the guard who usually escorted Trevor to the conference room, and who usually pocketed a couple of twenties on each visit, told the warden that the lawyer and Mr. Spicer talked about cases and appeals and such. 'Just a bunch of law crap,' Link said.

'And you always search his briefcase?' the warden had asked.

'Always,' Link had replied.

Out of courtesy, the warden dialed the number of Mr. Trevor Carson in Neptune Beach. The phone was answered by a woman who said rudely, 'Law office.'

'Mr. Trevor Carson, please.'

'Who's calling?'

'This is Emmitt Broon.'

'Well, Mr. Broon, he's taking a nap right now.'

'I see. Could you possibly wake him? I'm the warden at the federal prison at Trumble, and I need to speak with him.'

'Just a minute.'

He waited for a long time, and when she returned she said, 'I'm sorry. I couldn't wake him up. Could I have him return your call?'

'No, thank you. I'll just fax him a note.'

The idea of a reverse scam was hatched by York, while playing golf on a Sunday, and as his game progressed, occasionally on the fairways but more often in the sand and trees, the scheme grew and grew and became brilliant. He abandoned his pals after fourteen holes and called Teddy.

They would learn the tactics of their adversaries.

And they could divert attention away from Al Konyers. There was nothing to lose.

The letter was created by York, and assigned to one of the top forgers in Documents. The pen pal was christened Brant White, and the first note was handwritten on a plain, white, but expensive correspondence card.

Dear Ricky:

Saw your ad, liked it. I'm fifty-five, in great shape, and looking for more than a pen pal. My wife and I just bought a home in Palm Valley, not far from Neptune Beach. We'll be down in three weeks, with plans to stay for two months.

If interested, send photo. If I like what I see, then I'll give more details.

Brant

The return address was from Brant, P.O. Box 88645, Upper Darby, PA 19082.

To save two or three days, a Philadelphia postmark was applied in Documents, and the letter was flown to Jacksonville where agent Klockner himself delivered it to Aladdin North's little box in the Neptune Beach post office. It was a Monday.

After his nap the following day, Trevor picked up the mail and headed west, out of Jacksonville, along the familiar route to Trumble. He was greeted by the same guards, Mackey and Vince, at the front door, and he signed the same logbook Rufus shoved in front of him. He followed Link into the visitors' area and to a corner where Spicer was waiting in one of the small attorney-conference rooms.

'I'm catchin some heat,' Link said as they stepped into the room. Spicer did not look up. Trevor handed two twenties to Link, who took them in a flash.

'From who?' Trevor asked, opening his brief-case. Spicer was reading a newspaper.

'The warden.'

'Hell, he's cut back on my visits. What else does he want?'

'Don't you understand?' Spicer said, without lowering the newspaper. 'Link here is upset because he's not collecting as much. Right, Link?'

'You got that right. I don't know what kinda funny business you boys are runnin here, but if I tightened up on my inspections you'd be in trouble, wouldn't you?'

'You're being paid well,' Trevor said.

'That's what you think.'

'How much do you want?' Spicer said, staring at him now.

'A thousand a month, cash,' he said, looking at Trevor. 'I'll pick it up at your office.'

'A thousand bucks and the mail doesn't get checked,' Spicer said.

'Yep.'

'And not a word to anybody.'

'Yep.'

'It's a deal. Now get outta here.'

Link smiled at both of them and left the room. He positioned himself outside the door, and for the benefit of the closed-circuit cameras looked through the window occasionally.

Inside, the routine varied little. The exchange of mail happened first and took only a second. From a worn manila folder, the same one every time, Joe Roy Spicer removed the outgoing letters and handed them to Trevor, who took the incoming mail from his briefcase and gave it to his client.

There were six letters to be mailed. Some days there were as many as ten, seldom less than five. Though Trevor didn't keep records, or copies, or documents in a file that would serve as proof that he had anything whatsoever to do with the Brethren's little scam, he knew there had to be twenty or thirty potential victims currently being set up. He recognized some of the names and addresses.

Twenty-one to be exact, according to Spicer's precise records. Twenty-one serious prospects, with another eighteen who were marginal. Almost forty pen pals currently hiding in their various closets, some terrified of their shadows, others getting bolder by the week, still others on the verge of kicking down the door and dashing off to meet Ricky or Percy.

The difficult part was being patient. The scam was working, money was changing hands, the temptation was to squeeze them too quickly. Beech and Yarber were proving to be workhorses, laboring over their letters for hours at a time while Spicer directed operations. It took discipline to hook a new pen pal, one with money, then ply him with enough pretty words to earn his trust.

'Aren't we due for a bust?' Trevor said.

Spicer was flipping through the new letters. 'Don't tell me you're broke,' he said. 'You're making more than we are.'

'My money's tucked away just like yours. I'd just like to have some more of it.'

'So would I.' Spicer looked at the envelope from Brant in Upper Darby, Pa. 'Ah, a new one,' he mumbled to himself, then opened it. He read it quickly, and was surprised by its tone. No fear, no wasted words, no peeking around corners. This man was ready for action.

'Where's Palm Valley?' he asked.

'Ten miles south of the beaches. Why?'

'What kinda place is it?'

'It's one of the gated golf communities for rich retirees, almost all from up North.'

'How much are the houses?'

'Well, I've never been there, okay. They keep the damned gate locked, guards everywhere like somebody might break in and steal their golf carts, but –'

'How much are the houses?'

'Nothing less than a million. I've seen a couple advertised for three million.'

'Wait here,' Spicer said, gathering his file and walking to the door.

'Where you going?' Trevor asked.

'To the library. I'll be back in half an hour.'

'I got things to do.'

'No you don't. Read the newspaper.'

Spicer said something to Link, who escorted him through the visitors' area and out of the administration building. He walked quickly along the manicured grounds. The sun was warm, and the gardeners were earning their fifty cents an hour.

So were the keepers of the law library. Beech

219

and Yarber were hiding in their little conference room, taking a break from their writings with a game of chess, when Spicer entered in a rush, with an uncharacteristic smile. 'Boys, we've finally hooked the big one,' he said, and tossed Brant's letter on the table. Beech read it aloud.

'Palm Valley is one of the golf communities for rich folks,' Spicer explained proudly. 'Houses go for about three million. The boy's got plenty of dough and he ain't much for letters.'

'He does seem anxious,' Yarber observed.

'We need to move fast,' Spicer said. 'He wants to come down in three weeks.'

'What's the upside potential?' Beech asked. He loved the jargon of those who invested millions.

'At least a half a million,' Spicer said. 'Let's do the letter now. Trevor is waiting.'

Beech opened one of his many files and displayed his wares; sheets of paper in soft pastels. 'I think I'll try the peach,' he said.

'Oh definitely,' Spicer said. 'Gotta do peach.'

Ricky wrote a scaled-down version of the initial contact letter. Twenty-eight years old, college graduate, locked down in rehab but on the verge of release, probably in ten days, very lonely, looking for a mature man to start a relationship. How convenient that Brant would be living nearby, because Ricky had a sister in Jacksonville and he'd be staying with her. There were no obstacles, no hurdles to cross. He'd be ready for Brant when he came South. But he'd like a photo first. Was Brant really married? Would his wife be living at Palm Valley too? Or would she stay up there in Pennsylvania? Wouldn't it be great if she did?

They enclosed the same color photo they'd used a hundred times. It had proved to be irresistible.

The peach envelope was taken by Spicer back to the attorney-conference room where Trevor was napping. 'Mail this immediately,' Spicer barked at him.

They spent ten minutes on their basketball bets, then said goodbye without a handshake.

Driving back to Jacksonville, Trevor called his bookie, a new one, a bigger bookie, now that he was a player. The digital line was indeed more secure, but the phone wasn't. Agent Klockner and his band of operatives were listening as usual, and tracking Trevor's bets. He wasn't doing badly, up $4,500 in the past two weeks. By contrast, his law firm had put $800 on the books during the same period.

In addition to the phone, there were four mikes in the Beetle, most of them of little value but operational nonetheless. And under each bumper was a transmitter, both wired to the car's electrical system and checked every other night when Trevor was either drinking or sleeping. A powerful receiver in the rental across the street tracked the Beetle wherever it went. As Trevor puttered down the highway, talking on his phone like a big shot, tossing money around like a Vegas high roller, sipping scalded coffee from a quick-stop grocery, he was emitting more signals than most private jets.

March 7. Big Super Tuesday. Aaron Lake bounced triumphantly across the stage in a large banquet room of a Manhattan hotel, while thousands cheered and music roared and balloons fell from above. He'd taken New York with 43 percent of the vote. Governor Tarry had a rather weak 29 percent, and the other also-rans got the rest. Lake hugged people he'd never seen before and waved to people he'd never see again, and he delivered without notes a stirring victory speech.

Then he was off, on his way to L.A. for another victory celebration. For four hours, in his new Boeing jet that would hold a hundred and leased for $1 million a month and flew at a speed of five hundred miles per hour, thirty-eight thousand feet above the country, he and his staff monitored the returns from the twelve states participating in big Super Tuesday. Along the East Coast, where the polls had already closed, Lake barely won in Maine and Connecticut, but put up big margins in New York, Massachusetts, Maryland, and Georgia. He lost Rhode Island by eight hundred votes, and won Vermont by a thousand. As he was flying over Missouri, CNN declared him the winner of that state by four percentage points over Governor Tarry. Ohio was just as close.

By the time Lake reached California, the rout was over. Of the 591 delegates at stake, he'd captured 390. He'd also solidified the momentum. And most important, Aaron Lake now had the money. Governor Tarry was falling hard and fast, and all bets were on Lake.

TWENTY

Six hours after claiming victory in California, Lake awoke to a frenzied morning of live interviews. He suffered through eighteen in two hours, then flew to Washington.

He went straight to his new campaign headquarters, on the ground floor of a large office building on H Street, a stone's throw from the White House. He thanked his workers, almost none of whom were volunteers. He worked his crowd, shook their hands, all the while asking himself, 'Where did these people come from?'

We're gonna win, he said over and over, and everybody believed it. Why not?

He met for an hour with his top people. He had $65 million, no debt. Tarry had less than $1 million on hand and he was still trying to count the money he owed. In fact, the Tarry campaign had missed a federal filing deadline because its books were in such a mess. All cash had vanished. Contributions had stopped. Lake was getting all the money.

The names of three potential Vice Presidents were debated with great enthusiasm. It was an exhilarating exercise because it meant the nomination was in the bag. Lake's first choice, Senator Nance from Michigan, was drawing fire because he'd had some shady business deals in another life. His partners had been of Italian extraction, from Detroit, and Lake could close his eyes and see the press peeling skin off Nance. A committee was appointed to explore the issue further.

And a committee was appointed to begin planning Lake's presence at the convention in Denver. Lake wanted a new speech-writer, now, and he wanted him working on the acceptance speech.

Lake secretly marveled at his own overhead. His campaign chairman was getting $150,000 for the year, not for twelve months, but until Christmas. There was a chairman of finance, of policy, of media relations, of operations, and of strategic planning, and all had contracts for $120,000 for about ten months of work. Each chairman had two or three immediate underlings, people Lake hardly knew, and they earned $90,000 apiece. Then there were the campaign assistants, or CAs, not the volunteers that most candidates attracted, but real employees who earned $50,000 each and kept the offices in a frenzy. There were dozens of them. And dozens of clerks and secretaries and, hell, nobody made less than $40,000.

And on top of all this waste, Lake kept telling himself, if I make it to the White House then I'll have to find jobs for them there. Every damned one of them. Kids now running around with Lake buttons on every lapel will expect to have West Wing clearances and jobs paying $80,000 a year.

It's a drop in the bucket, he kept reminding

himself. Don't get hung up on the small stuff when so much more is at stake.

Negatives were pushed to the end of the meeting and given short shrift. A reporter for the *Post* had been digging into Lake's early business career. Without too much effort he'd stumbled upon the GreenTree mess, a failed land development, twenty-two years in the past. Lake and a partner had bankrupted GreenTree, legally shafting creditors out of $800,000. The partner had been indicted for bankruptcy fraud, but a jury let him walk. No one laid a glove on Lake, and seven times after that the people of Arizona elected him to Congress.

'I'll answer any question about GreenTree,' Lake said. 'It was just a bad business deal.'

'The press is about to shift gears,' said the chairman of media relations. 'You're new and you haven't been subjected to enough scrutiny. It's time for them to get nasty.'

'It's already started,' Lake said. 'I have no skeletons.'

For an early dinner he was whisked away to Mortimer's, the current power place to be seen, just down Pennsylvania, where he met Elaine Tyner, the lawyer running D-PAC. Over fruit and cottage cheese she laid out the current financials of the newest PAC on the block. Cash in hand of $29 million, no significant debt, money being churned around the clock, coming in from all directions, from everywhere in the world.

Spending it was the challenge. Since it was considered 'soft money,' or money that couldn't go directly to the Lake campaign, it had to be used elsewhere. Tyner had several targets. The first was a series of generic ads similar to the doomsday ads Teddy had put together. D-PAC was already buying prime-time spots for the fall. The second, and by far the most enjoyable, were the Senate and congressional races. 'They're lining up like ants,' she said with great amusement. 'It's amazing what a few million bucks can do.'

She told the story of a House race in a district in Northern California where the incumbent, a twenty-year veteran Lake knew and despised, started the year with a forty-point lead against an unknown challenger. The unknown found his way to D-PAC and surrendered his soul to Aaron Lake. 'We've basically taken over his campaign,' she said. 'We're writing speeches, polling, doing all his print and TV ads, we even hired a new staff for him. So far we've spent one-point-five million, and our boy has cut the lead to ten points. And we have seven months to go.'

In all, Tyner and D-PAC were meddling in thirty House races and ten in the Senate. She expected to raise a total of $60 million, and spend every dime of it by November.

Her third area of 'focus' was taking the pulse of the country. D-PAC was polling nonstop, every day, fifteen hours a day. If labor in western Pennsylvania was bothered by an issue, D-PAC would know it. If the Hispanics in Houston were pleased with a new welfare policy, D-PAC would know it. If the women in greater Chicago liked or disliked a Lake ad, D-PAC knew yes or no and by what percentage. 'We know everything,' she boasted. 'We're like Big Brother, always watching.'

The polling cost $60,000 a day, a bargain. No one could touch it. For the important matters, Lake was nine points ahead of Tarry in Texas, even in Florida, a state Lake had yet to visit, and very close in Indiana, Tarry's home state.

'Tarry's tired,' she said. 'Morale is low because he won in New Hampshire and the money was rolling in. Then you came from nowhere, a fresh face, no baggage, new message, you start winning, and suddenly the money finds you. Tarry can't raise fifty bucks at a church bake sale. He's losing key people because he can't pay them, and because they smell another winner.'

Lake chewed a piece of pineapple and savored the words. They weren't new; he'd heard them from his own people. But coming from a seasoned insider like Tyner, they were even more reassuring.

'What are the Vice President's numbers?' Lake asked. He had his own set, but for some reason trusted her more.

'He'll squeak out the nomination,' she said, offering nothing new. 'But the convention will be bloody. Right now, you're only a few points behind him on the big question: Who will you vote for in November?'

'November is far away.'

'It is and it isn't.'

'A lot can change,' Lake said, thinking of Teddy, and wondering what sort of crisis he'd create to terrify the American people.

The dinner was more of a snack, and from Mortimer's Lake he was driven to a small dining room at the Hay-Adams Hotel. It was a long, late dinner with friends, two dozen of his colleagues

227

from the House. Few of them had rushed to endorse him when he'd entered the race, but now they were all wildly enthusiastic about their man. Most had their own pollsters. The bandwagon was rolling down the mountain.

Lake had never seen his old pals so happy to be around him.

The letter was prepared in Documents by a woman named Bruce, one of the agency's three best counterfeiters. Tacked to the corkboard just above the worktable in her small lab were letters written by Ricky. Excellent samples, much more than she needed. She had no idea who Ricky was, but there was no doubt his handwriting was contrived. It was fairly consistent, with the more recent samples clearly showing an ease that came only with practice. His vocabulary was not remarkable, but then she suspected he was trying to downplay it. His sentence structure showed few mistakes. Bruce guessed him to be between the ages of forty and sixty, with at least a college education.

But it wasn't her job to make such inferences, at least not in this case. With the same pen and paper as Ricky, she wrote a nice little note to Al. The text had been prepared by someone else, she did not know who. Nor did she care.

It was, 'Hey, Al, where have you been? Why haven't you written? Don't forget about me.' That kind of letter, but with a nice little surprise. Since Ricky couldn't use the phone, he was sending Al a cassette tape with a brief message from deep inside rehab.

Bruce fit the letter onto one page, then worked

for an hour on the envelope. The postmark she applied was from Neptune Beach, Florida.

She didn't seal the envelope. Her little project was inspected, then taken to another lab. The tape was recorded by a young agent who'd studied drama at Northwestern. In a soft, accentless voice he said, 'Hey, Al, this is Ricky. Hope you're surprised to hear my voice. They won't let us use the phones around here, I don't know why, but for some reason we can send tapes back and forth. I can't wait to get out of this place.' Then he rambled for five minutes about his rehab and how much he hated his uncle and the people who ran Aladdin North. But he did concede that they had rid him of his addictions. He was certain he would look back and not judge the place too harshly.

His entire narrative was nothing but babble. No plans were discussed for his release, no hint of where he might go or what he might do, only a vague reference about seeing Al one day.

They were not yet ready to bait Al Konyers. The sole purpose of the tape was to hide within its casing a transmitter strong enough to lead them to Lake's hidden file. A tiny bug in the envelope was too risky. Al might be smart enough to find it.

At Mailbox America in Chevy Chase, the CIA now controlled eight boxes, duly rented for one year by eight different people, each of whom had the same twenty-four-hour access that Mr. Konyers had. They came and went at all hours, checking their little boxes, picking up mail they'd sent themselves, occasionally taking a peek at Al's box if no one was looking.

Since they knew his schedule better than he

knew it himself, they waited patiently until he'd made his rounds. They felt certain he'd sneak out as before, dressed like a jogger, so they held the envelope with the tape until almost ten one night. Then they placed it in his box.

Four hours later, with a dozen agents watching every move, Lake the jogger jumped from a cab in front of Mailbox America, darted inside, his face hidden by the long bill of a running cap, went to his box, pulled out the mail, and hurried back into the cab.

Six hours later he left Georgetown for a prayer breakfast at the Hilton, and they waited. He addressed an association of police chiefs at nine, and a thousand high school principals at eleven. He lunched with the Speaker of the House. He taped a stressful Q&A session with some talking heads at three, then returned home to pack. His itinerary called for him to depart Reagan National at eight and fly to Dallas.

They followed him to the airport, watched the Boeing 707 take off, then called Langley. When the two Secret Service agents arrived to check the perimeter of Lake's townhouse, the CIA was already inside.

The search ended in the kitchen ten minutes after it began. A handheld receptor caught the signal from the cassette tape. They found it in the wastebasket, along with an empty half-gallon milk jug, two torn packages of oatmeal, some soiled paper towels, and that morning's edition of the *Washington Post*. A maid came twice a week. Lake had simply left the garbage for her to take care of.

They couldn't find Lake's file because he didn't have one. Smart man, he tossed away the evidence.

Teddy was almost relieved when he got word. The team was still in the townhouse, hiding and waiting for the Secret Service to leave. Whatever Lake did in his secret life, he worked hard not to leave a trail.

The tape unnerved Aaron Lake. Reading Ricky's letters and looking at his handsome face had given him a nervous thrill. The young man was far away and odds were they'd never meet. They could be pen pals and play tag at a distance and move slowly, at least that's what Lake had contemplated initially.

But hearing Ricky's voice had brought him much closer, and Lake was rattled. What had begun a few months earlier as a curious little game now held horrible possibilities. It was much too risky. Lake trembled at the thought of getting caught.

It still seemed impossible, though. He was well hidden behind the mask of Al Konyers. Ricky had not a clue. It was 'Al this' and 'Al that' on the tape. The post office box was his shield.

But he had to end it. At least for now.

The Boeing was packed with Lake's well-paid people. They didn't make an airplane big enough to haul his entire entourage. If he leased a 747, within two days it would be filled with CAs and advisers and consultants and pollsters, not to mention his own growing army of bodyguards from the Secret Service.

The more primaries he won, the heavier his

plane became. It might be wise to lose a couple of states so he could jettison some of the baggage.

In the darkness of the plane, Lake sipped tomato juice and decided to write a final letter to Ricky. Al would wish him the best, and simply terminate the correspondence. What could the boy do?

He was tempted to write the note right then, sitting in his deep recliner, his feet in the air. But at any moment an assistant of some variety would emerge with another breathless report that the candidate had to hear immediately. He had no privacy. He had no time to think or loaf or daydream. Every pleasant thought was interrupted by a new poll or a late-breaking story or an urgent need to make a decision.

Surely he'd be able to hide in the White House. Loners had lived there before.

TWENTY-ONE

The case of the stolen cell phone had fascinated the inmates at Trumble for the past month. Mr. T-Bone, a wiry street kid from Miami serving twenty for drugs, had taken original possession of the phone by means that were still unclear. Cell phones were strictly prohibited at Trumble, and the method by which he got one had created more rumors than T. Karl's sex life. The few who'd actually seen it had described it, not in court, but around the camp, as being no larger than a stopwatch. Mr. T-Bone had been seen lurking in the shadows, hunched at the waist, chin to his chest, back to the world, mumbling into the phone. No doubt he was still directing street operations in Miami.

Then it disappeared. Mr. T-Bone let it be known that he might kill whoever took it, and when the threats of violence didn't work he offered a reward of $1,000 cash. Suspicion soon fell upon another young drug dealer, Zorro, from a section of Atlanta just as rough as Mr. T-Bone's. A killing seemed likely, so the guards and the suits up front intervened and convinced the two that they'd be

233

shipped away if things got out of hand. Violence was not tolerated at Trumble. The punishment was a trip to a medium-security pen with inmates who understood violence.

Someone told Mr. T-Bone about the weekly dockets the Brethren held, and in due course he found T. Karl and filed suit. He wanted his phone back, plus a million bucks in punitive damages.

When it was first set for trial, an assistant warden appeared in the cafeteria to observe the proceedings, and the matter was quickly postponed by the Brethren. The same thing happened just before the second trial. Allegations of who did or did not have possession of an outlawed cell phone could not be heard by anyone in administration. The guards who watched the weekly shows wouldn't repeat a word.

Justice Spicer finally convinced a prison counselor that the boys had a private matter to reconcile, without interference from the front. 'We're trying to settle a little matter,' he whispered. 'And we need to do it in private.'

The request worked its way upward, and at the third trial date the cafeteria was packed with spectators, most of whom were hoping to see bloodshed. The only prison official in the room was a solitary guard, sitting in the back, half asleep.

Neither of the litigants was a stranger to courtrooms, so it was no surprise that Mr. T-Bone and Zorro acted as their own attorneys. Justice Beech spent most of the first hour trying to keep the language out of the gutter. He finally gave up. Wild accusations spewed forth from the plaintiff, charges that couldn't have been proved with the aid of a thousand FBI agents. The denials were just as loud and preposterous from the defense. Mr. T-Bone scored heavy blows with two affidavits, signed by inmates whose names were revealed only to the Brethren, which contained eyewitness accounts of seeing Zorro trying to hide while talking on a tiny phone.

Zorro's angry response described the affidavits in language the Brethren had never before encountered.

The knockout punch came from nowhere. Mr. T-Bone, in a move that even the slickest lawyer would admire, produced documentation. His phone records had been smuggled in, and he showed the court in black and white that exactly fifty-four calls had been made to numbers in southeast Atlanta. His supporters, by far the majority but whose loyalty could vanish in an instant, whooped and hollered until T. Karl slammed his plastic gavel and got them quiet.

Zorro had trouble regrouping, and his hesitation killed him. He was ordered to immediately turn over the phone to the Brethren within twenty-four hours, and to reimburse Mr. T-Bone $450 for long-distance charges. If twenty-four hours passed with no phone, the matter would be referred to the warden, along with a finding of fact from the Brethren that Zorro did indeed possess an illegal cell phone.

The Brethren further ordered the two to maintain a distance of at least fifty feet from one another at all times, even when eating.

T. Karl rapped a gavel and the crowd began a

noisy exit. He called the next case, another petty gambling dispute, and waited for the spectators to leave. 'Quiet!' he shouted, and the racket only grew louder. The Brethren went back to their newspapers and magazines.

'Quiet!' he barked again, slamming his gavel.

'Shut up,' Spicer yelled at T. Karl. 'You're making more noise than they are.'

'It's my job,' T. Karl snapped back, the curls of his wig bouncing in all directions.

When the cafeteria was empty, only one inmate remained. T. Karl looked around and finally asked him, 'Are you Mr. Hooten?'

'No sir,' the young man said.

'Are you Mr.Jenkins?'

'No sir.'

'I didn't think so. The case of Hooten versus Jenkins is hereby dismissed for failure to show,' T. Karl said, and made a dramatic entry into his docket book.

'Who are you?' Spicer asked the young man, who was sitting alone and glancing around as if he wasn't sure he was welcome. The three men in the pale green robes were now looking at him, as was the clown with the gray wig and the old maroon pajamas and the lavender shower shoes, no socks. Who were these people!

He slowly got to his feet and moved forward with great apprehension until he stood before the three. 'I'm looking for some help,' he said, almost afraid to speak.

'Do you have business before the court?' T.Karl growled from the side.

'No sir.'

'Then you'll have to –'

'Shut up!' Spicer said. 'Court's adjourned. Leave.'

T.Karl slammed his docket book, kicked back his folding chair, and stormed out of the room, his shower shoes sliding on the tile, his wig bouncing behind him.

The young man appeared ready to cry. 'What can we do for you?' Yarber asked.

He was holding a small cardboard box, and the Brethren knew from experience that it was filled with the papers that had brought him to Trumble. 'I need some help,' he said again. 'I got here last week, and my roommate said you guys could help with my appeals.'

'Don't you have a lawyer?' Beech asked.

'I did. He wasn't very good. He's one reason I'm here.'

'Why are you here?' asked Spicer.

'I don't know. I really don't know.'

'Did you have a trial?'

'Yes. A long one.'

'And you were found guilty by a jury?'

'Yes. Me and a bunch of others. They said we were part of a conspiracy.'

'A conspiracy to do what?'

'Import cocaine.'

Another druggie. They were suddenly anxious to get back to their letter writing. 'How long is your sentence?' asked Yarber.

'Forty-eight years.'

'Forty-eight years! How old are you?'

'Twenty-three.'

The letter writing was momentarily forgotten.

They looked at his sad young face and tried to picture it fifty years later. Released at the age of seventy-one; it was impossible to imagine. Each of the Brethren would leave Trumble a younger man than this kid.

'Pull up a chair,' Yarber said, and the kid grabbed the nearest one and placed it in front of their table. Even Spicer felt a little sympathy for him.

'What's your name?' Yarber asked.

'I go by Buster.'

'Okay, Buster, what'd you do to get yourself forty-eight years?'

The story came in torrents. Balancing his box on his knees, and staring at the floor, he began by saying he'd never been in trouble with the law, nor had his father. They owned a small boat dock together in Pensacola. They fished and sailed and loved the sea, and running the dock was the perfect life for them. They sold a used fishing boat, a fifty-footer, to a man from Fort Lauderdale, an American who paid them in cash – $95,000. The money went in the bank, or at least Buster thought it did. A few months later the man was back for another boat, a thirty-eight-footer for which he paid $80,000. Cash for boats was not unusual in Florida. A third and fourth boat followed. Buster and his dad knew where to find good used fishing boats, which they overhauled and renovated. They enjoyed doing the work themselves. After the fifth boat, the narcs came calling. They asked questions, made vague threats, wanted to see the books and records. Buster's dad refused initially, then

238

they hired a lawyer who advised them not to cooperate. Nothing happened for months.

Buster and his father were arrested at 3 A.M. on a Sunday morning by a pack of goons wearing vests and enough guns to hold Pensacola hostage. They were dragged half-dressed from their small home near the bay, lights flashing all over the place. The indictment was an inch thick, 160 pages, eighty-one counts of conspiracy to smuggle cocaine. He had a copy of it in his box. Buster and his dad were barely mentioned in the 160 pages, but they were nonetheless named as defendants and lumped together with the man they'd sold the boats to, along with twenty-five other people they'd never heard of. Eleven were Colombians. Three were lawyers. Everybody else was from South Florida.

The U.S. Attorney offered them a deal – two years each in return for guilty pleas and cooperation against the other codefendants. Pleading guilty to what? They'd done nothing wrong. They knew exactly one of their twenty-six coconspirators. They'd never seen cocaine.

Buster's father remortgaged their home to raise $20,000 for a lawyer, and they made a bad selection. At trial, they were alarmed to find themselves sitting at the same table with the Colombians and the real drug traffickers. They were on one side of the courtroom, all the coconspirators, sitting together as if they'd once been a well-oiled drug machine. On the other side, near the jury, were the government lawyers, groups of pompous little bastards in dark suits, taking notes, glaring at them as if they were child molesters. The jury glared at them too.

239

During seven weeks of trial, Buster and his father were practically ignored. Three times their names were mentioned. The government's principal charge against them was that they had conspired to procure and rebuild fishing boats with souped-up engines to transport drugs from Mexico to various drop-offs along the Florida panhandle. Their lawyer, who complained that he wasn't getting paid enough to handle a seven-week trial, proved ineffective at rebutting these loose charges. Still, the government lawyers did little damage and were much more concerned with nailing the Colombians.

But they didn't have to prove much. They had done a superior job of picking the jury. After eight days of deliberation, the jurors, obviously tired and frustrated, found every conspirator guilty of all charges. A month after they were sentenced, Buster's father killed himself.

As the narrative wound down, the kid looked as if he might cry. But he stuck out his jaw, gritted his teeth, and said, 'I did nothing wrong.'

He certainly wasn't the first inmate at Trumble to declare his innocence. Beech watched and listened and remembered a young man he'd sentenced once to forty years for drug trafficking back in Texas. The defendant had a rotten childhood, no education, a long record as a juvenile offender, not much of a chance in life. Beech had lectured him from the bench, high and lordly from above, and had felt good about himself for handing down such a brutal sentence. Gotta get these damned drug dealers off the streets!

A liberal is a conservative who's been arrested.

After three years on the inside of a prison Hatlee Beech agonized over many of the people he'd thrown the book at. People far guiltier than Buster here. Kids who just needed a break.

Finn Yarber watched and listened and felt immense pity for the young man. Everybody at Trumble had a sad story, and after a month or so of hearing them he'd learned to believe almost nothing. But Buster was believable. For the next forty-eight years he would wither and decline, all at taxpayer expense. Three meals a day. A warm bed at night – $31,000 a year was the latest guess of what a federal inmate cost the government. Such a waste. Half the inmates at Trumble had no business being there. They were non-violent men who should've been punished with stiff fines and community service.

Joe Roy Spicer listened to Buster's compelling story, and he sized the boy up for future use. There were two possibilities. First, in Spicer's opinion, the telephones were not being properly utilized in the Angola scam. The Brethren were old men writing letters as if they were young. It would be too risky to call Quince Garbe in Iowa, for example, and pretend to be Ricky, a robust twenty-eight-year-old. But with a kid like Buster working for them, they could convince any potential victim. There were plenty of young guys at Trumble, and Spicer had considered several of them. But they were criminals, and he didn't trust them. Buster was fresh off the streets, seemingly innocent, and he was coming to them for help. The boy could be manipulated.

The second possibility was an offshoot of the

first. If Buster joined their conspiracy, he would be in place when Joe Roy was released. The scam was proving too profitable to simply walk away from. Beech and Yarber were splendid at writing the letters, but they had no business sense. Perhaps Spicer could train young Buster here to fill his shoes, and to divert his share to the outside.

Just a thought.

'Do you have any money?' Spicer asked.

'No sir. We lost everything.'

'No family, no uncles, aunts, cousins, friends who could help you with your legal fees?'

'No sir. What kinda legal fees?'

'We usually charge for reviewing cases and helping with the appeals.'

'I'm dead broke, sir.'

'I think we can help,' Beech said. Spicer didn't work on the appeals anyway. The man never finished high school.

'Sort of a pro bono case, wouldn't you say?' Yarber said to Beech.

'A pro what?' Spicer asked.

'Pro bono.'

'What's that?'

'Free legal work,' Beech said.

'Free legal work. Done by whom?'

'By lawyers,' Yarber explained. 'Every lawyer is expected to donate a few hours of his time to help people who can't afford to hire him.'

'It's part of the Old English common law,' Beech added, further clouding the issue.

'It never caught on over here, did it?' Spicer said.

'We'll review your case,' Yarber said to Buster. 'But please do not be optimistic.'

'Thank you.'

They left the cafeteria in a group, three ex-judges in green choir robes followed by a scared young inmate. Frightened, but also quite curious.

TWENTY-TWO

Brant's reply from Upper Darby, Pa., had an urgent tone to it:

Dear Ricky:
  Wow! What a photo! I'm coming down even sooner. I'll be there on April 20. Are you available? If so, we'll have the house to ourselves because my wife will stay here for another two weeks. Poor woman. We've been married for twenty-two years and she doesn't have a clue.
  Here's a picture of me. That's my Learjet in the background, one of my favorite toys. We'll buzz around in it if you want.
  Write me immediately, please.
                              Sincerely, Brant

There was still no last name, not that that was a problem. They would dig for it soon enough.

Spicer inspected the postmark, and for a passing moment thought about how quickly the mail was running between Jacksonville and Philadelphia. But the photo kept his attention. It was a four-by-six candid shot, very similar to an ad for a get-rich-quick scheme where the huckster is pictured with a proud smile, flanked by his jet, his Rolls, and possibly his latest wife. Brant was standing beside a plane, smiling, dressed neatly in tennis shorts and a sweater, with no Rolls in sight but with an attractive middle-aged woman next to him.

It was the first photo, in their growing collection, in which one of their pen pals had included his wife. Odd, thought Spicer, but then Brant had mentioned her in both letters. Nothing surprised him anymore. The scam would work forever because there was an endless supply of potential victims willing to ignore the risks.

Brant himself was fit and tanned, short dark hair with shades of gray, and a mustache. He was not particularly handsome, but what did Spicer care?

Why would a man with so much be so careless? Because he'd always taken chances and never been caught. Because it was a way of life. And after they squeezed him and took his money, Brant would slow down for a while. He'd avoid the personal ads, and the anonymous lovers. But an aggressive type like Brant would soon return to his old ways.

Spicer figured the thrill of finding random partners overshadowed the risks. He was still bothered by the fact that he, of all people, spent time each day trying to think like a homosexual.

Beech and Yarber read the letter and studied the photo. The small cramped room was completely silent. Could this be the big one?

'Reckon how much that jet cost,' Spicer said, and all three laughed. It was nervous laughter, as if they weren't sure they could believe it.

'A couple of million,' Beech said. Since he was from Texas, and had been married to a rich woman, the other two assumed he knew more about jets than they. 'It's a small Lear.'

Spicer would settle for a small Cessna, anything that would lift him off the ground and take him away. Yarber didn't want a plane. He wanted tickets, in first class where they brought you champagne and two menus and you had your choice of movies. First class over the ocean, far away from this country.

'Let's bust him,' Yarber said.

'How much?' asked Beech, still staring at the photo.

'At least a half a million,' Spicer said. 'And if we get that, we'll go back for more.'

They sat in silence, each playing with his portion of half a million dollars. Trevor's third was suddenly getting in the way. He'd take $167,000 off the top, leaving each of them $111,000. Not bad for prisoners, but it should be a helluva lot more. Why was the lawyer making so much?

'We're going to cut Trevor's fee,' Spicer announced. 'I've been thinking about this for some time. Beginning now, the money will be split four ways. He takes an equal share.'

'He won't do it,' Yarber said.

'He has no choice.'

'It's only fair,' Beech said. 'We're doing the work, and he's getting more than each of us. I say we cut it.'

'I'll do it Thursday.'

Two days later, Trevor arrived at Trumble just

after four with a particularly bad hangover, one deadened by neither the two-hour lunch nor the one-hour nap.

Joe Roy seemed particularly edgy. He passed across the outgoing mail, but held a large, red, oversized envelope. 'We're getting ready to bust this guy,' he said, tapping it on the table.

'Who is he?'

'Brant somebody, near Philadelphia. He's hiding behind the post office, so you need to flush him out.'

'How much?'

'A half a million bucks.'

Trevor's red eyes narrowed and his dry lips fell open. He did the math – $167,000 in his pocket. His sailing career was suddenly drawing closer. Perhaps he didn't need a full million bucks before he slammed his office door and left for the Caribbean. Maybe half that would do it. And he was getting so close.

'You're kidding,' he said, knowing that Spicer was not. Spicer had no sense of humor, and he certainly took his money seriously.

'No. And we're changing your percentage.'

'I'll be damned if we are. A deal's a deal.'

'Deals can always be changed. From now on you get the same piece we do. One fourth.'

'No way.'

'Then you're fired.'

'You can't fire me.'

'I just did. What, you think we can't find another crooked lawyer to run mail for us?'

'I know too much,' Trevor said, his cheeks flashing pink and his tongue suddenly parched.

247

'Don't overestimate yourself. You're not that valuable.'

'Yes I am. I know everything that's going on here.'

'And so do we, hotshot. Difference is, we're already in jail. You're the one with the most to lose. You play hardball with me and you'll be sittin on this side of the table.'

Bolts of pain shot through Trevor's forehead and he closed his eyes. He was in no condition to argue. Why had he stayed at Pete's so late last night? He had to be sharp when he met with Spicer. Instead, he was tired and half-drunk.

His head spun and he thought he might be sick again. He did the math. They were arguing over the difference between $167,000 and $125,000. Frankly, both sounded good to Trevor. He couldn't run the risk of being fired because he'd managed to alienate what few clients he had. He spent less time in the office; he wouldn't return their calls. He'd found a far richer source of income, so to hell with the small-time foot traffic along the beaches.

And he was no match for Spicer. The man had no conscience. He was mean and conniving and desperate to stash away as much money as possible.

'Are Beech and Yarber in favor of this?' he asked, knowing damned well they were, and knowing that even if they weren't he'd never know the difference.

'Sure. They're doing all the work. Why should you make more than them?'

It did seem a little unfair. 'Okay, okay,' Trevor said, still in pain. 'There's a good reason you're in prison.'

'Are you drinking too much?'

'No! Why do you ask?'

'I've known drunks. Lots of them. You look like hell.'

'Thanks. You take care of your business, I'll take care of mine.'

'It's a deal. But nobody wants a drunk for a lawyer. You're handling all our money, in an enterprise that's very illegal. A little loose talk in a bar and somebody starts asking questions.'

'I can handle myself.'

'Good. Watch your back too. We're squeezing people, making them hurt. If I were on the other end of our little sting, I'd be tempted to come down and try to get some answers before I coughed up the money.'

'They're too scared.'

'Keep your eyes open anyway. It's important for you to stay sober and alert.'

'Thank you very much. Anything else?'

'Yeah, I got some games for you.' On to the important stuff. Spicer opened a newspaper and they began making their bets.

Trevor bought a quart of beer at a country store on the edge of Trumble, and sipped it slowly as he puttered back to Jacksonville. He tried his best not to think of their money, but his thoughts were out of control. Between his account and their account, there was just over $250,000 sitting offshore, money he could take anytime he wanted. Add a half a million bucks to it, and, well, he just couldn't stop adding – $750,000!

He'd never get caught stealing dirty money; that was the beauty of it. The victims of the Brethren weren't complaining now because they were too ashamed. They weren't breaking any laws. They were just scared. The Brethren, on the other hand, were committing crimes. So who would they run to if their money disappeared?

He had to stop thinking such thoughts.

But how could they, the Brethren, catch him? He'd be on a sailboat drifting between islands they'd never heard of. And when they were finally released, would they have the energy and money and willpower to track him down? Of course not. They were old men. Beech would probably die at Trumble.

'Stop it,' he yelled at himself.

He walked to Beach Java for a triple-shot latte, and returned to his office determined to do something productive. He went online and found the names of several private investigators in Philadelphia. It was almost six when he began calling. The first two went to answering machines.

The third, to the offices of Ed Pagnozzi, was answered by the investigator himself. Trevor explained that he was a lawyer in Florida and needed a quick job in Upper Darby.

'Okay. What kinda job?'

'I'm trying to track some mail here,' Trevor said glibly. He'd done this enough to have it well rehearsed. 'Pretty big divorce case. I got the wife, and I think the husband's hiding money. Anyway,

I need somebody up there to find out who's renting a certain post office box.'

'You gotta be kiddin.'

'Well, no, I'm pretty serious about this.'

'You want me to go snoopin around a post office?'

'It's just basic detective work.'

'Look, pal, I'm very busy. Call somebody else.'

Pagnozzi was gone, off to more important matters. Trevor cursed him under his breath and punched the next number. He tried two more, and hung up on both when the machines answered. He'd try again tomorrow.

Across the street, Klockner listened to the brief chat with Pagnozzi one more time, then called Langley. The final piece of the puzzle had just fallen into place, and Mr. Deville would want to know it immediately.

While dependent on fancy words and smooth talk and compelling photos, the scam was basic in its operation. It preyed on human desire and it paid off by sheer terror. Its mechanics had been solved by Mr. Garbe's file, and by the Brant White reverse scam, and by the other letters they'd intercepted.

Only one question had gone unanswered: When aliases were used to rent post office boxes, how did the Brethren find the real names of their victims? The phone calls to Philadelphia had just given them their answer. Trevor simply hired a local private detective, evidently one with less business than Mr. Pagnozzi.

It was almost ten when Deville was finally

cleared to see Teddy. The North Koreans had shot another American soldier in the DMZ, and Teddy had been dealing with the fallout since noon. He was eating cheese and crackers and sipping a Diet Coke when Deville entered the bunker.

After a quick briefing, Teddy said, 'That's what I thought.'

His instincts were uncanny, especially with hindsight.

'This means, of course, that the lawyer could hire a local here to somehow uncover the real identity of Al Konyers,' Deville said.

'But how?'

'We can think of several ways. First is surveillance, the same way we caught Lake sneaking to his box. Watch the post office. That's somewhat risky because there's a good chance you'll get noticed. Second is bribery. Five hundred bucks cash to a postal clerk will work in a lot of places. Third is computer records. This is not highly classified material. One of our guys just hacked his way into the central post office in Evansville, Indiana, and got the list of all box leases. It was a random test, took him about an hour. That's high tech. Low tech is to simply break into the post office at night and have a look around.'

'How much does he pay for this?'

'Don't know, but we'll find out soon when he hires an investigator.'

'He has to be neutralized.'

'Eliminated?'

'Not yet. I'd rather buy him first. He is our window. If he's working for us, then we know everything and we keep him away from Konyers. Put together a plan.'

'And for his removal?'

'Go ahead and plan it, but we're in no hurry. Not yet anyway.'

TWENTY-THREE

The South did indeed like Aaron Lake, with his love of guns and bombs and tough talk and military readiness. He flooded Florida, Mississippi, Tennessee, Oklahoma, and Texas with ads that were even bolder than his first ones. And Teddy's people flooded the same states with more cash than had ever changed hands the night before an election.

The result was another rout, with Lake getting 260 of the 312 delegates at stake on little Super Tuesday. After the votes were counted on March 14, 1,301 of the 2,066 total delegates had been decided. Lake held a commanding lead over Governor Tarry – 801 to 390.

The race was over, barring an unforeseen catastrophe.

Buster's first job at Trumble was running a Weed Eater, for which he earned a starting wage of twenty cents an hour. It was either that or mopping floors in the cafeteria. He chose the weed eating because he liked the sun and vowed that his skin would not turn as pale as some of the bleached-out inmates he'd seen. Nor would he get fat like some of them. This is prison, he kept telling himself, how can they be so fat?

He worked hard in the bright sun, kept his tan, vowed to keep his flat stomach, and tried gamely to go through the motions. But after ten days Buster knew he would not last for forty-eight years.

Forty-eight years! He couldn't begin to comprehend such time. Who could?

He'd cried for the first forty-eight hours.

Thirteen months earlier he and his father were running their dock, working on boats, fishing twice a week in the Gulf.

He worked slowly around the concrete edge of the basketball court where a rowdy game was in progress. Then to the big sandbox where they sometimes played volleyball. In the distance, a solitary figure was walking around the track, an old-looking man with his long gray hair in a ponytail and with no shirt. He looked vaguely familiar. Buster worked both edges of a sidewalk, making his way to the track.

The lone walker was Finn Yarber, one of the judges who was trying to help him. He moved around the oval at a steady pace, head level, back and shoulders stiff and erect, not a picture of athleticism but not bad for a sixty-year-old man. He was barefoot and barebacked, sweat rolling off his leathery skin.

Buster turned off the Weed Eater and placed it on the ground. When Yarber drew near, he saw the kid and said, 'Hello, Buster. How's it goin?'

'I'm still here,' the kid said. 'Mind if I walk with you?'

'Not at all,' Finn said without breaking stride.

They did an eighth of a mile before Buster could find the courage to say, 'So how about my appeals?'

'Judge Beech is lookin at it. The sentencing appears to be in order, which is not good news. A lot of guys get here with flaws in their sentencing, and we can usually file a couple of motions and knock off a few years. Not so with you. I'm sorry.'

'That's okay. What's a few when you have forty-eight? Twenty-eight, thirty-eight, forty-eight, what does it matter?'

'You still have your appeals. There's a chance the decision can be overturned.'

'A slim chance.'

'You can't give up hope, Buster,' Yarber said, without the slightest trace of conviction. Keeping some measure of hope meant keeping some faith in the system. Yarber certainly had none. He'd been framed and railroaded by the same law he'd once defended.

But at least Yarber had enemies, and he could almost understand why they came after him.

This poor boy had done nothing wrong. Yarber had read enough of his file to believe Buster was completely innocent, another victim of an over-zealous prosecutor.

It appeared, at least from the record, that the kid's father may have been hiding some cash, but nothing serious. Nothing to warrant a 160-page conspiracy indictment.

Hope. He felt like a hypocrite for even thinking the word. The appeals courts were now packed with right-wing law and order types, and it was a rare drug case that got reversed. They'd slamdunk the kid's appeal with a rubber stamp, and tell themselves they were making the streets safer.

The biggest coward had been the trial judge. Prosecutors are expected to indict the world, but the judges are supposed to weed out the fringe defendants. Buster and his father should've been separated from the Colombians and their cohorts, and sent home before the trial began.

Now one was dead. The other was ruined. And nobody in the federal criminal system gave a damn. It was just another drug conspiracy.

At the first curve of the oval, Yarber slowed, then stopped. He looked off in the distance, beyond a grassy field to the edge of a treeline. Buster looked too. For ten days he'd been looking at the perimeter of Trumble, and seeing what wasn't there – fences, razor wire, guard towers.

'Last guy who left here,' Yarber said, gazing at nothing, 'left through those trees. They're thick for a few miles, then you come to a country road.'

'Who was he?'

'A guy named Tommy Adkins. He was a banker in North Carolina, got caught with his hand in the cookie jar.'

'What happened to him?'

'He went crazy and walked away one day. He was gone six hours before anybody knew it. A month later they found him in a motel room in Cocoa Beach, not the cops but the maids. He was curled in the fetal position on the floor, naked, suckin his thumb, his mind completely gone. They put him in some mental joint.'

'Six hours, huh?'

'Yeah, it happens about once a year. Somebody just walks away. They notify the cops in your hometown, put your name in the national computers, the usual drill.'

'How many get caught?'

'Almost all.'

'Almost.'

'Yeah, but they get caught because they do dumb things. Get drunk in bars. Drive cars with no taillights. Go see their girlfriends.'

'So if you had a brain you could pull it off?'

'Sure. Careful planning, a little cash, it would be easy.'

They began walking again, a bit slower. 'Tell me something, Mr. Yarber,' Buster said. 'If you were facing forty-eight years, would you take a walk?'

'Yes.'

'But I don't have a dime.'

'I do.'

'Then you'll help me.'

'We'll see. Give it some time. Settle in here. They're watchin you a bit closer because you're new, but with time they'll forget about you.'

Buster actually smiled. His sentence had just been reduced dramatically.

'You know what happens if you get caught?' Yarber said.

'Yeah, they add some more years. Big deal. Maybe I'll get fifty-eight. No sir, if I get caught, I blow my brains out.'

'That's what I'd do. You have to be prepared to leave the country.'

'And go where?'

'Go someplace where you look like the locals, and where they don't extradite to the U.S.'

'Anyplace in particular?'

'Argentina or Chile. You speak any Spanish?'

'No.'

'Start learnin. We have Spanish lessons here, you know. Some of the Miami boys teach them.'

They walked a lap in silence as Buster reconsidered his future. His feet were lighter, his shoulders straighter, and he couldn't keep a grin off his face.

'Why are you helping me?' he asked.

'Because you're twenty-three years old. Too young and too innocent. You've been screwed by the system, Buster. You have the right to fight back any way you can. Do you have a girlfriend?'

'Sort of.'

'Forget about her. She'll only get you in trouble. Besides, you think she'll wait forty-eight years?'

'She said she would.'

'She's lyin. She's already playin the field. Forget about her, unless you want to get caught.'

Yeah, he's probably right, thought Buster. He'd yet to get a letter from her, and though she lived only four hours away she hadn't made it to Trumble. They'd talked twice on the phone, and all she seemed to care about was whether he'd been attacked.

'Any kids?' asked Yarber.

'No. Not that I know of.'

'What about your mother?'

'She died when I was very young. My dad raised me. It was just the two of us.'

'Then you're the perfect guy to walk away.'

'I'd like to leave now.'

259

'Be patient. Let's plan it carefully.'

Another lap, and Buster wanted to sprint. He couldn't think of a damned thing he'd miss in Pensacola. He'd made As and Bs in Spanish in high school, and while he couldn't remember any of it, he hadn't struggled with the material. He'd pick it up fast. He'd take the courses and hang out with the Latins.

The more he walked the more he wanted his conviction to be affirmed. And the quicker the better. If it got reversed, he'd be forced to have another trial, and he had no confidence in the next jury.

Buster wanted to run, starting over there in the grassy field, to the treeline, through the woods to the country road where he wasn't sure what to do next. But if an insane banker could walk away and make it to Cocoa Beach, so could he.

'Why haven't you walked away?' he asked Yarber.

'I've thought about it. But in five years they'll let me go. I can last that long. I'll be sixty-five, in good health, with a life expectancy of sixteen years. That's what I'm livin for, Buster, the last sixteen years. I don't wanna be lookin over my shoulder.'

'Where will you go?'

'Don't know yet. Maybe a little village in the Italian countryside. Maybe the mountains of Peru. I've got the whole world to choose from, and I spend hours every day just dreamin about it.'

'So you have plenty of money?'

'No, but I'm gettin there.'

That raised a number of questions, but Buster

let them pass. He was learning that in prison you kept most of your questions to yourself.

When Buster was tired of walking, he stopped near his Weed Eater. 'Thanks, Mr. Yarber,' he said.

'No problem. Just keep it between the two of us.'

'Sure. I'm ready whenever you are.'

Finn was off, pacing another lap, his shorts now soaked with sweat, his gray ponytail dripping with moisture. Buster watched him go, then for a second looked across the grassy field, into the trees.

At that moment, he could see all the way to South America.

261

TWENTY-FOUR

For two long, hard months Aaron Lake and Governor Tarry had gone head to head, toe to toe, coast to coast, in twenty-six states with almost 25 million votes cast. They'd pushed themselves with eighteen-hour days, brutal schedules, relentless travel, the typical madness of a presidential race.

Yet they'd worked just as hard to avoid a face-to-face debate. Tarry didn't want one in the early primaries because he was the front-runner. He had the organization, the cash, the favorable polls. Why legitimize the opposition? Lake didn't want one because he was a newcomer to the national scene, a novice at highstakes campaigning, and besides it was much easier to hide behind a script and a friendly camera and make ads whenever needed. The risks of a live debate were simply too high.

Teddy didn't like the thought of one either.

But campaigns change. Front-runners fade, small issues become big ones, the press can create a crisis simply out of boredom.

Tarry decided he needed a debate because he was broke, and losing one primary after another. 'Aaron Lake is trying to buy this election,' he said over and over. 'And I want to confront him, man to man.' It sounded good, and the press had beaten it to death.

'He's running from a debate,' Tarry declared, and the pack liked that too.

'The governor's been dodging a debate since Michigan' was Lake's standard response.

And so for three weeks they played the he's-running-from-me game until their people quietly worked out the details.

Lake was reluctant, but he also needed a forum. Though he was winning week after week, he was rolling over an opponent who'd been fading for a long time. His polls and D-PAC's polls showed a great deal of voter interest in him, but mainly because he was new and handsome and seemingly electable.

Unknown to outsiders, the polls also showed some very soft areas. The first was on the question of Lake's single-issue campaign. Defense spending can excite the voters for only so long, and there was great concern, in the polls, about where Lake stood on other issues.

Second, Lake was still five points behind the Vice President in their hypothetical November matchup. The voters were tired of the Vice President, but at least they knew who he was. Lake remained a mystery to many. Also, the two would debate several times prior to November. Lake, who had the nomination in hand, needed the experience.

Tarry didn't help matters with his constant query, 'Who is Aaron Lake?' With some of his few remaining funds, he authorized the printing of

bumper stickers with the now famous question –
Who is Aaron Lake?

(It was a question Teddy asked himself almost
every hour, but for a different reason.)

The setting of the debate was in Pennsylvania at
a small Lutheran college with a cozy auditorium,
good acoustics and light, a controllable crowd.
Even the smallest of details were haggled over by
the two camps, but because both sides now needed
a debate agreements were eventually reached. The
precise format had nearly caused fistfights, but
once ironed out it gave everybody something. The
media got three reporters on the stage to ask direct
questions during one segment. The spectators got
twenty minutes to ask about anything, with nothing screened. Tarry, a lawyer, wanted five minutes
for opening remarks and a ten-minute closing
statement. Lake wanted thirty minutes of one-on-
one debate with Tarry, no holds barred, no one to
referee, just the two of them slugging it out
without rules. This had terrified the Tarry camp,
and had almost broken the deal.

The moderator was a local public radio figure,
and when he said, 'Good evening, and welcome to
the first and only debate between Governor Wen-
dell Tarry and Congressman Aaron Lake,' an
estimated 18 million people were watching.

Tarry wore a navy suit his wife had selected,
with the standard blue shirt and the standard red
and blue tie. Lake wore a dashing light brown suit,
a white shirt with a spread collar, and a tie of red
and maroon and a half-dozen other colors. The
entire ensemble had been put together by a fashion
consultant, and was designed to complement the

colors of the set. Lake's hair had received a tinting. His teeth had been bleached. He'd spent four hours in a tanning bed. He looked thin and fresh, and anxious to be onstage.

Governor Tarry was himself a handsome man. Though he was only four years older than Lake, the campaign was taking a heavy toll. His eyes were tired and red. He'd gained a few pounds, especially in his face. When he began his opening remarks, beads of sweat popped up along his forehead and glistened in the lights.

Conventional wisdom held that Tarry had more to lose because he'd already lost so much. Early in January, he'd been declared, by prophets as prescient as *Time* magazine, to have the nomination within his grasp. He'd been running for three years. His campaign was built on grassroots support and shoe leather. Every precinct captain and poll worker in Iowa and New Hampshire had drunk coffee with him. His organization was impeccable.

Then came Lake with his slick ads and single-issue magic.

Tarry badly needed either a stunning performance by himself, or a major gaffe by Lake.

He got neither. By a flip of the coin, he was chosen to go first. He stumbled badly in his opening remarks as he moved stiffly around the stage, trying desperately to look at ease but forgetting what his notes said. Sure he'd once been a lawyer, but his specialty had been securities. As he forgot one point after another, he returned to his common theme – Mr. Lake here is trying to buy this election because he has nothing to say. A

265

nasty tone developed quickly. Lake smiled handsomely; water off a duck's back.

Tarry's weak beginning emboldened Lake, gave him a shot of confidence, and convinced him to stay behind the podium where it was safe and where his notes were. He began by saying that he wasn't there to throw mud, that he had respect for Governor Tarry, but they had just listened to him speak for five minutes and eleven seconds and he'd said nothing positive.

He then ignored his opponent, and briefly covered three issues that needed to be discussed. Tax relief, welfare reform, and the trade deficit. Not a word about defense.

The first question from the panel of reporters was directed at Lake, and it dealt with the budget surplus. What should be done with the money? It was a soft pitch, lobbed by a friendly reporter, and Lake was all over it. Save Social Security, he answered, then in an impressive display of financial straight talk he outlined precisely how the money should be used. He gave figures and percentages and projections, all from memory.

Governor Tarry's response was simply to cut taxes. Give the money back to the people who'd earned it.

Few points were scored during the questioning. Both candidates were well prepared. The surprise was that Lake, the man who wanted to own the Pentagon, was so well versed in all other issues.

The debate settled into the usual give and take. The questions from the spectators were thoroughly predictable. The fireworks began when the candidates were allowed to quiz one another. Tarry went first, and, as expected, asked Lake if he was trying to buy the election.

'You weren't concerned about money when you had more than everybody else,' Lake shot back, and the audience came to life.

'I didn't have fifty million dollars,' Tarry said.

'Neither do I,' Lake said. 'It's more like sixty million, and it's coming in faster than we can count it. It's coming from working people and middle-income folks. Eighty-one percent of our contributors are people earning less than forty thousand dollars a year. Something wrong with those people, Governor Tarry?'

'There should be a limit on how much a candidate should spend.'

'I agree. And I've voted for limits eight different times in Congress. You, on the other hand, never mentioned limits until you ran out of money.'

Governor Tarry looked Quayle-like at the camera, the frozen stare of a deer in headlights. A few of Lake's people in the audience laughed just loud enough to be heard.

The beads of sweat returned to the governor's forehead as he shuffled his oversized notecards. He wasn't actually a sitting governor, but he still preferred the title. In fact, it had been nine years since the voters of Indiana sent him packing, after only one term. Lake saved this ammo for a few minutes.

Tarry then asked why Lake had voted for fifty-four new taxes during his fourteen years in Congress.

'I don't recall fifty-four taxes,' Lake said. 'But a lot of them were on tobacco and alcohol and gambling. I also voted against increases in personal income taxes, corporate income taxes, federal withholding taxes, and Social Security taxes. I'm not ashamed of that record. And speaking of taxes, Governor, during your four years in Indiana, how do you explain the fact that individual tax rates increased by an average of six percent?'

No quick response was forthcoming, so Lake plowed ahead. 'You want to cut federal spending, yet in your four years in Indiana state spending increased eighteen percent. You want to cut corporate income taxes, yet during your four years in Indiana, corporate income taxes went up three percent. You want to end welfare, yet when you were governor forty thousand people were added to the welfare rolls in Indiana. How do you explain this?'

Each blow from Indiana drew blood, and Tarry was on the ropes. 'I disagree with your figures, sir,' he managed to say. 'We created jobs in Indiana.'

'Is that so?' Lake said sardonically. He pulled up a sheet of paper from his podium as if it were a federal indictment against Governor Tarry. 'Maybe you did, but during your four years almost sixty thousand ex-workers signed up for unemployment,' he announced without looking at the paper.

Sure Tarry had had a bad four years as governor, but the economy had gone south on him. He had explained all this before and he'd love to do it again, but, gosh, he had only a few short minutes on national television. Surely he shouldn't waste it splitting hairs about the past. 'This race is not about Indiana,' he said, managing a smile. 'It's about all fifty states. It's about working people everywhere who'll be expected to pay more taxes to finance your gold-plated defense projects, Mr. Lake. You can't be serious about doubling the Pentagon's budget.'

Lake looked hard at his opponent. 'I'm very serious about it. And if you wanted a strong military, you'd be serious too.' He then rattled off a string of statistics that went on and on, each building on the other. It was conclusive proof of our military unreadiness, and when he finally finished our armed forces would've been hard-pressed to invade Bermuda.

But Tarry had a study to the contrary, a thick glossy manuscript produced by a think tank run by ex-admirals. He waved it for the cameras and argued such a buildup was unnecessary. The world was at peace, with the exception of a few civil and regional wars, disputes in which we had no national interest, and the United States was by far the only superpower left standing. The cold war was history. The Chinese were decades away from achieving anything remotely resembling parity. Why burden the taxpayers with tens of billions in new hardware?

They argued for a while about how to pay for it, and Tarry scored minor points. But they were on Lake's turf, and as the issue dragged on it became evident that Lake knew far more than the governor.

Lake saved his best for last. During his ten-minute recap, he returned to Indiana and continued the miserable list of Tarry's failures there during his sole term. The theme was simple, and very effective: If he can't run Indiana, how can he run the entire nation?

'I'm not knocking the people of Indiana,' Lake said at one point. 'In fact, they had the wisdom to return Mr. Tarry to private life after only one term. They knew he was doing a terrible job. That's why only thirty-eight percent of them voted for him when he asked for four more years. Thirty-eight percent! We should trust the people of Indiana. They know this man. They've seen him govern. They made a mistake, and they got rid of him. It would be sad if the rest of the country now made the same mistake.'

The instant polls gave a solid win to Lake. D-PAC called a thousand voters immediately after the debate. Almost 70 percent thought Lake was the better of the two.

On a late flight from Pittsburgh to Wichita, several bottles of champagne were opened on Air Lake and a small party began. The debate poll results were flowing in, each better than the last, and the mood was victorious.

Lake hadn't banned alcohol on his Boeing, but he had discouraged it. If and when a member of his staff took a drink, it was always a quick one, and always on the sly. But some moments called for a little celebration. He enjoyed two glasses of champagne himself. Only his closest people were present. He thanked them and congratulated them, and just for fun they watched the highlights of the debate while another bottle was opened. They paused the video each time Governor Tarry looked particularly puzzled, and the laughs grew louder.

But the party was brief; fatigue hit hard. These were people who'd been sleeping five hours a night for weeks. Most had slept even less the night before the debate. Lake himself was exhausted. He finished a third glass, the first time in many years he'd drunk that much, and settled into his massive leather recliner with a heavy quilt. Bodies sprawled everywhere in the darkness of the cabin.

He couldn't sleep; he seldom did on airplanes. There were too many things to think and worry about. It was impossible not to savor the victory in the debate, and as he kicked around under the quilt Lake repeated his best lines of the night. He had been brilliant, something he'd never admit to anyone else.

The nomination was his. He would be showcased at the convention, then for four months he and the Vice President would slug it out in the grandest of American traditions.

He turned on the small overhead reading light. Someone else was reading down the aisle, near the flight deck. Another insomniac, with the only other light on in the cabin. People were actually snoring under their blankets, the sleep of hurried young people running on fumes.

Lake opened his briefcase and pulled out a small leather folder filled with his personal correspondence cards. They were four by six, heavy stock, off-white in color, and in light black Old English print had the name of 'Aaron Lake' printed at the top. With a thick, antique Mont Blanc pen, Lake scribbled a brief word to his college roommate, now a professor of Latin at a small college in Texas. He wrote a thank-you to the moderator of the debate, and one to his Oregon coordinator. Lake loved Clancy novels. He'd just finished the latest one, the thickest yet, and he wrote the author a complimentary note.

Sometimes his notes ran long, and for this reason he had plain cards, same size and color but without his name. He looked around to make sure everyone was sound asleep, and he quickly wrote:

Dear Ricky:
   I think it's best if we end our correspondence. I wish you well with your rehab.

                              Sincerely, Al

He addressed an unmarked envelope. The address of Aladdin North came from memory. Then he returned to his personalized cards and wrote a series of thank-you notes to serious contributors. He wrote twenty of them before fatigue finally settled in. With the cards still in front of him, and his reading light still on, he yielded to exhaustion and within minutes was napping.

He'd slept less than an hour when panicked voices awakened him. Lights were on, people were moving, and there was smoke in the cabin. A buzzer of some sort was ringing loudly from the cockpit, and once he got his bearings Lake realized the nose of the Boeing was pointed downward. Total panic set in quickly as the air masks dropped from above. After years of half-watching flight attendants give their routine demonstrations before takeoff, the damned masks were actually going to be used. Lake snapped his into place and inhaled mightily.

The pilot announced they were making an emergency landing in St. Louis. The lights flickered, and someone actually screamed. Lake wanted to move about the cabin and reassure everyone, but the mask wouldn't move with him. In the section behind him were two dozen reporters and about that many Secret Service people.

Maybe the air masks didn't drop back there, he thought, then felt guilty.

The smoke got thicker, and the lights faded. After the onset of panic, Lake managed a rational thought or two, if only for a brief second. He quickly gathered the correspondence cards and envelopes. The one to Ricky got his attention just long enough to place it in the envelope to Aladdin North. He sealed it, and stuffed the folder back into his briefcase. The lights flickered again, then went out for good.

The smoke burned their eyes and warmed their faces. The plane was descending at a rapid pace. Warning bells and sirens shrieked from the flight deck.

This can't be happening, Lake told himself as he gripped his armrests. I'm about to be elected President of the United States. He thought of Rocky Marciano, Buddy Holly, Otis Redding, Thurman Munson, Senator Tower of Texas, Mickey Leland from Houston, a friend of his. And JFK, Jr., and Ron Brown.

The air suddenly turned cold and the smoke

dissipated rapidly. They were below ten thousand feet, and the pilot had somehow managed to vent the cabin. The plane leveled and from the windows they could see lights on the ground.

'Please continue to use the oxygen masks,' the pilot said in the darkness. 'We'll be on the ground in a few minutes. The landing should be uneventful.'

Uneventful? He must be kidding, thought Lake. He needed to find the nearest toilet.

Relief settled uneasily through the plane. Just before it touched down, Lake saw the flashing lights of a hundred emergency vehicles. They bounced a little, a typical landing, and when they stopped at the end of the runway the emergency doors flew open.

A controlled stampede occurred, and within minutes they were grabbed by rescue personnel and rushed to ambulances. The fire, in the luggage area of the Boeing, was still spreading when they landed. As Lake jogged away from the plane, firemen rushed toward it. Smoke boiled from under the wings.

Just a few more minutes, Lake said to himself, and we would be dead.

'That was a close one, sir,' a paramedic said as they raced away. Lake clutched his briefcase, with his little letters inside, and for the first time went rigid with horror.

The near miss, and the obligatory nonstop media barrage after it, probably did little to boost Lake's popularity. But the publicity certainly didn't hurt. He was everywhere on the morning news, one moment talking about his decisive victory over Governor Tarry in the debate, and the next giving details of what could've been his last flight.

'I think I'll take the bus for a while,' he said with a laugh. He used as much humor as he could muster, and took the high road of aw-shucks-it-was-nothing. His staff members had different stories, of breathing oxygen in the dark while the smoke grew thicker and hotter. And the reporters on board were eager sources of information, providing detailed narratives of the terror.

Teddy Maynard watched it all from his bunker. Three of his men were on the plane, and one had called him from the hospital in St. Louis.

It was a perplexing event. On the one hand, he still believed in the importance of a Lake presidency. The security of the nation depended on it.

On the other hand, a crash wouldn't have been a catastrophe. Lake and his double life would be gone. A huge headache wiped out. Governor Tarry had learned firsthand the power of unlimited cash. Teddy could cut a deal with him in time to win in November.

But Lake was still standing, taller than ever now. His tanned face was on the front of every newspaper and close to every camera. His campaign had progressed far faster than Teddy had dreamed.

So why was there so much angst in the bunker? Why was Teddy not celebrating?

Because he had yet to solve the puzzle of the Brethren. And he couldn't simply start killing people.

TWENTY-FIVE

The team in Documents used the same laptop they'd used to write the last letter to Ricky. This letter was composed by Deville himself, and approved by Mr. Maynard. It read:

Dear Ricky:
   Good news about your release to the halfway house in Baltimore. Give me a few days and I think I'll have a full-time job lined up for you there. It's a clerical position, not a lot of money, but a pretty good place to start.
   I suggest we go a bit slower than you want. Maybe a nice lunch at first, then we'll see where things go. I'm not the type to rush in.
   Hope you're doing well. I'll write you next week with the details of the job. Hang in there.

                                        Best Wishes, Al

Only the 'Al' was handwritten. A D.C. postmark was applied, and the letter was flown and hand-delivered to Klockner in Neptune Beach.
Trevor happened to be in Fort Lauderdale,

oddly enough tending to legitimate legal business, and so the letter sat in the Aladdin North box for two days. When he returned, exhausted, he stopped by his office just long enough to commence a nasty argument with Jan, then stormed out, got back in his car, and went straight to the post office. To his delight, the box was full. He sorted out the junk mail, then drove a half mile to the Atlantic Beach post office and checked the box for Laurel Ridge, Percy's fancy rehab spa.

Once all the mail was collected, and much to the dismay of Klockner, Trevor left for Trumble. He made one call en route, to his bookie. He'd lost $2,500 in three days on hockey, a sport Spicer knew nothing about and refused to bet on. Trevor was picking his own favorites, with predictable results.

Spicer didn't answer the page at the courtyard at Trumble, so Beech met with Trevor in the attorney-conference room. They did their mail swap – eight letters going out, fourteen coming in.

'What about Brant in Upper Darby?' Beech asked, flipping through the envelopes.

'What about him?'

'Who is he? We're ready to bust him.'

'I'm still searching. I've been out of town for a few days.'

'Get it done, okay. This guy could be the biggest fish yet.'

'I'll do it tomorrow.'

Beech had no Vegas lines to ponder and he didn't want to play cards. Trevor left after twenty minutes.

★

Long after they should've eaten dinner, and long after the library should've been closed, the Brethren remained locked in their little room, saying little, avoiding eye contact with one another, each staring at the walls, deep in thought.

On the table were three letters. One was from Al's laptop, postmarked two days earlier in D.C. One was Al's handwritten note ending his correspondence with Ricky, postmarked from St. Louis, three days earlier. These two conflicted sharply, and were obviously written by different people. Someone was tampering with their mail.

The third letter had stopped them cold. They'd read it over and over, one by one, collectively, in silence, in unison. They'd picked at its corners, held it up to the light, even smelled it. There was a very faint smoky odor, same as the envelope and the note from Al to Ricky.

Handwritten in ink, it was dated April 18, at 1:20 A.M., and addressed to a woman named Carol.

Dear Carol:
What a great night! The debate couldn't have gone better, thanks in part to you and the Pennsylvania volunteers. Many thanks! Let's push harder and win this thing. We're ahead in Pennsylvania, let's stay there. See you next week.

It was signed by Aaron Lake. The card had his name personalized across the top. The handwriting was identical to that on the terse note Al had sent Ricky.

The envelope was addressed to Ricky at Aladdin North, and when Beech opened it he did not notice the second card stuck behind the first. Then it fell on the table, and when he picked it up he saw the name 'Aaron' Lake engraved in black.

That had happened sometime around 4 P.M., not long after Trevor had left. For almost five hours they'd studied the mail, and they were now almost certain that (a) the laptop letter was a fake, with the name 'Al' signed by someone who was quite good at forging; (b) the forged 'Al' signature was virtually identical to the original 'Al,' so the forger at some point had gained access to Ricky's correspondence with Al; (c) the notes to Ricky and Carol were handwritten by Aaron Lake; and (d) the one to Carol had obviously been sent to them by mistake.

Above all, Al Konyers was really Aaron Lake.

Their little scam had snared the most famous politician in the country.

Other, less important pieces of evidence also pointed toward Lake. His front was a mailbox service in the D.C. area, a place where Congressman Lake spent almost all of his time. Being a high-profile elected official, subject to the whims of voters every so often, he would certainly hide behind an alias. And he'd use a machine with a printer to hide his handwriting. Al had not sent a photograph, another sign that he had a lot to conceal.

They'd checked recent newspapers in the library to get the dates straight. The handwritten notes had been mailed from St. Louis the day after the debate, when Lake was there because his airplane had caught fire.

The timing seemed perfect for Lake to call off the letters. He'd started the correspondence before he entered the race. In three months he'd taken the country by storm and become very famous. Now, he had so much to lose.

Slowly, with no concern for time, they built their case against Aaron Lake. And when it looked airtight, they tried to break it down. The most compelling counterpoint came from Finn Yarber.

Suppose, he said, someone on Lake's staff had access to his stationery? Not a bad question, and one they'd kicked around for an hour. Wouldn't Al Konyers do such a thing in order to hide himself? What if he lived in the D.C. area and worked for Lake? Suppose Lake, a very busy man, trusted this assistant to write personal notes for him. Yarber couldn't remember allowing an assistant such authority back when he was Chief Justice. Beech had never let anyone write his personal notes. Spicer had never fooled with such nonsense. That's what phones were for.

But Yarber and Beech had never known the stress and fury of anything remotely similar to a presidential campaign. They'd been busy men in their times, they reflected with sadness, but nothing like Lake.

Say it was an assistant to Lake. So far he had a perfect cover because he'd told them almost nothing. No photo. Only the vaguest details about career and family. He liked old movies and Chinese food, and that was about all they'd extracted. Konyers was on their list of pen pals to soon dispose of because he was too timid. Why, then, would he call off the relationship at this moment?

There was no ready answer.

And the argument was a long shot anyway. Beech and Yarber concluded that no man in Lake's position, someone with a good chance of becoming President of the United States, would allow anyone else to write and sign personal notes. Lake had a hundred staff members to type letters and memos, all of which could be signed by him at a rapid clip.

Spicer had posed a more serious question. Why would Lake run the risk of a handwritten note? His prior letters had been typed on plain white paper, and mailed in a plain white envelope. They could spot a coward by his choice of stationery, and Lake was as fainthearted as anyone who'd answered their ad. The campaign, rich as it was, had plenty of word processors and typewriters and laptops, no doubt the latest in technology.

To find the answer, they went back to the little evidence they had. The letter to Carol had been written at 1:20 A.M. According to a newspaper, the emergency landing happened around 2:15, less than an hour later.

'He wrote it on the plane,' Yarber said. 'It was late, the plane was filled with people, almost sixty according to the paper, these people were exhausted, and maybe he couldn't get his hands on a computer.'

'Then why not wait?' asked Spicer. He'd proved to be excellent at asking questions no one, especially him, could answer.

'He made a mistake. He thought he was being smart, and he probably was. Somehow the mail got mixed.'

'Look at the big picture,' Beech said. 'The nomination is in the bag. He's just wiped out his only opponent, before a national audience, and he's finally convinced that his name will be on the ballot in November. But he's got this secret. He's got Ricky, and he's been thinking for weeks about what to do with Ricky. The boy's going to be released, he wants to have a rendezvous, etc. Lake feels the pressure on both fronts – from Ricky, and from the realization that he might just be elected President. So he decides to stiff Ricky. He writes a note that has one chance in a billion of getting screwed up, then the plane catches on fire. He makes a small mistake, but it turns into a monster.'

'And he doesn't know it,' Yarber added. 'Yet.'

Beech's theory settled in. They absorbed it in the heavy stillness of their little room. The gravity of their discovery weighed down their words and thoughts. The hours passed, and it slowly sank in.

For the next great question they grappled with the baffling reality that someone was meddling with their mail. Who? And why would anyone want to? How had they intercepted the letters? The puzzle seemed hopeless.

Again, they argued the scenario that the culprit was someone very close to Lake, perhaps an assistant with access who'd stumbled across the letters. And maybe he was trying to protect Lake from Ricky by commandeering the correspond-ence, with the goal of somehow, someday ending the relationship.

But there were too many unknowns to build any evidence. They scratched their heads and bit their nails, and finally admitted they would have to sleep on it. They couldn't plot the next move because the situation before them had more riddles than answers.

They slept little, and they were red-eyed and unshaved when they reconvened just after 6 A.M. with black coffee steaming from Styrofoam cups. They locked the door, pulled out the letters, placed them exactly where they'd been the night before, and began thinking.

'I think we should scope out the box in Chevy Chase,' said Spicer. 'It's easy, safe, usually quick. Trevor's been able to do it almost everywhere. If we know who's renting it, then a lot of questions will be answered.'

'It's hard to believe a man like Aaron Lake would be renting a box so he could hide letters like these,' Beech said.

'It's not the same Aaron Lake,' Yarber said. 'When he rented the box and began writing to Ricky, he was just a simple congressman, one of four hundred and thirty-five. You'd never heard of him. Now, things have changed dramatically.'

'And that's exactly why he's trying to end the relationship,' Spicer said. 'Things are very different now. He has much more to lose.'

The first step would be to get Trevor to investigate the post office box in Chevy Chase.

The second step was not as clear. They were concerned that Lake, and they assumed that Lake was Al and Al was Lake, might realize his screwup

283

with the letters. He had tens of millions of dollars (a fact they had certainly not overlooked), and he could easily use some of it to track down Ricky. Given the enormity of the stakes, Lake, if he did realize his mistake, would do almost anything to neutralize Ricky.

So they debated whether to write him a note, in which Ricky would beg Al not to slam the door like this. Ricky needed his friendship, nothing more, etc. The purpose would be to give the impression that everything was fine, nothing out of the ordinary. They hoped Lake would read it and scratch his head and wonder to himself just where, exactly, did that damned card to Carol get off to.

Such a note was unwise, they decided, because someone else was also reading the letters. Until they knew who, they couldn't risk any more contact with Al.

They finished their coffee and walked to the cafeteria. They ate alone, cereal and fruit and yogurt, healthy stuff because they would now live again on the outside. They walked four smoke-free laps together, at a leisurely pace, then returned to their chamber to finish the morning deep in thought.

Poor Lake. He was scrambling from one state to the next with fifty people in tow, late for three engagements at once, a dozen aides whispering in both ears. He had no time to think for himself.

And the Brethren had all day, hours upon hours to sit with their thoughts and their schemes. It was not an equal match.

TWENTY-SIX

There were two types of phones at Trumble; secured and unsecured. In theory, all calls made on unsecured lines were taped and subject to review by little elves in a booth somewhere who did nothing but listen to a million hours of useless chatter. In reality, about half the calls were actually taped, at random, and only about 5 percent were ever heard by anybody working for the prison. Not even the federal government could hire enough elves to handle all the listening.

Drug dealers had been known to direct their gangs from unsecured lines. Mafia bosses had been known to order hits on their rivals. The odds were very high against getting caught.

The secured lines were fewer in number, and by law could not be wired for surveillance. The secured calls went only to lawyers, and always with a guard posted nearby.

When Spicer's turn finally came to make a secured call, the guard had drifted away.

'Law office,' came the rude hello from the free world.

'Yes, this is Joe Roy Spicer, calling from the Trumble prison, and I need to speak with Trevor.'

'He's asleep.'

It was 1:30 P.M. 'Then wake the sonofabitch up,' Spicer growled.

'Hang on.'

'Would you please hurry? I'm on a prison phone.'

Joe Roy glanced around and wondered, not for the first time, what kind of lawyer they'd crawled in bed with.

'Why are you calling?' were Trevor's first words.

'Never mind. Wake your ass up and get to work. We need something done quickly.'

By now, the rental across from Trevor's office was buzzing. This was the first call from Trumble.

'What is it?'

'We need a box checked out. Quickly. And we want you to go supervise it. Don't leave until it's finished.'

'Why me?'

'Just do it, dammit, okay? This could be the biggest one yet.'

'Where is it?'

'Chevy Chase, Maryland. Write this down. Al Konyers, Box 455, Mailbox America, 39380 Western Avenue, Chevy Chase. Be very careful because this guy could have some friends, and there's a good chance someone else is already watching the box. Take some cash and hire a couple of good investigators.'

'I'm pretty busy around here.'

'Yeah, sorry I woke you up. Do it now, Trevor.

Leave today. And don't come back until you know who rented the box.'

'All right, all right.'

Spicer hung up, and Trevor put his feet back on his desk and appeared to return to his nap. But he was just contemplating matters. A moment later he yelled for Jan to check the flights to Washington.

In fourteen years as a field supervisor, Klockner had never seen so many people watch one person do so little. He made a quick call to Deville at Langley, and the rental sprang into action. It was time for the Wes and Chap show.

Wes walked across the street and entered the creaking and peeling door of Mr. L. Trevor Carson, Attorney and Counselor-at-Law. Wes was dressed in khakis and a pullover knit, loafers, no socks, and when Jan offered him her customary sneer she couldn't tell if he was a native or a tourist. 'What can I do for you?' she asked.

'I really need to see Mr. Carson,' Wes said with an air of desperation.

'Do you have an appointment?' she asked, as if her boss was so busy she couldn't keep track of his meetings.

'Well, no, it's sort of an emergency.'

'He's very busy,' she said, and Wes could almost hear the laughter from the rental.

'Please, I've got to talk to him.'

She rolled her eyes and didn't budge. 'What kind of matter is it?'

'I've just buried my wife,' he said, on the verge of tears, and Jan finally cracked a bit. 'I'm very sorry,' she said. Poor guy.

'She was killed in a car wreck on I–95, just north of Jacksonville.'

Jan was standing now and wishing she'd made fresh coffee. 'I'm so sorry,' she said. 'When did this happen?'

'Twelve days ago. A friend recommended Mr. Carson.'

Not much of a friend, she wanted to say. 'Would you like some coffee?' she asked, putting the top on her nail polish. Twelve days ago, she thought. Like all good legal secretaries, she read the newspapers with a keen eye on the accidents. Who knows, one might walk in the door.

Never Trevor's door. Until now.

'No, thanks,' Wes said. 'She was hit by a Texaco truck. The driver was drunk.'

'Oh my god!' she exclaimed, hand over her mouth. Even Trevor could handle this one.

Serious money, big fees, right here in the reception area, and that fool back there snoring off his lunch.

'He's in a deposition,' she said. 'Let me see if I can disturb him. Please have a seat.' She wanted to lock the front door so he couldn't escape.

'The name's Yates. Yates Newman,' he said, trying to help her.

'Oh yes,' she said, racing down the hall. She knocked politely on Trevor's door, then stepped inside. 'Wake up, asshole!' she hissed through clenched teeth, loud enough for Wes to hear up front.

'What is it?' Trevor said, standing, ready for a fistfight. He wasn't sleeping after all. He'd been reading an old *People*.

'Surprise! You have a client.'

'Who is it?'

'A man whose wife got run over by a Texaco truck twelve days ago. He wants to see you right now.'

'He's here?'

'Yep. Hard to believe, isn't it? Three thousand lawyers in Jacksonville and this poor guy falls through the cracks. Said a friend recommended you.'

'What'd you tell him?'

'I told him he needed to find new friends.'

'No, really, what did you tell him?'

'That you're in a deposition.'

'I haven't had a deposition in eight years. Send him back.'

'Be cool. I'll make him some coffee. Act like you're finishing some important stuff back here. Why don't you straighten this place up?'

'You just make sure he can't get out.'

'The Texaco driver was drunk,' she said, opening the door. 'Don't screw this up.'

Trevor froze, slack-jawed, glassy-eyed, his deadened mind suddenly springing to life. One third of $2 million, $4 million, hell, $10 million if he was really drunk and punitive damages kicked in. He wanted to at least straighten his desk, but he couldn't move.

Wes stared out the front window, stared at the rental, where his buddies were staring at him. He kept his back to the ruckus down the hall because he was struggling to keep a straight face. Footsteps, then Jan said, 'Mr. Carson will see you in just a moment.'

'Thanks,' he said softly, without turning around.

Poor guy's still grieving, she thought, then walked to the dirty kitchen to make coffee.

The deposition was over in a flash, and the other participants miraculously vanished without a trace. Wes followed her down the hall to Mr. Carson's cluttered office. Introductions were made. She brought them fresh coffee, and when she was finally gone, Wes made an unusual request.

'Is there any place to get a strong latte around here?'

'Why, certainly, yes, of course,' Trevor said, the words jumping across the desk. 'There's a place called Beach Java just a few blocks away.'

'Could you send her to get me one?'

Absolutely. Anything!

'Yes, of course. Tall or grande?'

'Tall's fine.'

Trevor bounced out of his office, and a few seconds later Jan hit the front door and practically ran down the street. When she was out of sight, Chap left the rental and walked to Trevor's. The front door was locked, so he opened it with a key of his own. Inside, he latched the chain, so poor Jan would be stuck on the porch with a cup of scalding latte.

Chap eased down the hall and made a sudden entrance into the lawyer's office.

'Excuse me,' Trevor said.

'It's okay,' Wes said. 'He's with me.'

Chap closed and locked the door, then he yanked a 9-millimeter pistol from his jacket and almost pointed it at poor Trevor, whose eyes bulged and heart froze.

'What –' he managed to emit in a high-pitched painful voice.

'Just shut up, okay,' said Chap, handing the pistol to Wes, who was sitting. Trevor's wild eyes followed it from one to the other, then it disappeared. *What have I done? Who are these thugs? All my gambling debts are paid.*

He was very happy to shut up. Whatever they wanted.

Chap leaned on the wall, pretty damned close to Trevor, as if he might lunge at any moment. 'We have a client,' he began. 'A wealthy man, who has been snagged in the little scam run by you and Ricky.'

'Oh my god,' Trevor mumbled. His worst nightmare.

'It's a wonderful idea,' Wes said. 'Extorting from rich gay men who are still hiding in the closet. They can't complain. Ricky's already in prison, so what does he have to lose?'

'Almost perfect,' Chap said. 'Until you hook the wrong fish, which is exactly what you've done.'

'It's not my scam,' Trevor said, his voice still two octaves above normal, his eyes still searching for the pistol.

'Yes, but it wouldn't work without you, would it?' Wes asked. 'There has to be a crooked lawyer on the outside to shuttle mail. And Ricky needs someone to direct the money and do a little investigative work.'

'You're not cops, are you?' Trevor asked.

'No. We're private thugs,' Chap said.

'Because if you're cops then I'm not sure I wanna talk anymore.'

291

'We're not cops, okay.'

Trevor was breathing and thinking again, the breathing going much faster than the thinking, but his training kicked in. 'I think I'll record this,' he said. 'Just in case you're cops.'

'I said we're not cops.'

'I don't trust cops, especially the FBI. The fibbies would walk in here just like the two of you, wave a gun around, and swear that they weren't fibbies. I just don't like cops. I think I'll get this on tape.'

Don't worry, pal, they wanted to say. It was all being recorded, live and in high-density digital color from a tiny camera in the ceiling a few feet behind where they were sitting. And there were mikes planted all around Trevor's littered desk so that when he snored or burped or even cracked his knuckles somebody across the street heard it.

The pistol was back. Wes held it with both hands and examined it carefully.

'You're not recording anything,' Chap said. 'As I told you, we're private boys. And we're calling the shots right now.' He took a step closer along the wall. Trevor watched him with one eye, and with the other helped Wes examine the pistol.

'In fact, we come in peace,' Chap said.

'We have some money for you,' Wes said, and put the damned thing away again.

'Money for what?' Trevor asked.

'We want you on our side. We want to retain your services.'

'To do what?'

'To help us protect our client,' Chap said. 'Here's the way we see it. You're a conspirator in an extortion scheme operating from inside a federal prison, and you've been discovered by us. We could go to the feds, get you and your client busted, you'd be sent away for thirty months, probably to Trumble, where you'd fit right in. You'd be automatically disbarred, which means you'd lose all this.' Chap casually waved his right hand, dismissing the clutter and dust and heaps of old files untouched in years.

Wes jumped right in. 'We're prepared to go to the feds right now, and we could probably stop the mail out of Trumble. Our client would probably be spared any embarrassment. But there's an element of risk our client is not willing to take. What if Ricky has another cohort, either inside or out of Trumble, somebody we haven't found yet, and he somehow manages to expose our client in retaliation?'

Chap was already shaking his head. 'It's too risky. We'd rather work with you, Trevor. We'd rather buy you off, and kill the scam from this office.'

'I cannot be bought,' Trevor said with only a trace of conviction.

'Then we'll lease you for a while, how about that?' Wes said. 'Aren't all lawyers leased by the hour anyway?'

'I suppose, but you're asking me to sell out a client.'

'Your client is a felon who's committing crimes every day from inside a federal prison. And you're just as guilty as he is. Let's not get too sanctimonious here.'

'When you become a criminal, Trevor,' Chap

said gravely, 'you lose the privilege of being self-righteous. Don't preach to us. We know it's just a question of how much money.'

Trevor forgot about the gun for a moment, and he forgot about his law license hanging on the wall behind him, slightly crooked. As he so often did these days when faced with yet another unpleasantry from the practice of law, he closed his eyes and dreamed of his forty-foot schooner, anchored in the warm, still waters of a secluded bay, topless girls on the beach a hundred yards away, and himself barely clad, sipping a beverage on the deck. He could smell the salt water, feel the gentle breeze, taste the rum, hear the girls.

He opened his eyes and tried to focus on Wes across the desk. 'Who is your client?' he asked.

'Not so fast,' Chap said. 'Let's cut the deal first.'

'What deal?'

'We give you some money, and you work as a double agent. We get access to everything. We wire you when you talk to Ricky. We see all the mail. You don't make a move until we discuss it.'

'Why don't you just pay the extortion money?' Trevor asked. 'It'd be a whole lot easier.'

'We've thought of that,' Wes said. 'But Ricky doesn't play fair. If we paid him, then he'd come back for more. And more.'

'No, he wouldn't.'

'Really? What about Quince Garbe in Bakers, Iowa?'

Oh my god, thought Trevor, and he almost said it aloud. How much do they know? All he could manage was a very weak 'Who's he?'

'Come on, Trevor,' Chap said. 'We know where

the money is hidden in the Bahamas. We know about Boomer Realty, and about your little account, currently with a balance of almost seventy thousand bucks.'

'We've dug as far as we can dig, Trevor,' Wes said, jumping in with perfect timing. Trevor was watching tennis, back and forth, back and forth. 'But we've finally hit a rock. That's why we need you.'

Truthfully, Trevor had never liked Spicer. He was a cold, ruthless, nasty little man who'd had the gall to cut Trevor's percentage. Beech and Yarber were okay, but what the hell. It wasn't as if Trevor had a lot of choices here. 'How much?' he asked.

'Our client is prepared to pay a hundred thousand dollars, cash,' Chap said.

'Of course it's cash,' Trevor replied. 'A hundred thousand is a joke. That would be Ricky's first installment. My self-respect is worth a helluva lot more than a hundred thousand.'

'Two hundred thousand,' Wes said.

'Let's do it this way,' Trevor said, trying to willfully suppress his racing heart. 'How much is it worth to your client to have his little secret buried?'

'And you're willing to bury it?' Wes asked.

'Yep.'

'Give me a second,' Chap said, yanking a tiny phone from his pocket. He punched numbers as he opened the door and stepped into the hallway, then mumbled several sentences Trevor could barely hear. Wes stared at a wall, the gun lying peacefully beside his chair. Trevor couldn't see it, though he tried.

Chap returned and stared hard at Wes, as if his

eyebrows and wrinkles could somehow deliver a crucial message. In the brief hesitation, Trevor rushed in. 'I think it's worth a million bucks,' he said. 'It could be my last case. You're asking me to divulge confidential client information, a rather egregious act for a lawyer. It would get me disbarred in an instant.'

Disbarment would be a step up for old Trevor, but Wes and Chap let it pass. Nothing good could come from an argument about how valuable his law license might be.

'Our client will pay a million dollars,' Chap said.

And Trevor laughed. He couldn't help it. He cackled as if he'd just heard the perfect punch line, and across the street in the rental they laughed because Trevor was laughing.

Trevor managed to control himself. He stopped chuckling but couldn't wipe off the smile. A million bucks. Cash. Tax-free. Hidden offshore, in another bank, of course, away from the clutches of the IRS and every other branch of the government.

Then he managed to arrange a lawyerly frown, a little embarrassed that he'd reacted so unprofessionally. He was about to say something important when three sharp raps on glass came from the front. 'Oh yes,' he said. 'That would be the coffee.'

'She's gotta go,' Chap said.

'I'll send her home,' Trevor said, standing for the first time, a little light-headed.

'No. Permanently. Get her out of the office.'

'How much does she know?' Wes asked.

'She's dumb as a rock,' Trevor said happily.

'It's part of the deal,' Chap said. 'She goes, and

now. We have a lot to discuss, and we don't want her around.'

The knocking grew louder. Jan had unlocked the door but was caught by the security chain. 'Trevor! It's me!' she shouted through the two-inch crack.

Trevor walked slowly down the hall, scratching his head, searching for words. He came face to face with her through the window of the front door, and he looked very confused.

'Open up,' she growled. 'This coffee is hot.'

'I want you to go home,' he said.

'Why?'

'Why?'

'Yes, why?'

'Because, well, uh –' Words failed him for a second, then he thought of the money. Her exit was part of the deal. 'Because you're fired,' he said.

'What?'

'I said you're fired!' he yelled, loud enough for his new pals in the back to hear.

'You can't fire me! You owe me too much money.'

'I don't owe you a damned thing!'

'How about a thousand bucks in back salary!'

The windows of the rental were crowded with faces hidden by one-way shading. The voices echoed down the quiet street.

'You're crazy!' Trevor screamed. 'I don't owe you a dime!'

'One thousand forty bucks, to be exact!'

'You're nuts.'

'You sonofabitch! I stick with you for eight years, making minimum wage, then you finally get the big case, and you fire me. Is that what you're doing, Trevor!?'

'Something like that! Now leave!'

'Open the door, you little coward!'

'Leave, Jan!'

'Not until I get my things!'

'Come back tomorrow. I'm meeting with Mr. Newman.' With that, Trevor took a step back. When she saw he wasn't opening the door, she lost it. 'You sonofabitch!' she screamed even louder, then hurled the tall latte at the door. The thin, rickety window shook but didn't break, and was instantly covered with creamy brown liquid.

Trevor, safe on the inside, flinched anyway and watched in horror as this woman he knew so well lost her mind. She stormed away, red-faced and cursing, and took a few steps until a rock caught her attention. It was a remnant of a long-forgotten, low-budget landscaping project he'd once okayed at her insistence. She grabbed it, gritted her teeth, cursed some more, then launched it toward the door.

Wes and Chap had done a masterful job of playing it straight, but when the rock crashed through the door window, they couldn't help but laugh. Trevor yelled, 'You crazy bitch!' They laughed again and looked away from each other, trying gamely to tighten up.

Silence followed. Peace had broken out in and around the reception area.

Trevor appeared in the doorway of his office, unscathed, no visible injuries. 'Sorry about that,' he said softly, and went to his chair.

'You okay?' Chap asked.

298

'Sure. No problem. How about plain coffee?' he asked Wes.

'Forget about it.'

The details were hammered out during lunch, which Trevor insisted they enjoy at Pete's. They found a table in the back, near the pinball machines. Wes and Chap were concerned with privacy, but they soon realized that nobody listened because nobody conducted business at Pete's.

Trevor knocked down three longnecks with his french fries. They had soft drinks and burgers.

Trevor wanted all the money in hand before he betrayed his client. They agreed to deliver a hundred thousand cash that afternoon, and immediately start a wire transfer for the balance. Trevor demanded a different bank, but they insisted on keeping Geneva Trust in Nassau. They assured him their access was limited only to observing the account; they could not tamper with the funds. Besides, the money would arrive there by late afternoon. If they changed banks, then it might take a day or two. Both sides were anxious to complete the deal. Wes and Chap wanted full, immediate protection for their client. Trevor wanted his fortune. After three beers he was already spending it.

Chap left early to fetch the money. Trevor ordered a longneck to go, and they got into Wes' car for a ride around town. The plan was to meet Chap at some spot and take possession of the cash. As they rode south on Highway A1A, along the beach, Trevor began talking.

'Isn't it amazing,' he said, his eyes hidden behind cheap sunglasses, his head back on the headrest.

'What's amazing?'

'The risks people are willing to take. Your client, for example. A rich man. He could hire all the young boys he wanted, yet he answers an ad in a gay magazine and starts writing letters to a complete stranger.'

'I don't understand it,' Wes said, and the two straight boys bonded for a second. 'It's not my job to ask questions.'

'I suppose the thrill is in the unknown,' Trevor said and took a small sip.

'Yeah, probably so. Who's Ricky?'

'I'll tell you when I get the money. Which one's your client?'

'Which one? How many victims are you working on right now?'

'Ricky's been busy lately. Probably twenty or so in the works.'

'How many have you extorted?'

'Two or three. It's a nasty business.'

'How'd you get involved?'

'I'm Ricky's lawyer. He's very bright, very bored, somehow he cooked up this scheme to put the squeeze on gays still in the closet. Against my better judgment, I signed on.'

'Is he gay?' Wes asked. Wes knew the names of Beech's grandchildren. He knew Yarber's blood type. He knew who Spicer's wife was dating back in Mississippi.

'No,' said Trevor.

'He's a sicko then.'

300

'No, he's a nice guy. So who's your client?'

'Al Konyers.'

Trevor nodded and tried to remember how many letters he'd handled between Ricky and Al. 'What a coincidence. I was making plans to go to Washington to do some background work on Mr. Konyers. Not his real name, of course.'

'Of course not.'

'Do you know his real name?'

'No. We were hired by some of his people.'

'How interesting. So none of us knows the real Al Konyers?'

'That's correct. And I'm sure it'll stay that way.'

Trevor pointed to a convenience store and said, 'Pull in there. I need a beer.'

Wes waited near the gas pumps. It had been determined that they would not say anything about his drinking until the money changed hands and he'd told them everything. They would build some trust, then gently try to nudge him closer to sobriety. The last thing they needed was Trevor at Pete's every night, drinking and talking too much.

Chap was waiting in a matching rental car, in front of a Laundromat five miles south of Ponte Vedra Beach. He handed Trevor a thin, cheap briefcase and said, 'It's all there. A hundred thousand. I'll meet you guys back at the office.'

Trevor didn't hear him. He opened the briefcase and began counting the money. Wes turned around and headed north. Ten stacks of $10,000, all in $100 bills.

Trevor closed it, and crossed over to the other side.

TWENTY-SEVEN

Chap's first task as Trevor's new paralegal was to organize the front desk and rid it of anything remotely female. He put Jan's things in a cardboard box, everything from lipstick tubes and nail files to peanut candy and several X-rated romance novels. There was an envelope with eighty dollars and change. The boss claimed it for himself, said it was petty cash.

Chap wrapped her photos in old newspapers and placed them carefully in another box, along with the breakable knickknacks you find on most front desks. He copied her appointment books so they would know who was scheduled to appear in the future. The traffic would be light, he saw with little surprise. Not a single court date anywhere on the horizon. Two office appointments this week, two the next, then nothing. As Chap studied the calendars, it was obvious that Trevor had shifted to a slower gear at about the time the money arrived from Quince Garbe.

They knew Trevor's gambling had picked up in recent weeks, and probably his drinking. Several times Jan had told friends on the phone that

302

Trevor was spending more time at Pete's than at the office.

As Chap busied himself in the front room, packing her junk, rearranging her desk, dusting and vacuuming and throwing away old magazines, the phone rang occasionally. His job description covered the phone, and he stayed close to it. Most of the calls were for Jan, and he politely explained that she no longer worked there. 'Good for her' seemed to be the general feeling.

An agent dressed as a carpenter arrived early to replace the front door. Trevor marveled at Chap's efficiency. 'How'd you find one so quick?' he asked.

'You just have to work the yellow pages,' Chap said.

Another agent posing as a locksmith followed the carpenter and changed every lock in the building.

Their agreement included the provision that Trevor would see no new clients for at least the next thirty days. He'd argued long and hard against this, as if he had a stellar reputation to protect. Think of all the people who might need him, he'd complained. But they knew how slow the last thirty days had been, and they pressed him until he conceded. They wanted the place to themselves. Chap called those clients with scheduled appointments and told them that Mr. Carson would be tied up in court on the day they were supposed to stop by. Rescheduling would be difficult, Chap explained, but he'd give them a call when there was a break in the action.

303

'I didn't think he went to court,' one of them said.

'Oh yes,' Chap said. 'It's a really big case.'

When the client list was pared to the core, only one case required an office visit. It was an ongoing child support matter, and Trevor had represented the woman for three years. He couldn't simply give her the boot.

Jan stopped by to cause trouble, and brought with her a boyfriend of sorts. He was a wiry young man with a goatee, polyester pants, white shirt, and tie, and Chap figured he probably sold used cars. No doubt he could have easily thrashed Trevor, but he wanted no part of Chap.

'I'd like to speak to Trevor,' Jan said, her eyes darting around her newly organized desk.

'Sorry. He's in a meeting.'

'And who the hell are you?'

'I'm a paralegal.'

'Yeah, well get your money up front.'

'Thank you. Your things are in those two boxes over there,' Chap said, pointing.

She noticed the magazine racks were purged and neat, the wastebasket was empty, the furniture had been polished. There was a smell of antiseptic, as if they'd fumigated the place where she'd once sat. She was no longer needed.

'Tell Trevor he owes me a thousand dollars in unpaid salary,' she said.

'I will,' Chap replied. 'Anything else?'

'Yeah, that new client yesterday, Yates Newman. Tell Trevor I checked the newspapers. In the past two weeks there's been no accident deaths on

I-95. No record of a female named Newman getting killed either. Something's up.'

'Thank you. I'll tell him.'

She looked around for the last time, and smirked again when she saw the new door. Her boyfriend glared at Chap as if he might just step over and break his neck anyway, but the glaring was done as he headed for the door. They left without breaking anything, both of them carrying a box as they lumbered down the sidewalk.

Chap watched them leave, then began preparing for the challenge of lunch.

Dinner the night before had been nearby, at a crowded new seafood place two blocks from the Sea Turtle Inn. Given the size of the portions, the prices were outrageous, and that was exactly why Trevor, the newest millionaire in Jacksonville, had insisted they eat there. Of course the evening was on him and he spared no expense. He was drunk after the first martini, and didn't remember what he ate. Wes and Chap had explained that their client did not allow them to drink. They sipped designer water and kept his wineglass full.

'I'd find me another client,' Trevor said, laughing at his own humor.

'Guess I'll have to drink for all three of us,' he said halfway through dinner, then proceeded to do just that.

Much to their relief, they learned that he was a docile drunk. They kept pouring, in an effort to see how far he would go. He got quieter and lower in his seat, and long after dessert he tipped the waiter

$300 in cash. They helped him to their car and drove him home.

He slept with the new briefcase across his chest. When Wes turned off his light, Trevor was lying on his bed in his rumpled pants and white cotton shirt, bow tie undone, shoes still on, snoring, and clutching the briefcase tightly with both arms.

The wire had arrived just before five. The money was in place. Klockner had told them to get him drunk, see how he behaved in that condition, then start working in the morning.

At 7:30 A.M. they returned to his house, unlocked the door with their key, and found him pretty much as they'd left him. One shoe was off, and he was curled on his side with the briefcase tucked away like a football.

'Let's go! Let's go!' Chap had yelled while Wes turned on lights and raised shades and made as much noise as possible. Trevor, to his credit, scrambled from bed, raced to the bathroom, took a quick shower, and twenty minutes later walked into his den with a fresh bow tie and not a wrinkle anywhere. His eyes were slightly swollen, but he was smiling and determined to tackle the day.

The million dollars helped. In fact, he'd never conquered a hangover as quickly.

They had a quick muffin and strong coffee at Beach Java, then attacked his little office with vigor. While Chap took care of the front, Wes kept Trevor in his office.

Some of the pieces had fallen into place over dinner. The names of the Brethren had finally been extracted from Trevor, and Wes and Chap had done a splendid job of being surprised.

'Three judges?' they'd both repeated, in apparent disbelief.

Trevor had smiled and nodded with great pride, as if he and he alone had been the architect of this masterful scheme. He wanted them to believe that he'd had the brains and skill to convince three former judges that they should spend their time writing letters to lonely gay men so he, Trevor, could rake off a third of their extortion. Hell, he was practically a genius.

Other pieces of the puzzle remained unclear, and Wes was determined to keep Trevor locked away until he had answers.

'Let's talk about Quince Garbe,' he said. 'His post office box was rented to a fake corporation. How'd you learn his true identity?'

'It was easy,' Trevor said, very proud of himself. Not only was he a genius now, but he was a very rich one. He had awakened yesterday morning with a headache, and had spent the first half hour in bed, worrying about his gambling losses, worrying about his dwindling law practice, worrying about his increasing reliance on the Brethren and their scam. Twenty-four hours later, he'd awakened with a worse headache, but one soothed with the balm of a million bucks.

He was euphoric, giddy, and anxious to finish the task at hand so he could get on with life.

'I found a private investigator in Des Moines,' he said, sipping coffee, his feet on his desk, where they belonged. 'Sent him a check for a thousand bucks. He spent two days in Bakers – you been to Bakers?'

'Yep.'

'I was afraid I'd have to go. The scam works best if you can snare some prominent guy with money. He'll pay anything to keep you quiet. Anyway, this investigator found a postal clerk who needed some money. She was a single mother, houseful of kids, old car, small apartment, you get the picture. He called her at night and said he'd give her five hundred dollars cash if she could tell him who was renting Box 788 in the name of CMT Investments. Next morning he called her at the post office. They met in a parking lot during her lunch break. She gave him a piece of paper with the name of Quince Garbe, and he gave her an envelope with five one-hundred-dollar bills. She never asked who he was.'

'Is that a typical method?'

'It worked with Garbe. Curtis Cates, the guy in Dallas, the second one we scammed, was a little more complicated. The investigator we hired there couldn't find anyone on the inside, so he had to watch the post office for three days. Cost eighteen hundred dollars, but he finally saw him and got his license number.'

'Who's next?'

'Probably this guy in Upper Darby, Pennsylvania. His alias is Brant White, and he appears to be a hot prospect.'

'Do you ever read the letters?'

'Never. I don't know what's being said back and forth; don't wanna know. When they're ready to bust somebody, they'll tell me to scope out the box and get a real name. That's if their pen pal is using a front, like your client Mr. Konyers. You'd be amazed how many men use their real names. Unbelievable.'

'Do you know when they send the extortion letters?'

'Oh yeah. They tell me so I can alert the bank in the Bahamas that a wire might be on the way. The bank calls me as soon as the money hits.'

'Tell me about this Brant White in Upper Darby,' Wes said. He was taking pages of notes, as if something might be missed. Every word was being recorded on four different machines across the street.

'They're ready to bust him, that's all I know. He seems hot to trot because they've just swapped a couple of letters. Some of these guys, it's like pulling teeth, judging by the number of letters.'

'But you don't keep track of the letters?'

'There are no records here. I was afraid the feds would show up one day with a search warrant, and I wanted no evidence of my involvement.'

'Smart, very smart.'

Trevor smiled and savored his shrewdness. 'Yeah, well, I've done a lot of criminal law. After a while, you start thinking like a criminal. Anyway, I've been unable to find the right investigator in the Philadelphia area. Still working on it though.'

Brant White was a Langley creation. Trevor could hire every investigator in the Northeast and they'd never find a real person behind the post office box.

'In fact,' he continued, 'I was preparing to go up there myself when I got the call from Spicer telling me to go to Washington and track down Al Konyers. Then you guys showed up, and, well, the

309

rest is history.' His words trailed away as he once again thought of the money. Sure it was a coincidence that Wes and Chap entered his life just hours after he was supposed to go searching for their client. But he didn't care. He could hear the seagulls and feel the hot sand. He could hear the reggae from the island bands, and feel the wind pushing his little boat.

'Is there another contact on the outside?' Wes asked.

'Oh no,' he said vainly. 'I don't need any help. The fewer people involved, the easier the operation works.'

'Very smart,' Wes said.

Trevor leaned back even deeper in his chair. The ceiling above him was cracked and peeling and in need of a fresh coat of enamel. A couple of days ago that might have worried him. Now he knew it would never get painted, not if they expected him to foot the bill. He'd walk out of the place one day very soon, once Wes and Chap here had finished with the Brethren. He'd spend a day or two boxing up his files to store for what reason he was not certain, and he'd give away his outdated and unused law books. He'd find some broke rookie fresh out of law school and looking for a few crumbs around city court, and he'd sell him the furniture and computer for a very reasonable price. And when all the loose ends were covered, he, L. Trevor Carson, Attorney and Counselor-at-Law, would walk out of the office and never look back.

What a glorious day that would be.

Chap interrupted the brief daydream with a sack

of tacos and soft drinks. Lunch had not been discussed among the three, but Trevor had already been checking his watch in anticipation of another long meal at Pete's. He grudgingly took a taco and seethed for a moment. He needed a drink.

'I think it's a good idea to lay off the booze during lunch,' Chap said as they huddled around Trevor's desk and tried not to spill black beans and ground beef.

'Do as you please,' Trevor said.

'I was talking to you,' Chap said. 'At least for the next thirty days.'

'That wasn't part of our deal.'

'It is now. You need to be sober and alert.'

'Why, exactly?'

'Because our client wants you that way. And he's paying you a million dollars.'

'Does he want me to floss twice a day and eat my spinach?'

'I'll ask him.'

'Tell him to kiss my ass while you're at it.'

'Don't overreact, Trevor,' Wes said. 'Just cut back on the drinking for a few days. It'll be good for you.'

If the money had set him free, these two were beginning to choke him. They'd now spent twenty-four hours together, and they showed no signs of leaving. In fact, the opposite was happening. They were moving in.

Chap left early to collect the mail. They'd convinced Trevor that he'd been very sloppy in his habits, and that's how they'd tracked him so easily. Suppose other victims were lurking out there? Trevor'd had little trouble in finding the real names of their victims. Why couldn't the victims do the same to the person behind Aladdin North and Laurel Ridge? From now on, Wes and Chap would take turns collecting the mail. They'd mix things up, visit the post offices at different times, use disguises, real cloak-and-dagger stuff.

Trevor eventually agreed. They seemed to know what they were doing.

There were four letters for Ricky waiting in the Neptune Beach post office, and two for Percy in Atlantic Beach. Chap quickly made the rounds, with a team behind him, watching anyone who might be watching him. The letters were taken to the rental, where they were quickly opened, and copied, then put back together.

The copies were read and analyzed by agents anxious to have something to do. Klockner read them too. Of the six, they'd seen five of the names before. All were lonely middle-aged men trying to muster the nerve to take the next step with Ricky or Percy. None seemed particularly aggressive.

One wall in a converted bedroom of the rental had been painted white and a large map of the fifty states had been stenciled on it. Red pushpins were used to mark Ricky's pen pals. Green for Percy. The names and hometowns of the correspondents were printed in black under the pins.

The nets were getting wider. Ricky had twenty-three men actively writing him; Percy, eighteen. Thirty states were represented. The Brethren were fine-tuning their venture with each passing week. They were now running ads in three magazines, as far as Klockner could tell. They held firm to their profile, and by the third letter they usually knew if a new guy had any money. Or a wife.

It was a fascinating game to watch, and now that they had complete access to Trevor they wouldn't miss a letter.

The day's mail was summarized in two pages, then given to an agent who took off to Langley. Deville had it in hand by 7 P.M.

The first call of the afternoon, at three-ten, came when Chap was washing windows. Wes was still in Trevor's office, grilling him with one question after another. Trevor was weary. He'd missed his nap and he desperately needed a drink.

'Law office,' Chap answered.

'Is this Trevor's office?' the caller asked.

'It is. Who's calling?'

'Who are you?'

'I'm Chap, the new paralegal.'

'What happened to the girl?'

'She no longer works here. What can I do for you?'

'This is Joe Roy Spicer. I'm a client of Trevor's, and I'm calling from Trumble.'

'Calling from where?'

'Trumble. It's a federal prison. Is Trevor there?'

'No sir. He's in Washington, and he should be back here in a couple of hours.'

'Okay. Tell him I'll call back at five.'

'Yes sir.'

Chap hung up and took a deep breath, as did Klockner across the street. The CIA had just had its first live contact with one of the Brethren.

★

313

The second call came at exactly five. Chap answered the phone and recognized the voice. Trevor was waiting in his office. 'Hello.'

'Trevor, this is Joe Roy Spicer.'

'Hello, Judge.'

'What'd you find in Washington?'

'We're still working on it. It's gonna be a tough one, but we'll find him.'

There was a long pause, as if Spicer didn't like this news and was uncertain about how much to say. 'Are you comin tomorrow?'

'I'll be there at three.'

'Bring five thousand dollars cash.'

'Five thousand dollars?'

'That's what I said. Get the money and bring it here. All in twenties and fifties.'

'What are you gonna do –'

'Don't ask stupid questions, Trevor. Bring the damned money. Put it in an envelope with the other mail. You've done it before.'

'All right.'

Spicer hung up without another word. Then Trevor spent an hour discussing the economics of Trumble. Cash was prohibited. Every inmate had a job and his wages were credited to his account. Expenditures, such as long-distance calls, commissary charges, copying expenses, stamps, were all debited against his account.

But cash was present, though seldom seen. It was smuggled in and hidden, and it was used to pay gambling debts and bribe guards for small favors. Trevor was afraid of it. If he, as the attorney, got caught sneaking it in, his visiting privileges would be permanently eliminated. He'd smuggled on two previous occasions, both times $500, in tens and twenties.

He couldn't imagine what they wanted with $5,000.

TWENTY-EIGHT

After three days of stepping over and around Wes
and Chap, Trevor needed a break. They wanted
breakfast, lunch, and dinner together. They
wanted to drive him home and pick him up for
work, very early in the morning. They were
running what was left of his practice – Chap the
paralegal, Wes the office manager, both of them
drilling him with endless questions because there
was precious little lawyering to be done.

So it was no surprise when they announced they
would drive him to Trumble. He didn't need a
driver, he explained. He'd made the trip many
times, in his trusty little Beetle, and he'd go it
alone. This upset them, and they threatened to call
their client for guidance.

'Call the damned client, for all I care,' Trevor
yelled at them, and they backed down. 'Your client
is not running my life.'

But the client was, and they all knew it. Only the
money mattered now. Trevor had already per-
formed his Judas act.

He left Neptune Beach in his Beetle, alone,
followed by Wes and Chap in their rental car, and

behind them was a white van occupied by people Trevor would never see. Nor did he want to see them. Just for the hell of it, he made a sudden turn into a convenience store for a six-pack, and laughed when the rest of the caravan slammed on brakes and barely avoided a wreck. Once out of town, he drove painfully slow, sipping his beer, savoring his privacy, telling himself he could suffer through the next thirty days. He could suffer through anything for a million bucks.

As he neared the village of Trumble, he had the first pangs of guilt. Could he pull this off? He was about to face Spicer, a client who trusted him, a prisoner who needed him, a partner in crime. Could he keep a straight face and act as if things were fine, while every word was being captured by a high-frequency mike in his briefcase? Could he swap letters with Spicer as if nothing had changed, knowing that the mail was being monitored? Plus, he was throwing away his law career, something he'd worked hard to attain and had once been proud of.

He was selling his ethics, his standards, even his morals for money. Was his soul worth a million bucks? Too late now. The money was in the bank. He took a sip of beer and washed away the fading twinges of guilt.

Spicer was a crook, and so were Beech and Yarber, and he, Trevor Carson, was just as culpable. There's no honor among thieves, he kept repeating silently.

Link got a whiff of the beer wafting off Trevor as they walked down the hall and into the visitors' area. At the lawyers' room Trevor looked inside.

He saw Spicer, partially hidden by a newspaper, and was suddenly nervous. What kind of low-life lawyer carries an electronic listening device into a confidential meeting with a client? The guilt hit Trevor like a brick, but there was no turning back.

The mike was almost as big as a golf ball, and had been meticulously installed by Wes in the bottom of Trevor's beaten-up and scruffy black leather briefcase. It was extremely powerful, and would easily transmit everything to the faceless boys in the white van. Wes and Chap were there too, ready with their earphones, anxious to hear it all.

'Afternoon, Joe Roy,' Trevor said.

'Same to you,' Spicer said.

'Lemme see the briefcase,' Link said. He gave a cursory look, then said, 'It looks fine.' Trevor had warned Wes and Chap that Link sometimes took a peek into the briefcase. The mike was covered by a pile of papers.

'Here's the mail,' Trevor said.

'How many?' Link asked.

'Eight.'

'You got any?' Link asked Spicer.

'No. None today,' Spicer replied.

'I'll be outside,' Link said.

The door closed; feet shuffled, and suddenly there was silence. A very long silence. Nothing. Not a word between lawyer and client. They waited in the white van for an eternity, until it was obvious something had gone wrong.

As Link stepped from the small room, Trevor quickly and deftly set the briefcase outside the door, on the floor, where it rested benignly during the remainder of the attorney-client conference. Link noticed it, and thought nothing about it.

'What'd you do that for?' Spicer asked.

'It's empty,' Trevor said, shrugging. 'Let the closed-circuit see it. We have nothing to hide.' Trevor had had one final, brief attack of ethics. Maybe he'd bug the next chat with his client, but not this one. He'd simply tell Wes and Chap that the guard took his briefcase, something that happened occasionally.

'Whatever,' Spicer said, riffling through the mail until he came to two envelopes that were slightly thicker. 'Is this the money?'

'It is. I had to use some hundreds.'

'Why? I plainly said twenties and fifties.'

'That's all I could find, okay. I didn't anticipate needing that much cash.'

Joe Roy studied the addresses on the other letters. Then he asked, rather caustically, 'So what happened in Washington?'

'It's a tough one. One of those rent-a-box outfits in the suburbs, open twenty-four hours, seven days a week, always somebody on duty, lots of traffic. Security is tight. We'll figure it out.'

'Who are you using?'

'Some outfit in Chevy Chase.'

'Gimme a name.'

'Whatta you mean, gimme a name?'

'Give me the name of the investigator in Chevy Chase.'

Trevor drew a blank; invention failed him. Spicer was on to something, his dark liquid eyes glowing with intensity. 'I can't remember,' Trevor said.

'Where'd you stay?'

'What is this, Joe Roy?'

'Give me the name of your hotel.'

'Why?'

'I have the right to know. I'm the client. I'm paying for your expenses. Where did you stay?'

'Ritz-Carlton.'

'Which one?'

'I don't know. The Ritz-Carlton.'

'There are two. Which one was it?'

'I don't know. Not downtown.'

'What flight did you take?'

'Come on, Joe Roy. What is this?'

'What airline?'

'Delta.'

'The flight number?'

'I don't remember.'

'You got back yesterday. Less than twenty-four hours ago. What was your flight number?'

'I don't recall.'

'Are you sure you went to Washington?'

'Of course I went,' Trevor said, but his voice broke a little from a lack of sincerity. He had not planned his lies, and they were breaking down as fast as he put them up.

'You don't know your flight number, which hotel you stayed in, or the name of the investigator you spent the last two days with. You must think I'm stupid.'

Trevor didn't answer. He could only think of the mike in the briefcase and how lucky he was to have it outside. Getting flogged like this was something he'd rather Wes and Chap not hear.

'You've been drinking, haven't you?' Spicer asked, on the attack.

'Yes,' Trevor said, a temporary pause in the lying. 'I stopped and bought a beer.'

'Or two.'

'Yes, two.'

Spicer leaned on his elbows, his face halfway across the table. 'I got some bad news for you, Trevor. You're fired.'

'What?'

'Terminated. Sacked. Gone for good.'

'You can't fire me.'

'I just did. Effective immediately. By unanimous vote of the Brethren. We're notifying the warden so your name will be removed from the list of attorneys. When you leave today, Trevor, don't come back.'

'Why?'

'Lying, drinking too much, sloppy habits, a general lack of trust on behalf of your clients.'

It sounded true enough, but Trevor nevertheless took it hard. It had never crossed his mind that they'd have the guts to fire him. He clenched his teeth and asked, 'What about our little enterprise?'

'It's a clean break. You keep your money, we'll keep ours.'

'Who'll run it on the outside?'

'We'll worry about that. You can pursue an honest living, if you're able.'

'What would you know about an honest living?'

'Why don't you just leave, Trevor? Get up, walk out, it's been lovely.'

'Sure,' he mumbled, his thoughts a blur but two coming to the forefront. First, Spicer had brought no letters, the first time that had happened in many weeks. Second, the cash. What did they need the five grand for? Probably to bribe their new lawyer. They'd planned their ambush well, which was always an advantage they held because they had so much time on their hands. Three very bright men, with lots of idle time. It wasn't fair.

Pride made him stand. He extended a hand and said, 'Sorry it had to happen.'

Spicer shook it reluctantly. Just get out of here, he wanted to say.

When they made eye contact for the last time, Trevor said, almost in a whisper, 'Konyers is the man. Very rich. Very powerful. He knows about you.'

Spicer leapt up like a cat. With their faces just inches apart, he said, also in a whisper, 'Is he watching you?'

Trevor nodded and winked. Then he grabbed the door. He picked up his briefcase without a word to Link. What was he supposed to say to the guard? Sorry, old boy, but the thousand bucks a month in cash you were getting under the table just got cut off. Sad about it? Then ask Judge Spicer here why it happened.

But he let it pass. He was reeling and almost dizzy, and the alcohol didn't help. What would he tell Wes and Chap? That was the question of the moment. They would hammer him as soon as they could catch him.

He said good-bye to Link, and Vince, Mackey,

322

and Rufus up front, same as always but now for the last time, and walked into the hot sun.

Wes and Chap were parked three cars down. They wanted to talk but played it safe. Trevor ignored them as he tossed his briefcase into the passenger's seat and got in the Beetle. The caravan followed him away from the prison, and slowly down the highway toward Jacksonville.

Their decision to dispose of Trevor had been reached with a maximum of judicial deliberation. They'd spent hours hiding in their little room, studying the Konyers file until every word of every letter was memorized. They'd walked miles around the track, just the three of them, playing one scenario against another. They ate together, played cards together, all the while whispering new theories of who might be watching their mail.

Trevor was the nearest culprit, and the only one they could control. If their victims got sloppy, they could do nothing about it. But if their lawyer had failed to watch his trail, then he had to be fired. He was not the type to evoke a lot of trust in the first place. How many good, busy lawyers would be willing to risk their careers in a gay extortion scheme?

The only hesitation in ridding themselves of Trevor was the fear of what he might do with their money. They expected him to steal it, frankly, and they couldn't stop him. But they were willing to run that risk in return for a bigger score with Mr. Aaron Lake. To get to Lake, they felt they had to eliminate Trevor.

Spicer gave them the details of their meeting,

word for word. Trevor's muted message at the end stunned them. Konyers was watching Trevor. Konyers knew about the Brethren. Did that mean Lake knew about the Brethren? Who was really Konyers now? Why did Trevor whisper this and why did he leave his briefcase outside the door?

With the scrutiny that only a team of bored judges could generate, the questions poured forth. And then the strategies.

Trevor was making coffee in his newly cleaned and shined kitchen when Wes and Chap made their quiet entry and came straight at him.

'What happened?' Wes asked. They were frowning and gave the impression they'd been fretting for some time.

'What do you mean?' Trevor asked, as if things were splendid.

'What happened to the mike?'

'Oh that. The guard took the briefcase and kept it outside.'

They frowned at each other some more. Trevor poured the water into his coffee machine. The fact that it was almost five and he was making coffee was duly noted by the agents.

'Why did he do that?'

'It's routine. About once a month the guard will keep the briefcase during the visit.'

'Did he search it?'

Trevor busied himself by watching the coffee drip. Absolutely nothing was wrong. 'He made his usual quick exam, which I think he does with his eyes closed. He removed the ingoing letters, then took it. The mike was safe.'

'Did he notice the thick envelopes?'

'Of course not. Relax.'

'And the meeting went well?'

'It was routine, except that Spicer had no outgoing mail, which is a bit unusual these days, but it happens. I'll go back in two days and he'll have a stack of letters, and the guard will not even touch the briefcase. You'll get to hear every word. Want some coffee?'

They relaxed in unison. 'Thanks, but we'd better go,' Chap said. There were reports to make, questions to answer. They started for the door, but Trevor stopped them.

'Look, fellas,' he said very politely. 'I'm perfectly capable of getting dressed by myself, and of having a quick bowl of cereal, alone, the way I've done it for many years. And I like to open my office here no earlier than nine. Since it's my office, we'll open at nine, and not a minute sooner. You're welcome to be here at that unholy hour, but not at eight fifty-nine. Stay away from my house, and stay away from this office until nine. Understood?'

'Sure,' one of them said, and they were gone. It didn't really matter to them. They had bugs crawling all over the office, the house, the car, even the briefcase now. They knew where he bought his toothpaste.

Trevor drank the entire pot of coffee and sobered up. Then he began his movements, all carefully planned. He'd started preparing the moment he left Trumble. He assumed they were watching, back there with the boys from the white van. They had the gadgets and the toys, the mikes and the bugs, and Wes and Chap certainly knew

325

how to use them. Money was no object. He told himself to believe they knew everything, just let his imagination run wild and assume they heard every word, followed every turn, and knew exactly where he was at all times.

The more paranoid he was, the better his chances of escape.

He drove to a mall sixteen miles away near Orange Park, in the sprawl south of Jacksonville. He roamed and window-shopped and ate pizza in a near-empty food court. It was difficult not to dart behind a rack of clothes in a store and wait for the shadows to walk by. But he resisted. In a Radio Shack, he bought a small cell phone. One month of long distance with a local service came with the package, and Trevor had what he needed.

He returned home after nine, certain that they were watching. He turned the television on full volume, and made more coffee. In the bathroom he stuffed his cash into pockets.

At midnight, with the house dark and quiet and Trevor evidently asleep, he slipped out the back door and into the night. The air was brisk, the moon full, and he tried his best to look as though he was simply going for a walk on the beach. He wore baggy cargo pants with pockets from the waist down, two denim shirts, and an oversized windbreaker with money stuffed inside the liner. In all, Trevor had $80,000 hidden on himself as he wandered aimlessly south, along the edge of the water, just another beachcomber out for a midnight stroll.

After a mile his pace quickened. When he'd

gone three miles he was exhausted, but he was in a desperate hurry. Sleep and rest would have to wait.

He left the beach and walked into the grungy lobby of a rundown motel. There was no traffic along Highway A1A; nothing was open except for the motel and a convenience store in the distance.

The door rattled enough for the clerk to come to life. A television was on somewhere in the back. A chubby young man of no more than twenty emerged and said, 'Good evening. Need a room?'

'No sir,' Trevor said, as he slowly drew a hand from a pocket and produced a thick roll of bills. He began peeling them off and placing them in a neat row on the counter. 'I need a favor.'

The clerk stared at the money, then rolled his eyes. The beach attracted all kinds. 'These rooms ain't that expensive,' he said.

'What's your name?' Trevor asked.

'Oh, I don't know. Let's say it's Sammy Sosa.'

'All right, Sammy. There's a thousand bucks. It's yours if you'll drive me to Daytona Beach. Take you ninety minutes.'

'It'll take me three hours because I have to drive back.'

'Whatever. That's more than three hundred bucks an hour. When's the last time you made three hundred bucks an hour?'

'It's been a while. I can't do it. I run the night shift, you see. My job is to be on duty from ten until eight.'

'Who's the boss?'

'He's in Atlanta.'

'When's the last time he stopped by?'

'I've never met him.'

'Of course you haven't. If you owned a dump like this, would you stop by?'

'It's not that bad. We have free color TVs and most of the air-conditioning works.'

'It's a dump, Sammy. You can lock that door, drive away, and come back three hours later, and no one will ever know it.'

Sammy looked at the money again. 'You runnin from the law or something?'

'No. And I'm not armed. I'm just in a hurry.'

'So what's up?'

'A bad divorce, Sammy. I have a little money. My wife wants it all and she has some pretty nasty lawyers. I gotta get out of town.'

'You got money, but no car?'

'Look, Sammy. You want the deal or not? If you say no, then I'll walk down the street to the convenience store and find somebody smart enough to take my cash.'

'Two thousand.'

'You'll do it for two thousand?'

'Yep.'

The car was worse than Trevor had expected. It was an old Honda, uncleaned by Sammy or any of the previous five owners. But A1A was deserted, and the trip to Daytona Beach took exactly ninety-eight minutes.

At 3:20 A.M., the Honda stopped in front of an all-night waffle grill, and Trevor got out. He thanked Sammy, said good-bye, and watched him drive away. Inside, he drank coffee and chatted with the waitress long enough to persuade her to go fetch a local phone directory. He ordered pancakes and used his new Radio Shack cell phone to find his way around town.

The nearest airport was Daytona Beach International. A few minutes after four, his cab stopped at the general aviation terminal. Dozens of small planes sat in neat rows on the tarmac. He stared at them as the cab drove away. Surely, he told himself, one of them was available for a quick charter. He just needed one, preferably a twin-engine.

TWENTY-NINE

The back bedroom of the rental had been converted into the meeting room, with four folding tables pushed together to make one large one. It was covered with newspapers, magazines, and doughnut boxes. Every morning at seven-thirty Klockner and his team met over coffee and pastries to review the night and plan the day. Wes and Chap were always there, and six or seven others joined them, depending on who was in town from Langley. The technicians from the front room sometimes sat in, though Klockner did not require their attendance. Now that Trevor was on their side, they needed fewer people to track him.

Or so they thought. Surveillance detected no movement inside his home before seven-thirty, which was not altogether unusual for a man who often went to bed drunk and woke up late. At eight, while Klockner was still meeting in the back, a technician called the house under the ruse of a wrong number. After three rings, the recorder came on and Trevor announced he was not in, please leave a message. This happened occasionally when he was trying to sleep late, but it usually worked well enough to roust him from bed.

Klockner was notified at eight-thirty that the house was completely still; no shower, no radio, no television, no stereo, not a sound from the normal routine.

It was entirely possible he'd gotten drunk at home, by himself, but they knew he had not spent last night at Pete's. He'd gone to a mall and arrived home apparently sober.

'He could be sleeping,' Klockner said, unconcerned. 'Where's his car?'

'In his driveway.'

At nine, Wes and Chap knocked on Trevor's door, then opened it when there was no answer. The rental sprang to life when they reported there was no sign of him, and that his car was still there. Without panic, Klockner sent people to the beach, to the coffee shops near the Sea Turtle, even to Pete's, which was not yet open. They canvassed the area around his house and office, by foot and by car, and saw nothing.

At ten, Klockner called Deville at Langley. The lawyer's missing, was the message.

Every flight to Nassau was checked; nothing turned up, no sign of a Trevor Carson. Deville's contact in Bahamian customs could not be located, nor could he find the banking supervisor they'd been bribing.

Teddy Maynard was in the middle of a briefing on North Korean troop movements when he was interrupted by an urgent message that Trevor Carson, their drunken lawyer in Neptune Beach, Florida, was missing.

'How can you lose a fool like him?' Teddy growled at Deville, in a rare display of anger.

'I don't know.'

'I don't believe this!'

'Sorry, Teddy.'

Teddy shifted his weight and grimaced from the pain. 'Find him, dammit!' he hissed.

The plane was a Beech Baron, a twin-engine owned by some doctors and chartered by Eddie, the pilot Trevor had coaxed out of bed at six in the morning with the promise of cash on the spot and more under the table. The official quote was $2,200 for a round-trip between Daytona Beach and Nassau – two hours each way, total of four at $400 an hour, plus some fees for landing and immigration and pilot downtime. Trevor kicked in another $2,000 for Eddie's pocket if the trip took place immediately.

The Geneva Trust Bank in downtown Nassau opened at 9 EST, and Trevor was waiting when the doors were unlocked. He barged into the office of Mr. Brayshears and demanded immediate assistance. He had almost a million dollars in his account – $900,000 from Mr. Al Konyers, through Wes and Chap; about $68,000 from his dealings with the Brethren.

With one eye on the door, he pressed Brayshears to help him move the money, and quickly. The money was owned by Trevor Carson, and no one else. Brayshears had no choice. There was a bank in Bermuda managed by a friend of his, which suited Trevor just fine. He didn't trust Brayshears, and he planned to keep moving the money until he felt safe.

For a moment, Trevor cast a lustful eye at the account of Boomer Realty, currently with a balance of $189,000 and change. It was within his power, during that fleeting moment, to snatch their money too. They were nothing but felons – Beech, Yarber, the odious Spicer, all crooks. And they'd had the arrogance to fire him. They had forced him to run. He tried to hate them enough to take their money, but as he wavered back and forth he felt a soft spot for them. Three old men wasting away in prison.

A million was enough. Besides, he was in a hurry. If Wes and Chap suddenly charged in with guns, it wouldn't have surprised him. He thanked Brayshears and ran from the building.

When the Beech Baron lifted off the runway at Nassau International, Trevor couldn't help but laugh. He laughed at the heist, at the getaway, at his luck, at Wes and Chap and their rich client now minus a million, at his shabby little law office now mercifully idle. He laughed at his past and at his glorious future.

At three thousand feet he gazed downward at the still blue waters of the Caribbean. A lonely sailboat rocked along, its captain at the wheel, a scantily clad lady nearby. That would be him down there in just a few short days.

He found a beer in a carry-on cooler. He drank it and fell sound asleep. They landed on the island of Eleuthera, a place Trevor had seen in a travel magazine he'd bought the night before. There were beaches and hotels and all the water sports.

He paid Eddie in cash, then waited an hour at the small airport for a taxi to happen by.

He bought clothes at a tourist shop in Governor's Harbour, then walked to a hotel on the beach. He was amused at how quickly he stopped watching the shadows. Sure Mr. Konyers had plenty of money, but no one could afford a secret army big enough to track someone through the Bahamas. His future would be one of sheer delight. He would not ruin it by looking over his shoulder.

He drank rum by the pool as fast as the bar maid could bring it. At the age of forty-eight, Trevor Carson welcomed his new life in pretty much the same condition he'd left his old one.

The law office of Trevor Carson opened on time and things proceeded as if nothing was amiss. Its owner had fled, but its paralegal and office manager were on duty to take care of any business that might unexpectedly develop. They listened in all the right places, and heard nothing. The phone rang twice before noon, two misguided inquiries from souls lost in the yellow pages. Not a single client needed Trevor. Not a single friend called to say hello. Wes and Chap busied themselves by going through the few drawers and files they had not yet inspected. Nothing of consequence was found.

Another crew combed every inch of Trevor's house, primarily looking for the cash he'd been paid. Not surprisingly, they didn't find it. The cheap briefcase was in a closet, empty. There was no trail. Trevor had just walked away, with his cash.

The Bahamian banking official was tracked to New York, where he was visiting on government business. He was reluctant to get involved from such a long distance, but he eventually made his calls. Around 1 P.M. it was confirmed that the money had been moved. Its owner had done so in person, and the official would divulge nothing else.

Where did the money go? It was moved by wire, and that's all he would tell Deville. His country's banking reputation depended upon secrecy, and he could reveal only so much. He was corrupt, but he did have his limits.

U.S. Customs cooperated after some initial reluctance. Trevor's passport had been scanned at Nassau International early that morning, and so far he had not left the Bahamas, at least not officially. His passport was red-listed. If he used it to enter another country, U.S. Customs would know it within two hours.

Deville delivered a quick update to Teddy and York, his fourth of the day, then hung around for further instructions.

'He'll make a mistake,' York said. 'He'll use his passport somewhere, and we'll catch him. He doesn't know who's chasing him.'

Teddy seethed but said nothing. His agency had toppled governments and killed kings, yet he was constantly amazed at how the little things often got botched. One bumbling and witless lawyer from Neptune Beach slipped through their net while a dozen people were supposed to be watching. He thought he was beyond surprises.

335

The lawyer was to be their link, their bridge to the inside of Trumble. For a million dollars they thought they could trust him. There'd been no contingency plan for his sudden flight. Now they were scrambling to develop one.

'We need someone inside the prison,' Teddy said.

'We're close,' Deville answered. 'We're working with Justice and the Bureau of Prisons.'

'How close?'

'Well, in light of what's happened today, I think we can have a man there, inside Trumble, within forty-eight hours.'

'Who is he?'

'His name is Argrow, eleven years with the agency, age thirty-nine, solid credentials.'

'His story?'

'He'll transfer into Trumble from a federal prison in the Virgin Islands. His paperwork will be cleared by the Bureau here in Washington so the warden down there won't ask any questions. He's just another federal prisoner who requested a transfer.'

'And he's ready to go?'

'Almost. Forty-eight hours.'

'Do it now.'

Deville left, again with the burden of a difficult task that suddenly had to be done overnight.

'We have to find out how much they know,' Teddy said, almost in a mumble.

'Yes, but we have no reason to believe they suspect anything,' York said. 'I've read all their mail. There's nothing to indicate they are particularly excited about Konyers. He's just one of their

336

potential victims. We bought the lawyer to stop him from snooping around behind Konyers' post office box. He's off in the Bahamas now, drunk with his money, so he's not a threat.'

'But we still dispose of him,' Teddy said. It was not a question.

'Of course.'

'I'll feel better when he's gone,' Teddy said.

A guard with a uniform but no gun entered the law library in mid-afternoon. He first encountered Joe Roy Spicer, who was by the door to the chamber.

'The warden would like to see you,' the guard said. 'You and Yarber and Beech.'

'What's this about?' Spicer asked. He was reading an old copy of *Field & Stream.*

'None of my business. He wants you now. Up front.'

'Tell him we're busy.'

'I ain't tellin him nothin. Let's go.'

They followed him to the administration building, picking up other guards along the way until a regular entourage emerged from the elevator and stood before the warden's secretary. She and she alone somehow managed to escort the Brethren into the big office where Emmitt Broon was waiting. When she was gone, he said abruptly, 'I have been notified by the FBI that your lawyer is missing.'

No visible response from the three, but each instantly thought about the money hidden off-shore.

He continued, 'He disappeared this morning,

and there's some money missing. I don't have the details.'

Whose money? they wanted to ask. No one knew about their hidden funds. Had Trevor stolen from someone else?

'Why are you telling us?' Beech asked.

The real reason was that the Justice Department in Washington had asked Broon to inform the three of the latest news. But the reason he gave was 'Just thought you'd want to know in case you needed to call him.'

They'd fired Trevor the day before, and had not yet informed the administration that he was no longer their attorney of record.

'What're we gonna do for a lawyer?' Spicer asked, as if life couldn't go on.

'That's your problem. Frankly, I'd say you gentlemen have had enough legal counsel to last you many years.'

'What if he contacts us?' Yarber asked, knowing full well they'd never hear from Trevor again.

'You are to notify me immediately.'

They agreed to do so. Whatever the warden wanted. He excused them.

Buster's escape was less complicated than a trip to the grocery. They waited until the next morning, until breakfast was over and most of the inmates were busy with their menial jobs. Yarber and Beech were on the track, walking an eighth of a mile apart so that one was always watching the prison while the other watched the woods in the distance. Spicer loitered near the basketball court, on the lookout for guards.

With no fences or towers or pressing security concerns, guards were not that critical at Trumble. Spicer saw none.

Buster was lost in the whining noise of his Weed Eater, which he slowly worked toward the track. He took a break to wipe his face and look around. Spicer, from fifty yards away, heard the engine die. He turned and quickly gave a thumbs-up, the sign to do it quickly. Buster stepped onto the track, caught up with Yarber, and for a few steps they walked together.

'Are you sure you want to do this?' Yarber asked.

'Yes. I'm positive.' The kid appeared calm and ready.

'Then do it now. Pace yourself. Be cool.'

'Thanks, Finn.'

'Don't get caught, son.'

'No way.'

At the turn, Buster kept walking, off the track, across the freshly cut grass, a hundred yards to some brush, then he was gone. Beech and Yarber saw him go, then turned to watch the prison. Spicer was calmly walking toward them. There was no sign of alarm around the courtyards or dorms or any of the other buildings on the prison grounds. Not a guard in sight.

They walked three miles, twelve laps, at the leisurely pace of fifteen minutes per mile, and when they'd had enough they retired to the coolness of the chamber to relax and listen for news of the escape. It would be hours before they heard a word.

Buster's pace was much faster. Once into the

woods, he began to jog without looking back. Watching the sun, he moved due south for half an hour. The woods were not thick; the undergrowth was thin and did not slow him. He passed a deer stand twenty feet up in an oak tree, and soon found a trail that ran to the southwest.

In his left front pants pocket he had $2,000 cash, given to him by Finn Yarber. In his other front pocket he had a map Beech had drawn by hand. And in his rear pocket he had a yellow envelope addressed to a man named Al Konyers in Chevy Chase, Maryland. All three were important, but the envelope had received the most attention from the Brethren.

After an hour, he stopped to rest, and to listen. Highway 30 was his first landmark. It ran east and west and Beech figured he would find it within two hours. He heard nothing, and started running again.

He had to pace himself. There was a chance his absence would be noticed just after lunch, when the guards sometimes walked the grounds in a very casual inspection. If one of them thought to look for Buster, then other questions might follow. But after two weeks of watching the guards, neither Buster nor any of the Brethren thought this was a possibility.

So he had at least four hours. And probably a lot more because his workday ended at five when he turned in his Weed Eater. When he didn't show, they'd start looking around the prison. After two hours of that, they'd notify the surrounding police agencies that another one had walked away from Trumble. They were never armed and dangerous, and no one got too excited. No search parties. No bloodhounds. No helicopters hovering over the woods. The county sheriff and his deputies would patrol the main roads and warn the citizens to lock their doors.

The escapee's name went into a national computer. They watched his home and watched his girlfriend, and they waited for him to do something stupid.

After ninety minutes of freedom, Buster stopped for a moment and heard the whine of an eighteen-wheeler not far away. The woods stopped abruptly at a right-of-way ditch, and there was the highway. According to Beech's map, the nearest town was several miles to the west. The plan was to hike along the highway, dodging traffic by using ditches and bridges, until civilization in some form was found.

Buster wore the standard prison issue of khaki pants and an olive-colored short-sleeve shirt, both darkened with sweat. The locals knew what the prisoners wore, and if he were spotted walking down Highway 30 someone would call the sheriff. Get to town, Beech and Spicer had told him, and find different clothes. Then pay cash for a bus ticket, and never stop running.

It took him three hours of ducking behind trees and jumping over roadside ditches before he saw the first buildings. He moved away from the highway, and cut through a hay field. A dog growled at him as he stepped onto a street lined with house trailers. Behind one of them he noticed a clothesline with someone's laundry hanging in the windless air. He took a red and white pullover and threw away his olive shirt.

Downtown was nothing more than two blocks of stores, a couple of gas stations, a bank, some sort of town hall, and a post office. He bought denim shorts, a tee shirt, and a pair of boots at a discount store, and changed in the employee restroom. He found the post office inside the town hall. He smiled and thanked his friends at Trumble as he dropped their precious envelope into the Out-of-Town slot.

Buster caught a bus to Gainesville, where he purchased, for $480, the right to ride a bus anywhere in the United States for sixty days. He headed west. He wanted to get lost in Mexico.

THIRTY

The Pennsylvania primary on April 25 was to be
Governor Tarry's last mighty effort. Undaunted by
his dismal showing in the debate there two weeks
earlier, he campaigned with great enthusiasm, but
with very little money. 'Lake has it all,' he
proclaimed at every stop, feigning pride at being
the pauper. He did not leave the state for eleven
straight days. Reduced to traveling in a large
Winnebago camper, he ate his meals in the homes
of supporters, stayed in cheap motels, and worked
himself ragged shaking hands and walking neighborhoods.

'Let's talk about the issues,' he pleaded. 'Not
about money.'

Lake, too, worked very hard in Pennsylvania.
His jet traveled ten times faster than Tarry's RV.
Lake shook more hands, made more speeches, and
he certainly spent more money.

The result was predictable. Lake received 71
percent of the vote, a landslide so embarrassing to
Tarry that he openly talked about quitting. But he
vowed to hang on for at least another week, until
the Indiana primary. His staff had left him. He was

$11 million in debt. He'd been evicted from his campaign headquarters in Arlington.

Yet, he wanted the good people of Indiana to have the opportunity to see his name on the ballot.

And who knew, Lake's shiny new jet might catch on fire, just like the previous one.

Tarry licked his rather deep wounds, and the day after the primary he promised to fight on.

Lake almost felt sorry for him, and he sort of admired his determination to endure until the convention. But Lake, along with everybody else, could do the math. Lake needed just forty more delegates to lock up the nomination, and there were almost five hundred still out there. The race was over.

After Pennsylvania, newspapers across the country confirmed his nomination. His happy handsome face was everywhere, a political miracle. He was praised by many as a symbol of why the system works – an unknown with a message who came from nowhere and captured the attention of the people. Lake's campaign gave hope to every person who dreamed of running for President. It didn't take months of pounding the back roads of Iowa. Skip New Hampshire, it was such a small state anyway.

And he was condemned for buying his nomination. Before Pennsylvania, it was estimated he'd spent $40 million. A more precise number was difficult because the money was being burned on so many fronts. Another $20 million had been spent by D-PAC and half a dozen other high-powered lobbying groups, all working on Lake's behalf.

344

No other candidate in history had spent anything close.

The criticism stung Lake, and it dogged him day and night. But he'd rather have the money and the nomination than suffer the alternative.

Big money was hardly taboo. Online entrepreneurs were making billions. The federal government, of all bumbling entities, was showing a surplus! Nearly everybody had a job, and an affordable mortgage, and a couple of cars. Lake's nonstop polling led him to believe that the big money was not yet an issue with the voters. In a November matchup against the Vice President, Lake was now practically even.

He once again returned to Washington, from the wars of the West, as a triumphant hero. Aaron Lake, lowly congressman from Arizona, was now the man of the hour.

Over a quiet and very long breakfast, the Brethren read the Jacksonville morning paper, the only one allowed inside Trumble. They were very happy for Aaron Lake. In fact, they were thrilled with his nomination. They were now among his most ardent supporters. Run, Aaron, run.

The news of Buster's walk to freedom had created hardly a stir. Good for him, the inmates were saying. He was just a kid with a long sentence. Run, Buster, run.

The escape wasn't mentioned in the morning paper. They passed it around, reading every word but the want ads and the obituaries. They were waiting now. No more letters would be written; none would be brought in because they'd lost their courier. Their little scam was on hold until they heard from Mr. Lake.

Wilson Argrow arrived at Trumble in an unmarked green van, handcuffed, with two marshals pulling at his elbows. He'd flown with his escorts from Miami to Jacksonville, of course at the expense of the taxpayers.

According to his paperwork, he had served four months of a sixty-month sentence for bank fraud. He had requested a transfer for reasons that were not clear, but his reasons were of no concern to anyone at Trumble. He was just another low-security prisoner in the federal system. They moved around all the time.

He was thirty-nine years old, divorced, college-educated, and his home address, for prison records, was in Coral Gables, Florida. His real name was Kenny Sands, an eleven-year veteran of the CIA, and though he'd never seen the inside of a prison, he'd had much tougher assignments than Trumble. He'd be there a month or two, then request another transfer.

Argrow maintained the cool facade of an old prison hand as he was processed, but his stomach churned. He'd been assured that violence was not tolerated at Trumble, and he could certainly take care of himself. But prison was prison. He suffered through a one-hour orientation by an assistant warden, then was given a quick tour of the grounds. He began to relax when he saw Trumble for himself. The guards had no guns, and most of the inmates looked rather harmless.

His cell mate was an old man with a spotty white

346

beard, a career criminal who'd seen many prisons and loved Trumble. He told Argrow he planned to die there. The man took Argrow to lunch and explained the vagaries of the menu. He showed him the game room, where groups of thick men bunched around folding tables studying their cards, every one with a cigarette stuck to the lips. 'Gambling's illegal,' his cell mate said with a wink.

They walked to the lifting area outdoors where the younger men sweated in the sun, polishing their tans while their muscles expanded. He pointed to the track in the distance and said, 'You gotta love the federal government.'

He showed Argrow the library, a place he never visited, and he pointed to a corner and said, 'That's the law library.'

'Who uses it?' Argrow asked.

'We usually have some lawyers here. Right now we have some judges too.'

'Judges?'

'Three of 'em.'

The old man had no interest in the library. Argrow followed him to the chapel, then around the grounds again.

Argrow thanked him for the tour, then excused himself and returned to the library, which was empty except for an inmate mopping a floor. Argrow went to the corner, and opened a door to the law library.

Joe Roy Spicer glanced up from his magazine and saw a man he'd never seen before. 'Lookin for something?' he asked, with no effort at being helpful.

Argrow recognized the face from the file. An ex-

Justice of the Peace caught stealing bingo profits. What a low-life.

'I'm new,' he said, forcing a smile. 'Just got here. This is the law library?'

'It is.'

'I guess anybody can use it, huh?'

'I guess,' Spicer said. 'You a lawyer?'

'Nope, a banker.'

A few months earlier, Spicer would've hustled him for some legal work, under the table, of course. But not now. They no longer needed the nickel-and-dime stuff. Argrow looked around and did not see Beech and Yarber. He excused himself and returned to his room.

Contact was made.

Lake's plan to rid himself of any memories of Ricky and their ill-fated correspondence depended upon someone else. He, Lake, was simply too scared and too famous to sneak away again in the middle of the night, in a disguise, in the back of a taxi, dashing through the suburbs to an all-night mailbox. The risks were too great; plus he seriously doubted if he could shake the Secret Service anymore. He couldn't count the number of agents now assigned to protect him. Count, hell, he couldn't see them all.

The young lady's name was Jayne. She'd joined the campaign in Wisconsin and had quickly worked her way into the inner circle. A volunteer at first, she now earned $55,000 a year as a personal aide to Mr. Lake, who trusted her completely. She seldom left his side, and they'd already had two little chats about Jayne's future job in the White House.

At the right moment, Lake would give Jayne the key to the box rented by Mr. Al Konyers, and instruct her to get the mail, close out the rental, and leave no forwarding address. He would tell her it was a box he'd rented in an effort to monitor the sale of classified defense contracts, back when he was convinced the Iranians were buying data they should never see. Or some such tale. She would believe him because she wanted to believe him.

If he were incredibly lucky, there would be no letter from Ricky. The box would be forever closed. And if a letter was waiting for Jayne, and if she was the least bit curious, Lake would simply tell her he had no idea who the person was. She would ask nothing further. Blind allegiance was her strong suit.

He waited for the right moment. He waited too long.

THIRTY-ONE

It arrived safely with a million other letters, tons of paperwork shipped into the capital to sustain the government for one more day. It was sorted by zip code, then by street. Three days after Buster dropped it off, Ricky's last letter to Al Konyers made it to Chevy Chase. A routine check of Mailbox America by a surveillance team found it. The envelope was examined, then quickly taken to Langley.

Teddy was between briefings, alone for a moment in his office, when Deville rushed in, holding a thin file. 'We got this thirty minutes ago,' he said as he handed over three sheets of paper. 'It's a copy. The original is in the file.'

The Director adjusted his bifocals and looked at the copies before he began reading. There was the Florida postmark, same as always. The handwriting was too familiar. He knew it was serious trouble before he began reading.

Dear Al:
   In your last letter you tried to end our correspondence. Sorry, it won't be that easy.

I'll get right to the point. I'm not Ricky, and you're not Al. I'm in a prison, not some fancy drug rehab clinic.

I know who you are, Mr. Lake. I know you're having a great year, just wrapped up the nomination and all, and you have all that money pouring in. They give us newspapers here at Trumble, and we've been following your success with great pride.

Now that I know who Al Konyers really is, I'm sure you'd like for me to keep quiet about our little secret. I'll be happy to remain silent, but it will cost you dearly.

I need money, and I want out of prison. I can keep secrets and I know how to negotiate.

The money is the easy part, because you have so much of it. My release will be more complicated, but you're collecting all sorts of very powerful friends. I'm sure you'll think of something.

I have nothing to lose, and I'm willing to ruin you if you don't negotiate with me.

My name is Joe Roy Spicer. I'm an inmate at Trumble Federal Prison. You figure out a way to contact me, and do it quickly.

I will not go away.

Sincerely,
Joe Roy Spicer

The next briefing was canceled. Deville found York, and ten minutes later they were locked away in the bunker.

Killing them was the first option discussed.

Argrow could do it with the right tools; pills and poisons and such. Yarber could die in his sleep. Spicer could drop dead on the track. Beech the hypochondriac could get a bad prescription from the prison pharmacy. They were not particularly fit or healthy, and certainly no match for Argrow. A nasty fall, a broken neck. There were many ways to make it look natural or accidental.

It would have to be done quickly, while they were still waiting for a reply from Lake.

But it would be messy, and unduly complicated. Three dead bodies all at once, in a harmless little prison like Trumble. And the three were close friends who spent most of their time together, and they would each die in different ways within a very short period of time. It would create an avalanche of suspicion. What if Argrow became a suspect? His background was hidden to begin with.

And the Trevor factor frightened them. Wherever he was, there was the chance he would hear of their deaths. The news would scare him even more, but it might also make him unpredictable. There was a chance he knew more than they thought.

Deville would work on plans to take them out, but Teddy was very reluctant. He had no qualms about killing the three, but he was not convinced it would protect Lake.

What if the Brethren had told someone else?

There were too many unknowns. Make the plans, Deville was told, but they would be used only when every other option was gone.

All scenarios were on the table. York suggested, for the sake of argument, that the letter be returned to the box so Lake could find it. It was his screwup to begin with.

'He wouldn't know what to do,' Teddy said.

'Do we?'

'Not yet.'

The thought of Aaron Lake reacting to this ambush and somehow trying to silence the Brethren was almost amusing, but there was a strong element of justice to it. Lake had created this mess; let him handle it.

'Actually, we created this mess,' Teddy said, 'and we'll deal with it.'

They couldn't predict, and thus they couldn't control, what Lake would do. Somehow the fool had avoided their net long enough to drop something in the mail to Ricky. And he'd been so stupid that the Brethren now knew who he was.

Not to mention the obvious: Lake was the type of person who secretly swapped letters with a gay pen pal. He was living a double life, and didn't deserve a lot of confidence.

Confronting Lake was discussed for a moment. York had been advocating a showdown since the first letter from Trumble, but Teddy wasn't convinced. The sleep he'd lost fretting over Lake was always filled with thoughts and hopes of stopping the mail long before now. Quietly take care of the problem, then have a chat with the candidate.

Oh, how he'd love to confront Lake. He'd love to sit him in a chair over there and start flashing copies of all those damned letters up on a screen. And a copy of the ad from *Out and About*. He'd tell him about Mr. Quince Garbe in Bakers, Iowa, another idiot who fell for the scam, and Curtis

Vann Gates in Dallas. 'How could you be so stupid!?' he wanted to scream at Aaron Lake.

But Teddy kept his eye on the bigger picture. The problems with Lake were small when compared to the urgency of national defense. The Russians were coming, and when Natty Chenkov and the new regime seized power the world would change forever.

Teddy had neutralized men far more powerful than three felonious judges rotting away in a federal prison. Meticulous planning was his strong suit. Patient, tedious planning.

The meeting was interrupted by a message from Deville's office. Trevor Carson's passport had been scanned at a departure checkpoint at the airport in Hamilton, Bermuda. He left on a flight to San Juan, Puerto Rico, that was scheduled to land in about fifty minutes.

'Did we know he was in Bermuda?' York asked.

'No, we did not,' Deville answered. 'Evidently he entered without using his passport.'

'Maybe he's not as drunk as we thought.'

'Do we have someone in Puerto Rico?' Teddy asked, his voice only a shade more excited.

'Of course,' said York.

'Let's pick up the scent.'

'Have the plans changed for ole Trevor?' Deville asked.

'No, not at all,' Teddy said. 'Not at all.'

Deville left to deal with the latest Trevor crisis. Teddy called an assistant and ordered mint tea. York was reading the letter again. When they were alone, he asked, 'What if we separate them?'

'Yes, I was thinking of that. Do it quickly, before

they have time to confer. Send them to three prisons far apart, put them in isolation for a period of time, make sure they have no phone privileges, no mail. Then what? They still have their secret. Any one of them could conceivably ruin Lake.'

'I'm not sure we have the contacts within the Bureau of Prisons.'

'It can be done. If necessary, I'll have a chat with the Attorney General.'

'Since when did you become friends with the Attorney General?'

'It's a matter of national security.'

'Three crooked judges sitting in a federal prison in Florida can somehow affect national security? I'd like to hear that conversation.'

Teddy sipped his tea with his eyes closed, all ten fingers on the cup. 'It's too risky,' he whispered. 'We make them mad, they become even more erratic. We can't take chances here.'

'Suppose Argrow can find their records,' York said. 'Think about it – these are con men, convicted criminals. No one will believe their story about Lake unless they have proof. The proof is documentation, pieces of paper, originals and copies of the correspondence. The proof exists somewhere. We find it, take it from them, then who will listen?'

Another small sip with his eyes closed, another long pause. Teddy shifted slightly in his chair and grimaced from the pain. 'True,' he said softly. 'But I'm worried about somebody on the outside, somebody we know nothing about. These guys are a step ahead of us, and they always will be. We're trying to figure out what they've known for some time. I'm not sure we'll ever catch up. Maybe they've thought about losing their little files. I'm sure the prison has rules against maintaining such paperwork, so they're already hiding things. The Lake letters are much too valuable not to copy again and stash on the outside.'

'Trevor was their mailman. We've seen every letter he's carried out of Trumble for the past month.'

'We think we have. But we don't know for certain.'

'But who?'

'Spicer has a wife. She's been to see him. Yarber's getting a divorce, but who knows what they're doing. She's visited in the past three months. Or maybe they're bribing guards to run mail for them. These people are bored and they're smart and they're very creative. We can't just assume we know everything they're up to. And if we make a mistake here, if we assume too much, then Mr. Aaron Lake gets himself shoved out of the closet.'

'How? How would they do it?'

'Probably contact a reporter, feed him one letter at a time until he was convinced. It would work.'

'The press would go insane.'

'It can't happen, York. We simply cannot allow it to happen.'

Deville returned in a rush. U.S. Customs had been notified by the authorities in Bermuda ten minutes after the flight departed for San Juan. Trevor would be landing in eighteen minutes.

Trevor was just following his money. He had

quickly grasped the fundamentals of wire transfers, and was now perfecting the art. In Bermuda, he had sent half of it to a bank in Switzerland, and the other half to a bank in Grand Cayman. East or west? That had been the great question. The quickest flight out of Bermuda went to London, but the idea of sneaking through Heathrow scared him. He was not a wanted man, at least not by the government. No charges were filed or pending. But the Brits were so efficient at customs. He'd go west and take his chances in the Caribbean.

He landed in San Juan and went straight to a bar where he ordered a tall draft and studied the flights. No hurry, no pressure, a pocket full of cash. He could go anywhere, do anything, and take as long as he wanted. He had another draft and decided to spend a few days in Grand Cayman, with his money. He went to the Air Jamaica counter and bought a ticket, then back to the bar because it was almost five and he had thirty minutes before boarding.

Of course he flew first class. He boarded early so he could get another drink, and as he watched the other passengers file by he saw a face he'd seen before.

Where was it now? Just moments ago, somewhere in the airport. A long thin face, with a salt-and-pepper goatee, and little narrow slits for eyes behind square glasses. The eyes glanced at him just long enough to meet Trevor's, then looked away, down the aisle, as if nothing had been seen.

It had been near the airline counter, as Trevor was turning to leave after buying his ticket. The face was watching him. The man was standing nearby, studying the departure notices.

When you're on the run, the stray glances and second looks and drifting eyes all seem more suspicious. See a face once, and you don't even know it. See it again a half hour later, and somebody is watching every move you make.

Stop drinking, Trevor ordered himself. He asked for coffee after takeoff, and drank it quickly. He was the first passenger off the plane in Kingston, and he walked quickly through the terminal, through immigration. No sign of the man behind him.

He grabbed his two small bags and raced for the taxi stand.

THIRTY-TWO

The Jacksonville paper arrived at Trumble each morning around seven. Four copies were taken to the game room where they were to be read and left behind for any of the inmates who cared about life on the outside. Most of the time Joe Roy Spicer was the only one waiting at seven, and he usually took one paper for himself because he needed to study the Vegas lines throughout the day. The scene rarely changed: Spicer with a tall Styrofoam cup of coffee, feet on a card table, waiting for Roderick the guard to bring the papers.

So Spicer saw the story first, at the bottom of the front page. Trevor Carson, a local lawyer who'd been missing for some vague reason, found dead outside a hotel in Kingston, Jamaica, shot twice in the head last night, just after dark. The story had no picture of Trevor, Spicer noticed. Why would the paper have one on file? Why would anyone care if Trevor died?

According to Jamaican officials, Carson was a tourist who'd apparently been robbed. An unidentified source close to the scene had tipped the police as to the identity of Mr. Carson, since his wallet was missing. The source seemed to know a lot.

The paragraph recapping Trevor's legal career was quite brief. A former secretary, Jan something or other, had no comment. The story had been thrown together, and placed on the front page only because the victim was a murdered lawyer.

Finn was at the far end of the track, rounding the turn, walking at a rapid clip in the damp early morning air, his shirt already off. Spicer waited at the homestretch, and handed him the paper without a word.

They found Beech waiting in line in the cafeteria, holding his plastic tray and staring forlornly at the crude piles of freshly scrambled eggs. They sat together in a corner, away from everyone else, picking at their food, talking in muted voices.

'If he was running, who the hell was he running from?'

'Maybe Lake was after him.'

'He didn't know it was Lake. He didn't have a clue, did he?'

'Okay, then he was running from Konyers. The last time he was here he said Konyers was the big one. He said Konyers knew about us, then he disappeared the next day.'

'Maybe he was just scared. Konyers confronted him, threatened to expose his role in our scam, and so Trevor, who wasn't the most stable guy to begin with, decided to steal all he could and disappear.'

'Whose money was missing, that's what I want to know.'

'Nobody knows about our money. How could it be missing?'

360

'Trevor probably stole from everybody he could, then vanished. Happens all the time. Lawyers get in trouble, crack up. They raid their clients' trust funds and bolt.'

'Really?' asked Spicer.

Beech could think of three examples, and Yarber added a couple more for good measure.

'So who killed him?'

'There's a good chance he was just in the wrong part of town.'

'Outside the Sheraton Hotel? I don't think so.'

'Okay, what if Konyers iced him?'

'That's possible. Konyers somehow smoked out Trevor, learned he was the outside contact for Ricky. He put pressure on Trevor, threatened to nail him or whatever, and Trevor ran off to the Caribbean. Trevor didn't know Konyers was Aaron Lake.'

'And Lake certainly has the money and power to track down a drunken lawyer.'

'What about us? By now, Lake knows Ricky ain't Ricky, that Joe Roy here is the man, and that he has friends with him in prison.'

'Question is, can he get to us?'

'I guess I'll find out first,' Spicer said with a nervous laugh.

'And there's always the chance that Trevor was down there in Jamaica hanging around in the wrong part of town, probably drunk and trying to pick up a woman, and he got himself shot.'

They all agreed on this, that Trevor was perfectly capable of getting himself killed.

May he rest in peace. But only if he didn't steal their money.

They scattered for an hour or so. Beech went to the track, to walk and think. Yarber was on the clock, twenty cents an hour trying to fix a computer in the chaplain's office. Spicer went to the library, where he found Mr. Argrow reading law books.

The law library was open, no appointments were necessary, but the unwritten rule was that you should at least ask one of the Brethren before using their books. Argrow was new, and obviously had not yet learned the rules. Spicer decided to give him a break.

They acknowledged each other with a nod, then Spicer got busy clearing tables and straightening books.

'Rumor has it you guys do legal work,' Argrow said from across the room. No one else was present.

'You hear a lot of rumors around here.'

'My case is on appeal.'

'What happened at trial?'

'Jury nailed me on three counts of bank fraud, hiding money offshore, in the Bahamas. The judge gave me sixty months. I've served four. I'm not sure I'm gonna last for fifty-six more. I need some help with my appeals.'

'What court?'

'Virgin Islands. I worked for a big bank in Miami. Lots of drug money.'

Argrow was glib and fast and very anxious to talk, and this irritated Spicer, but only slightly. The reference to the Bahamas had his attention.

'For some reason, I developed a fascination for money laundering. I dealt with tens of millions every day, and it was intoxicating. I could move dirty money quicker than any banker in South Florida. Still can. But I made some bad friends, and bad choices.'

'You admit you're guilty?'

'Sure.'

'That puts you in the distinct minority around here.'

'No, I was wrong, but I think the sentence was too harsh. Somebody said you guys can get some time knocked off.'

Spicer was no longer concerned with the untidy tables and disorganized books. He took a chair nearby and had time to talk. 'We can take a look at your papers,' he said, as if he'd handled a thousand appeals.

You idiot, Argrow wanted to say. You dropped out of high school in the tenth grade, and stole a car when you were nineteen. Your father pulled some strings and got the charges dropped. You got yourself elected Justice of the Peace by voting dead people and stuffing absentee ballots, and now you're stuck in a federal pen and trying to play the big shot.

And, Argrow conceded, you, Mr. Spicer, now have the power to bring down the next President of the United States.

'What will it cost?' Argrow asked.

'How much do you have?' Spicer asked, just like a real lawyer.

'Not much.'

'I thought you knew how to hide money off-shore.'

'Oh, I do, believe me. And at one point I had a nice bundle, but I let it get away.'

'So you can't pay anything?'

'Not much. Maybe a couple of thousand or so.'

'What about your lawyer?'

'He got me convicted. I don't have enough to hire a new one.'

Spicer pondered the situation for a moment. He realized he did indeed miss Trevor. Things had been much simpler when they had him on the outside collecting money. 'You still got contacts in the Bahamas?'

'I have contacts all over the Caribbean. Why?'

'Because you'll have to wire the money. Cash is forbidden around here.'

'You want me to wire two thousand dollars?'

'No. I want you to wire five thousand dollars. That's our minimum fee.'

'Where's your bank?'

'In the Bahamas.'

Argrow's eyes narrowed. His eyebrows pushed together, and while he was deep in thought so was Spicer. The minds were in the process of meeting.

'Why the Bahamas?' Argrow asked.

'Same reason you used the Bahamas.'

Thoughts rattled around in both heads. 'Lemme ask you something,' Spicer said. 'You said you could move dirty money quicker than anybody else.'

Argrow nodded and said, 'No problem.'

'Can you still do it?'

'You mean, from in here?'

'Yes. From here.'

Argrow laughed and shrugged as if nothing could be easier. 'Sure. I still have some friends.'

'Meet me here in an hour. I might have a deal for you.'

An hour later, Argrow returned to the law library and found the three judges already in position, behind a table with papers and law books scattered about as if the Supreme Court of Florida were in session. Spicer introduced him to Beech and Yarber, and he took a seat across the table. No one else was present.

They talked for a moment about his appeal, and he was sufficiently vague on the details. His file was en route from the other prison, and they couldn't do much without it.

The appeal was a preliminary topic of conversation, and both sides of the table knew it.

'Mr. Spicer tells us you're an expert on moving dirty money,' Beech said.

'I was until I got caught,' Argrow said modestly. 'I take it you have some.'

'We have a little account offshore, money we've earned doing legal work and a few other things we can't be too open about. As you know, we can't charge for legal work.'

'But we do anyway,' added Yarber. 'And we get paid for it.'

'How much is in the account?' Argrow asked, knowing yesterday's closing balance to the exact penny.

'Let's wait on that,' Spicer said. 'There's a good chance the money may have disappeared.'

Argrow let the words hang for a second, and managed to appear confused. 'I'm sorry?' he said.

'We had a lawyer,' Beech said slowly, each word measured. 'He disappeared and he may have taken the money.'

'I see. And this account is in a bank in the Bahamas?'

'It was. We're not sure if it still is.'

'We doubt the money is still there,' Yarber added.

'But we'd like to know for sure,' Beech added.

'Which bank?' Argrow asked.

'Geneva Trust, in Nassau,' Spicer answered, glancing at his colleagues.

Argrow nodded smugly, as if he knew dark little dirty secrets about the bank.

'You know the bank?' Beech asked.

'Sure,' he said, and let them hang for a long second.

'And?' Spicer said.

Argrow was overcome with smugness and insider knowledge, so he stood rather dramatically and walked around the small library for a moment, deep in thought, then moved closer to the table again. 'Look, what do you guys want me to do? Let's cut to the chase.'

The three looked at him, then at each other, and it was obvious they weren't sure of two things: (a) how much they trusted this man they'd just met, and (b) what they really wanted from him.

But they figured the money was gone anyway, so what was there to lose. Yarber said, 'We're not too sophisticated when it comes to moving dirty money. That was not our original calling, you understand. Forgive our lack of knowledge, but is there any way to verify if the money is still where it once was?'

'We're just not sure if the lawyer stole it,' Beech added.

'You want me to verify the balance of a secret account?' Argrow asked.

'Yes, that's it,' said Yarber.

'We figure that maybe you still have some friends in the business,' Spicer said, treading water. 'And we're just curious as to whether there's any way to do this.'

'You're lucky,' Argrow said, and allowed the words to settle.

'How's that?' Beech asked.

'You picked the Bahamas.'

'Actually, the lawyer picked the Bahamas,' Spicer said.

'Anyway, the banks are pretty loose there. Lots of secrets get told. Lots of officials get bribed. Most of the serious money launderers stay away from the Bahamas. Panama is the current hot spot, and, of course, Grand Cayman is still rock solid.'

Of course, of course, they all three nodded. Offshore was offshore, wasn't it? Just another example of trusting an idiot like Trevor.

Argrow watched them with their puzzled faces and thought how truly clueless they were. For three men with the ability to totally wreck the American electoral process, they seemed awfully naive.

'You haven't answered our question,' Spicer said.

'Anything's possible in the Bahamas.'

367

'So you can do it?'

'I can try. No guarantees.'

'Here's the deal,' Spicer said. 'You verify the account, and we'll do your appeals for free.'

'That's not a bad deal,' Argrow said.

'We didn't think so. Agreed?'

'Agreed.'

For an awkward second they just looked at one another, proud of their mutual agreement but not sure who moved next. Finally, Argrow said, 'I'll need to know something about the account.'

'Such as?' Beech asked.

'Such as a name or a number.'

'The account name is Boomer Realty, Ltd. The account number is 144-DXN-9593.'

Argrow scribbled some notes on a sheet of scrap paper.

'Just curious,' Spicer said as they watched him closely. 'How do you plan to communicate with your contacts outside?'

'Phone,' Argrow said without looking up.

'Not these phones,' Beech said.

'These phones are not secure,' Yarber said.

'You can't use these phones,' Spicer said with an edge.

Argrow smiled and acknowledged their concerns, then he glanced over his shoulder and removed from his pants pocket an instrument of some sort, not much larger than a pocketknife. He held it between his thumb and index finger, and said, 'This is a phone, gentlemen.'

They stared in disbelief, then watched as he quickly unfolded it from the top and the bottom and from one side so that when properly opened it still looked much too small for any meaningful conversation. 'It's digital,' he said. 'Very secure.'

'Who gets the monthly bill?' asked Beech.

'I have a brother in Boca Raton. The phone and the service were gifts from him.' He snapped it back smartly, and it vanished before their eyes. Then he pointed to the small conference room behind them, to their chamber. 'What's in there?' he asked.

'Just a conference room,' Spicer said.

'It has no windows, right?'

'None, except for that small one in the door.'

'All right. What if I go in there, get on the phone, and go to work. You three stay here and watch out for me. If anyone enters the library, come knock on the door.'

The Brethren readily agreed, though they did not believe Argrow could pull it off.

The call went to the white van, parked a mile and a half from Trumble, on a gravel road sometimes maintained by the county. The road was next to a hay field, farmed by a man they'd yet to meet. The property line for the acreage owned by the federal government was a quarter of a mile away, but from where the van was sitting there was no sign of a prison.

Only two technicians were in the van, one fully asleep in the front seat, the other half asleep in the back with a headset on. When Argrow pressed the Send button on his fancy little gadget, a receiver in the van was activated, and both men came to life.

'Hello,' he said. 'This is Argrow.'

'Yes, Argrow, Chevy One here, go ahead,' said the technician in the back.

'I'm near the three stooges, going through the motions, supposedly making calls to friends on the outside to verify the existence of their account offshore. So far things are progressing even faster than I'd hoped.'

'Sounds like it.'

'Roger. I'll check in later.' He pushed the End button, but kept the phone at his head and appeared to be deep in conversation. He sat on the edge of the table, then he walked around some, glancing occasionally at the Brethren and beyond.

Spicer couldn't help but sneak a look through the window of the door. 'He's making calls,' he said excitedly.

'What do you expect him to be doing?' asked Yarber, who was actually reading recent court decisions.

'Relax, Joe Roy,' Beech said. 'The money disappeared with Trevor.'

Twenty minutes passed, and things became dull as usual. While Argrow worked the phones, the judges killed time, waiting at first, then returning to more pressing business. It had been six days since Buster had left with their letter. No word from Buster meant he'd walked away clean, dropped off the note to Mr. Konyers, and was now somewhere far away. Give it three days to travel to Chevy Chase, and the way they had it figured Mr. Aaron Lake should now be scrambling with a plan to deal with them.

Prison had taught them patience. Only one deadline worried them. Lake had the nomination,

370

which meant he would be vulnerable to their blackmail until November. If he won, they would have four years in which to torment him. But if he lost he would fade quickly away, like all the losers. 'Where's Dukakis now?' Beech had asked.

They had no plans to wait until November. Patience was one thing, release was another. Lake was their one fleeting opportunity to walk away with enough money to coast forever.

They intended to give it a week, then write another letter to Mr. Al Konyers in Chevy Chase. They weren't sure how to smuggle it out, but they would think of something. Link, the guard up front whom Trevor had been bribing for months, was their first prospect.

Argrow's phone presented an option. 'If he'll let us use it,' Spicer said, 'then we can call Lake, call his campaign office, his congressional office, call every damned number we can get from directory assistance. Leave the message that Ricky in rehab really needs to see Mr. Lake. That'll scare the hell out of him.'

'But Argrow will have a record of our calls, or at least his brother will,' Yarber said.

'So? We'll pay him for the calls, and so what if they know we're trying to call Aaron Lake. Right now, half the country is trying to call him. Argrow won't have a clue why we're doing it.'

A brilliant idea, one they pondered for a long time. Ricky in rehab could make the calls and leave the messages. Spicer in Trumble could do the same. Poor Lake would get hounded.

Poor Lake. The man had money pouring in so fast he couldn't count it.

After an hour, Argrow emerged from the chamber and announced he was making progress. 'I need to wait an hour, then make a few more calls,' he said. 'What about lunch?'

They were anxious to continue their discussion, and they did so over sloppy joes and coleslaw.

THIRTY-THREE

Pursuant to Mr. Lake's precise instructions, Jayne
drove alone to Chevy Chase. She found the
shopping center on Western Avenue, and parked
in front of Mailbox America. With Mr. Lake's key,
she opened the box, removed eight pieces of junk
mail, and placed them in a folder. There were no
personal letters. She walked to the counter and
informed the clerk that she wished to close the box
on behalf of her employer, Mr. Al Konyers.

The clerk pecked a few times on a keyboard.
The records indicated that a man named Aaron L.
Lake had rented the box in the name of Al
Konyers about seven months earlier. The rental
had been paid for twelve months, so nothing was
owed.

'That guy running for President?' the clerk
asked as she slid a form across the counter.

'Yes,' Jayne said, signing where indicated.

'No forwarding address?'

'No.'

She left with the folder and headed south, back
into the city. She had not stopped to question
Lake's story about renting the box in a clandestine

effort to expose fraud at the Pentagon. It didn't matter to her, nor did she have time to ask a lot of questions. Lake had them sprinting eighteen hours a day, and she had far more important things to worry about.

He was waiting in his campaign office, alone for the moment. The offices and hallways around him were choked with assistants of a dozen varieties, all running back and forth as if war were imminent. But Lake was enjoying a lull in the action. She gave him the folder and left.

Lake counted eight pieces of junk mail – taco delivery, long-distance service, a car wash, coupons for this and for that. And nothing from Ricky. The box was closed, there was no forwarding address. The poor boy would have to find someone else to help him through his new life. Lake fed the junk mail and the cancellation agreement through a small shredder under his desk, then paused a moment to count his blessings. He carried little baggage in life, and he'd made few mistakes. Writing to Ricky had been a stupid thing to do, yet he was walking away unscathed. What a lucky man!

He smiled and almost giggled to himself, then he bounced from his chair, grabbed his jacket, and rounded up his entourage. The candidate had meetings to attend, then a lunch with defense contractors.

Oh what a lucky man!

Back in the corner of the law library, with his three new friends guarding the perimeter like sleepy sentries, Argrow fiddled with the phone long enough to convince them he'd pulled strings all through the dark and murky world of offshore banking. Two hours of pacing and mumbling and holding the phone to his head like a frantic stockbroker, and he finally came out of the room.

'Good news, gentlemen,' he said with a tired smile.

They huddled around, eager for the results.

'It's still there,' he said.

Then the great question, the one they'd been planning, the one that would verify whether Argrow was a fraud or a player.

'How much?' asked Spicer.

'A hundred and ninety thousand, and small change,' he said, and they exhaled in unison. Spicer smiled. Beech looked away. Yarber looked at Argrow with a quizzical frown, but a rather pleasant one.

According to their figures, the balance was $189,000, plus whatever paltry rate of interest the bank was paying.

'He didn't steal it,' Beech mumbled, and they shared a pleasant memory of their dead lawyer, who suddenly was not the devil they'd made him out to be.

'I wonder why not,' Spicer mused, almost to himself.

'Well, it's still there,' Argrow said. 'That's a lot of legal work.'

It certainly appeared to be, and since neither of the three could think of a quick fib, they just let it pass.

'I suggest you move it, if you don't mind my

saying so,' Argrow said. 'This bank is known for its leaks.'

'Move it where?' Beech asked.

'If the money were mine, I'd move it to Panama immediately.'

This was a new issue, a train of thought they had not pursued because they had been obsessed with Trevor and his certain theft. But they weighed it carefully anyway, as if the matter had been discussed many times.

'Why would you move it?' Beech asked. 'It's safe, isn't it?'

'I guess,' Argrow answered, quick with a response. He knew where he was going, they did not. 'But you see how loose the confidentiality can be. I wouldn't use banks in the Bahamas these days, especially this one.'

'And we don't know if Trevor told anyone about it,' Spicer said, always anxious to nail the lawyer.

'If you want the money protected, move it,' Argrow said. 'It takes less than a day and you won't have to worry about it. And put the money to work. This account is just sitting there, drawing a few pennies in interest. Put it with a fund manager and let it earn fifteen or twenty percent. You're not gonna be using it any time soon.'

That's what you think, pal, they thought. But he made perfect sense.

'And I assume you can move it?' Yarber said.

'Of course I can. Do you doubt me now?'

All three shook their heads. No sir, they did not doubt him.

'I have some nice contacts in Panama. Think about it.' Argrow glanced at his watch as if he had lost interest in their account and had a hundred pressing matters elsewhere. A punch line was coming, and he didn't want to push.

'We've thought about it,' Spicer said. 'Let's move it now.'

He looked at three sets of eyes, all looking back at him. 'There's a fee involved,' he said, like a seasoned money launderer.

'What kinda fee?' Spicer asked.

'Ten percent, for the transfer.'

'Who gets ten percent?'

'I do.'

'That's rather steep,' said Beech.

'It's a sliding scale. Anything under a million pays ten percent. Anything over a hundred million pays one percent. It's pretty common in the business, and it's exactly the reason I'm wearing an olive prison shirt and not a thousand-dollar suit.'

'That's pretty sleazy,' said Spicer, the man who'd skimmed bingo profits from a charity.

'Let's not preach, okay. We're talking about a small cut from money that's already tainted, both here and there. Take it or leave it.' His tone was aloof, an icy veteran who'd cut much larger deals.

It was only $19,000, and this from a stash they'd been certain was gone. After his 10 percent, they still had $170,000, roughly $60,000 each, and it would've been more if treacherous Trevor hadn't raked so much off the top. And, besides, they were confident of greener pastures just around the corner. The loot in the Bahamas was pocket change.

'It's a deal,' Spicer said as he looked at the other two for approval. They both nodded slowly. All three were thinking the same thing now. If the shakedown of Aaron Lake proceeded as they dreamed it would, then serious money was coming their way. They would need a place to hide it, and maybe someone to help them. They wanted to trust this new guy Argrow. Let's give him the chance.

'Plus, you do my appeals,' Argrow said.

'Yes, we'll do the appeals.'

Argrow smiled and said, 'Not a bad deal. Lemme make some more calls.'

'There's one thing you should know,' Beech said.

'Okay.'

'The lawyer's name was Trevor Carson. He set up the account, directed the deposits, did everything really. And he was murdered night before last in Kingston, Jamaica.'

Argrow searched their faces for more. Yarber handed him a copy of the newspaper, which he read very deliberately. 'Why was he missing?' he asked after a long silence.

'We don't know,' Beech said. 'He left town, and we got word through the FBI that he was missing. We just assumed that he'd stolen our money.'

Argrow handed the paper back to Yarber, and crossed his arms over his chest. He cocked his head, narrowed his eyes, and managed to look suspicious. Let them sweat.

'How dirty is this money?' he asked, as if he might not want to get involved with it after all.

'It's not drug money,' Spicer said quickly, on the defensive, as if all other money was clean.

'We really can't say,' Beech replied.

'You've got a deal,' Yarber said. 'Take it or leave it.'

Good move, old boy, Argrow said to himself. 'The FBI is involved?' he asked.

'Only with the lawyer's disappearance,' Beech said. 'The feds know nothing about the offshore account.'

'Let me get this straight. You got a dead lawyer, the FBI, an offshore account hiding dirty money, right? What've you boys been up to?'

'You don't wanna know,' Beech said.

'I think you're right.'

'No one's forcing you to get involved,' Yarber said.

So a decision had to be made. For Argrow, the red flags were up, the minefield was marked. If he went forward, then he did so armed with sufficient warnings that his three new friends could be dangerous. This, of course, meant nothing to Argrow. But to Beech, Spicer, and Yarber, the opening in their tight little partnership, however slight it might be, meant they were admitting another conspirator. They would never tell him about their scam, and certainly not about Aaron Lake, nor would he share in any more of their loot, unless he earned it with his wiring prowess. But he already knew more than he should. They had no choice.

Desperation played no small role in their decision. With Trevor, they'd had access to the outside, something they'd taken for granted. Now that he was gone, their world had shrunk considerably.

Though they had yet to admit it, firing him had

been a mistake. With perfect hindsight, they should've warned him, and told him everything about Lake and the tampered mail. He'd been far from perfect, but they needed all the help they could get.

Perhaps they would've hired him back a day or two later, but they never had the chance. Trevor bolted, and now he was gone forever.

Argrow had access. He had a phone and friends; he had guts and he knew how to get things done. Perhaps they might need him, but they would take it slowly.

He scratched his head and frowned as if a headache was coming. 'Don't tell me anything else,' he said. 'I don't wanna know.'

He returned to the conference room and closed the door behind him, then perched on the edge of the table and once again seemed to be firing calls all over the Caribbean.

They heard him laugh twice, probably a joke with an old friend surprised to hear his voice. They heard him swear once, but had no idea at whom or for what reason. His voice rose and fell, and try as they might to read court decisions and dust off old books and study Vegas odds, they couldn't ignore the noise from the room.

Argrow put on quite a show, and after an hour of useless chatter he came out and said, 'I think I can finish it tomorrow, but we need an affidavit signed by one of you stating that you are the sole owners of Boomer Realty.'

'Who sees the affidavit?' Beech asked.

'Only the bank in the Bahamas. They're getting a copy of the story about Mr. Carson, and they want verification about the ownership of the account.'

The idea of actually signing any type of document in which they admitted they had anything to do with the dirty money terrified them. But the request made sense.

'Is there a fax machine around here?' Argrow asked.

'No, not for us,' Beech replied.

'I'm sure the warden has one,' Spicer said. 'Just trot up there and tell him you need to send a document to your offshore bank.'

It was unnecessarily sarcastic. Argrow glared at him, then let it pass. 'Okay, tell me how to get the affidavit from here to the Bahamas. How does the mail run?'

'The lawyer was our mail runner,' Yarber said. 'Everything else is subject to inspection.'

'How close do they inspect the legal mail?'

'They glance at it,' Spicer said. 'But they can't open it.'

Argrow paced around a bit, deep in thought. Then, for the benefit of his audience he stepped between two racks of books, so that he could not be seen from outside the law library. He deftly unfolded his gadget, punched numbers, and stuck it to his ear. He said, 'Yes, Wilson Argrow here. Is Jack in? Yes, tell him it's important.' He waited.

'Who the hell's Jack?' Spicer asked from across the room. Beech and Yarber listened but watched for passersby.

'My brother in Boca,' Argrow said. 'He's a real estate lawyer. He's visiting me tomorrow.' Then, into the phone, he said, 'Hey, Jack, it's me. You comin tomorrow? Good, can you come in the morning? Good. Around ten. I'll have some mail going out. Good. How's Mom? Good. I'll see you in the morning.'

The prospect of the resumption of mail intrigued the Brethren. Argrow had a brother who was a lawyer. And he had a phone, and brains, and guts.

He slid the gadget back into his pocket and walked from the racks. 'I'll give the affidavit to my brother in the morning. He'll fax it to the bank. By noon the next day the money will be in Panama, safe and sound and earning fifteen percent. Piece of cake.'

'We're assuming we can trust your brother?' Yarber said.

'With your life,' Argrow said, almost offended by the question. He was walking to the door. 'I'll see you guys later. I need some fresh air.'

THIRTY-FOUR

Trevor's mother arrived from Scranton. She was with her sister, Trevor's aunt Helen. They were both in their seventies and in reasonably good health. They got lost four times between the airport and Neptune Beach, then meandered through the streets for an hour before stumbling on Trevor's house, a place his mother hadn't seen in six years. She hadn't seen Trevor in two years. Aunt Helen hadn't seen him in at least ten, not that she particularly missed him.

His mother parked the rental car behind his little Beetle, and had a good cry before getting out.

What a dump, Aunt Helen said to herself.

The front door was unlocked. The place had been abandoned, but long before its owner fled the dishes had collected in the sink, the garbage had gone unattended, the vacuum hadn't left the closet.

The odor drove Aunt Helen out first, and Trevor's mother soon followed. They had no clue what to do. His body was still in Jamaica, in a crowded morgue, and according to the unfriendly young man she'd talked to at the State Department it would cost $600 to ship him home. The airlines would cooperate, but the paperwork was tied up in Kingston.

It took a half hour of bad driving to find his office. By then, word was out. Chap the paralegal was waiting at the reception desk, trying to look sad and busy at the same time. Wes the office manager was in a back room, just to listen and observe. The phone had rung constantly the day the news broke, but after a round of condolences from fellow lawyers and a client or two it went silent again.

On the front door was a cheap wreath, paid for by the CIA. 'Ain't that nice,' his mother said as they waddled up the sidewalk.

Another dump, thought Aunt Helen.

Chap greeted them and introduced himself as Trevor's paralegal. He was in the process of trying to close the office, a most difficult task.

'Where's the girl?' his mother asked, her eyes red from grieving.

'She left some time back. Trevor caught her stealing.'

'Oh dear.'

'Would you like some coffee?' he asked.

'That would be nice, yes.' They sat on the dusty and uneven sofa, while Chap fetched three coffees from a pot that just happened to be fresh. He sat across from them in an unstable wicker chair. The mother was bewildered. The aunt was curious, her eyes darting around the office, looking for any sign of prosperity. They were not poor, but at their ages affluence would never be attained.

'I'm very sorry about Trevor,' Chap said.

'It's just awful,' Mrs. Carson said, her lip quivering. Her cup shook and coffee splashed onto her dress. She didn't notice it.

'Did he have a lot of clients?' Aunt Helen asked.

'Yes, he was very busy. A good lawyer. One of the best I've ever worked with.'

'And you're a secretary?' Mrs. Carson asked.

'No, I'm a paralegal. I go to law school at night.'

'Are you handling his affairs?' Aunt Helen asked.

'Well, not really,' Chap said. 'I was hoping that's why the two of you were here.'

'Oh, we're too old,' his mother said.

'How much money did he leave?' asked the aunt.

Chap stepped it up a notch. This old bitch was a bloodhound. 'I have no idea. I didn't handle his money.'

'Who did?'

'I guess his accountant.'

'Who's his accountant?'

'I don't know. Trevor was very private about most things.'

'He certainly was,' his mother said sadly. 'Even as a boy.' She splashed her coffee again, this time on the sofa.

'You pay the bills around here, don't you?' asked the aunt.

'No. Trevor took care of his money.'

'Well, listen, young man, they want six hundred dollars to fly him home from down in Jamaica.'

'Why was he down there?' his mother interrupted.

'It was a short vacation,' Chap said.

'And she doesn't have six hundred dollars,' Helen finished.

'Yes I do.'

'Oh, there's some cash here,' Chap said, and Aunt Helen looked satisfied.

'How much?' she asked.

'A little over nine hundred dollars. Trevor liked to keep plenty of petty cash.'

'Give it to me,' Aunt Helen demanded.

'Do you think we should?' asked his mother.

'You'd better take it,' Chap said gravely. 'If not, it will just go into his estate and the IRS will get it all.'

'What else will go into his estate?' asked the aunt.

'All this,' Chap said, waving his arms at the office while he walked to the desk. He removed a wrinkled envelope stuffed with bills of all denominations, money they'd just transferred from the rental across the street. He gave it to Helen, who snatched it and counted the money.

'Nine twenty, and some change,' Chap said.

'Which bank did he use?' Helen asked.

'I have no idea. Like I said, he was very private about his money.' And in one respect, Chap was telling the truth. Trevor had wired the $900,000 from the Bahamas to Bermuda, and from there the trail had disappeared. The money was now hidden in a bank somewhere, in a numbered account accessible only by Trevor Carson. They knew he was headed for Grand Cayman, but the bankers there were famous for their secrecy. Two days of intense digging had revealed nothing. The man who shot him took his wallet and room key, and while the police were inspecting the crime scene the gunman searched the hotel room. There was about $8,000 in cash hidden in a drawer, and nothing else of any significance. Not a clue as to where Trevor had parked his money.

It was the collected wisdom at Langley that Trevor, for some reason, suspected he was being followed closely. The bulk of the cash was missing, though he could have deposited it in a bank in Bermuda. His hotel room had been secured without a reservation – he simply walked in from the street and paid cash for one night.

A person on the run, chasing $900,000 from one island to the next, would have, somewhere on his body or in his effects, evidence of banking activities. Trevor had none.

While Aunt Helen riffled through what would surely be the only cash they'd net from the estate, Wes thought about the fortune lost somewhere in the Caribbean.

'What do we do now?' Trevor's mother asked.

Chap shrugged and said, 'I guess you need to bury him.'

'Can you help us?'

'That's not really something I do. I –'

'Should we take him back to Scranton?' Helen asked.

'That's up to you.'

'How much would that cost?' Helen asked.

'I have no idea. I've never had to do anything like this.'

'But all his friends are here,' his mother said, touching her eyes with a tissue.

'He left Scranton a long time ago,' Helen said, her eyes cutting in all directions, as if there was a long story behind Trevor's leaving Scranton. No doubt, thought Chap.

'I'm sure his friends here will want a memorial service,' Mrs. Carson said.

'Actually, one is already planned,' Chap said.

'It is!' she said, thrilled.

'Yes, it's tomorrow at four o'clock.'

'Where?'

'A place called Pete's, just down the street a few blocks.'

'Pete's?' Helen said.

'It's, well, it's sort of a restaurant.'

'A restaurant. What about a church?'

'I don't think he went.'

'He did when he was a boy,' his mother said in defense.

In memory of Trevor, the five o'clock happy hour would begin at four, and run until midnight. Fifty-cent longnecks, Trevor's favorite.

'Should we go?' asked Helen, sensing trouble.

'I wouldn't think so.'

'Why not?' asked Mrs. Carson.

'It could be a rough crowd. A bunch of lawyers and judges, you know the scene.' He frowned at Helen, and she got the message.

They asked about funeral parlors and cemetery lots, and Chap felt himself getting dragged deeper and deeper into their problems. The CIA killed Trevor. Was it expected to send him off with a proper burial?

Klockner thought not.

After the ladies left, Wes and Chap finished the

removal of the cameras, wires, mikes, and phone taps. They tidied up the place, and when they locked the doors for the last time Trevor's office had never been so orderly.

Half of Klockner's team had already left town. The other half monitored Wilson Argrow inside Trumble. And they waited.

When the forgers at Langley finished with Argrow's court file it fit in a cardboard box, and was flown to Jacksonville on a small jet along with three agents. It contained, among many other things, a fifty-one-page indictment handed down by a grand jury in Dade County, a correspondence file filled with letters from Argrow's defense lawyer and the U.S. Attorney's office, a thick file of motions and other pretrial maneuverings, research memos, a list of witnesses and summaries of their testimonies, a trial brief, jury analysis, an abstract of the trial, presentencing reports, and the final sentence itself. It was reasonably well organized, though not too neat to arouse suspicion. Copies were smudged, and pages were missing, and staples were hanging off, little touches of reality carefully added by the good folks in Documents to create authenticity. Ninety percent of it would not be needed by Beech and Yarber, but its sheer heft made it impressive. Even the cardboard box had some age on it.

The box was delivered to Trumble by Jack Argrow, a semiretired real estate lawyer in Boca Raton, Florida, and brother of the inmate. Lawyer Argrow's state bar certification had been faxed to the proper bureaucrat at Trumble, and his name was on the approved list of attorneys.

Jack Argrow was Roger Lyter, a thirteen-year man with a law degree from Texas. He'd never met Kenny Sands, who was Wilson Argrow. The two shook hands and said hello while Link looked suspiciously at the cardboard box sitting on the table.

'What's in there?' he asked.

'It's my court records,' Wilson said.

'Just paperwork,' Jack said.

Link stuck a hand in the box and moved some files around, and in a few seconds the search was over and he stepped out of the room.

Wilson slid a paper across the desk, and said, 'This is the affidavit. Wire the money to the bank in Panama, then get me written verification so I'll have something to show them.'

'Less ten percent.'

'Yes, that's what they think.'

The Geneva Trust Bank in Nassau had not been contacted. To do so would've been futile and risky. No bank would release funds under the circumstances Argrow was creating. And questions would be raised if he tried.

The wire transfer going to Panama was new money.

'Langley is quite anxious,' the lawyer said.

'I'm ahead of schedule,' the banker replied.

The box was emptied on a table in the law library. Beech and Yarber began sifting through its contents while Argrow, their new client, watched with feigned interest. Spicer had better things to do. He was in the middle of his weekly poker game.

'Where's the sentencing report?' Beech asked, scratching through the pile.

'I want to see the indictment,' Yarber mumbled to himself.

They found what they wanted, and both settled into their chairs for a long afternoon of reading. Beech's choice was quite dull. Yarber's, however, was not.

The indictment read like a crime narrative. Argrow, along with seven other bankers, five accountants, five securities brokers, two lawyers, eleven men identified only as drug traffickers, and six gentlemen from Colombia, had organized and run an elaborate enterprise designed to take drug proceeds in the form of cash and turn them into respectable deposits. At least $400 million had been laundered before the ring was infiltrated, and it appeared as though their man Argrow was right in the thick of things. Yarber admired him. If half the allegations were true, then Argrow was a very smart and talented financier.

Argrow became bored with the silence, and left to stroll around the prison. When Yarber finished reading the indictment, he interrupted Beech and made him read it. Beech enjoyed it too. 'Surely,' he said, 'he's got some of the loot buried somewhere.'

'You know he does,' Yarber agreed. 'Four hundred million bucks, and that's just what they could find. What about his appeal?'

'Doesn't look good. The judge followed the guidelines. I see no error.'

'Poor guy.'

'Poor guy, my ass. He'll be out four years before me.'

'I don't think so, Mr. Beech. We've spent our last Christmas in prison.'

'Do you really believe that?' Hatlee asked.

'Indeed I do.'

Beech placed the indictment back on the table, then stood and stretched and paced around the room 'We should've heard something by now,' he said, very softly though no one else was there.

'Patience.'

'But the primaries are almost over. He's back in Washington most of the time. He's had the letter for a week.'

'He can't ignore it, Hatlee. He's trying to figure out what to do. That's all.'

The latest memo from the Bureau of Prisons in Washington baffled the warden. Who in hell's name up there had nothing better to do than to stare at a map of the federal prisons and decide which one to meddle with that day? He had a brother making $150,000 selling used cars, and there he was making half that much running a prison and reading idiotic memos from pencil-pushers making $100,000 and not doing a productive damned thing. He was so sick of it!

RE: Attorney Visitation, Trumble Federal Prison

Disregard prior order, said order restricting attorney visitation to Tuesdays, Thursdays, and Saturdays, from 3 to 6 P.M.

Attorneys are now permitted to visit seven days a week, from 9 to 7 P.M.

'It takes a dead lawyer to get the rules changed,' he mumbled to himself.

THIRTY-FIVE

Deep in a basement garage, they rolled Teddy Maynard into his van and locked the doors. York and Deville sat with him. A driver and a bodyguard handled the van, which had a television, a stereo, and a small bar with bottled water and sodas, all of which were ignored by Teddy. He was subdued, and dreading the next hour. He was tired – tired of his work, tired of the fight, tired of forcing himself through another day, then another. Fight it six more months, he kept telling himself, then give it up and let someone else worry about saving the world. He'd go quietly to his small farm in West Virginia where he'd sit by the pond, watch the leaves fall into the water, and wait for the end. He was so tired of the pain.

There was a black car in front of them and a gray one behind, and the little convoy made its way around the Beltway, then east across the Roosevelt Bridge and onto Constitution Avenue.

Teddy was silent, so therefore York and Deville were too. They knew how much he loathed what he was about to do.

He talked to the President once a week, usually

on Wednesday morning, always by phone if Teddy had his way. They last saw each other nine months earlier when Teddy was in the hospital and the President needed to be briefed.

The favors usually fell to an equal level, but Teddy hated to be on the same footing with any President. He'd get the favor he wanted, but it was the asking that humiliated him.

In thirty years he'd survived six Presidents, and his secret weapon had been the favors. Gather the intelligence, hoard it, rarely tell the President everything, and occasionally gift-wrap a small miracle and deliver it to the White House.

This President was still pouting over the humiliating defeat of a nuclear test ban treaty Teddy had helped sabotage. The day before the Senate killed it, the CIA leaked a classified report raising legitimate concerns about the treaty, and the President got flattened in the stampede. He was leaving office, a lame duck more concerned with his legacy than with the pressing matters of the country.

Teddy had dealt with lame ducks before, and they were impossible. Since they wouldn't face the voters again, they dwelt on the big picture. In their waning days, they liked to travel, with lots of their friends, to foreign lands where they held summits with other lame ducks. They worried about their presidential libraries. And their portraits. And their biographies, so they spent time with historians. As the clock ticked they became wiser and more philosophical, and their speeches became grander. They talked of the future, of the challenges and the way things ought to be, conveniently ignoring the fact that they'd had eight years to do all the things that needed to be done.

There was nothing worse than a lame duck. And Lake would be just as bad if and when he had the chance.

Lake. The very reason Teddy was trekking to the White House, hat in hand, to grovel for a while.

They were cleared through the West Wing, where Teddy suffered the indignity of having his wheelchair examined by a Secret Service agent. Then they rolled him to a small office next to the cabinet room. A busy appointment secretary explained with no apology that the President was running late. Teddy smiled and waved her off and mumbled something to the effect that this President had never been on time for anything. He'd suffered a dozen fussy secretaries just like her, in the same position she was now in, and the others were long gone. She led York and Deville and the others away, down to the dining room where they would eat by themselves.

Teddy waited, as he knew he would. He read a thick report as if time meant nothing. Ten minutes passed. They brought him coffee. Two years ago the President had visited Langley, and Teddy had made him wait for twenty-one minutes. He needed a favor then, the President did, needed a little matter kept quiet.

The only advantage to being crippled was that he didn't have to jump to his feet when the President entered the room. He finally arrived in a rush, with aides scrambling behind him, as if this would impress Teddy Maynard. They shook hands and made the required greetings as the aides got rid of themselves. A waiter appeared and placed small green salads before them.

'It's good to see you,' the President said with a soft voice and drippy smile. Save it for television, Teddy thought, and he couldn't bring himself to return the lie. 'You're looking well,' he said, only because it was partially true. The President had a new tint to his hair, and he looked younger. They ate their salads, and a quietness settled around them.

Neither wanted a long lunch. 'The French are selling toys to the North Koreans again,' Teddy said, offering a crumb.

'What kinds of toys?' the President asked, though he knew precisely about the trafficking. And Teddy knew he knew.

'It's their version of stealth radar, which is quite stupid because they haven't perfected it yet. But the North Koreans are even dumber because they're paying for it. They'll buy anything from France, especially if the French try to hide it. The French, of course, know this, so it's all cloak and dagger and the North Koreans pay top dollar.'

The President pushed a button and the waiter appeared to remove their plates. Another brought chicken and pasta.

'How's your health?' the President asked.

'About the same. I'll probably leave when you do.'

This pleased them both, the prospect of the other leaving. For no apparent reason, the President then launched into a windy narrative about his Vice President, and what a wonderful job he would do in the Oval Office. He ignored his lunch and became very earnest in his opinions of what a fine human being and brilliant thinker and capable leader the man was. Teddy played with his chicken.

'How do you see the race?' the President asked.

'I honestly don't care,' Teddy said, lying again. 'As I told you, I'm leaving Washington when you do, Mr. President. I'm retiring to my little farm where there's no television, no newspapers, nothing but a little fishing and a lot of rest. I'm tired, sir.'

'Aaron Lake scares me,' the President said.

You don't know the half of it, Teddy thought. 'Why?' he asked, taking a bite. Eat, and let him talk.

'A single issue. Nothing but defense. You give the Pentagon unlimited resources and they'll waste enough to feed the third world. And all this money worries me.'

It never worried you before. The last thing Teddy wanted was a long, useless conversation about politics. They were wasting time. The sooner he finished his business, the sooner he could return to the safety of Langley. 'I'm here to ask a favor,' he said slowly.

'Yes, I know. What can I do for you?' The President was smiling and chewing, enjoying both the chicken and the rare moment of having the upper hand.

'It's a little out of the ordinary. I'd like clemency for three federal prisoners.'

The chewing and smiling stopped, not out of shock but out of confusion. Clemency was usually a simple matter, unless it involved spies or terrorists or infamous politicians. 'Spies?' the President asked.

'No. Judges. One from California, one from Texas, one from Mississippi. They're serving their time together in a federal prison in Florida.'

'Judges?'

'Yes, Mr. President.'

'Do I know these people?'

'I doubt it. The one from California was once the Chief Justice of the Supreme Court out there. He got himself recalled, then had a little trouble with the IRS.'

'I think I remember that.'

'He was convicted of tax evasion and sentenced to seven years. He's served two. The one from Texas was a trial judge, a Reagan appointee. He got drunk and killed a couple of hikers in Yellowstone.'

'I do remember that, but vaguely.'

'It was several years ago. The one from Mississippi was a Justice of the Peace who got caught embezzling bingo profits.'

'I must've missed that one.'

There was a long pause as they considered the questions. The President was bewildered and not certain where to start. Teddy wasn't sure what was coming, so they finished eating in silence. Neither wanted dessert.

The request was an easy one, at least for the President. The felons were virtually unknown, as were their victims. Any fallout would be quick and painless, especially for a politician whose career was less than seven months from being over. He'd been pressured to grant far more difficult pardons. The Russians always had a few spies they lobbied to get back. There were two Mexican businessmen locked away in Idaho for drug trafficking, and every time a treaty of some sort was on the table their clemency became an issue. There was a Canadian Jew serving a life sentence for spying, and the Israelis were determined to get him out.

Three unknown judges? The President could sign his name three times and the matter would be over. Teddy would owe him.

It would be a simple matter, but that was no reason to make things easy for Teddy.

'I'm sure there's a good reason for this request,' he said.

'Of course.'

'A matter of grave national security?'

'Not really. Just a few favors for old friends.'

'Old friends? Do you know these men?'

'No. But I know their friends.'

The lie was so obvious the President almost jumped at it. How could Teddy know the friends of three judges who just happened to be serving time together?

Nothing would come from grilling Teddy Maynard, nothing but frustration. And the President would not stoop that low. He would not beg for information he'd never get. Whatever Teddy's motives were, he would take them to his grave.

'This is a bit confusing,' the President said with a shrug.

'I know. Let's leave it at that.'

'What's the fallout?'

'Not much. The families of the two kids who

were killed in Yellowstone might squawk, and I wouldn't blame them.'

'How long ago was it?'

'Three and a half years.'

'You want me to pardon a Republican federal judge?'

'He's not a Republican now, Mr. President. They have to swear off politics once they take the bench. Now that he's been convicted, he can't even vote. I'm sure if you granted clemency he'd become a big fan of yours.'

'I'm sure he would.'

'If it'll make matters easier, these gentlemen will agree to leave the country for at least two years.'

'Why?'

'It might look bad if they return home. Folks will know that they somehow got out early. This can be kept very quiet.'

'Did the judge from California pay the taxes he tried to evade?'

'He did.'

'And did the guy from Mississippi repay the money he stole?'

'Yes sir.'

All the questions were superficial. He had to ask something.

The last favor had dealt with nuclear spying. The CIA had a report documenting widespread infiltration of Chinese spies in and through virtually all levels of the U.S. nuclear arms program. The President learned of the report just days before he was scheduled to visit China for a highly touted summit. He asked Teddy to come have lunch, and over the same chicken and pasta he

401

asked that the report be held for a few weeks. Teddy agreed. Later, he wanted the report modified to place more blame on prior administrations. Teddy rewrote it himself. When it was finally released, the President deflected most of the blame.

Chinese spying and national security, versus three obscure ex-judges. Teddy knew he would get the pardons.

'If they leave the country, where will they go?' the President asked.

'We're not sure yet.'

The waiter brought coffee. When he was gone, the President asked, 'Will this in any way hurt the Vice President?'

And with the same expressionless face, Teddy said, 'No. How could it?'

'You tell me. I have no clue what you're doing.'

'There's nothing to worry about, Mr. President. I'm asking for a small favor. With a little luck, this will not be reported anywhere.'

They sipped their coffee and both wanted to leave. The President had a full afternoon with more pleasant matters. Teddy needed a nap. The President was relieved it was such a benign request. Teddy was thinking, If you only knew.

'Give me a few days to do the background,' the President said. 'These requests are pouring in, as you might guess. Seems everybody wants something now that my days are numbered.'

'Your last month here will be your happiest,' Teddy said with a rare grin. 'I've seen enough Presidents to know.'

After forty minutes together, they shook hands and promised to talk in a few days.

There were five ex-lawyers at Trumble, and the newest one was using the library when Argrow entered. Poor guy was up to his elbows in briefs and legal pads, working feverishly, no doubt pursuing his last feeble appeal.

Spicer was rearranging law books and managing to look sufficiently busy. Beech was in the chamber, writing something. Yarber was absent.

Argrow removed a folded sheet of white paper from his pocket, and gave it to Spicer. 'I just saw my lawyer,' he whispered.

'What is it?' Spicer asked, holding the paper.

'It's a wire confirmation. Your money is now in Panama.'

Spicer looked at the lawyer across the room, but he was oblivious to everything except his legal pad. 'Thanks,' he whispered. Argrow left the room, and Spicer took the paper to Beech, who examined it carefully.

Their loot was now safely guarded by the First Coast Bank of Panama.

THIRTY-SIX

Joe Roy had dropped eight more pounds, was down to ten cigarettes a day and averaging twenty-five miles a week around the track. Argrow found him there, walking and pacing in the late afternoon heat.

'Mr. Spicer, we need to talk,' Argrow said.

'Two more laps,' Joe Roy said without breaking stride.

Argrow watched him for a few seconds, then jogged fifty yards until he caught up. 'Mind if I join?' he asked.

'Not at all.'

They went into the first turn, stride for stride. 'I just met with my lawyer again,' Argrow said.

'Your brother?' Spicer asked, breathing heavily. His paces were not nearly as graceful as Argrow's, a man twenty years younger.

'Yes. He's talked to Aaron Lake.'

Spicer stopped as if he'd hit a wall. He glared at Argrow, then looked at something in the distance.

'Like I said, we need to talk.'

'I suppose we do,' Spicer said.

'I'll meet you in the law library in half an hour,'

Argrow said, and walked away. Spicer watched him until he disappeared.

There was no Jack Argrow, Attorney-at-Law, in the Boca Raton yellow pages, and this initially caused concern. Finn Yarber frantically worked the unsecured phone, seeking directory assistance all over South Florida. When he asked for Pompano Beach, the operator said, 'One moment, please,' and Finn actually smiled. He scribbled down the number, then dialed it. A recorded voice said, 'You've reached the law offices of Jack Argrow. Mr. Argrow keeps hours by appointment only, so please leave your name and number and a brief description of the real estate you're interested in, and we'll get in touch with you.' Finn hung up and walked quickly across the lawn to the law library, where his colleagues were waiting. Argrow was already ten minutes late.

A moment before he arrived, the same ex-lawyer entered the room carrying a bulky file, evidently ready to spend hours trying to save himself. To ask him to leave would cause a fight and create suspicion, and besides he wasn't the type who respected judges anyway. One by one they retired to the small conference room, where Argrow joined them. The room was cramped when Beech and Yarber worked there, writing their letters. With Argrow as the fourth man in, and bringing no small amount of pressure, the room had never felt so crowded. They sat around the small table, each able to reach and touch the other three.

'I know only what I've been told,' Argrow began. 'My brother is a semiretired lawyer in Boca

Raton. He has some money, and for years he's been active in Republican politics in South Florida. Yesterday he was approached by some people who work for Aaron Lake. They had investigated matters and knew that I was his brother, and that I was here in Trumble along with Mr. Spicer. They made promises, swore him to secrecy, and now he's sworn me to secrecy. Now that everything is nice and confidential, I think you can connect the dots.'

Spicer had not showered. His shirt and face were still wet, but his breathing had slowed. Not the slightest sound from either Beech or Yarber. The Brethren were in a collective trance. Keep going, they said with their eyes.

Argrow looked at the three faces, and pushed onward. He reached into his pocket and removed a sheet of paper, which he unfolded and laid before them. It was a copy of their last letter to Al Konyers, the outing letter, the extortion demand, signed by Joe Roy Spicer, current address of Trumble Federal Prison. They had the words memorized, so there was no need to read it again. They recognized the handwriting, that of poor little Ricky, and they realized that it had now come full circle. From the Brethren to Mr. Lake, from Mr. Lake to Argrow's brother, from Argrow's brother back to Trumble, all in thirteen days.

Spicer finally picked it up, and glanced at the words. 'I guess you know everything, don't you?' he asked.

'I don't know how much I know.'

'Tell us what they've told you.'

'You're running a scam, the three of you. You

advertise in gay magazines, you develop relationships with older men, by mail, you somehow learn their true identities, then you extort money from them.'

'That's a pretty fair summary of the game,' Beech said.

'And Mr. Lake made the mistake of answering one of your ads. I don't know when he did this, and I don't know how you found out who he was. There are some gaps in the plot, as far as I'm concerned.'

'It's best to keep it that way,' Yarber said.

'Fair enough. I didn't volunteer for this job.'

'What will you get out of it?' Spicer asked.

'Early release. I'll spend a few more weeks around here, then they'll move me again. I'll walk by the end of the year, and if Mr. Lake gets elected then I'll get a full pardon. Not a bad deal. My brother gets a huge favor from the next President.'

'So you're the negotiator?' Beech said.

'No, I'm the messenger.'

'Then shall we begin?'

'The first move belongs to you.'

'You've got the letter. We want some money and we want out of this place.'

'How much money?'

'Two million each,' Spicer said, and it was obvious this had been discussed many times already. All six eyes watched Argrow, waiting for the twitch, the frown, the shock. But there was no reaction, just a pause as he returned their stares. 'I have no authority here, okay? I can't say yes or no to your demands. All I do is relay the details to my brother.'

'We read the newspaper every day,' Beech said. 'Mr. Lake has more money than he can spend right now. Six million is a drop in the bucket.'

'He has seventy-eight million on hand, with no debt,' Yarber added.

'Whatever,' Argrow said. 'I'm just the courier, the mail runner, sort of like Trevor.'

They froze again, with the mention of their dead lawyer. They glared at Argrow, whose fingernails had caught his attention, and they wondered if the Trevor comment had been laid across the table as some sort of warning. How deadly had their game become? They were giddy with thoughts of money and freedom, but how safe were they now? How safe would they be in the future?

They would always know Lake's secret.

'And the terms of the money?' Argrow asked.

'Very simple,' Spicer said. 'All of it up front, all of it wired to some delightful little place, probably Panama.'

'Okay. Now what about your release?' Argrow asked.

'What about it?' asked Beech.

'Any suggestions?'

'Not really. We thought Mr. Lake could take care of that. He has lots of friends these days.'

'Yes, but he's not the President yet. He can't lean on the right people yet.'

'We're not waiting until January when he's inaugurated,' Yarber said. 'In fact, we're not waiting until November to see if he wins.'

'So you want to be released now?'

'Pretty damned quick,' Spicer said.

'Does it matter how you're released?'

They thought for a moment, then Beech said, 'It has to be clean. We're not running for the rest of our lives. We're not looking over our shoulders.'

'Do you leave together?'

'Yes,' Yarber said. 'And we have some definite plans on how we want to do it. First, though, we need to agree on the important things – money, and exactly when we walk out of here.'

'Fair enough. From this side of the table, they'll want your files, all of the letters and notes and records from your scam. Obviously, Mr. Lake has to receive assurances that the secrets will be buried.'

'If we get what we want,' Beech said, 'he has nothing to worry about. We'll gladly forget we ever heard of Aaron Lake. But we must warn you, so you can warn Mr. Lake, that if anything happens to us, his story will be told anyway.'

'We have an outside contact,' Yarber said.

'It's a delayed reaction,' Spicer added, as if he were helping explain the unexplainable. 'Something happens to us, like, for instance, the same thing that happened to Trevor, and a few days later a little delay bomb goes off. Mr. Lake gets himself outed anyway.'

'That won't happen,' Argrow said.

'You're the messenger. You don't know what will or will not happen,' Beech said, lecturing. 'These are the same people who killed Trevor.'

'You're not sure of that.'

'No, but we have our opinions.'

'Let's not argue something we can't prove, gentlemen,' Argrow said, ending the session. 'I'll see my brother at nine in the morning. Let's meet here at ten.'

Argrow left the room, left them sitting trance-like, deep in thought, counting their money but afraid to start spending it. He headed for the track, but turned away when he saw a group of inmates jogging. He roamed the grounds until he found a secluded spot behind the cafeteria, then he called Klockner.

Within an hour, Teddy was briefed.

THIRTY-SEVEN

The 6 A.M. bell shrieked through Trumble, through the corridors of the dorms, across the lawns, around the buildings, into the surrounding woods. It lasted for exactly thirty-five seconds, most inmates could tell you, and by the time it quit no one was left asleep. It jolted them to life, as if important events were planned that day, and they had to hurry and get ready. But the only pressing matter was breakfast.

The bell startled Beech, Spicer, and Yarber, but it didn't wake them. Sleep had been elusive, the reasons obvious. They lived in different dorms, but not surprisingly they met in line for coffee, at ten minutes after six. With their tall cups, and without a word, they walked to the basketball court where they sat on a bench and sipped in the early dawn. They watched the prison grounds; the track was behind them.

How many more days would they wear their olive shirts and sit in the Florida heat, getting paid pennies by the hour for doing nothing, just waiting, dreaming, drinking endless cups of coffee? Would it be a month, or two? Were they talking days now? The possibilities had robbed them of sleep.

'There are only two possible ways,' Beech was saying. He was the federal judge, and they listened carefully, though it was familiar ground. 'The first is to go back to the sentencing jurisdiction and file a motion for reduced time. Under very narrow circumstances, the trial judge has the authority to release an inmate. It's rarely done, though.'

'Did you ever do it?' Spicer asked.

'No.'

'Asshole.'

'For what reasons?' Yarber asked.

'Only when the prisoner has provided new information about old crimes. If the prisoner provides substantial assistance to the authorities, then he might get a few years off.'

'That's not encouraging,' Yarber said.

'What's number two?' Spicer asked.

'We're shipped out to a halfway house, a really nice one where they don't expect us to live by the rules. The Bureau of Prisons has sole authority in placing inmates. If the right pressure is applied by our new friends in Washington, then the Bureau could move us out and basically forget about us.'

'Don't you have to live in a halfway house?' Spicer asked.

'Yes, in most of them. But they're all different. Some are locked down at night, with strict rules. Others are very laid back. You can phone in once a day, or once a week. It's all up to the Bureau.'

'But we'll still be convicted felons,' Spicer said.

'Doesn't bother me,' Yarber said. 'I'll never vote again.'

412

'I have an idea,' Beech said. 'It came to me last night. As part of our negotiations, we make Lake agree to pardon us if he's elected.'

'I thought of that too,' Spicer said.

'So did I,' said Yarber. 'But who cares if we have a record? The only thing that matters is that we get out.'

'It won't hurt to ask,' Beech replied. They concentrated on their coffee for a few minutes.

'Argrow's making me nervous,' Finn finally said.

'How's that?'

'Well, he drops in here from nowhere, and suddenly becomes our best friend. He does a magic trick with our money, gets it wired to a safer bank. Now he's the point man for Aaron Lake. Keep in mind, somebody out there was reading our mail. And it wasn't Lake.'

'He doesn't bother me,' Spicer said. 'Lake had to find somebody to talk to us. He pulled some strings, did some research, found out that Argrow was here and that he had a brother they could talk to.'

'That's awfully convenient, don't you think?' Beech asked.

'You too, huh?'

'Maybe. Finn's got a point. We know for a fact that somebody else got involved.'

'Who?'

'That's the big question,' Finn said. 'That's why I haven't slept in a week. There's somebody else out there.'

'Do we really care?' Spicer asked. 'If Lake can get us outta here, fine. If somebody else can get us outta here, what's wrong with that?'

'Don't forget Trevor,' Beech said. 'Two bullets in the back of the head.'

'This place might be safer than we think.'

Spicer was not convinced. He finished a drink and said, 'Do you really think that Aaron Lake, a man about to be elected President of the United States, would order a hit on a worthless lawyer like Trevor?'

'No,' replied Yarber. 'He would not. It's much too risky. And he wouldn't kill us. But the mystery man would. The guy who killed Trevor is the same guy who read our mail.'

'I'm not convinced.'

They were together where Argrow expected to find them, in the law library, and they seemed to be waiting. He entered in a rush, and when he was sure they were alone, he said, 'I just met with my brother again. Let's talk.'

They scurried into their little conference room, closed the door, and crowded around the table.

'Things are about to happen very fast,' Argrow said nervously. 'Lake will pay the money. It'll be wired anywhere you want it. I can help if you want; otherwise you can handle it any way you wish.'

Spicer cleared his throat. 'That's two million each?'

'That's what you asked for. I don't know Mr. Lake, but evidently he moves fast.' Argrow glanced at his watch, then looked over his shoulder at the door. 'There are some people from Washington here to meet with you. Big shots.' He yanked some papers from his pocket, unfolded them, and laid a single sheet before each of the three. 'These are presidential pardons, signed yesterday.'

With great reserve, they reached forward, took the papers, and tried to read them. The copies certainly looked official. They gawked at the bold letters across the top, the paragraphs of fussy prose, the compact signature of the President of the United States, and not a single word could be summoned. They were just stunned.

'We've been pardoned?' Yarber finally managed to ask, his voice dry.

'Yes. By the President of the United States.'

They kept reading. They fidgeted and chewed their lips and clenched their jaws, and tried to quietly hide their shock.

'They're gonna come get you, take you to the warden's office where the big shots from Washington will deliver the good news. Act surprised, okay?'

'No problem.'

'That should be easy.'

'How did you get these copies?' Yarber asked.

'They were given to my brother. I have no idea how. Lake has powerful friends. Anyway, here's the deal. You'll be released within the hour. A van will take you to Jacksonville, to a hotel where my brother will meet you. You will wait there until the wire transfers are confirmed, then you will hand over all of your dirty little files. Everything. Understood?'

They nodded in unison. For two million bucks, they could have it all.

'You will agree to leave the country immediately, and not to return for at least two years.'

415

'How can we leave the country?' Beech asked. 'We have no passports, no papers.'

'My brother will have all of that. You will be given new identities, with a complete set of papers, including credit cards. It's all waiting for you.'

'Two years?' Spicer asked, and Yarber looked at him as if he'd lost his mind.

'That's right. Two years. It's part of the deal. Agreed?'

'I don't know,' Spicer said, his voice shaking. Spicer had never left the United States.

'Don't be foolish,' Yarber snapped at him. 'A complete pardon, a million bucks a year for two years to live abroad. Hell, yes, we'll take the deal.'

A sudden knock on the door terrified them. Two guards were looking in. Argrow grabbed the copies of the pardons and stuffed them in his pocket. 'Do we have a deal, gentlemen?'

They nodded yes, and all three shook hands with him.

'Good,' he said. 'Remember, act surprised.'

They followed the guards to the warden's office where they were introduced to two very stern-faced men from Washington, one from Justice, one from the Bureau of Prisons. The warden completed the stiff introductions without getting any of the names confused, then he handed each of the three a legal-sized document. They were the originals of what Argrow had just shown them.

'Gentlemen,' the warden announced with as much drama as he could muster, 'you've just been pardoned by the President of the United States.' He smiled warmly as if he were responsible for this good news.

416

They stared at their pardons, still in shock, still dizzy with a thousand questions, the biggest of which was, How in the world did Argrow scoop the warden and show them the documents first?

'I don't know what to say,' Spicer managed to mumble, then the other two mumbled something else.

The man from Justice said, 'The President reviewed your cases, and he felt that you have served enough time. He feels very strongly that you have more to offer your country and your communities by once again becoming productive citizens.'

They stared blankly at him. This fool didn't know they were about to assume new names and flee their country and their communities for at least two years? Who was on which side here?

And why was the President granting them clemency when they had enough dirt to destroy Aaron Lake, the man who was primed to defeat the Vice President? It was Lake who wanted them silenced, not the President? Right?

How could Lake convince the President to pardon them?

How could Lake convince the President to do anything, at this stage of the campaign?

They clutched their pardons and sat speechless, their faces drawn tight as the questions hammered away inside.

The man from the Bureau said, 'You should feel honored. Clemency is very rare.'

Yarber managed to acknowledge him with a quick nod, but even then he was thinking, Who's waiting for us on the outside?

'I think we're in shock,' Beech said.

It was a first for Trumble, inmates so important that the President decided to pardon them. The warden was quite proud of the three, but uncertain as to how the moment should be commemorated. 'When would you like to leave?' he asked, as if they might want to stick around for a party.

'Immediately,' Spicer said.

'Very well. We'll drive you to Jacksonville.'

'No thanks. We'll have someone pick us up.'

'Okay, then, well, there's some paperwork.'

'Make it quick,' Spicer said.

They were each given a duffel bag to collect their things in. As they walked rather briskly across the grounds, all still very close together and in perfect step, with a guard trailing behind, Beech said, under his breath, 'So who got us the damned pardons?'

'It wasn't Lake,' Yarber said, just barely loud enough to be heard.

'Of course it wasn't Lake,' Beech said. 'The President wouldn't do a damned thing Aaron Lake asked him to.'

They walked faster.

'What difference does it make?' Spicer asked.

'It doesn't make any sense,' Yarber said.

'So what're you gonna do, Finn?' Spicer asked without looking. 'Stay here for a few days and ponder the situation? And then if you figure out who's responsible for the pardon, then maybe you won't accept it? Gimme a break.'

'Somebody else is behind this,' Beech said.

'Then I love this somebody else, okay?' Spicer said. 'I'm not sticking around to ask questions.'

They ransacked their rooms in a mad rush, never slowing to say good-bye to anyone. Most of their friends were scattered around the camp anyway.

They had to hurry before the dream was over, or before the President changed his mind.

At eleven-fifteen, they walked through the front door of the administration building, the same door they'd each entered years ago, and waited on the hot sidewalk for their ride. None of the three looked back.

The van was driven by Wes and Chap, though they gave other names. They used so many.

Joe Roy Spicer lay down on the backseat, and covered his eyes with a forearm, determined not to see anything until he was far away. He wanted to cry and he wanted to scream, but he was numb with euphoria – sheer, uncut, unabashed euphoria. He hid his eyes and smiled a goofy smile. He wanted a beer and he wanted a woman, preferably his wife. He'd call her soon. The van was rolling now.

The suddenness of the release had them rattled. Most inmates count the days, and in doing so know with some measure of accuracy when the moment will come. And they know where they're going, and who's waiting for them there.

But the Brethren knew so little. And the few things they knew, they didn't really believe. The pardons were a hoax. The money was nothing but bait. They were being taken away to be slaughtered, same as poor Trevor. The van would stop any minute, and the two goons up front would search their bags, find their dirty files, then murder them in a roadside ditch.

Maybe. But, at the moment, they did not miss the safety of Trumble.

Finn Yarber sat behind the driver and watched the road ahead. He held his pardon, ready to present it to anyone who might stop them and tell them the dream was over. Next to him was Hatlee Beech, who after a few minutes on the road began to cry, not loud, but with his eyes tightly closed and his lips quivering.

Beech had reason to cry. With almost eight and a half years to go, clemency meant more to him than to his two colleagues combined.

Not a word was uttered between Trumble and Jacksonville. As they approached the city, and the roads became wider and the traffic heavier, the three watched the scenery with great curiosity. People were driving, moving about. Planes overhead. Boats on the rivers. Things were normal again.

They inched through the traffic on Atlantic Boulevard, thoroughly enjoying every moment of the congestion. The weather was hot, the tourists were out, ladies with long bronze legs. They saw the seafood restaurants and bars with signs advertising cold beer and cheap oysters. When the street ended, the beach began, and they pulled under the veranda of the Sea Turtle. They followed one of their escorts through the lobby, where they caught a look or two because they were still dressed alike. Up to the fifth floor, and off the elevator before Chap said, 'Your rooms are right here, these three.' He was pointing down the hall. 'Mr. Argrow would like to see you as soon as possible.'

'Where is he?' Spicer asked.

Chap pointed again. 'Over there, in the corner suite. He's waiting.'

'Let's go,' Spicer said, and they followed Chap into the corner, their duffel bags bouncing against one another.

Jack Argrow looked nothing like his brother. He was much shorter, and his hair was blond and wavy where his brother's was dark and thinning. It was just a casual observation, but the three noticed it and mentioned it later. He shook their hands quickly, but only to be polite. He was edgy and talked very fast. 'How's my brother?' he asked.

'He's doing well,' Beech said.

'We saw him this morning,' Yarber added.

'I want him out of prison,' Jack snapped, as if they'd put him there in the first place. 'That's what I'll get outta this deal, you know. I'll get my brother out of prison.'

They glanced at each other; nothing could be said.

'Have a seat,' Argrow said. 'Look, I don't know how or why I'm in the middle of this, you understand. It makes me very nervous. I'm here on behalf of Mr. Aaron Lake, a man I believe will be elected, and make a great President. I suppose I can then get my brother outta prison. But anyway, I've never met Mr. Lake. Some of his people approached me about a week ago, and asked me to get involved in a very secret and delicate matter. That's why I'm here. It's a favor, okay? I don't know everything, you understand?' The sentences were clipped and rapid. He talked with his hands and his mouth, and he couldn't be still.

The Brethren offered no response, none was really expected.

Two hidden cameras captured the scene and sent it immediately to Langley, where Teddy, York, and Deville watched it on a wide screen in the bunker. The ex-judges, now ex-inmates, looked like freshly released POWs, dazed and subdued, still in uniform, still in disbelief. They sat close together, watching Agent Lyter give a splendid performance.

After trying to outthink and outmaneuver them for three months, it was fascinating to finally see them. Teddy studied their faces, and grudgingly admitted a little admiration. They'd been shrewd and lucky enough to hook the right victim; now they were free and about to be well compensated for their ingenuity.

'Okay, look, the first thing is the money,' Argrow barked. 'Two million each. Where do you want it?'

It was not the sort of question they'd had much experience with. 'What are the options?' asked Spicer.

'You have to wire it somewhere,' Argrow snapped back.

'How about London?' Yarber asked.

'London?'

'We'd like the money, all of it, all six million, to be wired at one time, to one account, to a bank in London,' Yarber said.

'We can wire it anywhere. Which bank?'

'Can you help us with the details?' Yarber asked.

422

'I'm told we can do anything you want. I'll have to make a few calls. Why don't you go to your rooms, take a shower, change clothes. Give me fifteen minutes.'

'We don't have any clothes,' Beech said.

'There are some things in your rooms.'

Chap led them down the hall and gave them their keys.

Spicer stretched out on his king-sized bed and stared at the ceiling. Beech stood in the window of his room and looked north, for miles along the beach, the blue water gently rolling onto the white sand. Children played near their mothers. Couples strolled hand in hand. A fishing boat inched along on the horizon. Free at last, he said to himself. Free at last.

Yarber took a long hot shower – complete privacy, no time limit, plenty of soap, thick towels. Someone had placed a selection of toiletries on the vanity – deodorant, shaving cream, razors, toothpaste, toothbrush, floss. He took his time, then changed into a pair of Bermuda shorts, sandals, and a white tee shirt. He'd be the first to leave, and he needed to find a clothing store.

Twenty minutes later they reconvened in Argrow's suite, and they brought with them their collection of files wrapped neatly in a pillowcase. Argrow was just as anxious as before. 'There's a large bank in London called Metropolitan Trust. We can send the money there, then you can do with it whatever you want.'

'That's fine,' Yarber said. 'The account will be in my name only.'

Argrow looked at Beech and Spicer, and they

nodded their approval. 'Very well. I assume you have a plan of some sort.'

'We do,' Spicer said. 'Mr. Yarber here will leave for London this afternoon, and when he gets there he'll go to the bank and take care of the money. If all goes well, then we'll leave soon afterward.'

'I assure you things will go well.'

'And we believe you. We're just being careful.'

Argrow handed two sheets of paper to Finn. 'I need your signature to start the wire and open the account.' Yarber scribbled his name.

'Have you had lunch?' he asked.

They shook their heads. Lunch was certainly on their minds, but they weren't sure how to proceed.

'You're free men now. There are some nice restaurants just a few blocks from here. Go enjoy yourselves. Give me an hour to start the wire. Let's meet here at two-thirty.'

Spicer was holding the pillowcase. He sort of waved it at Argrow and said, 'Here are the files.'

'Right. Just throw them on the sofa there.'

THIRTY-EIGHT

They left the hotel on foot, without escorts, without restrictions, but with their pardons in their pockets, just in case. And though the sun was warmer near the beach, the air was certainly lighter. The sky was clearer. The world was pretty again. Hope filled the air. They smiled and laughed at almost anything. They strolled along Atlantic Boulevard, and mixed easily with the tourists.

Lunch was steak and beer at a sidewalk café, under an umbrella, so they could watch the foot traffic. Little was said as they ate and drank. Everything was seen, though, especially the younger ladies in shorts and skimpy tops. Prison had turned them into old men. Now they felt the urge to party.

Especially Hatlee Beech. He'd had wealth and status and ambition, and as a federal judge he'd had what was all but impossible to lose – a lifetime appointment. He'd fallen hard, lost everything, and during his first two years at Trumble he'd existed in a state of depression. He had accepted the fact that he would die there, and he'd seriously considered suicide. Now, at the age of fifty-six, he was emerging from the darkness in a rather splendid fashion. He was fifteen pounds lighter, nicely tanned, in good health, divorced from a woman who had money but not much else to offer, and about to collect a fortune. Not a bad middle-aged rally, he told himself. He missed his children, but they'd followed the money and forgotten about him.

Hatlee Beech was ready for some fun.

Spicer was also looking for a party, preferably one at a casino. His wife had no passport, so it would be a few weeks before she could join him in London, or wherever he might land. Did they have casinos in Europe? Beech thought so. Yarber had no idea, and didn't care.

Finn was the most reserved of the three. He drank a soda instead of beer, and he wasn't as interested in the flesh passing by. Finn was already in Europe. He'd never leave, never return to his native land. He was sixty, very fit, now with lots of money, and was about to bum around Italy and Greece for the next ten years.

Across the street, they found a small bookstore and bought several travel books. In a shop specializing in beachwear, they found just the right sunglasses. Then it was time to see Jack Argrow again, and finish the deal.

Klockner and company watched them stroll back to the Sea Turtle. Klockner and company were weary of Neptune Beach and Pete's and the Sea Turtle and the crowded rental. Six agents, including Chap and Wes, were still there, all very anxious for another assignment. The unit had discovered the Brethren, plucked them from inside Trumble, brought them to the beach, and now they just wanted them to leave the country.

Jack Argrow had not touched the files, or at least they appeared untouched. They were still wrapped in the pillowcase, on the sofa, in the exact spot Spicer had left them.

'The wire is under way,' Argrow said as they settled into his suite.

Teddy was still watching from Langley. The three were now wearing all manner of beach garb. Yarber had a fishing cap with a six-inch bill. Spicer had a straw hat and a yellow tee shirt of some variety. Beech, the Republican, wore khaki shorts, a knit pullover, and a golf cap.

There were three large envelopes on the dining table. Argrow handed one to each of the Brethren. 'Inside, you'll find your new identities. Birth certificates, credit cards, Social Security cards.'

'What about passports?' asked Yarber.

'We have a camera set up in the next room. The passports and driver's licenses will need photos. It'll take thirty minutes. There's also five thousand dollars cash in those small envelopes there.'

'I'm Harvey Moss?' Spicer asked, looking at his birth certificate.

'Yes. You don't like Harvey?'

'I guess I do now.'

'You look like a Harvey,' Beech said.

'And who are you?'

'Well, I'm James Nunley.'

'Nice to meet you, James.'

Argrow never cracked a smile, never relaxed for

a second. 'I need to know your travel plans. The people in Washington really want you out of the country.'

'I need to check flights to London,' Yarber said.

'We've already done that. A flight to Atlanta leaves Jacksonville in two hours. At seven-ten tonight, there's a flight leaving Atlanta for London Heathrow that arrives early tomorrow morning.'

'Can you get me a seat?'

'It's already done. First class.'

Finn closed his eyes and smiled.

'And what about you?' Argrow asked, looking at the other two.'

'I kinda like it here,' Spicer said.

'Sorry. We have a deal.'

'We'll take the same flights tomorrow afternoon,' Beech said. 'Assuming all goes well with Mr. Yarber.'

'Do you want us to handle the reservations?'

'Yes, please.'

Chap eased into the room without making a sound, and took the pillowcase from the sofa. He left with the files.

'Let's do the photos,' Argrow said.

Finn Yarber, now traveling as a Mr. William McCoy of San Jose, California, flew to Atlanta without incident. For an hour he walked the concourses of the airport, rode the underground shuttles, and thoroughly enjoyed the frenzy and chaos of being in the midst of a million people in a hurry.

His first-class seat was a massive leather recliner. After two glasses of champagne, he began to drift, and to dream. He was afraid to sleep because he was afraid to wake up. He was certain he would be back on his top bunk, staring at the ceiling, counting off another day at Trumble.

From a pay phone next to Beach Java, Joe Roy finally caught his wife. At first, she thought the call was a hoax and refused to accept the collect charges. 'Who is this?' she asked.

'It's me, dear. I'm no longer in prison.'

'Joe Roy?'

'Yes, now listen. I'm out of prison, okay. Are you there?'

'I think so. Where are you?'

'I'm staying at a hotel near Jacksonville, Florida. I was released from prison this morning.'

'Released? But how –'

'Don't ask, okay. I'll explain everything later. I'm leaving tomorrow for London. I want you to go to the post office first thing in the morning, and get an application for a passport.'

'London? Did you say London?'

'Yes.'

'England?'

'That's it, yes. I have to go there for a while. It's part of the deal.'

'For how long?'

'A couple of years. Listen, I know it's hard to believe, but I'm free and we're gonna live abroad for a couple of years.'

'What kinda deal? Have you escaped, Joe Roy? You said it'd be easy to do.'

'No. I have been released.'

'But you got more than twenty months to go.'

'Not anymore. Listen, get the application for a passport and follow the instructions.'

'Why do I need a passport?'

'So we can meet in Europe.'

'For two years?'

'Yes, that's it.'

'But Mother's sick. I can't just run off and leave Mother.'

He thought of all the things he'd like to say about her mother, then let it pass. A deep breath, a glance down the street. 'I'm going away,' he said. 'I have no choice.'

'Just come home,' she said.

'I can't. I'll explain it later.'

'An explanation would be nice.'

'I'll call you tomorrow.'

Beech and Spicer ate seafood in a restaurant crowded with people much younger. They roamed the sidewalks and eventually found their way to Pete's Bar and Grill, where they watched the Braves and enjoyed the noise.

Finn was somewhere over the Atlantic, following their money.

The customs agent at Heathrow barely glanced at Finn's passport, which was a marvel of forgery. It was well used and had accompanied Mr. William McCoy around the world. Aaron Lake did indeed have powerful friends.

Finn took a taxi to the Basil Street Hotel in Knightsbridge, and paid cash for the smallest room available. He and Beech had selected the hotel at random from a travel guide. It was an old-fashioned place, filled with antiques, and it rambled from floor to floor. At the small restaurant upstairs, he had breakfast of coffee, eggs, and black sausage, then went for a walk. At ten, his taxi stopped in front of the Metropolitan Trust in the City. The receptionist didn't care for his attire – jeans and a pullover – but when she realized he was an American she shrugged and seemed to tolerate it.

They made him wait for an hour, but he didn't mind it at all. Finn was nervous, but didn't show it. He'd wait for days, weeks, months to get the money. He'd learned how to be patient. The Mr. MacGregor who was in charge of the wire finally came for him. The money had just arrived, sorry for the delay. All six million bucks had crossed the Atlantic safely, and was now on British soil.

But not for long. 'I'd like to wire it to Switzerland,' Finn said, with the proper dose of confidence and experience.

That afternoon, Beech and Spicer flew to Atlanta. Like Yarber, they roamed the airport with unrestrained freedom while waiting for their London flight. They sat together in first class, ate and drank for hours, watched movies, tried to sleep as they crossed the ocean.

Much to their surprise, Yarber was waiting when they cleared customs at Heathrow. He delivered the wonderful news that the money had come and gone. It was hidden in Switzerland. He surprised them again with the idea of leaving immediately.

'They know we're here,' he said over coffee in an airport bar. 'Let's shake them.'

'You think they're following us?' Beech asked.

'Let's assume they are.'

'But why?' Spicer asked.

They discussed it for half an hour, then began looking for flights. Alitalia to Rome caught their attention. First class, of course.

'Do they speak English in Rome?' Spicer asked as they were boarding.

'Actually, they speak Italian,' Yarber said.

'You think the Pope will see us?'

'He's probably busy.'

THIRTY-NINE

Buster zigzagged westward for days until he made his final bus stop in San Diego. The ocean attracted him, the first water he'd seen in months. He hung around the docks looking for odd jobs and chatting with the regulars. A charter boat captain hired him as a gopher, and he jumped ship in Los Cabos, Mexico, at the southern tip of the Baja. The harbor there was filled with expensive fishing boats, much nicer than the ones he and his father once traded. He met a few of the captains, and within two days had a job as a deckhand. The customers were wealthy Americans from Texas and California, and they spent more time drinking than fishing. He earned no wages or salary, but worked for tips, which invariably got larger the more the clients drank. A slow day would net him $200; a good day, $500, all cash. He lived in an inexpensive motel, and after a few days stopped looking over his shoulder. Los Cabos quickly became his home.

Wilson Argrow was suddenly transferred out of

Trumble and sent to a halfway house in Milwaukee, where he stayed exactly one night before walking away. Since he didn't exist he couldn't be found. Jack Argrow met him at the airport with tickets, and they flew together to D.C. Two days after leaving Florida, the Argrow brothers, Kenny Sands and Roger Lyter, reported to Langley for their next assignment.

Three days before he was scheduled to depart D.C. for the convention in Denver, Aaron Lake arrived at Langley for lunch with the Director. It was to be a joyful occasion, the conquering candidate once again thanking the genius who'd asked him to run. His acceptance speech had been written for a month, but Teddy had a few suggestions he wanted to discuss.

He was escorted to Teddy's office, where the old man was waiting under his quilt, as always. He looked so pale and tired, Lake thought. The aides vanished, the door was closed, and Lake noticed that no table had been prepared. They sat away from the desk, face to face, very close together.

Teddy liked the speech and made just a few comments. 'Your speeches are getting too long,' he said quietly. But Lake had so much to say these days.

'We're still editing,' he said.

'This election belongs to you, Mr. Lake,' Teddy said, quite feebly.

'I feel good, but it will be a brawl.'

'You'll win by fifteen points.'

Lake stopped smiling and listened hard. 'That's, uh, quite a margin.'

'You're up slightly in the polls. Next month the Vice President will be up. It will go back and forth until the middle of October. Then, there will be a nuclear situation that will terrify the world. And you, Mr. Lake, will become the messiah.'

The prospect frightened even the messiah. 'A war?' Lake asked quietly.

'No. There will be casualties, but they won't be Americans. Natty Chenkov will get the blame, and the good voters of this republic will flock to the polls. You could win by as much as twenty points.'

Lake breathed deeply. He wanted to ask more questions, even perhaps object to the bloodshed. But it would be futile. Whatever terror Teddy had planned for October was already in the works. There was nothing Lake could say or do to stop it.

'Keep beating the same drum, Mr. Lake. The same message. The world is about to become a lot crazier, and we have to be strong to protect our way of life.'

'The message has worked so far.'

'Your opponent will become desperate. He'll attack you for the single issue, and he'll whine about the money. He'll beat you up and score some points. Don't panic. The world will be turned upside down in October, trust me.'

'I do.'

'You've got this thing won, Mr. Lake. Keep preaching the same message.'

'Oh, I will.'

'Good,' Teddy said, and closed his eyes for a moment as if he needed a quick nap. Then he opened them and said, 'Now, on an entirely different topic, I'm a little curious about your plans once you get to the White House.'

Lake was puzzled, and his face showed it.

Teddy continued the ambush: 'You need a partner, Mr. Lake, a First Lady, someone to grace the White House with her presence. Someone to entertain and decorate, a pretty woman, one young enough to have children. It's been a long time since we had children in the White House, Mr. Lake.'

'You must be kidding.' Lake was flabbergasted.

'I like this Jayne Cordell on your staff. She's thirty-eight, smart, articulate, quite pretty though she needs to drop fifteen pounds. Her divorce was twelve years ago, and it's forgotten. I think she'd make a fine First Lady.'

Lake cocked his head to one side, and was suddenly angry. He wanted to lash out at Teddy, but for the moment words failed him. He managed to mumble, 'Have you lost your mind?'

'We know about Ricky,' Teddy said, very coolly, with his eyes penetrating Lake's.

The wind was sucked out of Lake's lungs, and as he exhaled he said, 'Oh my god.' He studied his feet for a moment, his entire body frozen in shock.

To make matters worse, Teddy handed over a sheet of paper. Lake took it, and instantly recognized it as a copy of his last note to Ricky.

Dear Ricky:
I think it's best if we end our correspondence. I wish you well with your rehab.

Sincerely, Al

Lake almost said that he could explain things; they were not as they seemed. But he decided to say nothing, at least not for a while. The questions flooded his thoughts – How much do they know? How in hell did they intercept the mail? Who else knows?

Teddy let him suffer in silence. There was no hurry.

When his thoughts cleared somewhat, the politician in Lake came to the surface. Teddy was offering a way out. Teddy was saying, 'Just play ball with me, son, and things will be fine. Do it my way.'

And so Lake swallowed hard and said, 'I actually like her.'

'Of course you do. She's perfect for the job.'

'Yes. She's very loyal.'

'Are you sleeping with her?'

'No. Not yet.'

'Start soon. Hold hands with her during the convention. Let the gossip start, let nature take its course. A week before the election, announce a Christmas wedding.'

'Big or small?'

'Huge. The social event of the year in Washington.'

'I like that.'

'Get her pregnant quickly. Just before your inauguration, announce that the First Lady is expecting. It'll make a marvelous story. And it will be so nice to see young children in the White House again.'

Lake smiled and nodded and appeared to like

the thought, then he suddenly frowned. 'Will anyone ever know about Ricky?' he asked.

'No. He's been neutralized.'

'Neutralized?'

'He'll never write another letter, Mr. Lake. And you'll be so busy playing with all your little children that you won't have time to think about people like Ricky.'

'Ricky who?'

'Atta boy, Lake. Atta boy.'

'I'm very sorry, Mr. Maynard. Very sorry. It won't happen again.'

'Of course it won't. I've got the file, Mr. Lake. Always remember that.' Teddy began rolling himself backward, as if the meeting was over.

'It was an isolated moment of weakness,' Lake said.

'Never mind, Lake. Take care of Jayne. Get her a new wardrobe. She works too hard and she looks tired. Ease up on her. She's going to make a wonderful First Lady.'

'Yes sir.'

Teddy was at the door. 'No more surprises, Lake.'

'No sir.'

Teddy opened the door and rolled himself away.

By late November, they had settled in Monte Carlo, primarily because of its beauty and warm weather, but also because so much English was spoken there. And there were casinos, a must for Spicer. Neither Beech nor Yarber could tell if he was winning or losing, but he was certainly enjoying himself. His wife was still tending to her mother, who'd yet to die. Things were tense because Joe Roy wouldn't go home, and she wouldn't leave Mississippi.

They lived in the same small but handsome hotel on the edge of town, and they usually had breakfast together twice a week before scattering. As the months passed and they settled into their new lives, they saw less and less of each other. They had differing interests. Spicer wanted to gamble and drink and spend time with the ladies. Beech preferred the sea and enjoyed fishing. Yarber traveled and studied the history of southern France and northern Italy.

But each always knew where the others were. If one disappeared, the other two wanted to know it.

They'd read nothing about their pardons. Beech and Yarber had spent hours in a library in Rome, reading American newspapers just after they fled. Not a word about them. They'd had no contact with anyone from home. Spicer's wife claimed to have told no one that he was out of prison. She still thought he'd escaped.

On Thanksgiving Day, Finn Yarber was enjoying an espresso at a sidewalk café in downtown Monte Carlo. It was warm and sunny, and he was only vaguely aware that it was an important holiday back home. He didn't care because he would never go back. Beech was asleep in his hotel room. Spicer was in a casino three blocks away.

A vaguely familiar face appeared from nowhere. In a flash, the man sat across from Yarber and said, 'Hello, Finn. Remember me?'

Yarber calmly took a sip of coffee and studied the face. He'd last seen it at Trumble.

'Wilson Argrow, from prison,' the man said, and Yarber put down his cup before he dropped it.

'Good morning, Mr. Argrow,' Finn said slowly, calmly, though there were many other things he wanted to say.

'I guess you're surprised to see me.'

'Yes, as a matter of fact.'

'Wasn't that exciting news about Aaron Lake's landslide?'

'I suppose. What can I do for you?'

'I just want you to know that we're always close by, just in case you need us.'

Finn actually chuckled, then said, 'That doesn't seem likely.' It had been five months since their release. They had moved from country to country, from Greece to Sweden, from Poland to Portugal, slowly heading south as the weather changed. How on earth could Argrow track them down?

It was impossible.

Argrow pulled a magazine from inside his jacket. 'I ran across this last week,' he said, handing it over. The magazine was turned to a page in the back where a personal ad was circled with a red marker:

> SWM in 20s looking for kind and
> discreet American gentleman in
> 40s or 50s to pen pal with.

Yarber had certainly seen it before, but he shrugged as if he hadn't a clue.

'Looks familiar, doesn't it?' Argrow asked.

'They all look the same to me,' Finn said. He

tossed the magazine on the table. It was the European edition of *Out and About*.

'We traced the address to the post office here in Monte Carlo,' Argrow said. 'A brand-new box rental, with a fake name and everything. What a coincidence.'

'Look, I don't know who you work for, but I have a very strong hunch that we're not in your jurisdiction. We haven't broken a single law. Why don't you bug off?'

'Sure, Finn, but two million bucks isn't enough?'

Finn smiled and looked around the lovely café. He took a sip of coffee and said, 'You gotta keep busy.'

'I'll see you around,' Argrow said, then jumped to his feet and vanished.

Yarber finished his coffee as if nothing had happened. He watched the street and the traffic for a while, then left to gather his colleagues.

The Last Juror

John Grisham

In 1970, The *Ford County Times*, one of Mississippi's more colourful weekly newspapers, went bankrupt. To the surprise and dismay of many, ownership was assumed by 23-year-old college drop-out, Willie Traynor. The future of the paper looked grim until a young mother was brutally raped and murdered by a member of the notorious Padgitt family. Traynor reported all the gruesome details,and his newspaper began to prosper.

The murderer, Danny Padgitt, was tried before a packed courtroom in Clanton, Mississippi. The trial came to a startling, dramatic end when the defendant threatened revenge against the jurors if they convicted him. Nevertheless, they found him guilty, and he was sentenced to life in prison.

But in Mississippi in 1970 'life' didn't necessarily mean 'life', and nine years later Danny Padgitt managed to get himself paroled. He returned to Ford County, and the retribution began.

'Masterful . . . When Grisham gets in the courtroom he lets rip, drawing scenes so real they're not just alive, they're pulsating . . . Quality thriller writing' *Daily Mirror*

'*The Last Juror* does not need to coast on its author's megapopularity. It's a reminder of how the Grisham juggernaut began' *New York Times*

arrow books